Angels

and

Manners

CYNN CHADWICK

Ann Arbor
2010

Bywater Books

Copyright © 2010 by Cynn Chadwick

BYWATER BOOKS FIRST EDITION

First Printing November 2010

ISBN 13: 978-1-932859-71-3
ISBN 10: 1-932859-71-3

Cover designer: Bonnie Liss (Phoenix Graphics)

Printed in the United States of America
on acid-free paper.

Bywater Books
PO Box 3671
Ann Arbor MI 48106-3671
www.bywaterbooks.com

For my beautiful sons, Zac and Sam,
who have survived and thrived in spite of it all.

Chapter One

Carrie stopped at the threshold to the Mediation Center. Standing on the far side of the room with his back to her was Dill, her ex-husband, looking through a magazine. She could see the pages flipping between his outstretched hands. He was slouched; his head tilted into his lean. She had seen the same pose in their son Casper when he was lost in thought. Dill's hair curled over his collar and was much longer than when she had met him—a lifetime ago—with his Air Force buzz cut. He had gone a little paunchy around the middle, love handles easing over his jeans. She would recognize that mannered posture anywhere. Seeing him like this—unawares—conjured the image of that boy she had met one dismal night in a musty tavern where she was tending bar.

Back then, she saw right away that he was beautiful, pretty, the way men had no right being—plump full lips, long feathery lashes, and each angle a delicate cut, right down to the cleave of his chin. When he smiled, more a mischievous grin, a deep dimple appeared in his cheek; she remembered dropping a metal shaker. He laughed, watching her fumble it to the counter, only to knock it off again. His voice was soft and friendly.

He'd worn a dark blue flight suit with shiny silver wings, but she didn't need the wings to tell her he was a pilot; his swagger alone reeked flyboy, she'd seen a million of them. He ordered a beer from the tap and said his name was Dill, *for Dilbert*, he'd confessed, reddening, which softened her to him.

He liked the military life and was training to be a fighter pilot. He

1

had ambitions, she could tell, and she liked the way he seemed to smell of confidence. Finally, after the last of the stragglers had sifted out, they were alone.

Carrie touched a stripe of a scar across his knuckles. "What's this from?"

"Oh, just a little action I saw out in the field," he'd said, leaning close. He slowly pressed his lips against her fingers, wrist, neck, and mouth, his tongue urgently exploring. She'd propped herself on top of the bar and felt his palm cup her breast, springing her nipples to attention. It was then that the manager came around the corner yelling, "Get a room!"

They had most of their clothes off by the time they made it through the rain to Carrie's car. It had been a quick eight minutes of fumbling in the backseat of the Chevy before they each huffed their way to adolescent ecstasy. And in those eight minutes a seed planted and rooted inside Carrie's womb. Nine months and a quick Las Vegas wedding later, they were the proud parents of Amarillo Texas Angel— aka Tex.

After they married, and had begun to settle down to life on base, Dill did not pass the test that would've turned him into the fighter pilot he'd so confidently believed he'd become. Rather than being away on secret missions, he was instead relegated to freight transport: mail, supplies, and equipment. *I'm like a fucking flying UPS driver*, he'd complain. When his job wore on his ego and he became more sullen, his grumbling at her began. *Before I met you, everything was on track*, he'd shouted at her one early anniversary, making everything go still the way it does before a storm, and she guessed that's exactly what it foreshadowed.

There were no other people in the Mediation Center's waiting room. The only sounds to be heard were the Beatles' *Yesterday* and the clicking of a keyboard from somewhere down a hallway. Watching Dill shift his weight, splitting his gaze between the outside and the slick pages in his hands, she wondered what had happened to them, those two kids falling in love that night. They'd gone from being strangers to lovers to enemies within months, it seemed.

2

About the same time their lovemaking had been replaced by *Leno*, their conversations turned to kids, the house, or whatever was on the news. Just as that first tumble in the back of the Chevy had produced Tex, their final robotic rotation produced Casper, born after they had transferred to Wyoming. Then Dill started running around. Never again had they been intimate, at least not with each other.

Too many transfers and affairs later they were stationed at Pope Air Force base outside Fayetteville, North Carolina, or *Fayette-Nam*, as Dill liked to call it, where they'd each been trapped these many years since. No longer married or military, they continued to wage their own private battles with each other. After months of fighting across phone lines, e-mails, thresholds, and over the heads of the very sons they both sought to protect, they were here at Mediation to try to figure things out. What a pair of idiots we are, Carrie thought, and shook her head, feeling warmth toward the father of her children.

She sidled toward him. Placing her hand on his back, she felt the familiar tremble of his heat, the slight shiver of his skin beneath her palm, and the hum of their old life together; the one where they had made love and babies.

"Dill," she said softly, "Please," she whispered, feeling him stiffen. "We can work this out. We don't have to make it horrible."

Like a ramrod, his back straightened and he stood motionless, planted in his spot. She could feel his breathing getting faster and the muscles beneath her hand constricting, as if pulling away from her.

"We used to be able to talk," Carrie quickened her speech, holding onto him, desperate to make him listen.

He did not turn, but said evenly, "We used to be able to do a lot of things."

"How did we get here?"

It was as if he had turned himself to stone. Silent and solid in his position.

"The boys are afraid, Dill. I'm afraid." She swallowed back the confession. "Just tell me what you want," she begged, feeling him begin to shake. "I'll do anything; just don't take my babies away from me."

3

"They're not babies, anymore, and they need a man's influence."

She felt her throat thicken. "They're all I've got, Dill. They are all that's good in my life."

He pulled away, turning and heading for the exit, bypassing her. Not even looking at her.

"Dill, come on, I'm not some monster." Carrie started to follow when the door behind them opened.

"Mr. Angel? Mrs. Angel?" The woman's voice called. "Dr. Solomon is ready to see you."

She sat at the round table in a small, square room across from Dill and beside the mediator. He was a long tall man, Abe Lincoln-ish in stature as well as demeanor; his beard and hair were gray, and he had deep blue eyes. He was quietly shuffling paperwork in front of him. His name was Dr. Solomon, and he had not said a word beyond this introduction.

I'm a pretty good mother, Carrie thought. Mostly. Tex and Casper are good boys. The three of them have a rhythm together. What would the apartment feel like without them? She imagined the silence. There would be no loud music to shout down, no late night rummaging through the fridge; when she called out for help in the kitchen, a companion for a TV movie, or a couple of rounds of Spades, there would be no begrudging groans or easily cajoled participation. Only silence.

No, it had not all been perfect, she knew. She could admit that. Sure, she got mad. What mother didn't? Mother Teresa, maybe, but Carrie suspected she had been a closeted pillow puncher. There were times when Carrie yelled, got out of control inside herself and then on the outside. If she were going to be real, she had said things she wished she hadn't. There was evidence of punched walls and kicked doors, and a couple of telephones that had cracked under her pressure. Once, she hated to recall, she and Tex had gotten into it.

Inwardly cringing, she conjured the image of the two of them, squared off like boxers. In spite of the fact that Tex towered above her, Carrie had him backed into a corner. Screaming into his face, seeing spittle hit his chin. While she could imagine the scene, she could not remember what the fight was even about. When the words

4

Fuck You came out of Tex's mouth, she had slapped him—hard. Her handprint raising red on his white, still baby-soft skin. Holding her wrist, she stared at her hand as if it did not belong to her. As if it had been a weapon thrust upon her. She looked up at her child, whose own hand covered the welt of her imprint. Tears had sprung to his eyes, and the betrayal she saw lingering in them shamed her.

Dill had filed a motion for full custody. He'd named Carrie's job insecurity, and the lack of a male role model for Tex as the reasons for his case, but Carrie knew the real reason Dill wanted the boys to live with him; he was about to have another kid and he needed the child support money. However, temper had inspired this latest round of legal battling. It had been over a month ago when Carrie had come home from work and caught Dill inside the apartment, rummaging through her desk.

"What are you doing?" she asked.

"Waiting for Casper," Dill looked up from his investigation.

"Did he let you in?"

"He's upstairs. So, I see that you're making good money, now." He pointed to a pay stub that was amongst her paperwork.

"That's none of your fucking business," she pushed him aside. "How dare you go through my stuff?"

"I dare because I'm paying for half of everything around here. I'm just making sure I'm not getting ripped off."

"My God, do you see me taking vacations? Driving a Jag?"

"I see you living off me and Uncle Sam just fine."

She threw her keys down and slid the paperwork into a drawer. She glared when he refused to move, and she stood facing him. "Look, I'm working full time, I'm in school full time, and for all you do for these boys, I'm pretty much parenting for two—full time."

"I'm here, now."

"Oh, did you get free tickets to something? Is Dodi too pregnant to get out nowadays?"

The front door swung open, and Tex pranced in wearing mint-green vinyl pants and a zebra-striped tank top of his own design and making.

"Oh for God's sakes!" Dill said as he saw his son.

"Do you like it?" Tex twirled for his parents. "I just finished it in Home-Ec today!"

"Don't think you're wearing that to the movies," Dill said.

Tex's smile wilted. "Why not?" He looked from one parent to the other, confused hurt in his eyes. "Mom?"

"It's great, sweetie. Amazing. You are amazing!" Carrie said.

"You look like a fag."

With that, Carrie lunged at her ex-husband and pushed him toward the door. "Get out! Get out of my fucking house!" She shoved him, this time into the wall. She took a couple of swings, grazing his chin.

"Mom! It's okay." Tex grabbed her, pulling her off his father.

Casper jumped down the steps. "What's going on?"

"Get the fuck out of here!" She wiggled from Tex's hold and grabbed a stapler from the desk; she held it above her head.

"You are a nutcase," Dill said, sidling out the door. "I'll wait for you in the car, Casper."

"What about me?" Tex asked.

"Not dressed like that."

"Then I won't come."

"Good. Stay with your mother, I'm sure you girls have plenty to talk about."

Carrie hurled the stapler, just barely missing the top of Dill's scalp, lodging deep into the sheetrock above his head.

His eyes grew large as he registered the size of the hole torn in the wall. "You're a fucking nut job."

"Get out!" She felt Tex's hand on her arm, readying to hold her back if needed.

"Come on, Casp, the movie's about to start." Dill looked at her disgustedly.

Reluctantly, her younger son followed his father while his brother stood beside their mother. They were all being torn every which way. That incident had led to this particular session of mediation. In North Carolina, parents filing custody matters were ordered to mediation

6

before the case could be heard by a judge. And so here they were, all ready to mediate.

Dr. Solomon cleared his throat, and then, with long graceful fingers, he lifted a pitcher of water and doled out three paper cups. He pulled his reading glasses down to the end of his nose. Peering over them, first at Carrie and then at Dill, he attempted a sober smile.

"We'll begin with the rules of mediation," he said, his voice low and soulful, almost like James Earl Jones, Carrie thought. "As court ordered, you are both here to try to resolve some custody issues. Agreed?" He waited.

She watched as Dill sat motionless, like a palace guard, staring straight ahead.

Solomon continued, "We believe that children benefit from having their parents rather than judges make decisions about their lives."

"Makes sense," Carrie said, glancing across the table at Dill, whose jaw was twitching. She saw that his once reddish mustache was peppered gray, as was his hair. He was looking a little haggard.

"You will each have a chance to speak," Solomon said, solemnly. "And hopefully, with some careful negotiations, we can all come to a mutual agreement without having to take this before a judge. Mr. Angel? Do you agree?"

Dill finally looked up from his fingernails and said, "Sure, whatever."

As his lips parted, Carrie was startled by the glaring whiteness of Dill's teeth. Brilliant caps of gleaming square pegs freakishly radiated from his mouth. Interesting how he had money to bleach his *own* teeth, Carrie thought, but could not afford (or so he said) braces for Tex's. Those once good looks were fading, and Dill's vanity was obviously working overtime.

"Mr. Angel, you do understand that we are here to *cooperatively* resolve these custody issues?" Dr. Solomon asked again.

"Hey, good luck if you can get her to cooperate about anything."

"Ms. Angel. Is this going to be a problem for you?"

"No, because there are no *custody issues* here to *resolve*. My boys have been perfectly fine living with me their whole lives. There's nothing to cooperate about."

Dr. Solomon allowed an uncomfortable amount of silence to pass between them before continuing. "You both want the best for your children. You have differing ideas about what that might be. Together we are going to try to resolve this list of complaints brought by Mr. Angel. That's what the court has ordered."

Both Carrie and Dill shifted, each equally chastised.

"Ms. Angel. Carrie, may I call you Carrie?" Solomon asked, gently. "Let's start with this motion brought by Dill, is that right?"

He nodded.

"Dill? Why don't you tell us why you think that your sons . . . let's see . . ." he mumbled, sliding a finger under a line of type on the paper in front of him. ". . . *Amarillo Texas*, I see he's nearly sixteen. And *Casper Wyoming* just turned fourteen." Solomon looked up from the paper. "Those are some unusual names," he tried engaging them.

Carrie said, "I wanted Jason both times." She looked across the table. "*He* filled out the paperwork."

Dill shook his head but did not say anything.

"Let's look at the least emotionally charged issue here in the summons," Solomon said. "It says here that you have concerns about your ex-wife's employment status and its impact on the boys living in Section Eight housing." Solomon read.

"That's right, those kids have suffered that neighborhood long enough," Dill elaborated. "Crack addicts on corners, rats in gutters, and a bunch of illegals scurrying around. I'm tired of my sons being exposed to all that."

"It's not like that," Carrie interjected. "We're in a good school district. It's near Knob Hill, even."

"What about your employment situation, Carrie?"

She turned to face Solomon. "You know, it's interesting." Thumbing across the table toward Dill, she said, "He manages to climb his way *down* the corporate ladder, enough to get his child support payments reduced, and nobody's asking him about his *employment status*."

"At least I've got one."

Solomon asked, "Carrie, are you employed now?"

8

"Of course. You think I can actually *live* on five hundred dollars a month child support?"

"And subsidized housing and healthcare," Dill said.

"I'm in school, raising two kids, working my ass off . . ."

"Here we go," Dill interrupted. "Get out the violin, Dr. Solomon, you're about to hear a sob story."

"Well, do you see yourself *gainfully* employed anytime soon?" Solomon asked.

"What's *that* supposed to mean?"

"I'm sorry," Solomon's deep voice had a soothing affect. "I just mean, might there be some future employment that will relieve you of all the juggling you have to do right now?"

She leaned back in her chair. "Look, I'm about to get my carpentry certification. When I do, I'll be getting the hell out of Section Eight, all right?"

"How long have I been hearing *that* story?" Dill asked, curling his lip, revealing his ghoulishly white teeth. "She's been failing that same damn test every year."

Solomon gently cajoled them away from their mounting anger. "Carrie, when will you take this exam?"

"In a few months."

"Then how about we agree to table this part of the complaint until we see what happens and where that leaves you?"

"I can already tell you where that will leave her," Dill said. "Sucking off the tit of the government like she's been doing since I met her. She doesn't know any better."

"Fuck you."

Dill spoke softly. "I want better for my sons. We are a good Christian family. We teach our children responsibility. Family and God. Hard work. Being frugal. These are the values I want for my sons. We are moral people."

"You are unbelievable!" Carrie could barely speak when she turned to Solomon, her voice rising. "This is the *married* asshole I caught in bed with our babysitter when I was *pregnant* with Casper!"

"That was a long time ago. I have a *good* marriage, and a stable life with Dodi."

9

"Stable? You've got a wife with a nervous tic so pronounced that she smiles and winks at the same time. Her fat son's got an eating disorder. There's a toddler who sleepwalks wearing underpants on her head, and a brand new baby on the way. Working your way up to those eight kids you wanted, aren't you?"

"Just sorry I had two with you."

Solomon interrupted. "What I'm hearing, Dill, is that you feel the boys might benefit from living with you?"

"Hell, yeah. Especially Tex." Dill bent down and lifted a briefcase in front of him.

"That's a joke," Carrie said. "You barely see them as it is, and when they do stay at your house, you leave them with Dodi, or make them do chores, or ignore them in front of whatever sport-of-the-season is on; no Disneyland Dad in this room!"

Dill ignored her and snapped open the locks and raised the lid. Pulling out a thick envelope, he placed it on the table. "Here are the pictures to prove *that* point."

Carrie recognized Tex in each of the photos. He was dressed in the creations he had been designing.

"Look at this!" Dill pointed to a picture of his son prancing along the sidewalk with multi-colored feathery boas wrapping around his neck and trailing behind like a couple of snakes slinking along a Mardi Gras parade.

"That was for school!" Carrie yelled. "You idiot! He was designing clothes for a dance recital."

"Yeah, well, if he were living with me he'd be playing football not prancing around on some stage."

"But, these are his *designs!*" Carrie slid toward Solomon the shot of Tex wearing a hot pink cape with a white sequined jump suit modeled after the one Elvis wore before he got fat. "He makes these outfits. It's pure genius!" she said.

"Oh yeah, check out this *genius,*" Dill's tone exuded disgust as he pulled out another shot, this one of Tex in a purple Afro wearing giant silver eyelashes and a dog collar. "He's turning into a homo."

"And so what if he is?" Carrie's voice rose with each syllable. "What if he is gay? What are you going to do about it?"

10

"He needs a male, role model—a father."

"Like you've ever been any of the above," she said.

"At least I'd put a stop to these queer shenanigans!" Dill shook his head.

Carrie turned to Solomon, "Am I supposed to let my son go live with this man?" She turned over one of the pictures and noted a stamp that read: Wiley's Detective Agency, and the address.

"You had a PI spying on your own kid?" Carrie leaned forward. "You piss and moan about child support, but you can afford a private detective?" She flung the photos across the table. "Can you fucking believe this?" She stood. "Do you see what's going on here?"

"Please, Carrie, sit down," Dr. Solomon said, quietly.

"You have no right, you prick." She leaned over the table.

"I have every right," Dill countered. "I'm not paying out child support just to watch *my* son turn into a fucking faggot!"

She hit him. Right in the face. Without thought, nearly without understanding, as her arm cocked back and her fist shot forward, landing one straight punch to his nose, smashing it; she could feel her knuckles crushing bone and sinew. Suddenly blood spurted across the neat stack of papers, dotting the table, and one glob of bright red mucus landed in Dr. Solomon's cup. Dill grabbed his face, "You bitch." He stood. "You goddamn bitch!"

Dr. Solomon rose, pulled a wad of tissues from the box near him, and shoved them at Dill. "Here, tilt your head back," he said.

Dill pushed him away. He grabbed the Kleenex and got to his feet. Reaching down, lifting the briefcase, he turned toward the door. The bunched wad pressing against his nose was blooming bright red, like a rosebud opening in slow motion. He paused and spoke quietly to the mediator, "I guess we don't need to discuss the case against her temper, now, do we?"

"Mr. Angel," Dr. Solomon said, reverting to the formal. "Why don't we calm down and . . ."

"I don't need to calm down," Dill said evenly. "I am calm. I'll see you both in court." He looked at Solomon. "I'm sure you'll dutifully testify to my crazy ex-wife's explosively dangerous temper." He punched open the door and left.

Simultaneously, Carrie and Dr. Solomon sat back down. Neither said a word for a moment, and then Solomon sighed and looked over at her.

"What?" she shook her head. "I'm just supposed to sit here and listen to that trash about my son?"

"There are other ways to handle these things."

"Mister, you don't have a clue about my life."

His voice was soft and low. "I see many women in your situation, all the time. I know it gets desperate . . ."

"It's beyond desperation, it's terror," she said. "Threaten the children and inspire raw terror. This breeds violence. I could kill him, Dr. Solomon. I know I could."

"Don't say that, Ms. Angel."

"It's the truth. Go ahead and testify against me. Go ahead and help get my son, yes, my *gay homo faggot queer* son, placed in daily proximity of *that* monster, just because I happened to give him what he deserved."

"Carrie." Solomon reached a long hand and placed it on her arm. "If I may offer some advice." He waited and when she did not pull away, he continued calmly. "It might be a good idea for you to enroll in an anger management class."

"Oh, great!" she shook him off and stood.

"No, wait." He rose with her. She could barely make out the color of his eyes as she craned her neck to meet them. He continued, "I just mean that if Mr. Angel is going to take this to court, it would be in your best interest to show that you recognize your *challenge* and have taken measures to help yourself."

"Fuck off," she turned toward the door.

"Ms. Angel," he stopped her. "If you don't want to lose your kids . . ." He looked pointedly at her. "Or worse, get thrown in jail, I suggest you take my advice."

She paused and turned. "Jail? But I'm a mother."

His sober expression did not change. "The court won't figure that into account. If you keep throwing punches, you'll find that out."

She bit the inside of her lip to stop the thickness tightening her throat.

"If you really do want to protect them—" he reached for a pen and scribbled on his tablet. Tearing the sheet away, he handed it to her. "—call this number. It's free. It will help you out in court."

She took the paper and stuffed it into her back pocket. "Thanks," she said. "I'll think about it." Then she left.

The Toyota limped into the parking lot of the Section Eight housing complex where Carrie lived with her sons in apartment Number Two. She finished smoking one last cigarette. Looking up at the brick exterior of the two-story, six-unit building that was one of four squaring off a grassy quad. *Just like a college campus*, Tex had remarked five years ago on the day they had moved into the low-income housing. A thumping loud bass of a low-riding Chevy slithered by, making its rounds, cruising drugs for kids, or kids for drugs, she'd bet.

Carrie inhaled the smoke cigarette, trying to shake off her day. Had it really been that long ago? She had sworn back then that the move to Section Eight would be temporary. So far, the boys had spent nearly a third of their lives here. Cracking the window further, she blew smoke into the night air. She noticed the lights on in the laundry facility across the way. There were a few folks milling around inside. There were too many hard-luck stories, and she had too many of her own to have any patience to listen to any tonight. She'd do the laundry on the weekend.

Carrie watched a couple of barefoot children lumbering up the slope from the playground. They were heading toward the end unit, where a porch light was flashing. It was the signal to come home. Carrie smiled knowing that she was the one who had started the *call* lights, back when the boys were little. It was safer back then, she thought, there were not as many strangers around like there are today. Nowadays, on weekend nights, hooded teenagers in baggy jeans who left beer cans on swings and cigarette butts or worse in the sandbox, inhabited the playground. Sometimes, on hot summer nights, raging voices roared from open windows, often concluding in the sharp report of a slammed door or slapped cheek.

When Carrie moved in, she felt like she had landed at the Ritz.

Lately, though, the once bright façade looked pale and weary. Paint chips scattered below windowsills, and rooftop shingles curled and crumbled under too many years of wind and weather. Each screen-door had its own unique squeak. In these close quarters, everyone knew who was coming and going. More and more sounds of police or ambulance sirens could be heard wailing in the compound rushing some sick baby, drunk boyfriend, or pregnant teenager to jail or the hospital.

And yet, it was the arm of forest wrapped around the perimeters that initially made Carrie feel good about living here. On one side, the slice of woods shielded the complex from the noise and notice of the highway. On the other side, the thick foliage and a tall wooden fence shielded the upscale Knob Hill gated-community from the noise and notice of the Section Eight housing. The good thing was that kids from Section Eight attended the same schools as the kids from Knob Hill. Over the years, however, little by little, the *knobbies*, as they were known, were transferring out of public school to attend the prestigious Harrington Academy, where they could avoid rubbing elbows with the *Sex8* kids, as Tex and Casper had early on been tagged. Once, there had been many benefits to living here. Now, it seemed there were fewer and fewer.

Through apartment Number Two's steamy kitchen window, she watched her sons readying dinner. There was blurry commotion as Tex scampered to and from the table with plates and silverware. She could see his dark red curls, like her own, bobbing up and down as he balanced water glasses and salad bowls. Casper's long, tall body stood at the sink as he tossed the pasta in the big stainless colander. It was Wednesday and that meant it was the boys' turn to cook, and that meant it was spaghetti night. When the lights dimmed inside, Carrie crushed out her cigarette. She knew that Tex was lighting candles, and Casper would be waiting by the door. She was grateful for the meal that (mostly) Casper would have cooked. Moreover, she appreciated the soft candlelight and matching music that would be Tex's usual spaghetti-night contribution. She would do her best to forget about today, and hauled herself out of the car.

◻◻◻

High above the landscape, Carrie maneuvered across the open framework of the three-story mansion like a sailor traversing the topmast of a schooner. She sidestepped each upright two-by-four, spaced and anchored sixteen inches on center, and climbed the skeleton of the structure. Feeling along the bottom plate, her nimble feet scooted in and out of the pine studs, measuring her way back to the ladder that would lead her to the ground. Earlier in her apprenticeship, the old-timers had warned her *Never look down,* and she never did.

At her waist, the tool belt tugged, holding her back, and she paused to see the claw of her hammer gripping a piece of board. The wind at this height was fast and sneaky. If you weren't careful, one quick gust could shove you loose from the framing. She wrapped her gloved hand tighter around the two-by and yanked the cold steel from the wood. Before continuing her skirt along the perimeters of the building, Carrie turned her gaze to the faraway valley. Pockets of bright green woods dotted the soft, yellow carpet of rolling hills. The air shimmered with heat. She loved doing carpentry, she thought, no matter how hot or cold it got. It could rain, snow, sleet, or scorch the earth, and she would be just fine as long as she was pounding a hammer or cutting a board.

The sun was sinking behind her; she could feel its warmth on her back. She knew it wouldn't last long. Soon one final dip behind the hillock and it would be dusk and cold. It was time to get down off this trussing and home to the boys. She reached the uprights where the ladder had last been resting and readied to place her boot on the top rung. As Carrie's foot swiped the empty air, her stomach lurched. Holding tight to the studs, she quickly dared a look between her legs to discover the ladder gone. What the heck? She wedged between the boards, wrapping both arms tightly as a blast of wind shook the structure, causing it to sway.

Three stories below, on the pad of concrete that was the floor of the house, stood a circle of men craning their necks up toward her. She noticed they were each squinting and grinning at the same time.

Fucking asshole Pressley was pointing at her and slapping Mick's shoulder. The other guys laughed loud enough for her to hear and then high-fived each other.

Pressley cupped his hands like a megaphone and shouted at her, "Lose somethin', Angel?"

Carrie's eyes and nose began to run as the wind whipped around her. Strands of dark red hair escaped from beneath her cap and stung her cheeks. *Don't look down,* she warned herself, and tightened her hold on the studs. *Don't let 'em see you sweat,* she commanded, as fear-induced trickles slid from her temples.

"Put the ladder back," she yelled, not knowing how many of her words were carried off in the wind.

"Ladder? What ladder?" Pressley shouted.

Carrie stared straight ahead. She counted the dozen or so near-mansions in various stages of completion. They were dotting the hillside that had once been a cow-pasture but would soon be a pricey gated community. She had worked on nearly every one of them under the supervision of one foreman or another. Some fellas were better than others. One or two seemed genuinely interested in helping women like her, who were training for jobs in the state-sponsored apprenticeship programs. Some ignored you, believing that you were just another pathetic welfare case. There were the few who let you know, right up front, they were against women working in the trades. There was only one, however, who tried to torture women right out of the program. That little prick was Pressley.

"We're headin' out, Angel," he yelled again. "Want us to bring you coffee in the mornin'?"

"Yeah, cream *and* sugar? Or just *cream?*" Don, the old pervert, hollered.

The sun on its descent angled a prism behind her. Bright rays of burnt orange and fiery yellow blazed a halo around her, casting a long shadow across the construction site. She saw her dark silhouette with outstretched arms, as if she really were an angel poised to take flight. The sway of the building brought her attention back to her predicament, and fear fueled her anger.

16

"Get the ladder, Pressley!" She yelled, hoping her panic was not audible in her words.

"Did you say *please?*"

She wouldn't. They could come back in the morning and find her clinging to the framework before she would beg. No, this bastard was not going to get that kind of satisfaction from her. Instead, she reached into the pouch of her tool belt, grabbed a handful of screws and tossed them.

"Hey!" one of them shouted.

Daring a glance below, she dropped another bunch. The men ducked, covering their heads with their arms. "Watch it!" someone yelled. They danced apart, splitting the circle.

"Are you crazy, Angel?" Pressley shouted. "Do you want to get down from there or not?"

This time Carrie did look down and met Pressley's skyward gaze. He was standing directly below her. She sucked as much phlegm as she could and chambered the glob into the curled barrel of her tongue. Taking a deep breath and accounting for wind, she squinted, aiming her shot right between Pressley's eyes. She fired. The hurling mass splattered on his chest.

"You bitch!" Pressley wiped the wet mess from his jacket. "Get the fucking ladder," he ordered Mick. "You'll be sorry for that, Angel," he warned.

"Not as sorry as you're gonna be," she muttered as she carefully climbed down thirty-odd feet of ladder. "Not funny," she said, again only to herself. When she got to the midpoint, a gust of wind pushed at her. She tightened her grip, feeling her temperature spike in spite of the chilling air. She took a couple of deep breaths before continuing, and glanced down to see Pressley with his hand on the ladder. He was not smiling. His eyes narrowed to slits and seemed to be daring her to finish her descent.

"Knock it off, Pressley," she said evenly but did not take her eyes off him as she made to take a step down. Suddenly, she felt a rattling shudder from below, and she clung to the cold metal. Pressley's lips curled into a smile, but his eyes remained dull. Before he could jostle the ladder again, Carrie quickly skimmed the rungs. Nearing bottom, she jumped, landed, and knocked into him. "You prick!" She was in his face. "You goddamn prick." She was spraying spit and jamming her finger against his chest. "I've got kids! You gonna explain *that* kind of *accident* to my boys?"

Surrendering, he raised his hands and backed up. "It was a joke. Can't you take a joke?"

"I'm a mother. It's no joke," she said, quietly.

"You're a *mother* all right . . ." Pressley snickered, looking to his lackeys for support.

She pushed past him. Mick and the others stood off to the side. None of them was daring a look at her.

"A *real* mother," Pressley said.

Carrie stopped and turned on him. "This'll get back to Ketchum," she said, referring to the director of the apprenticeship program. "I promise you that." She turned and double-timed it to her car. Just as she unlocked the door to the old Toyota, Pressley caught up and blocked her way into the vehicle.

"You'd better watch it, Angel." His breath was on her face, smelling of old coffee and stale cigarettes.

"You threatening me?" she asked, looking into his black eyes.

"I got a lot of friends in this business," he said.

"There isn't a homeless mutt in this town who'd be your friend."

"Think you're cute, dontcha?" Pressley backed Carrie up against the car. "Say a word about today and you'll never work in this town again."

"What are you, some kind of Hollywood producer?"

He grabbed her arm. "Get somethin' straight, Angel. Today was a *joke*. If it turns into anything else, you won't be laughin'."

Carrie turned to get in the car, but Pressley pinned her between the door and the frame. "And neither will you," she whispered.

He backed off a bit and seemed to be reconsidering. Carrie quickly slid into the vehicle. She pulled at the door but he held it open.

"When are you taking the certification exam?" he asked.

Carrie did not like his tone. It came singsong and snaky. She did not like the smirk on his lips, or the satisfied raise of his furry eyebrows.

He continued, "I hear the State's just limited the number of times you welfare cases get to take the test."

"What are you talking about?"

"New rules. *Three* strikes and you're O.U.T. Out."

"Hey! You can spell!" Carrie said, but could feel the turmoil roiling in her middle. She'd already failed the test twice.

"Oh, you're a riot, Angel. You won't be so smart when you get cut from the system, will you?"

"Says who?" she asked, wishing she didn't care. Sweat was building under her cap. She ripped it off, letting the cool air douse her.

"Says the memo that came from the state or senate . . ." Pressley frowned and rubbed his chin. "Or congress or one of those cabinets, whatever."

Pressley was dumber than dirt, Carrie knew, but regardless of its source, she was inclined to believe that there *had* been a memo announcing the limits. The rumors about the coming change had been on the wind for a while. She had heard about it from other women in the training program. Pressley just verified it. Again, she yanked on the door handle, but he held fast.

"How many times have you taken it, Angel? Once? Twice? Or maybe you're already *out* and don't even know it."

"Is that O.U.T.? or O.W.T?" She pulled again, this time wrenching it from his hold.

"Listen you, bitch," he said, and pushed his face into the open window. He hissed, "Like I said, I got friends all over this business. You just see if you pass that test."

Carrie shoved the door, slamming it against Pressley's forehead and kneecaps. He tripped backward, landing on his ass. She turned the key in the ignition and held her breath as the engine reluctantly clicked, clicked, and finally caught. She wheeled the old clunker off the job site.

All she wanted to do was get home and have a beer, a bath, or maybe a beer in a bath. "How 'bout a beer bath?" she asked out loud, nearly cracking herself up when the unmistakable thump, thump, thump of a flat tire resounded from below. "Goddamn it," she said, and pulled off the two-lane and onto the skinny shoulder.

"Shit," Carrie said, kicking the pancake of tire squished beneath the wheel. She popped the trunk, only to discover that it was full of all kinds of junk. Before she could even get to the spare, she had to empty the space of tools, full laundry basket, and a bag of books she'd been meaning to take back to the library. As she was pulling the donut from its well, a white work truck approached. Carrie could see Pressley behind the wheel. As if he was aiming for her, the truck swerved, and she dodged behind the Toyota. The few guys crammed into the cab and hollered out the window as they sped on by. "Assholes," Carrie said to no one in particular.

She could not get the last lug nut off. As she was just about ready to stick out her thumb, another truck came from the direction of the job site, and this time it did stop. Mick made his way to her. He was a rusty-colored Irishman with close-cropped orange hair and big green eyes.

"Hey," he said.

"Hey."

"What's going on?" he pointed to her flat.

"Can't get the nut off."

"Want me to try?" Mick seemed careful with his words, as if he were trying not to offend her.

"It's either that or give me a lift."

This prompt drove the Irishman to his knees. As he pulled on the wrench, the muscles in his neck bulged. When it finally broke loose, his face was the color of a cherry. In no time, the pair had the flat off and the spare on. Carrie wiped her hands with a towel from the laundry basket and passed it over to Mick.

"Thanks," she said.

He nodded. "Listen, I'm sorry about today, back at the jobsite."

"Why do you guys go along with Pressley?"

Mick shrugged. "He's the boss. I guess it's a survival instinct."

"Stupid if you ask me."

"I just try to do my job."

Carrie got back into her car. "Don't you know what Pressley is?"

Mick looked at her, "You mean beyond being an asshole?"

"He's every bully on every playground." She looked hard at him. "And I'm every bully's target. And you, Mick, are every kid who heard the taunts, watched the blows, and sped past, just glad it wasn't you."

"Hey, I stopped to help, didn't I?" He gestured toward the fixed flat.

"Sure. I knew you would. Knew I could count on you out here, with Pressley long gone. But can I count on you tomorrow, Mick? Tomorrow, after the dick fills my pouch with Liquid Nails, or puts bugs in my sandwich or maybe Quick Crete in my boots, all as a *joke*, of course. Where will you be then?"

"Look, Carrie, we all gotta do what we all gotta do. Right?"

"Right, Mick." She rolled up her window and rolled down the road.

Chapter Two

The waiting room was painted a pale green, and everything, including people, glowed beneath the hum of fluorescent lights. Backed up against the perimeter walls, plastic school chairs squared off as if readying for a contradance. There were others waiting here. One white teenager with a baby at her breast was chewing gum and rocking. There was a large black woman who took up two of the chairs and read a magazine while her toddlers climbed over and under her. Jen was startled to notice the bulging purple welt beneath the eye of a well-dressed, older woman who was in the corner, knitting furiously. It occurred to Jen that there were only women here. For such a feminine environment, this place was drab. The posters on the wall advertised battered women's shelters, community health facilities, and child day care centers—each frame containing hopeful messages that underscored harsh realities.

"Manners," a woman called, rousing Jen from her perch. Before going through the door, she was handed a manila file folder with her name and assigned case number typed on the tab. As instructed, Jen made her way down a long dark corridor and knocked on the last door on the right. A short stout woman with day-glo orange hair and square black glasses beckoned her inside.

"I'm Doris Martin. I'll be your case manager," she said and smiled widely, offering Jen the chair beside her metal desk. Doris took the folder and skimmed through the pages.

"First-timer, huh?" Doris asked without looking up.

"Yes. It's just temporary, though. Until I get back on my feet."

"Sure."

"I was working at the library, but you know, the economy tanked, state budget cuts."

Reading closely, Doris slid a pudgy finger beneath the lines in the folder. Jen noticed a hodgepodge of silver, gold, and oddly shaped gems bedecking each finger, including both thumbs.

"I'm going to be asking you some personal questions," Doris said. She leaned closer to Jen and touched her arm. "Just let me know if I'm going too fast for you. These are not meant to pry but to better help you. Do you understand?"

Why was the woman talking to her as if she was deaf or spoke a foreign language? "That's fine," Jen said.

"Good," Doris said, soothingly. "It'll go faster if you cooperate." Her smile crinkled the folds around her eyes and made her appear grandmotherly. She poised her pen above the page and with a smile she asked, "Okay, then, let's get started. Are you hungry?"

"What?"

"Are you hungry? When was the last time you ate?"

"This morning. Before I took my daughter to school."

Doris made a notation. "And your daughter, Emily?"

"Yes. Emily."

"Did Emily eat this morning, too?"

"Of course!" Jen sputtered. "I made eggs and turkey sausage. Wheat toast with raspberry preserves. Of course she ate."

Doris nodded vigorously. Her soft fleshy rolls jiggled beneath the bright red and black paisley blouse. "All right, then. Are you or Emily sick?"

"Sick like have a cold? Or sick like have a disease?"

"Either one."

"No. No, thankfully, neither of us is sick."

Doris's bangle bracelets clicked together as she scribbled in Jen's file.

"Do you have a criminal record?" she asked with the same upbeat tone that she had asked the previous questions.

"Good Lord, no. No, I don't have a criminal record." Jen's fingers fluttered to her throat and she sat up straight.

"Emily?"

"She's only sixteen."

Doris up looked over her glasses.

"No. She doesn't have a record, either."

"Are you able to read and write in English?"

"I have a B.A. in literature, will that do?"

Doris ignored the sarcasm in her tone. "How do you pay for your food?"

"Is this really necessary?"

Doris made checkmarks. "Drugs? Are either you or your daughter using drugs?"

"I don't mean to be impatient," Jen interrupted, "But what does any of this have to do with food stamps or subsidized housing?"

Doris placed the folder flat on the desk and carefully set her pen on the open page. She leaned back against her chair, and sighed.

"Ms. Manners, it is my job to determine how best to help my clients. I must find out the needs of the recipients in order to assign benefits."

"Benefits?"

"I can't do that unless I have all the information." She took a deep breath and exhaled, as if tired. "So, are you willing to be an asset to this process or remain a hindrance?" Doris's smile stretched but she did not show any teeth. She waited.

"Those questions just don't apply to my situation." Jen explained. "I am not like those other women. This is just a temporary situation for me and Emily."

Doris waited.

"We just need some place to live till I get a full-time job."

Doris continued to smile.

"No. Neither of us uses drugs."

Doris nodded, slid her body forward and her glasses up, and began scribbling again in the folder. "We want to decide how best to classify you. I'm wondering if you would be better served under TANF or SSI or possibly . . . SSDI . . ." She glanced over her glasses. "Are you disabled in any way? Unfit to work?"

24

"No! I'd love to work."

"Okay, scratch that. Medically needy?"

"I told you, we're not sick."

"Okay then, our best bet is to go under a TANF with a TFP chaser!"

"What?"

"Temporary Assistance for Needy Families."

"That's what it stands for? *Needy Families?*" Jen felt defensive. "We're not exactly a *needy* family."

"And the Thrifty Food Plan." The woman ignored Jen's lament. Doris then pulled out a drawer and brought out a stamp caddy. "Might need to get you an SLMB, as well."

"Excuse me?"

"Do you have health insurance?"

"No. Mine ran out. But Emily is on her father's."

"Then Specified Low-Income Medicaid Benefits is for you." Removing four blocky rubber stamps, she smacked them each into the open red inkpad and then onto Jen's folder: TANF, SLMB, TFP, and below this a fourth set of letters Jen could not identify. "There, I'm hooking you up with OSCCS, too!" she said, triumphantly.

"OSCCS?" Jen asked.

"One Stop Career Center System. We'll see about getting you back to work." Then Doris rose and waddled from the office. "I'll be right back."

By the time Jen had made her rounds through the *system*, she had been assigned more numbers and classifications than a monkey in the zoo. Doris told her that she would be called by the OFA (Office of Family Assistance) as soon as housing became available, and not to lose her ID number or they would have to go through the whole process all over again.

The OSCCS was the most intrusive of all the stops Jen made along the way. In addition to all sorts of tests, including a timed-fitting of pegs into matching holes, a speed and accuracy typing test, lastly she was expected to pee in a plastic cup.

"But I *told* my case worker that I don't use drugs," she explained

25

to the man in a white lab coat. He handed her the cup and said, "Either contribute or exit."

She peed.

The phone rang and she hesitated; lately, there'd been a decrease in friends calling and an increase in bill collectors with whom she'd become friendly. The caller ID read *Daddy*. Jen groaned. It was her ex-husband, Emily's father, Hempy. Jen tapped at the phone, deciding whether to pick it up. She glanced down at the pile of bills in her hands and pushed them under a magazine on the table, as if Hempy could see them through the ringing handset.

That morning, her boss Debra had delivered the news that Jen's position as the children's librarian had been cut. It was the economy: state and local jobs were being slashed, left and right; the stimulus money everybody was hoping for had not helped teachers or first responders, tradesmen or, apparently, librarians the way it was supposed to. Jen could tell by the way that Debra kept shaking her head that she was genuinely sorry. It seemed like everybody she knew was losing their jobs.

She looked at the clock, it was just two; she already felt guilty about those four p.m. wine coolers she had been justifying lately. If she started now, she might as well just go down and turn herself in to the local AA. Sinking into the kitchen chair, she reluctantly lifted the phone.

"Hello?"

"Jen, it's me."

"Hempy?"

"Of course," he said impatiently. "I need to discuss a matter with you."

"A *matter*?"

He cleared his throat before continuing, further convincing Jen that his matter was *the* matter.

"Since Virginia and Vanessa are going to Montessori, just like Emily did when she was their age, I'm not going to be able to pay for any special activities."

"What kind of special activities?"

"Harrington Academy, for one."

"Since when is Emily's education a *special activity?*" she asked, getting up from the chair, challenged by the conversation. Nervously flitting from room to room, she listened as Hempy justified. She stopped her pacing in front of the mirror, noticing that her long blond hair was in need of color.

"Since I had to re-mortgage the house when the twins signed up for Gym-For-Tots."

In the mirror, Jen watched herself sputter. Her big blue eyes widened, blinked, and widened again, and the manicured lines of her dark eyebrows knitted in disbelief. "Gym-For-Tots?" She tried to steady herself. "You're saying this is more important than Harrington Academy?"

"Jen," Hempy cleared his throat more, and said in his usual patronizing tone, "Emily's already extraordinary education could push her to the head of any public school class, possibly even Valedictorian."

"You're suggesting that this might be *good* for her?"

"I'm certain of it. She might even better her chances of getting into the Ivy League."

"But she's already an honor student," Jen said, picking up her trot around the duplex. "She'll have to leave all her friends."

"She's well rounded. She can start the new year fresh, like everyone else."

As she built up speed, Jen's long limbs bumped the big furniture that was over-crowding the small space.

"But, there's her prom, and senior project, and yearbook . . ." Jen's panic for Emily's situation increased her circling. Her daughter's plans for this last year of high school had been hatching all summer long.

"She'll have all that at the new school." Hempy's tone had turned off-handed—nearly annoyed, Jen could tell, as if he did not want to be bothered with these pesky details.

"Hempy, these are her friends since kindergarten . . ."

"Can't be helped, Jen."

"No? What about the royalties to the fiftieth-whatever edition of

America's Lit? You can't tell me that you're not still selling a million copies of that monstrosity every fall semester."

"That money is gone before it ever lands in my pocket. I'm still paying for the messy divorce you dragged me through."

"*I* dragged *you* through? No one told you to go off and have an affair."

"End of conversation, Jen," Hempy said, the weary tone in his voice apparent.

Suddenly, rounding the corner, she stubbed her pinky toe, snagging it on the corner cabinet. Repressing a string of expletives so that Hempy wouldn't think they were for him, she plunged backward onto the couch, biting down on a throw pillow, as tears stung her eyes.

'What was that?" Hempy asked.

"Nothing." Jen gritted her teeth. Reaching for her foot, she massaged the injured toe. "I just wonder if there's any other way."

"Well, Jen, if you want Emily to remain at Harrington, then you'll have to be the one to afford it."

Jen softened her tone. "This must be her idea, Hempy."

"Who's idea?"

"Tiffany's. You can't seriously think this is good for Emily." Gripping the pillow tighter, she crushed it to her chest in an attempt to alleviate her growing fears.

"Jen, that's enough," his voice became paternalistic. "You don't have to like Tiffany, but she is my wife."

Jen punched the couch pillow beside her; an activity her therapist said would help release her anger. "It's not about that, it's about Emily."

"It's time for us all to move on."

"How is Emily supposed to move on?" She picked up the pillow and smacked it against the armrest. A seam opened and tiny feathers spilled into the air. Jen beat harder, watching them fly with the gusts. White tufts of goose down swirled up toward the ceiling and twirled tiny twisters as she fanned them with the flailing pillow.

"She'll make the best of it." Hempy was saying. "I know my little princess, she'll bounce right back."

28

Jen shook the pillow's loose skin, and the room filled with floating feathers. No two alike, she thought, just like snowflakes.

"I thought you should break the news to her," Hempy said quietly. "You're so much better at this than I am."

"No, Hempy, not this time. I'm done doing your dirty work. You tell her."

"Fine. Be that way." He hung up on her.

Jen raked her fingers across her scalp and tried to breath through her nostrils. Carefully rising, testing her toe, she swatted at the air. Her mother used to say that bad things came in threes; if Jen believed this, she might breathe a sigh of relief since it was just midday and three disasters had already occurred. Emily was going to have a fit about this news, and as Jen's own tears welled, thinking of her daughter about to have her world turned upside down, she tried to swallow back the accompanying anger, because it always, always led back to that bitch Tiffany.

She reached above her head and stretched out her long limber body. Still looking *great* for thirty-*eight*, she rhymed. Cupping her palms under her breasts, she smiled at the firmness. Like ripe peaches, she decided. How could Hempy have dumped this body for that . . . that . . . little *cunt*, her brain blurted, and she quickly clamped her hand to her mouth, as if the little curse might escape. He was an idiot for a college professor, she thought. Emily adored her father, and he loved his little princess. This all had to be Tiffany's idea. Jen suddenly felt sorry for him. He obviously has no choice.

Why are you defending him? The voice of reason echoed in her mind. She had come to hear it more clearly nowadays. When it first began whispering to her, she ignored it. That was right before she had discovered Hempy's affair. Back then, its insistent nagging had awakened her in the night, often pounding her with doubts and clues.

She defended him because she had always defended him. Roaming through the darkened corridors of their home on Robin's Egg Lane, sometimes with warm milk, more frequently with a shot of whiskey, the signs of her endangered marriage had become undeniable. Considering her own past with the infamous Dr. Hemphill Manners, you would have thought she would have caught onto the affair long before she had actually caught them in the act of it. Hindsight is always easy, she thought, and always too late. She had spent the last bit of the marriage denying and then, in some odd way, defending Hempy's need for another woman. She justified it the same way that she had justified her own adulterous role, those many years before, when late night meetings, lingering perfume, and Jen's own name had wheedled into the conversations of the *first* Mrs. Manners who had once occupied the house on Robin's Egg Lane.

She had been so very young and adventurous about everything back then, really. Going to college had been a way to cut loose from her strict military family. She'd escaped—in-state—but out of the house. She'd smoked pot, partied, slept around, and not just with boys. She'd actually been having an affair with her roommate before she got involved with Hempy. It was the eighties; everybody was screwing everybody. Sex with Barb had been a delicious taboo. Then Barb shaved her head and moved to San Francisco, leaving Jen alone without a girlfriend or boyfriend to comfort her when her mother died suddenly. It was Hempy who stepped in to console her.

She stared down at the pile of bills covered with white feathers. She heard her father's voice in her head, telling her there were no free-rides in this life. Well, he could judge all he wanted. She did not see him coming up with any alternative solutions. Ever since Mom had died and Daddy had taken up with Helen, he offered more opinions than support.

The front door pushed noisily open, and a gust of wind sent feathers flying around the tiny living room-slash-kitchen in little tornados. Jen cringed, hearing her daughter's loud entry.

"Mother!"

"In here."

"Mother! Where are you?" Emily's voice was shaking. "Something horrible has happened!"

"I'm here, dear," Jen said, wishing that she wasn't. "What is it?"

"Oh, Mom," the girl sobbed and threw herself into Jen's arms. "She's a horrible, terrible, horrible liar!"

"Oh, sweetie, you're flushed. Here, let me get you a cool rag." Jen stepped away from the sweating teenager, pointed her toward the dining room table, and headed for the sink. Emily sobbed, following her into the dining area, she hiccupped, and then emitted a low guttural growl that startled Jen, who immediately rushed to her daughter's side and massaged the girl's shoulders, whispering *shh, shh, there now, there now.* When Emily finally composed herself, she scanned the room, her eyes landing on each feather-covered surface, and finally managed to gulp down her distress enough to ask, "What happened in here?"

Jen rolled up a hand towel and rinsed it under cool tap water. "Put this across your head," she said, placing it on her daughter's brow.

"Where did all these feathers come from?"

"Oh, one of the pillows seems to have exploded . . ." Jen started, realizing that there was really no explaining her tantrum to her daughter without explaining what had caused it. Emily seemed upset enough by something else right now.

"Exploded?"

"Never mind, honey. Nothing my good vacuum can't suck up." Jen pressed the cloth against Emily's brow. "Here, sweetie, just close your eyes for a minute and calm down."

"Calm down? Calm down? Emily yanked the cloth from her head and tossed it into the pile of down on the table. "How am I supposed to calm down when that bitch is trying to ruin my life?"

"Now, Em, I know you're mad, but we've talked about this language of yours."

"Mother! Stop! Me cursing is the last thing I want to talk about right now! My life is about to be completely wrecked forever!"

"I'm going to make you some tea. You'll feel better."

"No! Mom! You're not listening to me!" She grabbed her mother's arm and pulled her to the table. "This is nothing tea can fix!"

Jen stopped and slowly slid into the chair next to Emily. One by one, Jen plucked feathers from Emily's long, streaky hair. Looking into those sad brown eyes, Jen could not help but recognize herself those many years ago. Teen-hood was a terrible time. A crooked tooth or nose could determine the outcome of an entire high school career.

31

Luckily, for Emily, both her teeth and her nose were perfectly straight, as was her jaw, hair, and spine. Jen knew Emily was a pretty girl who would grow into a beautiful woman. "Okay." Jen said. "So why don't you tell me what's got you all upset."

"Tiffany picked me up from school today, instead of Daddy." Emily coughed and tears began to flow all over again.

"Take it easy, honey." Jen handed her a tissue.

"She said he supposedly had some kind of doctor's appointment." Emily blew and then continued. "Tiffany said that Daddy said that they can't pay for school for me any more and that I have to go to *public* school!"

Jen felt the blood draining from her face and puddling in her feet. This was not supposed to happen this way. Hempy was supposed to break the news to Emily. He was supposed to witness the effects of his poor judgment. Instead, he found another woman to do his dirty work. What a coward.

Emily continued through her sniffles, "And so I said that I was going to talk to you, and we'd see who was going to public school." She blew her nose, again. "Tiffany said that it didn't matter what you said. And I said, 'Well, you don't know my mother very well then, do you?' And she said that she knew you all too well."

"What's that supposed to mean?"

Emily seemed not to have heard. "And then I told her she was a liar and that my dad would never do this to me. And then she said that he'd already done it, and I could start packing up my books."

"Oh, really?" Jen set a glass of water down on the table.

"And I said, like *that's* ever going to happen. And then I made her bring me here instead of to their stupid house." Emily took a deep breath and sipped her water.

Jen scooped handfuls of feathers into her palm and dusting them into the trashcan. As she moved around the table, she distanced herself from Emily and the truth.

"She's such a liar," Emily said, seemingly feeling better for having relieved herself of the situation. "Wait till Dad finds out. Huh, Mom?"

The broom in Jen's hands busily hurried around the floor. The pile

32

seemed to be accumulating more feathers than had once filled the pillow, and there were still zillions more all over the place.

"Mom, Tiffany *is* lying, isn't she?" Emily whispered.

Jen leaned heavily on the broom handle. She looked at her beautiful daughter whose heart-shaped face was nearly angelic. By protecting Emily from Tiffany's scheming and shielding Hempy from Emily's scrutiny, she had done them all a disservice. She had hidden her own pain about the affair, about losing her marriage, about having to move from the big Colonial on Robin's Egg Lane to the dinky duplex on Fourth Street. She sat down beside her daughter and placed a palm over Emily's hand.

"I'm afraid Tiffany's not lying. I talked to your dad, and he is having some money problems right now."

Emily shot out of the chair. "You mean I *am* going to public school?" Her face crumpled and big tears welled, crested, and spilled over dark lashes down her cheeks. It broke Jen's heart to see such anguish on her child's face. She felt her own tears brimming.

"I'm so sorry, honey. I don't know what to do about it." She reached a hand toward Emily.

She pulled away. "Why can't *you* pay for it?" Her mascara smeared spidery webs across her cheeks.

"Sweetie, I can barely make the rent as it is." She did not want to tell Emily, just yet, that on top of having to change schools and leave all her friends, she might also be moving into Section Eight housing. *Oh, and by the way, Mommy will be working at McDonald's at the mall, so you might want to avoid that with your pals.*

"But I told Tiffany that you wouldn't let this happen!"

"Well, if your father can't afford it, I can't very well get blood from a stone, now can I?" Jen stood.

"What does that even *mean*, Mom?" Emily whirled around the room, her arms flailing about her. The school uniform's blue and black kilt that skirted just above her knee flared as she twirled. She then stomped her foot, and then stomped both feet. "I can't believe you would let them do this to me. I can't believe that *you* would do this to me!"

There was such bereaved betrayal in the girl's eyes that Jen wanted to take it all back, make it all right, remember that there were gold doubloons hidden somewhere in a box amongst their belongings. She tried to gather Emily into her arms, but the girl would not have it.

"Leave me alone!" Emily said through clenched teeth. "This is the end of my life!"

"Now, Em," Jen tried again. "We can make this okay. We'll find the best school district in the county . . ."

She pushed her mother aside. "I might as well be dead. Dead, dead, dead!" She stormed down the hall. "My life is over! I will lose everything!" Before she entered her bedroom, she turned on her mother and screamed, "I hate you! I hate you worse than I hate those bratty twins! I even hate you worse than I hate Tiffany! You've fucked up everything!" She slammed the door behind her.

Jen stood perfectly still in the middle of the room. She could not really blame Emily; she really had *fucked up everything*. The clock on the wall now did read four-thirty. It was past justification time. It was also past wine-cooler time. Jen went to her secret cabinet, reached inside, and pulled out a half empty bottle of scotch and poured herself a double.

The pair had arrived home from their respective days at the same time. Stepping out of her car, Jen watched Emily slouch off the school bus behind a couple of ruffians shoving each other down the steps. The girl passed by her mother without a glance.

"Hi," Jen attempted, and double-timed her step to catch up. "How was your first day?"

Emily unlocked the front door and flung her book bag onto the kitchen chair. She opened the refrigerator and stood staring at its innards.

"Did you make it to all your classes?"

Emily ducked and rifled through the shelves.

"How were the teachers?"

She emerged with an apple in her mouth and threw a dark look at her mother.

Jen persisted, "What about the other kids? How were they?" She knew she was babbling, hoping each question might spark an interest and deflect the oncoming assault.

Emily turned and faced her mother. She swallowed the bite of apple and said, "Let's see . . . yes, I made it to my classes *late* after every asshole kid I asked pointed me in the wrong direction. But since the idiot teachers had no record of my enrollment, *anyway*, they gave me a break and sent me to the principal instead of marking me absent."

"Oh. Did you get it straightened out?"

Emily kicked off her shiny sneakers, something she had never worn to school before, and flopped onto the couch. She had never worn pants to school, nor the expensive blouse she had guilted her father into buying. Street clothes were more costly than uniforms. "Straightened out?" Emily sat forward and turned toward her mother. "I don't know if I'd call it *that*, because the whole mess-up happened because *you* forgot to *sign* the paperwork! I spent the whole day trying to call you . . ." she pointed to the machine blinking new messages.

"I was out shopping," Jen offered lamely.

"Well, I don't have *that* phone number, now do I, Mother? Since you canceled our cell phones!" Emily pointed the remote and punched on the television. Its loud music raised the barrier zone meant to keep Jen out.

She raised her voice over the volume. "So what happened?"

Without turning her gaze from the screen Emily said, "I had to sit in that shitty office all day long."

"Emily, watch your language."

"Oh, Mom, you have no idea how public school is expanding my vocabulary. I got to sit next to this pimply-faced kid who called his French teacher *a fine piece of pussy*! Oh, yeah, and as they were hauling this girl by her hair into the principal's office, she kept calling *him* a *fucking prick*!"

"Emily, come on. It can't be that bad!"

"No?" She stood. "Then how 'bout the kid who brought a knife to school? Or the girl who had to leave her math class because her water

35

broke? *Bad* enough for you, yet?" She turned toward her bedroom. "One more thing, all those great new friends you said I was going to make? Well, you were right; this girl with three nose-rings invited me to a rave this weekend and promised that the Xtasy would be top shelf!" She stormed to her room and slammed the door. In moments, it reopened and she yelled, "If you don't go down tomorrow and sign that paperwork, I can't go back to public school!"

Jen sat for a moment, mostly feeling slammed against a wall. As she shook off the assault, her thoughts took turns so unexpected that she wondered if they were her own. This had been happening a lot lately. She had never heard of *ecstasy,* but figured it was some kind of drug, and then considered its *top-shelf* quality, and for one quick instance, Jen imagined herself at a *rave* on an *ecstasy* inspired trip, and as she closed her eyes swaying to some pulsing beat in her brain, she more than wished she was there.

Chapter Three

"I just don't see why I have to go in there with you," Emily said, scowling and shrinking down into the front seat. "It's a nasty looking building, with nasty looking cars in the parking lot, and nasty looking people going in and out!"

"That's exactly why you're coming inside; I will not leave you out here, alone." Jen looked around to see a shady looking gas station, blood donation center, and a check-cashing store squaring the intersection, and noticed two men standing on the corner passing a brown bag back and forth. She shivered and said, "It's not the best neighborhood."

"Oh, ya *think*?" Emily rolled her eyes. "And what about the neighborhood you're dragging me to *live* in next week? You think *that's* the best neighborhood? Government housing? Section Eight Housing? Do you know what kind of people live there? Drug addicts, alcoholics, ex-cons, wife-beaters, perverts, single mothers with millions of babies . . ."

"Emily, that's enough . . ." Jen said, and exited the vehicle. When Emily still had not emerged by the time Jen got to the sidewalk, she pressed the keypad, setting off the car alarm and flashing lights; Emily threw open the passenger side door, and stormed passed her mother. "You can be so annoying," she said.

"And you are the light of my life," Jen said.

Carrie watched as the woman ahead of her nervously sifted the layers of paperwork she was holding. Outfitted in an obviously expensive but somewhat outdated blue designer suit (even Carrie knew it was the wrong season for navy), the tall blond-haired woman was still way overdressed for the Welfare office. *A newbie,* Carrie decided. It was written all over her. The once stylish haircut had begun losing its shape and the L'Oreal-boxed blond almost but not quite matched the last long-ago salon coloring. Her heeled pumps had experienced their own home-dye job whose streaky swipes did not quite hide black scuffmarks.

A younger version of the woman stood beside her: the daughter, no doubt, the resemblance made clear when the teenager turned her bored gaze toward Carrie. Unlike her mother's growing anxiety, evidenced as she fumbled through her purse, the teenager's ennui revealed itself in the slouch of her shoulders. She was also over-dressed for the Welfare line. But this version of the latest shabby chic trend was working for the girl. Her jeans were torn in just the right places, and the hitch of her shirt revealed a diamond bellybutton ring. Where the mother sacrificed her own hair coloring to the bathroom sink, the blond streaking through the daughter's brown hair was definitely done by a professional.

As the line slowly inched toward the counter, the woman opened the manila folder she was carrying and flipped through the documents and then closed it. She glanced back over her shoulder, searching for nothing, Carrie knew, and then noticed worry lines across her fore-head. The woman's eyes darted from door to window to clock, and then roamed the faces around the room, landing on Carrie's for just a moment.

"Next!" came the sharp report from the beefy social worker behind the counter. This spun the tall blond in an about-face, as if she were at boot camp. She smoothed her palms across her thighs and straight-ened her back. Thin, birdlike shoulder blades revealed a drop in weight since she'd purchased the too large suit. *Two years in,* Carrie guessed. She'd seen 'em all. Hell, she'd been 'em all.

As the woman approached her turn, she began fumbling papers and pens and her purse with such shaky hands that just before she reached the counter the bag and all its contents—lipstick, wallet, checkbook, breath mints, and loose change—skidded in every direction across the tiled floor. As the woman knelt, her daughter distanced herself, ignoring the calamity as if she were an innocent bystander to the wreckage.

Carrie crouched down, corralling rolling coins before they made their escapes across the green linoleum. She leaned to grab a loose tampon that had wedged beneath the open sandal of the seemingly unattached daughter. She smacked the pink painted big toe with the wrapped tube.

"Hey," Carrie said, looking up into the widening brown eyes. "Get down here and help your mother!" Her tone seemed to startle the girl to her knees.

As they each stood and poured the contents back into the purse, Carrie saw that the shaky woman was now in tears. Her bottom lip was quivering and a few big droplets landed on Carrie's hand as she deposited the runaway change.

"Next!" the order barked again from the counter.

"Hang onto your shorts, sister," Carrie barked back. "Can't you see there's a situation here?"

"Line's waiting," the civil servant said.

"*Two* words! Good for you!"

"Next!"

Grabbing the small Latina woman standing behind her, Carrie said, "Go ahead, go on," and pushed her toward the station.

"Gracias." The woman smiled and bustled ahead of them.

The shaking woman seemed about to melt into the floor. Steadying her by the elbow, Carrie whispered, "Come on. Get hold of yourself. Everything's gonna work out just fine." She said this as if it had been her own experience. But it hadn't. Ever.

"First time?" Carrie asked.

"How can you tell?" Jen sniffed and patted her eyes with a crumpled Kleenex she'd retrieved from her purse.

"Somethin' in the way you move," she said and then pointed to the disheveled manila folder. "Here, let me show you what you need."

Gratefully, Jen handed over the paperwork.

Without much fanfare, Carrie whipped through the official documents in their colorful triplicates, tearing the sheets away from each other, stacking the colors together, and arranging them in the order she knew the old cow behind the counter would demand of them.

"Got your license? Birth certificate? Social?" Carrie asked, handing the folder back to Jen.

"Yes! Here! All of them!" she said, nearly exuberant to discover she had done something right after all.

"Good, then. You are all set. Congratulations and welcome to the wonderful world of welfare!"

"Next!"

This time, Jen fumbled nothing and turned over the folder to the warden at the counter, still a little flustered, Carrie noticed, but no longer shaking. When her business concluded, she turned, placing her hand on Carrie's shoulder. "Thank you. Thank you so much."

"No problem," she said, making her way to the counter.

"No. Really. I don't know what I would have done if you hadn't helped."

"Oh probably picked up all that shit by yourself, is my guess." She threw a dark glance at the moody young girl leaning against the far wall.

"I'd like to repay you."

"No need. Pay it forward."

"Pardon?" Jen was now obviously confused.

"You know, like the movie, *Pay it Forward*? Rent it. You'll see."

"Next!"

"But, at least tell me your name?"

At this, Carrie now anxious to do her own welfare business, said quickly, "Carrie, Carrie Angel," and brushed past Jen, turning her back on the gratitude. In addition to all that gratefulness making her uncomfortable, Carrie had learned during her first couple of anger-management classes that she held resentment for anyone willing to help her out—something to do with *beholding* to another inspired a kind of contempt in her. At least, that's what her new counselors Russ and Pam said, and then recommended that she watch the movie *Pay it Forward*, which she did, and it helped. Her negative responses had gone from 10 down to 5 according to the anger-management temper-scale, all the counselors noticed. She was already at the top of her class. And so, she smiled at the government drone behind the counter.

"God! That was so humiliating!" Emily hissed as soon as they got in the car. "Wasn't bad enough that we had to stand there with all those germ-y homeless people, but did you *really* have to drop your purse in front of everybody? Do you know how embarrassing that was? Thank *God* none of my friends are destitute, and didn't have to witness that disaster."

"Well, it wasn't as if I'd planned it . . ."

Emily wiped her hands up and down her thighs. "I just want to get in the shower. Are there any wet-napkins in this car?" she demanded, flipping open the glove box, and rummaging around. "Where's that box of wipes?"

"Honey, I haven't had wipes in this car in months. We used them up."

"Ugh!" Emily grabbed a napkin from a bunch leftover from a drive-thru. "Why didn't you buy new ones?"

"Things are tight, in case you hadn't noticed . . ."

"Duh, we just came out of a welfare office . . ."

"So, I'm cutting back on our budget."

Emily twisted the napkin around each finger. "Great! You're willing to forego hygiene at the risk to my health!"

"Oh, Emily, you picked up three pennies and a cough drop, how dirty could they be?"

"And that's another thing! Who did that bitch think she was, yelling at me, anyway?"

"She didn't yell," Jen said, gently. "And she wasn't a bitch. She just asked you to help your mother. Was that so very difficult for you?"

"Yes, Mother! Yes, it really was so very difficult for me! I mean, look at all the horror you're exposing me to! No one whose parents are college educated, never mind someone whose father's a college *professor*, should ever have to spend time in a welfare office! Do have you any idea what I'm going through?"

41

Jen was losing her patience. She had tolerated Emily's contempt for the past month—ever since she learned that she'd have to leave Harrington Academy and move to subsidized housing, she hadn't spoken in more than monosyllables or at a decibel that didn't hurt Jen's ears, or with such disdain in her tone that it was just easier not to engage, but Jen was about fed up with the dramatics. It wasn't only Emily who'd been dealt a blow. It wasn't only Emily's life that had been turned upside down.

"Well, Emily, if you don't like it, you can always go live with that college *professor* on Robin's Egg Lane."

"What? And have to deal with that, that, that . . ."

"Don't say it," Jen warned. "I mean it. Do not say it."

"Uggghh!! Fine! And have to put up with that big-breasted tiny-brained slut for a wife my father married, and baby-sit for the twin spawns of the devil they bred? Really, Mother? Is that what you want for your only daughter?"

Jen would not answer, because at this moment all she wanted to do was drive the kid, bags packed, right up to Hempy and Tiffany's door, dump her, and head west—she didn't care where, just west of all this mess.

Emily quietly sulked into her own personal corner, and stared out the window at a life she believed some version of hell. As Jen threw the SUV into gear, she slid the big envelope on her lap to the seat and pretended the keys bulging inside belonged to a sea-side condo rather than government housing, the thick booklet of perforated tickets was full of coupons instead of food stamps, and the Medicaid ID card was actually for a membership to a luxury spa.

Someday, she thought to herself, making a pact with whatever God still had faith in her, when she finally got out of this mess, she would *pay it forward*, just as the woman in line—Carrie Angel—had done for her.

Chapter Four

As she sat waiting in her car for the final school bell to ring and let her kids loose, Carrie flipped through the *Finish Carpenter's Certification* handbook. She had been studying it forever. She would leave the Welfare to Work Program that she had begun years ago once she passed this last whopping test. Not that it took all these years to complete the course and fieldwork. According to the brochure, this could (supposedly) be done in a fast, breezy, twenty-four months. The only problem was that nobody had factored the kids into the formula. Sick ones keep you home. Absentee fathers cancel last minute. Babysitters forget or feign freakishly frequent periods. Then there were the teachers with so-called emergencies, like the time she was summoned to school because Tex, in the fourth grade, would not remove the bridal veil he had fashioned out of the plastic netting that comes wrapped around a frozen turkey.

Carrie swiped her palm across the thick, floppy book. Three dense inches of paper stood between her and a real job. No more welfare if she could just pass this test. No more of that prick Pressley. And no more Dill threatening to take the boys away. This telephone book-sized text was the only obstacle between Carrie and the real world. For the life of her, she could not pass a fucking multiple-choice test. In her mind, the match-ups could almost always be A, B, C, *or* D. She could often make a case for each. One instructor told her she was over-thinking and that she just needed to *dumb down*. Memorize the terms, spit them back, and forget about it. It was that simple, the instructor instructed. Not to her, she thought. She patted the cover of

43

the wearied book and took a deep breath. If she didn't pass it this time, she was screwed. Pressley had been right about the new limits. Three strikes and she'd be O.U.T. out. Then what would she do?

The distant rumbling sound of a motorcycle brought her from her thoughts. She caught a glimpse of the familiar white and black Harley that belonged to Sheckie. He passed and she waved. Sheckie was probably her best friend in this town. They'd met when she moved into the Section Eight housing where he was the superintendent. He could always make her laugh, and he was a good listener. He didn't say a lot, but when he did, you wanted to hear it. As he waved back, a quick rush of desire surged through her. She'd been intimate with him, once. After one long summer evening of drinking beers and revealing conversation, it had been easy to wind up in bed with him.

It was that night he told her about his daughter, Amy, who lived nearby with her mother, Mary Jo. Carrie had never met the girl or the mother, but Carrie knew that even though they were divorced, Sheckie and his ex had been determined to be good co-parents together. Which he was, but the rest of his life was kind of a mess. He was always broke for starters—and, she considered, for enders. Once she got on her feet, she wasn't going to let some guy who couldn't manage a simple budget bring her down.

While there were times since she'd been with Sheckie that Carrie wanted to feel his arms around her, his hands and his lips on hers, she'd never invited him in again, not into her bed or her heart. She would not let another troubled man rescue her. Next time she got involved with someone, it would not be out of desperation or loneliness. Next time (if there ever was one), she would marry for love—or money, whichever came first.

Just then, the bells from Dorothy Ivy Central High School shrilled, announcing the release of hundreds of hormonal teenage inmates charging through the front doors.

Approaching her car was the eldest of her two sons. Tex was dressed in a red and black plaid kilt. His socks reached his knees. Carrie had confiscated the knife he had tried to slide against his calf before he left home that morning. With a ruffled white shirt, a sporran at his waist, and a cape of the same tartan thrown jauntily across his shoulder, he looked almost as if he had stepped right out of the Scottish Highlands. What skewed this effect were the bright yellow and green clumps of hair sprouting from his scalp like a field of dandelions. He had spent hours in the bathroom the night before, carefully dipping each one.

"Mom!" Tex blurted, as he blurted everything. "Mr. O'Dell, the drama teacher, came by while I was working on the costumes for the school play; he loved my kilt and asked me to try out for a part in *Brigadoon!*" His sporran caught in his crotch and he wrestled it free. "Isn't that fabulous?"

"That's great, Tex. Did he say anything about your hair?"

"I was thinking of going back to my natural red anyway. It's so . . . *Scottish*, don't you think?" He flipped the mirrored visor down in front of his face and pulled a green strand to the tip of his freckled nose, cross-eyeing it carefully.

"We're Irish," she said.

"Irish, Scottish, whatever. Totally *Rob Roy.*"

"Where's your brother?" Carrie squinted across the lawn toward the doors where the deluge of kids had trickled to a drip. Just one fat kid hauling an oversized tuba case huffed into the sunlight. She caught a glimpse of herself in the side view mirror. She noticed freckles across the bridge of her. Her nose and chin both cut the same straight lines. The only sign of her thirty-five years were the deepening creases fanning around her eyes. These, like her freckles, were a symptom of the sun's bright rays.

"I last saw him walking an old lady across the street," Tex said, beginning a thorough examination of his own face in the mirror.

Just then, she did catch a glimpse of her younger son. He was hard to miss. The very tall, very skinny, fair-haired boy with the long easy stride loped across the schoolyard. Everything about him was long: his legs, his arms, his fingers and toes. He shouldered his backpack, and was hefting some kind of big yellow bag. He grinned and waved at Carrie, and picked up his pace. His khakis still held the crease he had pressed that morning, and his blue oxford shirt had stayed obediently tucked into his pants. Casper's fussiness was a little anal, to be truthful. Everything had to be in place. Every night before going to bed, he would flatten out his shirt, pants, and shoes on the floor, "Like a dead body lying there," she'd once confided to Sheckie.

As Casper rounded the car and before he got into the backseat, he swooped down to the open driver's side window and planted a kiss on his mother's forehead. Carrie saw that the canvas duffle bag sported the school logo (a giant ram's head) sprawled across its side.

"What's in there?" Carrie asked, pulling the car out of its spot.

"I joined the track team."

"You did? What brought that on?"

Tex answered, "He sprinted up the flag pole as the black sky was about to crack open, and saved Old Glory before the rain could reach one single star."

"Is that true?" Carrie asked, watching Casper in the rearview adjusting his long chin with a clench of his teeth.

"You're not supposed to let the flag get wet," he said, matter of factly. "By the time I saw the rain coming, I only had two minutes before the second homeroom bell rang, so I ran to get it down."

She noticed that his nose, recently too big for his head, had begun to align with his face. Bodies were so disloyal at fourteen. You could wake up one morning looking like freakin' Cyrano de Bergerac, with your nose hooking your chin like a macaw's beak. Two days later, the nose is back to normal, but no one notices because of the quarter-sized zit that has sprouted in the middle of your forehead. Which bones shifted or which glands erupted in the middle of the night could make or break your day.

"Coach said he had never seen anyone run so fast and asked did I want to join the track team. I told him I couldn't pay for the uniform and stuff, and so he said, no problem. Gave me the bag and all."

"You must have been hauling ass," Carrie said, thinking no coach would just give away a spot and a uniform without good cause.

"Flags are important," he said.

"Did you make the bell?"

"Of course."

46

"So, you've both had an equally impressive day! Your special gifts have been noticed and you've been rewarded!" Carrie was practicing her *encouragement skills*, something highly *encouraged* in anger-management. *When you take the negative focus off yourself and instead focus positively on those you love, your spirits lift and your temper dwindles,* said her hyper-*encouraging* counselors. Carrie was discovering, for the most part, that it was true, and so she tried her best. It was not always that easy to be happily focused on others' successes, especially when there always seemed some personal bullshit constantly blocking the view and making her own world, well, less than encouraging.

"What about you, Mamacita?" Tex asked while fussing with a loose curl in his visor mirror. "Were you noticed and rewarded for any of your special gifts today?" Carrie glanced at her older son who was seemingly more interested in his hair than his mother's answer, and so she said nothing.

It wasn't until they pulled into the slot at Sonic, and after the girl had skated away with their ice-cream order, that Casper leaned forward and asked, more soberly, "Well, Mom? Were you noticed and rewarded for any of your special gifts today?"

Carrie tried not to picture that morning's *notice* when the claw of Pressley's hammer tore into a piece of sheetrock she'd had the damnedest time hanging, pulling it from the ceiling's corner, screaming about how crooked it was, how incompetent she was, and making her do it all over again. Her reward was that she missed lunch—and that was probably good for her diet.

Carrie looked at her younger son in the rearview mirror, his eyes hopeful that something, one good thing, had come to her today, and so she winked at him. "I just noticed how rewarded I feel sitting here having ice cream with my two most special gifts."

Casper's cheeks pinked, and his mouth twitched into a small grin; he was both embarrassed and pleased by the intimacy; Carrie, sadly, admitted that she was less than generous with her kindnesses and felt shame to witness this in her son's cautious response. She promised herself that she'd try harder to focus better on the good in her life, which truly were her boys.

47

◻◻◻

Casper set out onto the cross-country track that ran around the perimeters and outskirts of Dorothy Ivy Central High School, or *DICHS* as it was mostly known to every teenager in the county. Why didn't people think about acronyms, he wondered. He thought about them all the time. Both those inadvertent and those deliberate, like *Mothers Against Drunk Driving* or *MADD;* that sure got your attention. Nothing worse than a mad-mom, he could guar-an-damn-tee that one. Made him never want to drink and drive; that was for sure. But really *D-I-C-H-S?* Did no one sitting on whatever board that picks names for high schools ever once consider the acronym? Most school jackets sported their names; his read **DICHS** arced across his back in large bold lettering. Did no one ever notice?

He checked his watch, put his finger to his neck and found his pulse. These after-school practices included this three-mile long route along hilly terrain, through a patch of woods, over downed logs, and across the same stream twice. Running was like taking a vacation, he thought. Out here, the only sounds were his own breath, the beating of his heart, and when he was really listening, he swore he could hear the push of blood flushing through his veins.

It had rained just before he'd set out behind the rest of the team. He liked to let everyone get ahead so he could run alone. These last couple of practices, he'd had to stretch extra-long and tie a shoelace twice to ensure that the pack was so far ahead that it wouldn't be till that last mile that he'd actually catch up. The ground was slick with wet leaves and slippery rocks, and he was glad for the new sneakers he wore.

Carrie had surprised him with a trip to the shoe store. She'd taken a side job, like she sometimes did. This one had been faux finishing cabinets for a kitchen remodel, she'd told him. It was a good chunk of change. Casper worried that the whole load had gone into his sneakers, but he didn't ask and tried not to feel guilty because he knew what effect his shoes had on their budget, and just exactly how poor they really were. He knew how bad things were in ways that Tex had no clue. He knew all the adult problems that his mom was dealing with, and had known all the ones that came before. He'd known it all since they'd moved into Sex8 because next to his bed was an air vent that was connected to another air vent below in the kitchen, above the table where all conversations in the house took place, including those on the telephone.

From his secret vantage, Casper could hear everything. He'd discovered this the first night they'd moved in, when the vent somehow amplified voices when the phone faced north. This discovery came when he'd actually recognized his mother's friend Lucy's voice on the other end.

After he and Tex went to bed, his mother would often make phone calls to friends, and some family. There weren't many in the family, though: no grandparents, no aunts or uncles, but there was a cousin or two, and Lucy who'd been Carrie's best friend since high school; but who'd recently moved away, so they talked less, and e-mailed more. Early on, he heard his mother crying on the phone about how broke she was, how scared she was, and then Casper was scared, too, and so he started mowing lawns, trimming hedges, raking leaves, but he was only a kid and a kid could only do so much.

With a pit in his stomach, he'd listened to Carrie's hissed pleas to Dill for extra money to buy the running shoes, only to hear his father complain about how poor he was, and to accuse Carrie of trying to *milk me for every penny I've got.*

A light drizzle had started, but Casper didn't mind the cool rain misting against his face. Sometimes, he'd imagine himself the gazelle, the antelope, the panther, and he could feel his muscles, tendons, bones, sinews, all working together like the limbs of the lion as he sprints across the plains. When Casper was an animal running like this, he could get away from his worries. And there were a bunch of 'em, he had to admit: money began and ended his list, but lately the Toyota was making a funny noise; Mom's carpentry test had him up at night trying to devise methods for her to study; Tex's mice kept copulating and multiplying; and other stuff, stuff that just made his brain hurt, like college and girls and whether or not America could survive two wars, an economic crisis, the worst unemployment rate in the history of the world, and on and on. Funny, but the thing all the *experts* think kids like him were supposed to be worrying about—*abandoned* by your dad—was the last thing on his mind. He hadn't actually been *totally* abandoned by Dill, if the truth was told, but he might as well have been. The frequency of weekend visits had diminished, the nightly phone calls had disappeared completely, and the canceling of trips and plans had increased. The currently sporadic contacts between father and sons were more bothersome than anything. When Dill did get in touch, it was usually to get them to do something for him, like clean out a garage or baby-sit the herd of kids he now had. The life of fun with his father that Casper had, once, for a minute known—before it got usurped by Dill's wife, Dodi; her chubby son Dusty; their daughter, Destiny; and the new baby on the way—was a dim memory.

Casper pumped faster, jumped higher, until there was nothing in his mind, not worry, not anger, not guilt, and especially not the longing for a phone call that might begin with his father's words: "How about *you and me* go for a run, a hike, a swim . . ." There had been a time when he'd wished for that call, but it never came, so he quit wishing. After Dill walked out on them for Dodi and Dusty, there had never again been just a *you and me*. There was no *Dill* without *Do*, as Tex always said.

Ahead of him, he caught a glimpse of a bright yellow jersey like his; a fellow teammate he'd pass by with a polite nod. Approaching, he could see that it was Sarah Lash, a junior and one of the team's captains. Her canter, as he thought of her running style, was *jaunty*; he grinned, pleased with his word choice.

Over the last few weeks, in his mind, he'd matched the running styles of his teammates with those in the animal world. Casper imagined himself the great gazelle easily gliding over and around tall grasses, riverbeds, and predators. His feet, especially in these new shoes, barely touched down before his toes pushed him ahead, propelling him along the trail.

Sarah, whose breath he could hear above his own, was a wild pony.

The pulsing symmetry of her muscles and limbs, packed tight and rippling as she galloped along: equine in motion. A mustang.

"Left," he called out, warning her of his approach. He made the mistake of tossing a glance and a smile over his shoulder as he passed. For one fatal second his eyes left the trail. The tip of his left shoe stubbing against a jutting rock sent him flying. Instinctively, he reached and grasped at air. Casper flew spread-eagle into a holly bush on the uphill bank. He landed face down with a thud. Sarah's concerned voice echoed behind him. He did not want to get up. Instead, he thought about burrowing deeper into the wet, loamy soil. Perhaps he would be swallowed into the earth that was filling his mouth. He pushed out a wad of dirt with his tongue.

"Hey, are you okay?" Sarah's worry shook in her voice.

He felt a cool hand on his shoulder. If he just stayed still, maybe she would leave, thinking he was dead, go for help. Then he would make his escape. He'd pack his clothes in the yellow DICHS duffle bag, leave a note for Mom and Tex, and sneak out in the middle of the night. He'd catch the first bus out, no matter where it was going. Maybe head down to Mexico. He'd grow a beard and work in a tequila bar . . .

"Hey." Sarah patted his damp skin. "Do I need to get help?"

Slowly, with all the dignity he could muster—not much— Casper heaved himself up and back. Wiping a hand across his face, he tried to slide the mud from between his teeth. Finally, when he realized he couldn't spit in front of Sarah, he worked up enough saliva to swallow.

"Oh, you're bleeding," she said, reaching for his cheek. "You've got a few good scratches." She dabbed with the cuff of her jersey. "Holly bushes are pretty, but they sure can be dangerous."

Casper coughed. He brushed clumps of mud from his knees and elbows, checking for any other harm done. The damage seemed to have focused on his face and pride. Sarah was pulling wet leaves out of his hair, and one from behind his ear. After they rid Casper of most of the evidence of his calamity with the holly bush, the pair leaned, panting, against the bank.

"You're Casper, right?"

He nodded, finding words elusive.

"I'm Sarah. Sarah Lash."

He nodded again. Worried that the dirt stuck in the back of his throat might choke his response, he wrangled his tongue around his mouth, divining one more wad of spit to take the clog of soil down his throat.

"You're a sophomore?"

Casper nodded, praying that when a question came that required more than a yes or no, his teeth would be unblemished and his throat would be clear. He swallowed hard.

"I've watched you run," Sarah said, easily, as if she was used to talking, Casper thought. "You are insanely fast. Did you run in middle school?"

"No," he was finally able to manage, relieved that all passages were open. "But a pack of bullies used to chase me home every day after school, so I got good at running."

"Bullies?" Sarah was immediately concerned. "Why would they do that?"

"My brother says that I look like the kind of guy a bully wants to beat up."

"Oh, you do not," Sarah said, turning to him. "Bullies beat up anybody that doesn't look, act, or spit like them."

He swallowed again and said, "Well then, my brother's right. These were a bunch of dwarves. Guess if I were a dwarf, I might want to beat up tall guys."

Sarah squinted, suspicious. Casper noticed how dark her eyes were, black inky pools like bulls-eyes on a target. "You're kidding, right?" she asked.

"No. They were dwarves, seven of 'em. All lived in this group home for orphaned dwarves. Left in baskets on the doorstep, I'd heard."

"Yeah, and a beautiful princess keeps house and cooks for them."

"You know about them?"

She swatted at him. "Funny kid." She put her hand on his arm and he thought it would singe his hairs off. He tried not to look down but

52

was acutely aware of her very fingerprints as they seared his skin. Casper stayed still, holding his breath a little, hoping she would forget that her hand was on his arm, leaving it long enough to impress her soul forever.

Rain had begun; a light but steady sprinkle. Sarah stood first and then reached her hand down to Casper, giving him a lift. She was strong, he could tell. He towered above her, and she tilted her head back as he rose. "Yeah, I could see how those dwarves might want to beat you up." They started to walk the last mile.

"Is it true that you made the team because you rescued the American flag from a storm?" Sarah asked.

"Sort of, I guess." Casper shrugged. "I think it was because I ran fast to get it."

Her shoulder bumped his as they maneuvered over the uneven path. "Why'd you do that?"

"Flags aren't supposed to get wet."

"No, but you don't see people leaping from buildings to haul them down every time it rains."

"It's not supposed to touch anything below it, either: not the ground, water, the floor, or merchandise," Casper said.

"Merchandise?"

He continued, "It's not supposed to hang upside down or be used as a receptacle for carrying stuff. You shouldn't wear it as clothing, drape it over a car, or use it as a covering for a ceiling. And did you know that when it gets hoisted to half-staff, it actually goes up to full staff, first, and then drops back down to half?"

"Why would you know any of that?"

"Why would you not?"

"Are you a Boy Scout or something?"

"You don't have to be a Boy Scout to be a good citizen."

Sarah looked over and this time bumped his shoulder on purpose. "You're serious, aren't you?"

He kicked at a stone as they entered the clearing that opened to the schoolyard.

"I'll race you," Sarah said, but she had already bolted. Casper leapt quickly after her, feeling a slight twinge in his knee where it had knocked against a rock in his fall. She was like a pony in full gallop. Casper sprinted, catching the earth with the balls of his feet, pushing himself along the ground, finally catching up with the speeding filly. He took one great stretch to overtake her and easily flew past, raising his arms as he passed through the gates into the schoolyard.

She was right on his heels; he could feel her wind as she whipped by. "Show off," she yelled to him.

"Me? Wasn't that you who jumped the race, before I even had a chance? I had to do something."

Just then, a black Mercedes sedan pulled to the curb. "Oh, there's my dad," Sarah waved at the vehicle. "Do you need a ride?"

Casper looked to the sky and prayed it wouldn't open full valve until after he got home. "Oh, thanks, but no thanks. My mom should be along any minute."

"Okay, then. I'll see you tomorrow." Sarah waved and ducked into the car. Casper watched as she leaned across the seat and pecked her father on the cheek. Then they both smiled and began talking.

Casper waited for the vehicle to round the corner and then he took off. He'd told Carrie last week that he wanted to start running home in order to build his stamina. But his real reasoning was, the fewer trips the Toyota had to make, the longer its life. At least, he hoped so. Crossing the street and into the exclusive Knob Hill neighborhood, he'd discovered a short cut through a couple of ritzy backyards, but nobody seemed to be around to care. As he was passing a large white two-story house, with side porches upstairs and down, a black Mercedes pulled into its driveway.

"Hey! Casper!" a voice called out.

He turned to see Sarah emerge from the sedan and wave to him. His cheeks were the first to flush, caught in the lie. He was glad he'd been running; she'd probably chalk it up to that.

"Oh, hey," he panted, slowing his stride. "I didn't see you." Casper looked to see a gray-haired man in a business suit getting out of the car. He was carrying a large black bag, and when he caught Casper's eye, he smiled and waved. Casper waved back. "You live here?"

Sarah nodded, glancing back over her shoulder toward the house, as if making sure it was the right one. "Since I was a baby."

A woman came to the door and greeted Sarah's father with a warm hug and a kiss. "Sarah, honey," she called. "We're going to eat in twenty minutes."

"Okay, Mom. I'll be there in a second." She turned back to Casper. "I thought your mom was picking you up?"

"Yeah. I forgot. She's working late this week. I told her I would just run home. I forgot about it. No big deal."

"Do you live around here?"

Casper looked around at all the large homes, manicured lawns, sprinklers going, and shiny cars in every drive. "Not far. Over that way," he mumbled, gesturing in no specific direction.

"How far is it from school?"

"Just a few miles."

"Do you do it every day?"

He shrugged. "Well, when my mom can't pick me up."

Sarah's brow was working, as if she were thinking beneath it. Her long body turned toward the direction of the school and then her eyes landed on her home. Seeming to have decided in her own mind, she turned back to Casper. "Could I run home with you, sometime?"

"To my house?" he blurted, panic rising, thinking of the run-down apartment complex and his own dinky little unit compared to these monstrosities. Maybe he could find an empty mansion along this street. Farther down, where Sarah might not know the neighbors, where the cars are missing and the lights are out. Then maybe he could remember that MacGyver episode where he picked a lock with a shoestring. Then Casper could take Sarah into his borrowed home and pray that his loaner family was clean.

"No, silly," she interrupted his scheme. "I mean if you run by my house after practice, maybe I could just run with you, to here. To my house."

"Oh, right," he grinned, feeling relief and embarrassment crowding each other inside him. "Sure. That'd be great. I'll wait for you tomorrow. By the gate, in case I don't throw myself across your path and into a holly bush along the trail."

Casper ran home at his greatest speed. He scaled walls in single leaps, hurdled fences, trashcans, and three little girls playing hopscotch. He flew into the apartment, past Tex sewing something glittery on the machine Carrie had given him for Christmas. He grabbed an apple, and in just two strides, he conquered the stairs. His room was a tidy haven of neatly arranged furniture and very few knick-knacks. Casper threw himself onto his back onto his bed. After just one bite and swallow of the apple, he closed his eyes, and smiling, he fell fast asleep.

Chapter Five

Carrie pulled into the parking lot of the housing complex. She noticed a large moving truck with its rear doors gaping in front of Number Four, just a couple of doors down from her own. She slid the beat-up Toyota into her allocated space. Leaning over, gathering grocery bags from the floor, Carrie felt a large shadow cast across her back. When she sat upright, there were two bulky elbows planted at her open window.

"Jesus, Sheckie, you scared the shit out of me!" she said, annoyed, but she wasn't. "You gotta quit sneaking up on me like that."

The giant leaned back and yanked open her door. As usual, the rusted hinge squealed like chalk on a board. Carrie cringed, as she always cringed, and thought what she always thought: WD-40 would take care of that.

"I'm a six foot four, two hundred and fifty pound man, Carrie, how can I sneak up on anybody?" He grinned wide from beneath the thick black mustache that reached to his jaw line. A single, thick black braid snaked to mid-spine. "Here, let me get those for you," he said, taking the grocery bags out of her arms. He wore what he always wore: denim overalls and heavy leather boots. And a T-shirt. His massive chest pushed tight against the bib front. He cradled the two brown grocery bags like babies, tiny in his muscular arms. Tattooed sleeves of red and black fiery flames cuffed his forearms from wrist to elbow. On one shoulder was a pink heart with *MOM* ribboned across it. In a macabre juxtaposition, a skull clenching a dripping bloody knife between its teeth grinned hideously.

Standing together on the sidewalk, she dusted the day from her jeans. Carpentry was dirty work that got all over you, and sometimes into you, and sometimes not even a hot shower and a good scrub brush could get it off. Sometimes she could taste a job in the back of her throat days after it was over.

"How was work?" Sheckie asked.

Carrie rolled her eyes. "You want the long version or the short version?"

"How about the short long version?"

"Well, if picking up bent nails and screws all day long is the heart of carpentry, then I was the pulse today."

"Pressley got you on your knees?"

"Ever since I went to Ketchum about the *missing ladder* incident, Pressley's been dumping every pissant job there is on me. I feel like I'm back to being an apprentice instead of a journeyman."

"It'll all be over soon," Sheckie reassured. "You'll be done with him before you know it."

"One way or another," she said, but did not mention the anxiety she was feeling about the upcoming test that would either make or break her career. Carrie shaded her brow from the sun and squinted at the big truck. Changing the subject, she asked, "Who's movin' in?"

"Guess," he dared.

"Bet?" she dug into her jeans pocket for a quarter.

"Nah, too easy for you."

"Chicken." She slid the coin back.

"Divorced mother of . . .?"

"Four kids," she guessed, watching a couple of movers hump furniture and boxes out the back of the van into the apartment.

"Never mind, just give up." The big man nudged her.

"Okay, I give up."

"One girl!"

"One?" She was surprised. Most of the women who landed here had at least two kids, more often three, and even sometimes more. No one had just one. "A baby?" She ventured, curious.

"No, actually a teenager. Pretty girl. Looks kind of grim, though."

"Aren't they all?"

"I suppose," he said. A faraway look fleetingly crossed his brow. But then he quickly brightened. "Speaking of grim teenagers, yours just got home."

"I'm surprised the vultures aren't out here circling you with those grocery bags. The cupboard inside is bare." Feeding teenaged boys was a never-ending task. Had they been stranded on an island, she was convinced they would have cannibalized her by now. Casper especially never seemed to fill up. He was like a cow, always grazing. She once had the doctor check him for tapeworms but there were none. *Just a growing boy,* the doc had declared.

Carrie felt her own stomach rumble. One thing about being on a shoestring, it kept her skinny. She placed a hand on her belly and felt its firmness. Most of her life she had felt small at five foot three. Standing next to Sheckie always made her feel like a midget. She slipped a strand of curly reddish hair behind her ear.

"Casper's gonna come down to the shop with me later," Sheckie said. Casper was crazy for motorcycles too.

Sheckie had been working on them since he was in diapers; he told her one night over a beer. His old man had been the nut before him. Sheckie's first restore was a '59 Duo Glide. A red and white pedigreed beauty, he had described with the same lusty grin he was wearing now.

"I got a '65 Electra Glide on the slab down there, ready to take apart." His eyes were gleaming.

Without actually verifying it with a glance, Carrie could tell by the look on Sheckie's face that he had a hard-on. Say the word *Softail* and every one of them (she would stake the ranch on it) simultaneously imagines pussy and bike. Probably pussy *on* bike.

"I asked Tex if he wanted to come," Sheckie said.

"Let me guess. No."

"Said he had to finish making a costume for some party."

Carrie set her bag on the ground and lit a cigarette. "Why do you persist in trying to get Tex down to that shop? You know he hates anything that will get him dirty."

"I know. I just wanted to include him."

"Well, I know he appreciates that much. At least you try. It's more than I can say about that so-called dick-weed of a father he got saddled with."

"Another round with the mighty Dilbert?"

"Let's just say that last round of mediation didn't go the way we'd all hoped," Carrie blew smoke into the air.

"No? What now?"

"Court, if Dill actually follows through with his threat."

"Mr. Sheckmeyer?" The voice was coming from the far side of the moving van. Fast moving heels clicked along the pavement, carrying the voice into the open. "Oh, there you are, Mr. Sheckmeyer." The woman emerged from behind.

"Who the hell's Mr. Sheckmeyer?" Carrie whispered.

"Shut up."

"Oh my, it's you!" the woman called, hurrying toward them. "Carrie Angel, right? From the Welfare office? It's me, Jen Manners, remember? You helped me out."

"You *helped* someone out, Carrie Angel?" Sheckie asked.

"Fuck off," she said under her breath, and smiled at the approaching woman. "Sure, I remember," she called. "So, this is you movin' in?"

Jen glanced back at the moving van and sighed. "I'm afraid so. I have way too much furniture." She looked from Sheckie to Carrie. "Do you live here?"

"Yeah. Number Two." Carrie thumbed over her shoulder.

"Well now I really *can* pay it forward. And right back to *you*." She smiled. "I did see that movie. I was just confused."

"All right, then," Carrie said, remembering their previous conversation, but not really wanting to revisit it. She took the brown bags from Sheckie's arms and said to him, "Looks like your superpowers are being called upon."

"Tell Casper to come find me when he's done."

"Nice seeing you again," Jen said. "I'm glad we'll be neighbors. I could use a friend right now."

Carrie nodded and made her way to the door thinking: This is what happens, be nice just *one* friggin' time and the next thing you know you got a new best friend. Last thing I need is a new best friend. What I need is a job and out of Section Eight.

"Carrie?" Jen called, stopping her mid-stride.

She turned to see the woman standing beside a dark leather sofa and chair. "I was wondering; I can't use these here, there's not enough space. They were in our rumpus room."

Rumpus room?

"Could you use them?"

Carrie looked them over. They were beautiful. Italian leather, she guessed. Not some pleather or vinyl shit, and in good shape.

"How much?"

"Oh no, I wouldn't sell them to you."

"Then no can do. Thanks anyway."

Jen stepped away from the suite and moved toward her. "You helped me out so much down at the welfare office. Please."

"Sorry. It's not an even trade, I'd owe ya."

"How do you know, though?" Jen was looking intently into Carrie's blue eyes. "I was desperate. You told me to pay it forward. Who are you to decide what it was worth to me? Maybe *I* don't want to owe *you*."

This stopped Carrie. She had been standing right there in Jen's skin, feeling this same indebtedness too many times not to feel the woman's need to make it even. Carrie shrugged. "Okay, fine. I'll have my boys come get them."

"Thank you so . . ." Jen started.

Carrie held up her palm. "Enough. We're even. You're all paid up. Got it?"

"Got it."

Carrie and the boys were on their way to the grocery store, a Saturday chore that none of them liked and each of them grumbled equally about, when she spied the mail truck pulling away and noticed a clump of people in front of the cluster of mail boxes. As she got close she saw that it was Sheckie, Jen Manners, and her spoiled daughter, huddled together on the sidewalk. When she met Sheckie's eyes, she saw something helpless in them, something pleading, and so she and the boys wandered over to the threesome.

Jen was shaking.

"What's happening?" Carrie asked, sliding a cigarette from her pack.

"Jen here got some bad news," Sheckie said.

"My ex . . . reduced child support . . . hardship, it says," Jen stammered.

Sheckie gently took the paper from Jen and handed it to Carrie. Oh yeah, she had seen this before, another court order denying another single mother something: health insurance, custody, child support, visitation, the list went on. She didn't recognize this next part. "Health hardship?" she asked, looking up at Jen. "He got off on a *health* hardship? What's the matter with him?"

"His heart, supposedly. Irregular beats, is what he told Emily. Personally, I think his ticker is finally giving out after screwing his way through the entire university."

"So is it bad?" Carrie asked.

"Who knows? When we first met, he was this virile giant of a man. The last I saw him, he was hunched over and all that great hair that even I envied is thinning."

"So, he's getting old." Carrie consoled.

The boys and Emily were eyeing each other. They had not yet been introduced, and so Carrie decided to change the subject. "Tex, Casper, these are our new neighbors, Jen and—."

"Emily. I'm Emily."

They all fumbled, nodded, and mumbled some stuff and finally Carrie said, "Tex, why don't you and Casper take Emily to our place? Have a snack, watch some TV, and clean up your mice."

"Mice?" Emily perked up, suddenly animated. "You have mice?"

Tex nodded. "Millions."

"Can I see them?"

"Sure. Nice Prada," Tex said, pointing to Emily's shoes.

"Thanks, my dad got them for me."

The threesome headed for Number Two.

"Would you like to come inside?" Jen offered the grown-ups an invitation to her apartment. "The place is a mess from the move. But I can make us some tea."

"Coffee?" Sheckie ventured.

Jen smiled. "We're all set."

Stepping into Jen's apartment, Carrie felt like she had entered some underworld, like Alice in Wonderland. Jen's giant furniture dwarfed her. It was too big, clunky, and opulent for the size of the place. High-backed dining room chairs reached for the ceiling. A large plush sofa and chair covered the postage stamp of a carpet, nearly pressing the giant oak armoire up against the wall as if it were under arrest. Crystal and silver and what Carrie could see to be fine pieces of antiques, art, and sculptures cramped up against each other, into corners and along walls; there was little room to move around. Jen cleared a space at the large dark mahogany table and got them each their pleasure.

Carrie pulled a pack of Bicycle playing cards from her purse and whacked them on the table. She carried them with her at all times, an old trick she learned when she first got thrown into a system whose sole purpose was to make you hurry up and wait. The cards could help pass the time in any government *support* office. She'd been through them all. "Spades, anyone?"

"Sure," Sheckie said, clearing a space in front of him. They had been playing together for years.

Jen looked up, startled. "Cards?"

"Don't you know how to play?" Carrie asked.

"Well, yes. But it's been years. I mean, it's the middle of the morning." As if that somehow mattered greatly at the moment. "I'm not sure I can play right now. Things are so upsetting."

"Spades'll fix that," Sheckie said.

Carrie explained the rules to Jen and dealt them each a hand.

After a few rounds, Jen confessed, "Even with those lousy food stamps I just got, I'm broke. It's all gone. I have nothing."

Carrie grabbed her hand and held it in front of her face. "Whatdya call these?" She was pointing to the two hulking diamonds on Jen's fingers.

"Those are my engagement and anniversary rings."

"Got any more like that?"

Jen nodded, taking a deep breath, but a look of confusion remained on her face. "Yes."

"Anything else?" Sheckie asked, slapping the cards down in front of him.

Jen smiled nostalgically, "I have a storage unit full of antiques, silver, my furs, some of Emily's things, and stuff I can't remember."

"Then you don't have nothing, you've got plenty to sell," Carrie said.

"Sell?" Alarm replaced Jen's confusion. "I couldn't possibly *sell* any of it. It's all priceless. As soon as I get out of this mess, I'll need it all again."

Carrie laid down her cards. "Look, lady," she said quietly. "You don't seem to get it. Women do not wind up in Section Eight as if it's a stopover between hot vacation spots. Women in Section Eight are here because it is the last stop. Do you understand? You need that stuff now. To sell. So that you can make it into next month. Understand?"

Tears welled up and spilled down Jen's cheeks. Sheckie shuffled his big frame uncomfortably, finally reaching a hand to the woman's shoulder. "It'll be okay," he tried.

Carrie had no patience or pity. She wanted to shake the woman. Tell her to get a grip. Buck up. Instead she said, "Where is this storage unit?"

"Over by the new mall."

"All right, then. Tomorrow we'll go get some of your stuff and I'll show you where we can get a good price for it."

Jen sniffed and then sipped. "I can always get rid of my furs; I hardly go anywhere, lately. By the time things get right, they'll be out of fashion anyway."

"Well, there you go," Carrie said, raising her eyebrows at Sheckie, who frowned, shaking his head, warning her to keep her comments to herself.

Later that day, long after Carrie and Sheckie left, Jen was surprised to see Emily tiptoeing into the house with a smile on her face.

"Did you have fun?" Jen ventured, viewing the smile like a crack in a usually closed door, a gentle tap to see if it would widen.

Emily shrugged but did not leave. Instead, she flopped down on the couch beside her mother, who covertly lowered the volume of the TV with the remote on her lap. She didn't turn off the set. No, to do that would cause alarm in the young girl, like the sudden quiet of a forest that alerts deer to their enemy.

"Tex has a closet full of costumes."

"For Halloween?" Jen asked, then wished she hadn't when she saw Emily begin the impatient eyelash flutter. Instead of abandoning her mother to her own un-coolness, Emily remained slouched on the sofa, wrapping a long strand of silky auburn hair around her finger. Her big brown eyes always reminded Jen of a fawn's, making her want to hug her daughter, but she did not dare. Emily had been such an affectionate little girl; this pubescence-inspired distance was hard on Jen.

"He makes them. For anytime. Not just Halloween," Emily said, kicking off her shoes. "He gets ideas from movies and books and stuff. First, he draws the costumes on sketchpads. Then he takes Barbie dolls . . ."

"Barbies?"

Emily nodded and sat forward. "Yeah, Barbie and Ken, he's got dozens of them. All made up in these little versions of his life-size costumes. He cuts their hair, draws makeup on them with markers," Emily said, warming up to her description.

"My God . . ."

"You wouldn't believe it really. He's got bags full of scrap cloth, pleather, silk, old buttons, sequins, feathers . . . I mean, it's mind-blowing. He designs them, sews them, hot glues them, first for the dolls; then, if he likes them, he makes them for himself. He showed me pictures of him dressed like Farrah Fawcett at a drag show, and—"

"Drag show?" Jen interrupted.

"Yeah, drag show," Emily stopped and sat back.

"Is he gay?"

"So what if he is?" Her voice rose as quickly as she did.

"Nothing," Jen said carefully. "I just didn't realize . . ."

The girl swung around and marched across the room. "No, Mother, you wouldn't have realized it. You rarely realize anything." She poised at the bottom of the stairs. "Even when it's right under your very nose. Had you noticed that stupid teaching assistant when she was screwing my father, maybe she wouldn't have gotten pregnant. Maybe he wouldn't have married her. And maybe we wouldn't be living in this shit-hole next door to a *gay* boy." She stomped up the stairs.

What just happened? Jen listened as her daughter slammed her bedroom door. Instead of going after her, which she had done so many times during one of these *incidences,* as she'd come to view them, Jen got up and poured herself the last swallow from the wine bottle into her glass. She returned to the sofa but did not raise the volume of the television. Everything that Emily accused her of had at one time or another crossed her own mind.

My God, she thought, I *should* have seen the signs. She recalled sitting alongside Hempy's students and colleagues, listening as her husband read from his short story about a thinly veiled version of himself, *Billy,* in this case, a tortured *psychology* professor, wrestling his *duty* to his young wife and young *son* against his passionate lust for a *student* named *Brittany.* The slam-dunk came at the end of his reading, in the appalled pause preceding the applause, when not one pair of eyes would meet her own, including her husband's. She was the laughing stock of the campus. She guessed she got what she deserved.

Jen twirled the glass and wished for a cigarette. She *should* have seen it all coming. It was like a familiar ride through an old home-town. She had watched from the sidelines as Hempy's first marriage wrecked, as if she had played no part. As if she was an innocent bystander just waiting for the smoke to clear.

After all, back then, it was Hempy's *first* wife, Ruth, who had been in Jen's current shoes. The irony was not lost on her. Ruth had been frigid, Hempy had confided one evening as they sat in front of Jen's apartment with the engine running. He ran his fingers through his thick salt and pepper hair, only just beginning to gray at his temples. He was tortured, he had confessed. He loved Ruth so much; he had said this choking back tears. "I just can't seem to *please* her anymore. She has shut down to my very touch. It's been years, and my God," he clenched his fist, "I *have* been faithful! A man can only take so much. I feel cut off from my own blood supply."

She had believed him, then. Today, she'd bet the farm that she wasn't the first or the last woman he'd used that line on. He was a *man* in bed, she had discovered. Not like the college boys that she would let fondle her nipples as she fondled their dicks, coming quickly because there seemed nothing else to do. Actually, if she really thought about it, he was more like a woman-lover, with slow, knowing fingers, enticing and exciting, and had he not been this way in bed, Jen sometimes wondered if she might have wound up with women. She had been that close with Barb, and had nearly ran off to California with her.

All that was so long ago, as if it had happened to another person. She supposed it had; that sexy young adventurous woman had turned into something of an old frumpy boring *mother*. She wondered if she would ever feel sexual again. She'd not even had a satisfying moment with herself in the last year that was anything more than obligatory. After Emily was born, sex was like a holiday, it happened during certain times of the year: like all the old traditions, it was accompanied by baubles, ornaments, feasts, and a nostalgic intimacy in low-lighting. Of course there was a certain satisfaction amped-up by little blue pills, and then, the next morning all the accoutrements packed up and put away until the next holiday.

She imagined that this had also been the case for the first Mrs. Manners after their daughter Sylvia (for Plath) was born. Like Emily (for Dickinson), Sylvia resented Jen as much as Emily now resented Tiffany. Like Sylvia, Emily had been a daddy's girl. Treated as the princess until Daddy needed a new queen and bore new princesses.

This time around, the twins were named Virginia and Vanessa, for the Woolf sisters. *The man is a freak,* Jen thought, and drained her wine glass. *Those of us who agreed to name our daughters after tortured literary figures are even bigger freaks.*

"Mom?" A small voice came from the bottom of the stairs.

"Emily?" Jen startled and turned around. "I thought you went to bed."

"I couldn't sleep."

"Do you want to watch TV?"

Emily shook her head but did not move from her place. "I didn't mean it," she mumbled. "I didn't mean what I said about you and Tiffany and—well, all of it."

"I know. But sometimes I think you might be right. I was in La-La Land, as they say." Jen patted the seat beside her.

Emily joined her on the couch. "You were always home for me. Driving me everywhere, taking me shopping, waiting for practices to be over. I mean all that *and* volunteering at school, Junior League, Mothers Against Rap Music. I mean, how could you have known?"

Jen was surprised to know Emily had even noticed.

"I would have been better off having a job all those years instead of those volunteer things. At least now I'd have work experience. I've wasted my degree."

"Casper said his mother's getting some kind of carpentry certificate, and when she does they'll move out of here."

"You think I should do *carpentry?* Can you picture me?"

"In a tool belt?" Emily said, impishly.

The words shocked Jen. She hadn't heard this kind of playfulness in her daughter's tone since the day Emily found out she'd be leaving Harrington. Jen didn't quite trust it. At any moment, the girl could turn on her.

"Do they come in taupe?" Jen tried. "Will they match my boots?"

This time Emily did not smile, but instead became serious. "I didn't mean carpentry, but maybe something else. Maybe you could take another class. Casper says that they have training programs for free."

68

Jen considered, listening, as her child carefully maneuvered through an adult conversation. Emily's brown eyes were warm like her father's, and her soft oval face and matching lips assured a coming beauty. This time last year, Emily had been away on a school trip to England. She had been gone three weeks, and when she returned, she had a British accent. That was how Emily was meant to be living. Not like this. She was worried. Worried about living, Jen thought. That was not right; she should not have to be worried about living. She should just be happily living. Like she used to be.

"I'll ask Carrie about it tomorrow," Jen said, tapping Emily on the toe. She did not move away. "Maybe there is something else I could do. It is a good idea, sweetie. Thank you."

Emily shrugged, but was obviously pleased. "Tex has mice," she ventured.

"How many?"

"Hundreds. No kidding. He started off with two, and of course the little buggers were just humping the hell out of each other . . ."

"Emily!"

They both laughed.

"He doesn't want to get rid of them, but he's tired of them. The house kind of smells like cedar."

"Oh, dear."

"You get used to it. Casper, he cleans out every single one of those cages every day."

"I thought you said they belonged to Tex?"

"Yeah. But he's very busy making costumes. It's like his passion. He's going to show me how to *shop* the GW with flair." She flipped her hair dramatically.

"What's the GW?"

"Good Will, Tex says it's a goldmine. People get rid of fabulous clothes and sell them for, like, a dollar. Tex has a pair of vintage Donna Karan Jeans that he got for fifty cents—no joke."

"No joke?"

"I'm telling you, Mom, we're going soon."

"I might go with you."

"Well, maybe some other time. Once I get the hang of it."

"I want you to know that I don't care one way or the other if Tex is gay."

"I know."

"I truly had just not thought about it. I'm relieved. He seems like a safe, if not odd, kind of boy." Jen waited, suddenly aware that she could be misunderstood, again. She braced herself for her daughter's tirade.

"I like that he's odd," Emily said quietly.

"So do I."

Emily got up, kissed the top of her mother's head, and went upstairs.

Chapter Six

With a cup of coffee in her hand, Carrie stood on the sidewalk in front of her apartment, talking with Sheckie and Jen. On this sunny Saturday morning, one of the few remaining before the season completely changed from summer to autumn, Tex and Emily had found a patch of grass and spread a blanket. They were undressing all of Tex's Barbie dolls, bagging the outfits and cataloguing them. *"With new season comes new fashion,"* Carrie had overheard him say as he carried boxes of dolls from his room to the yard. Not far from the designing couple, Casper was doing push-ups. He had already done chin-ups on the swing set belonging to the housing area, and he'd told her that he was up to one hundred crunches a day. The thing about Casper was that whatever he was into, he was into big time. This could be a good thing, he was constantly wiping down countertops, scrubbing toilets, and changing the mice bedding, but sometimes she worried about his compulsive behavior. She watched him effortlessly pump his nose to the ground.

Suddenly, breaking into the idyllic scene was the loud humming engine of a monstrous silver king-cab truck as it roared into the parking lot. The detailed orange and yellow flames flickering over the hood and across the sides made it unmistakably Dill's. He pulled up directly behind her Toyota.

"Fuck," Carrie said. Also riding in Dill's latest acquisition was his wife and their combined brood. "What a way to wreck a day."

"Boys!" Dill called to his sons as he descended from the truck. "Come on over here, I need your help."

71

Casper and Tex hesitated.

"Now!" he bellowed.

"Dill, what the hell are you doing here?" Carrie stepped off the curb.

He turned on her. "I need to drop off their stuff."

"What stuff?"

"All of it."

"What do you mean?" She followed him around to the bed of the truck where a giant washing machine box was sitting. The boys joined their parents, standing nearer their mother. "Help me get this down, you two," Dill directed his sons, yanking down the gate and hoisting himself up into the bed. It was mostly Casper who held the weight of the box. Tex only made a display of putting his hands under a corner. Suddenly the box slipped from Tex's grip, tipping the large container and spilling its innards onto the pavement.

"Oh, for crying out loud," Dill shouted.

Carrie watched Dodi leaving the cab. Waddling, obviously pregnant, she made her way over to her husband. "I folded all those clothes before I packed them," she said. "Now look."

They all did. Jen and Sheckie moved closer; Emily had left the blanket. Only sleeping Destiny and her chubby brother, Dusty, sitting in the backseat and stuffing a fistful of cookie into his mouth, did not join the viewing. On the ground were rumpled piles of clothes, CD cases, electronic games, books and action figures. Casper's baseball card collection lay spilled from its case. In delight, Tex leapt to the pile and retrieved a sketchpad. "Thank god," he said, clutching it to his chest, "I thought I'd lost this." The beret he had been sporting fell to the ground and his bright pink locks tumbled out. He knelt to fetch the hat.

"What's *that* mess?" Dill flicked a finger at Tex's neon tresses.

Carrie cautiously watched both her sons. Tex remained crouched but turned a flat stare on his father. Looking at Casper, she saw his hands clench fists, his newly growing muscles flexing, and knew he was holding himself back.

"Enough, Dill," she said, stepping between her boys and the unstoppable asshole.

"Move this shit so we can get out of here," Dill yelled, kicking a football out of the way.

There were pillows and stuffed animals and pictures in frames. Pens and paper, paint tubes and airplane models had scattered. A splintered Popsicle stick structure crumpled in disarray, as if it had been blown apart by a hurricane. The group had circled, hovering over Tex and the contents of a life that was lived somewhere else. Casper moved in on his property; slipping a baseball glove onto his hand, punching its pocket.

"What the hell is going on?" Carrie took in the strewn belongings of her children, the stuff that was theirs at their *other* home. While she had confronted Dill, Dodi answered.

"Dusty has to come live with us full-time. His father left town without a word. Ran off with the cashier from the Bubble Lounge. We need the room."

"What about us?" Casper directed his question to his father. "Where are we supposed to sleep when we come over?" Up until then, since the three boys seemed unable to get along, the visitation arrangements placed them with their respective fathers on the opposite weekends. This avoided the fights that had afflicted them in the beginning, when they were pretending to be one big happy family.

"We've got the pull-out in the den," Dill said, not looking at his son.

Carrie leaned over and picked up a toothbrush. She held it up. "And what? There's not even enough room for their toothbrushes?"

Dill looked at Carrie. "They can bring them when they *visit*. As if they ever do."

Dodi broke in, "He doesn't mean that, it just hurts your father when you cancel a weekend." She directed her gaze to the brothers. "You haven't been in a long time."

"Who cancelled last?" Carrie interjected, knowing it was Dill.

"Look," Dill said. "I know they don't want to come. So, why force them. I do my duty. I pay child-support," he said, defensively. "Isn't that enough?

Carrie's voice rose and she stepped closer to him. "Are we really going to get into this?"

73

"I pay it, don't I?"

"No Dill, you work, and the government garnishes your wages because you keep having kids you can't afford. You're a flying sperm donor, spreading your seed like a dandelion blowing in the wind. Quit working and let's see how that works out for all of us." She looked at Dodi. "Don't put it past him, sister. You don't think you could be living here with *your* three kids someday?"

Dodi's twitch quickened, pulling at her eyelid and making her appear to be winking.

"Why would *you* even *want* us to visit?" Tex asked—his tone overly sympathetic. "Can we be frank, Dodi, when we're around, Dad's even angrier than usual and your twitch gets crazier than usual. I mean, can we just *say* it?"

"Hey, now," Dill stepped in. "Don't you talk to your *stepmother* that way!"

"You left out the *wicked* part," Tex said, seemingly emboldened by the troops that had gathered around him. "Don't worry, *Dad*," he said with a sneer. "I, for one, won't be huddling cramped up on your *pullout* waiting for a word from you." He stepped onto the sidewalk.

Carrie, Casper, and Jen had pushed most of the contents back into the box and righted its position. A few scattered items lay across the asphalt, and Emily was gathering those at her feet. Carrie caught a glimpse of Sheckie as he distanced himself from the group, stepping up to the curb, observing from the sidelines. *Another man who can't take the heat,* she thought, disgustedly. He folded his arms protectively across his big barrel chest.

"Come on, Dodi," Dill took his wife's chubby arm. "Let's get out of here." The pair climbed back into the cab. Carrie and Jen parted away from the backing up truck, while Casper just barely pulled the box from its path. Monster wheels crushed both Superman and Wonder Woman, flattening the plastic heroes like characters under a cartoon steamroller.

As the vehicle passed, Carrie saw Dusty placidly staring out the passenger window chomping a chocolate Moon Pie and swigging from a bottle of Mountain Dew.

"Is that her son?" Jen asked. The pudgy boy waved at the group.

"Yup," Carrie answered.

"What's he like?"

"He eats."

"No, I mean what's he like?"

Tex answered, "He eats. That's it."

"But does he . . ."

Casper cut her off, "Believe us. He eats. That's what he does, that's what he's like."

All but Sheckie had bunched together on the sidewalk.

"There go the *Dildos*," Tex said and waved as the truck pulled away.

Before it left the parking lot, Carrie hurled her coffee cup at its taillights, barely missing the custom protective grillwork. The mug smashed into a million pieces and the group turned to her, collectively startled.

"They're *all* nothing but a bunch of fucking sperm-donors," Carrie said, tossing a dark glance at Sheckie, seeing the hurt in his eyes. Nevertheless, she could not feel his pain. Not today. She could tell that he knew it. Catching Jen's horrified stare, she said, "Still wanna be my new best friend?" She stomped her way into the house.

The boys had made themselves scarce, keeping out of her way, knowing the black cloud that was hovering over their mother could strike lightning at any minute over any small provocation. They had tiptoed around their rooms, readying themselves for a day out of the house. When Carrie got like this, it was best to duck for cover. *Mom aka Boadicea*, Tex would sometimes whisper behind her back, as if she didn't hear. *Ready to tear through somebody's village*, her elder son had once explained to his brother. *When she's on a rampage, get out of the way.* And they had.

Before the boys exited, they had hauled the big box up the stairs and into Casper's room. Carrie stood, unbeknownst to them, at the threshold, watching as they sifted through their stuff. They were quiet together in a way that they were hardly ever quiet. Carrie noticed how when their shoulders touched, they did not pull away like they would any other time or maybe even punch each other for having spread cooties, but instead they leaned and lingered against each other. What would it be like, she wondered, to have a parent reject you? She could not imagine it. Her own parents had died together. Left her but didn't abandon her. Carrie had been an only child. Her folks were well into their forties when she was born, had declared her a miracle baby and had treated her as such. Their love for her had been unconditional. She had known it as she knew her own heartbeat. How would it feel to be unsure?

She could see the confusion in her children's postures as they bent tentatively into the box. They reminded her of the little boys they had been, reaching into Christmas boxes, hoping for a prize. Casper lifted an art project; Carrie recognized the cigar box covered with gold spray-painted macaroni noodles glued on in random patterns. Casper had made it one year for Father's Day.

When, earlier, Dill had announced that he was bringing *all* their stuff, he was not kidding. As if he had gathered every shred of evidence of his parenthood and by returning it to the source alleviated himself of any connection at all. She could feel her anger igniting. Those boys did not deserve this. They were good boys. Sweet boys, she considered. They should not be picking over a life, not at this age, not when it was barely off the ground.

Tex held up a picture in a frame. From her vantage, Carrie could not quite make out the particulars of the photo, but in it were three figures. She guessed they were of Dill and his two sons. Casper looked over his brother's shoulder and then without warning smashed his fist against the glass, cracking it, dislodging the frame from Tex's grasp, landing it on the floor between them. Each took a turn at stomping a foot and grinding a heel against the broken glass and picture, pulverizing the image. Then they did push against each other. "Muther-fucker," Tex said, seemingly to Casper, but directing his words to the mess at his feet.

"Fucker-muther," Casper added grinning, toeing a shard of glass, and then they both started laughing.

Before leaving Carrie to her own raging storm, her sons approached carefully as she was sweeping up the kitchen. They hugged her extra long, kissed her twice as much, and pronounced their love aloud in front of each other. Again, "We love you, Mom," they choroused as they fled. She followed them, opening the door they had just closed. She called and they turned, "You're both good boys," she said, not knowing what else to say. They waved and then ran across the parking lot.

Years before, Carrie had discovered that cleaning was a good outlet for pent-up frustration, and this had been reinforced by her anger management classes. She'd come to know that it was a way to get her fury under control. Instead of punching walls and kicking doors, when she got like this, she cleaned. And so when she closed the door on her kids, she turned and attacked her house like a famished lioness, tearing into the clutter, wiping away the dust and dinginess that seemed to coat everything, no matter how often she made her rounds. She cranked up Aretha Franklin on the stereo and danced around the room.

In the mirror she had just wiped clean she saw flushed cheeks, more from anger than from cleaning, and wild red curls flying loose around her head. She looked like a regular *banshee*, as her dad would say with a faked brogue, when she got her *Irish up*.

How could she let that lousy motherfucker ruin a perfectly good day? How *you* could let that motherfucker ruin *your* perfectly good day is the real question, Carrie Angel. Sometimes it just gets so hard on mothers. It's not like we don't love the kids. We do, that's why mothers are mainly the ones to stay. Everybody expects it. No one is surprised when the dad bugs out. And when he does, no one seems to understand how tired we get. How frustrated we get. How desperate we get with them *always* around. Once those deadbeats finally get *forced* to pay, it's like: *you wanted 'em, you got 'em.* We're expected to be everything: the coach, the disciplinarian, chef, maid, nurse, shrink, chauffer—the list goes on and on. It makes you nuts, makes you think about drowning the little bastards yourself. And OK, you don't, most mothers don't, but some do. Some do and you know what? Take a survey of mothers—anonymous, obviously—and ask them *How many of you*—even if just the once—*how many of you had that thought cross your mind?* Go on, ask.

Carrie shuddered to think of her own capacity.

□□□

Just as she was sitting down with a beer in her shiny kitchen, there was a tentative knock on her door. She pulled it open to find Sheckie standing before her with a six-pack and a couple of cartons of Chinese. His sheepish smile and the shrug of his shoulders, as if offering to restore the peace that he hadn't even been responsible for disturbing, touched her like it always touched her when Sheckie made his gestures.

"Come on in," she said, stepping aside. "The house is clean."

"Of course it is," he said, knowing the pattern. They sat at the kitchen table, at first silent, and then Sheckie cleared his throat. "I made up a poem for you today."

"What?"

He grinned. "I did. It came to me when I was working on a '59 fiddle-head Harley. Kept running through my head."

"Are you gonna recite it?"

He straightened his big shoulders. "It's more like a rap," he warned.

"Baited breath, here."

He inhaled and began, "Fuck the asshole! Fuck the stupid asshole . . ." He grinned and scooped up noodles with his chopsticks.

"That's it?" She asked.

"That's all I got so far."

Carrie couldn't help but laugh. She leaned over and hugged his neck. "You're a freak," she said softly. He kissed her gently on the cheek.

Chapter Seven

From the small safe, Jen scooped the jewelry and laid out the rings, necklaces, earrings, and bracelets onto the towel she had spread out on the bed. There were lots, she noticed. Lining up the gold, platinum, and silver, some clunky with stones and gems, others relying on their own shining qualities, she lovingly caressed them. It was the same way she had caressed Emily's cheek, right after she was born: *the only thing more precious than diamonds*, she had joked to Hempy after he had presented the earrings shimmering with teardrop stones. She held them at eye level. They reminded her of little candelabras. She put them in the *sell* pile. Sentimentality could starve her if she wasn't careful, Carrie had pointed out. She did pull her grandmother's engagement ring and her mother's wedding band from the lot and placed them in the *keep* pile. Neither would bring much money, and since both women were dead, their sentimental value was warranted. She wanted something to remember them by, something for Emily to have when she was old enough to know their worth in memory, if not money.

She had filled out an application at Edible Feast, the only gourmet food store in town, and was praying she would get it. At one time, when she could afford it, the Edible Feast had been her favorite grocery stop. The shopping experience was sensual: wafting aromas of French roast coffee mingled with baking breads and pastries; splashes of colorful, locally grown, organic vegetables were displayed artistically, as if on canvas; wines from around the world could be tasted with the help of the on-premises' sommelier. Soft music, low-lights, and intimate conversations over samples of caviar and pâté de fois gras, always made Jen feel like she was at a cocktail party, instead of at the grocery store. Everyone who was anyone shopped at Edible Feast. If she landed the check-out clerk position, she would get the employee discount, and that alone would make it worth the humiliation she would no doubt suffer when she would be forced to check out her old country club friends; the ones who never called anymore.

Jen heard whispering hisses coming from Emily's room, and so she crept close to find her daughter talking quietly but adamantly on the phone.

"No, Dad, I can't ask Mom. She is sleeping."

Pause.

Jen watched Emily's foot stomp once. "I never said I even *wanted* to babysit. I thought we were going to the movies. You and me? Alone?"

Pause.

"How long will the game last?" Emily's shoulders slouched. "All right, I'll ask her but I don't think she's going to be happy." She then turned, surprised to face Jen. "Dad wants to know if you can bring me over to his house, like now. He has a golf date." She clamped her hand over the phone. "Him and Tiffany. For *four* hours! I have to *babysit* for those friggin' brats! But then Dad and I are going to the movies."

Jen felt her daughter's pain. She didn't want to go *and* she wanted to be with her father. "I'll throw something on. Tell him he might be a little late for his tee-off, I have to call Carrie and see if she can be ready now."

The women had made plans to go sell off Jen's jewelry, and then go shopping at Good Will, and so the three packed the car on the way to dropping Emily at her father's. A solemn Emily was in the backseat as if on her way to her own funeral.

"I *hate* them," she said, lying prone across the entire length of the seat with her arms folded across her chest.

"You look like a corpse," Carrie said.

"That's the idea," Emily replied, eyes remaining closed. "I'm wishing it before I have to go spend hours with the two most spoiled rotten little brats you ever want to meet. Not to mention their *cunt* of a mother!"

Jen slammed on her brakes. "Emily!" The car behind nearly rear-ended her and laid on the horn. She began driving but kept trying to catch a glimpse of her daughter, out of sight of the rearview. "How dare you use that word? You should *never* use that word! It's . . . it's . . . horrible. *I* never use that word! It's a very bad word!"

"For Christ's sakes, Jen," Carrie started. "It's just a word! Maybe the kid's got it right? Maybe she *is* a *cunt!*"

"Carrie, please . . . I'm trying to have a conversation with my daughter."

"Well, then, have an honest one, for God's sakes. Stop acting like you haven't called that bitch a cunt at least once in your own mind."

Emily sat bolt upright and caught her mother's eye in the rearview. Jen didn't speak.

"You have! I knew it!" Carrie thumped the dashboard.

"Have you, Mom?"

"I didn't say I hadn't. You just don't say it out loud."

"Oh, go on," Carrie dared.

"Pardon?"

"Say it. Go ahead. Say Tiffany is a cunt."

"Say it, Mom. You should. It'll make you feel better."

Jen couldn't help smiling. And then the three were giggling.

"Promise. We won't tell a soul," Carrie crossed her heart.

"Swear to God, Mom. Scout's honor. Just say it."

As Jen swerved into the long driveway of 21 Robin's Egg Lane, she caught a glimpse of Tiffany standing on the porch in a pink cardigan and white golfing pants, and wearing a stylish straw hat. She was pluck-ing the dead leaves from the flowers in the planter, the one that Jen had originally bought for those very mums. After dusting her hands against each other, Tiffany turned toward the approaching vehicle.

"How do you like Tiffany's new tits, Mom?"

Jen eyed the younger woman's especially perky and largely round breasts. "*Tittany* is a cunt," she said.

Emily and Carrie howled, and both clapped at the same time.

Jen was startled to see Hempy as he emerged from the garage. His once shiny mane of long, thick hair was cropped short, fringed and sprouting in the front. His ears, she had never realized, were quite large and seemed jutting, like handles from his head. The stylish cut may have suited twenty-somethings, Jen thought, but on the graying fifty-five year old man, well, he just looked ridiculous. She smiled and waved.

Hempy approached the car with Tiffany and his toddling daughters at his heels. He was dressed similarly to his young wife, although his cardigan was mint green and sported the country club logo on its left breast. Remembering the recent court order reducing child support, Jen could feel her temperature rise.

"Nice that he can afford his club but not his daughter," she muttered.

"Doesn't *look* sick," Carrie said. "Looks kind of old, though."

"Hi, princess," Hempy said, leaning toward Emily through the back passenger window. "Ready?" He looked at his watch and tapped its face. "Already ten minutes past tee-off. We really need to get a move on, here."

At that moment, one of the toddlers pushed the other onto her bottom, landing her hard on the pavement. The downed girl let out a wail that could peel the bark off a tree. The piercing cry caused all three women in the car to cover their ears. Hempy spun about, leapt across the drive, and picked up the screaming child. Her yelps were joined by those of her sister, who was being reprimanded by Tiffany.

"Mom," Emily whispered. "I don't want to babysit."

"Honey, you have to . . ." she started, but Carrie interrupted with a hand on Jen's arm.

"No, she doesn't," Carrie's voice equally as low as Emily's. "Let's get out of here."

"What?"

"Throw it into reverse. Come on. The kid shouldn't have to take over *that* mess." She pointed to the chaotic scene. "*I* wouldn't want to, would you?"

82

In a moment of exhilarated rebelliousness, Jen floored the vehicle back down the driveway. At the end of the pavement, she swung the car around to face the road. Before pulling away, she caught a glimpse of Hempy and Tiffany and their screaming daughters, posturing a tableau, immobile with their mouths wide open.

"Holy shit! Mom!" Emily said, her grin taking up the entire rearview mirror. "You did it! You really did it!"

Jen giggled and cast her glance toward Carrie, "Why do I suddenly feel so liberated? Like I just burned my bra or something!"

"Mom!" Emily sounded shocked.

"What, you don't think I could have burned my bra? Done something rebellious in my life? Well, little lady, you might be surprised about some things your old mother has done!"

"Like what? Smoke pot? Have you ever smoked pot? LSD? Go to Woodstock?"

"How old do you think I am, honey?"

"Well, did you? Did you ever smoke pot? At least tell me that . . ."

With the small burst of adrenaline rushing through her veins, Jen was feeling powerful, so powerful that she wanted to bust out with every truth of every reckless thing she'd ever done just to prove to her daughter, and herself, that she hadn't always been some uptight, upright, prude. Thanks to Carrie Angel, she was pushing her limits all over again, just like she when she was a kid.

"Well—" she warmed up to her first toke, when Carrie put a hand on Jen's arm, and discreetly shook her head. Jen looked over to see her frowning, and nearly undetectably slicing her fingers across her throat, the universal *cut it* sign.

Emily craned forward, eager for the information. "Well?" she asked, hopefully.

"Well, I knew people back in the day who did, but I just, well, I just didn't find it that interesting," Jen said, holding back her enthusiasm for all things not prudish; not exactly lying but not exactly telling the truth either.

"Oh, come on, Mom, you can tell me."

And this is when Carrie turned around in her seat. "No she can't,"

83

she said. "It's in the parenting rule book. Any stupid thing a parent may have done before he or she was a parent, and before his or her brains were fully formed, usually between the ages of 18 to 21 years old, is privy information from their children."

"You're making this up," Emily said.

"Am I making this up, Jen?" Carrie looked at her friend. "Isn't it true, anyone under 18 is kind of a little retarded."

"Carrie! That's not nice," Jen said. "We don't use that word."

"No? What's with the word-thing? I can't say cunt, I can't say re-tard; okay, fine, so what word can I use to describe these under-formed brains found in teenagers? Disabled? You want me to say that? Fine, I'll say it."

Carrie looked at Emily. "Those of you disabled by unformed brains would use this information in any number of unformed ways, accompanied by your unformed temper tantrums, trying to manipulate unformed situations developed in your unformed brain."

"That's not true . . ."

"I've seen your tantrums, little sister," Carrie righted herself in the seat. "I believe you're capable of many unformed things."

"You don't even know me," Emily slouched back in her seat. Roping her arms around each other, preparing to pout, her bottom lip pushed plump.

"Doesn't matter what you think, you poor unformed thing," Carrie said.

"Hey! You can't talk to me like that!" Emily said. "Mom, are you going to let her talk to me like that?"

Jen turned left onto Ridge Road, where the housing complex was huddled along the woods.

"It's not your fault, really," Carrie said. "It's just that you, not only you, but, all of you teenagers, only have partial capacity for fully formed thinking due to your unformed brains. That is until around 21 years old. It's a fact, go ahead and Google it, you'll see. It has something to do with a crease in your frontal lobe.

"I don't believe you. You're just being mean."

"See, here's the way it works." Carrie seemed to have warmed to her notions. "You're opinion has no value since it has come from an under-formed brain."

"What does that even mean, *Mom*?" Emily said, but glared at Carrie.

"It means your mother isn't going to tell you anything," Carrie answered.

"I think my mother can speak for herself."

"Actually, she can't," Carrie said. "In fact, as another parent, it's my duty to speak for her."

"What are you talking about?"

"It's in that parenting rule book. You see, your mother's not going to tell you if she smoked pot, or went to Woodstock, or snorted coke off the tip of a porn-star's cock. . ."

Jen's shock met Emily's awe in the rearview.

Carrie continued, ". . . because anything that *she* may have done when *her* brain was still unformed is privileged information. So, lie down in your coffin back there and think about what kind of sacrifice your mother just made on your behalf, today, never mind all the ones she makes every day."

Emily quietly huddled against the window.

"And be grateful," Carrie said.

Jen turned the car into the complex and pulled up to the apartment door.

"What are we doing here?" Emily asked.

"I'm dropping you off," Jen said.

"But I thought I could go out with you guys. You're going shopping, right?"

"Yes, but Carrie and I made plans."

"What's the big deal? Why can't I just come along? I won't bother you."

"No, Emily. You were supposed to be at your father's today, remember? I just stopped you from having to babysit."

Emily jerked the door handle. "Right and you just stopped me from going out to the movies with my father, too!" She pushed her way out the door. "Thanks, Mom! You just ruined my whole day. I

85

hope you and your new *friend* here have a really great Saturday while I sit home all alone, by myself, without a soul who gives one crap about me! One more missed chance to spend an afternoon with my father!" She slammed the car door, stomped to the apartment, and after some fidgeting with the key in the lock, she went through and then slammed that door, too.

After a moment, Carrie said, "The unformed brain in action, don't you see?"

"I do. I never thought of it that way."

"Makes you feel kind of sorry for them, doesn't it?"

"It does."

"The way you feel for a moth when it throws itself against a flame."

"Nothing you can do to stop it," Jen said.

"Nope, but it doesn't mean you don't pity just how stupid it is."

"True."

"Rule number one," Carrie said, "Never tell your kid you smoked pot. She'll use it against every chance she gets."

"I see your point."

"You can't trust 'em, even when things seem friendly, as much as you love 'em."

They stood at the counter of *Evan's Fine Antique Jewelry Appraisers.* The sales clerk was a fop of a boy but one who knew enough to know that the hulking diamond and gold rings Jen had pulled from her fingers were more worthy of an expert's appraisal than his own novice eye; he dashed to the back to get Evan himself.

The jittery young clerk returned with Evan (pronounced E-von). The owner, for whom the store was named, was a tall, willowy fellow with a long face fringed by wispy strands of yellow hair. His smile lingered a little too long as he held Jen's hand. Not until he pushed the monocle to the diamonds did his cool patronizing manner shake, just a bit, as the glass popped from his socket to the countertop.

"My, my," he muttered, seemingly trying to compose himself. "These are Cartier, are they not?"

"Of course," Jen said. "Why do you think I brought them to you?"

"May I ask why you are interested in selling them?" Evan seemed concerned. "I hope it's not some sad situation that brought you here?"

Jen sniffed his contrived sympathy. If she knew anything, she knew about jewelry. It had been a passion, she admitted. She knew what she had, she knew their worth, and she knew what was about to happen *if* she let him sniff *her* desperation. "Oh, no, just the opposite, in fact," she said, casually. "These belonged to an old, recently deceased aunt, who left them to me. They're not exactly my style, so I'd like to get rid of them and find something more to my liking."

A flutter of disappointment crossed Evan's face, but his frozen smile remained.

At his first quoted price, Jen nearly jumped, but instead said. "You and I both know they're worth twice that!"

"I'm sorry, but I'm not sure the settings would be desired. They are *so* . . . Eighties, if you know what I mean."

Now the insults come. Jen held her composure. "These are from the Etruscan collection of Carlos Montevedo, the Italian designer. I thought surely that you would have recognized them, given your reputation." She glanced around the store. "Perhaps I was mistaken."

Evan bristled, but became conciliatory, "Well, of course, I did. Montevedo is one of our best sellers. We might be able to go a little higher."

Before Jen had a chance to respond, Carrie scooped the rings from the counter. "Come on Jen. This pansy's all about jerkin' your chain. I know a guy, name's Vinny, over in Raeford. He'll give you what they're worth. And he won't be pussyin' around about it, either."

They turned in unison and headed for the door. When Jen slowed, hoping not to make it to the threshold, Carrie poked a finger in her back, prodding her more quickly. Suddenly Evan came rushing around the counter, calling them back, groveling and begging their return to the conversation.

Not until she watched her glittering beauties stowed away in Evan's dark safe did she fully feel the magnitude of her situation. That was it, she realized, the end; there was not one more parachute to open, not one more safety net beyond the money she was depositing.

She had never known this poverty before. She'd always had someone taking care of her; she'd gone from her father's house to her husband's house, and the burden of survival, her own and Emily's, had always fallen on someone else. No more. She got it. The future was not looking bright for the whole country; not with the spiraling economy, skyrocketing unemployment, the villainous health-care system, and real estate in a tenuous condition. On her own account she was completely unprepared, with an outdated, overrated skill-set in children's literature, which was becoming obsolete. Kiddie-librarians weren't exactly in high demand nowadays, at least not the kind of librarian she'd been; part-time, local-branch training, mostly checking books in and out. Today's *real* librarians, those who worked in academia, had advanced degrees and were highly specialized computer geniuses trained in research, who could waltz through giant databases. Not to mention that forty was right around the corner. For the first time in her life, Jen understood that she was completely on her own and unprepared for it. This terrified her. With one quick swipe of her ringless, naked fingers across her tear stained-cheeks, she took a deep breath, threw back her shoulders, and decided to grow up.

They had made their way to Fear River Forks, which was somewhere between Lillington and Cokesbury, near Raven Rock, and had recently become a hangout for college students and a growing community of artists, musicians, and writers who'd been migrating down from Chapel Hill. Old abandoned warehouses along the Cape Fear River were being renovated into artists' studios, residential lofts, and retail space. They found easy parking around the corner from the small clustering of shops located in a renovated old brick factory.

Jen had never been to this part of the county and was surprised to see the bustling of people. As Emily had suggested, there were many kids from the local colleges, identified by their weighted backpacks and shiny laptops. There were older people, too, even older than Jen. She could see them sitting in the small diner as they passed by the window. These senior citizens were different from those in the suburbs who wore golf shirts and khaki pants and drove Lincolns and other, equally, obnoxious vehicles. No, these graying folks seated around the restaurant wore ponytails and braids, men and women alike, had necklaces of silver and leather, were cloaked in woolen ponchos, fringed suede jackets, and one, she saw, in a hooded sweatshirt that read *Remember Kent State.* These old hippies had taken refuge from the world and the cold and warmed their hands around mugs of hot tea and coffee. The diner was having a two-for-one *seniors' special*, the chalkboard on the outside of the building read. Finally, after meandering through the shops, they came to their true destination.

At the Good Will, Carrie surfed through the jeans-rack while Jen slid silk and linen blouses across the bar. She *was* stunned, as Emily had suggested she would be. She had to admit it was startling to see the designer labels with the mismatched prices scrawled in on tags dangling from sleeves. Jones of New York, Ralph Lauren, Vanderbilt—heavy hitters that once garnered prices in the hundreds—were marked down to four and five dollars, or less if a button were loose or missing.

Jen carefully chose pieces, reminding herself that the fifty she'd kept back from her deposit was all she was allowed. She came to a beautiful burgundy silk blouse, and pulled it off the hanger to see it was exactly her size. Even more significantly, it looked just like one she'd once owned. Where that blouse had gotten to, she hadn't a clue. She remembered loving that shirt, though. She threw it in her cart.

As she skimmed along the rack, another blouse, this time emerald green and shimmering, caught her eye. A beauty just her size and an exact replica of another blouse she'd once owned and lost track of. Pulling this shirt from its hanger, Jen immediately searched the seam at the sleeve and shoulder, noting the mismatched blue cotton thread stitched over a loosened opening.

"Oh my God!"

All heads turned and Carrie sidled over.

"What's the matter?"

"This is *my* shirt!"

Carrie looked down. "Yeah, it's *you* all right."

"No. I mean it's *mine.* Used to belong to me. Look." Jen turned up the stitched sleeve. "*I* sewed this. This shirt was mine. So was *this* one!"

She grabbed the burgundy blouse from the cart, scrutinizing it for proof. "See, it's an Armani, one of my favorites. These were all in my storage unit. How on earth did they get here?"

"Have you paid your bill? Because if you haven't, they'll get in there and auction off your stuff."

"Without even telling me?"

"No, they have to give you notice. Did you get a notice?"

"No, the storage unit is in Hempy's name. He's been paying the rent on it. He would have told me if he'd stopped."

"When was the last time you were there?"

"Right before we moved into Section Eight. Why?"

"Well, if it's in Hempy's name, the notices would've gone to him."

"So, he cancelled it?"

"I don't know, did he?"

"Can I borrow your cell phone?" Jen asked Carrie, holding out her hand. When there was no answer at Hempy's, she called the directory and got the number of the storage company. By the time she'd gotten off the phone, she had paced around the entire Good Will building twice. Quickly paying for her purchases, she and Carrie headed out the door.

She drove like a fiend out of the parking lot. "Well, it wasn't the rental company that auctioned off my stuff."

"Hey, you wanna slow down here, a little?" Carrie put her hand on the dash.

"Sorry," Jen eased the pedal, and braked some. "They didn't send the notice because the customer came and cleared it out."

"The customer? You mean Hempy? He cleared out your stuff without telling you? Man, that's low," Carrie shook her head.

"The guy said it was two days ago."

"Seriously?" Carrie considered.

"More than that? The guy said it was a woman who had come and emptied it. When I asked if her name was Tiffany, he said he couldn't remember, but when I asked if she was a blond with big tits, he was sure it was her!"

"Jen?"

"Yeah."

"Tittany's a cunt."

"I know."

Neither said much on the way home. On top of everything, this new development felt like an assault, Jen thought. Lately, it seemed like every single time she tried to turn things around, another something awful got in the way. It felt like this was becoming her norm. "Seems like it's always one step forward and two steps back, lately," she said aloud, but mostly to herself.

"Well, the laws of attraction work both ways," Carrie said. "Negativity attracts negativity just as much as abundance brings abundance."

"They tell you that in your anger management classes?"

"Yeah, and in other stuff I've been reading. Mostly about focusing on the positive things in life. Appreciating even the small good stuff. That kind of philosophy. The outcome is mostly all about where you focus."

Jen knew her attention had been on the negative, lately, but when bad things happen, there didn't seem anywhere else to focus. "I don't know how I'm going to be able to do this, Carrie." Jen finally interrupted their quiet. She felt her throat swelling with her confession.

"Do what?"

"Survive, move on, get off the government, and get my life back."

Carrie looked out the window.

"It's easy to think life is so easy when you don't have to contribute much to its functioning."

"What do you mean?"

"I mean, my whole life, I feel like I've been playing some kind of role. Like a part in a play, that all I had to do was memorize my lines, remember my cues, hit my marks, and all around me would support my role: set, director, crew otherwise known as home, husband, and all those that kept us functioning: gardeners, housekeepers, hair stylists, therapists, our own personal masseurs—"

Carrie shifted. "Yeah, sounds tough, having to give all that up."

Jen noted the sarcasm. "Carrie, I'm not complaining about losing it all. I know it sounds petty and spoiled, and to be frank, I guess I have been petty and spoiled, but I'm not saying this for pity or to build resentment."

"Then why are you saying it?" Carrie turned in her seat. There was no challenge in her tone, but a curiosity.

Jen leveled a look at her. "I'm saying it, I guess, because for the first time, I get it. I actually understand that I am picking up where I, me—the original Jen Quinn—left off, only it's twenty years later, and I'm more ill-prepared for life, than I ever was then."

Carrie shrugged. "No, you're not."

"I feel like I am. I just don't know how I'm going to manage."

"But you're already surviving, Jen." For a change, there was softness in Carrie's tone. She'd shed her usual flippant brusqueness for something more thoughtful. "You're already doing it. You've been doing it—okay, with your eyes closed and your head buried in the sand, but somehow you're getting to the next day, right?"

Jen nodded, trying not to allow the threatening tears.

"You'll just keep doing it. You'll get closer to where you want to be, and you'll figure it out along the way."

"Is that how you've been doing it?" Jen dared the question.

Carrie laughed, "Don't you mean *all these years later* and you're still in the hole?"

"No, I didn't say that—"

"But you meant it."

"I guess I suppose I did," Jen admitted.

"Look, I'm done apologizing and beating myself up for all my bad decisions. Life is gonna happen no matter what, crap is going to roll in, crap you never even thought about, you never even believed you'd ever be up against, but there you are, knee-deep in crap."

"I feel like I'm up to my waist."

"So, the only thing we can do about it is react and respond, and sometimes those reactions make it better, sometimes they make it worse. All we can do is hope that we'll know better when the next round of crap rolls in."

"The only thing I feel like I know better is just how stupid I really have been."

"Listen, the only difference between reacting and responding is the intention," Carrie said, and smiled. "If there's anything I'm learning in my anger-management classes it's this: Life's going to roll in, you can either put up your dukes or your walls or your shields; you can try to ignore it, swat at it, fend it off, push it away, kick it the fuck out of your world, or, instead, you can try to see it from a different angle. *Try something different*, an old carpenter I know says. Funny how I never applied that to life until I saw it work out in carpentry. If the board don't fit, no mount of bangin' on it is going to work. Go take off a saw-blades' worth and see what happens—like butter, she'll slip right in."

Jen smiled. "Do you know that you have a carpentry analogy for almost everything?"

"Do I?"

"Yes, it's one of those things I love about you."

"It's what I love about carpentry," Carrie considered. "It's a lot like life."

"Thank you," Jen reached and patted Carrie's arm. "I needed that."

"Good, cause it's all I got," Carrie said, and laughed.

"Why do these men all seem to always win?" Jen asked, and smacked the steering wheel. "I don't get it. You know, I once heard a woman at church talking about how bad gay adoption is because children deserve both a mother *and* a father!"

"You need to find a different church."

"I know, but when she said that I thought, How about starting with straight people?"

"I hear ya, sister."

"Straight people aren't doing such a bang-up job of marriage or child-rearing. I'd rather see two happy gay guys happily raising a little happy Chinese baby than a miserable heterosexual couple fucking up another one. And what about all the single-mothers from the beginning of time? Whether by choice or circumstance, women have brought up the world." Jen was on a roll. She had a lot of things to say, suddenly, about her own liberation, and that of women, suddenly aware of her gender and its timeless oppression. "And mothers, we stay. I mean no matter how crummy it gets, at least we stay. Men only want to win, whoever has the most or the biggest or the shiniest or, in Hempy's case, youngest. It's so caveman."

"Well, that's why it's us who really wins. Not them," Carrie said, quietly. "And that's how we survive."

"What do you mean?"

"We might be poor, it might be hard and all that, but our kids love us—unconditionally."

Jen rolled her eyes in protest. Carrie cut her off.

"Oh sure, they can be little fuckers. But the reason they are with us is that they know we're *not* going to leave them. They know we'll go down on the mat for them. So, they take the shit out on us. Watch how they treat their fathers and their wives."

"Emily walks around on eggshells. Never raises her voice. I was stunned when she told him she would no longer babysit. She's always trying to please him."

"See. Until recently, that is how both boys were with Dill. Well, Casper's like that with everybody. When Tex told Dill that he wouldn't be staying there anymore, that pretty much startled me."

"But why do *we* get punished by all this other stuff while they carry on with their lives?"

"Well, it's our own damn faults."

"What are you talking about?" Jen asked.

"Look, I never got an education. Never had a full-time job. Got pregnant and married, all way too young, all out of desperation, and so here I am. You squandered your degree."

Jen began to protest.

"You said so yourself," Carrie cut her off. "You devoted yourself to your family, your home, husband, and child. Rightfully so; you were led to believe you should and could and so you did. It was the *right* thing to do."

"It was." Jen said, softly. "Don't you think it was?"

"Sure. Whatever. It *was* because it *was*. Nuf said." Carrie leaned forward, her eyes narrowing. "Now, though, what do you want?"

Jen considered, "I want my own business, and home, and security. What about you?"

"I want all those things, too."

"Do you want your own carpentry business?" Jen asked.

Carrie smiled shyly. "It's hard to say out loud, like it might jinx everything."

"Or put it out there, so the Universe can help it along. Come on, if you tell me your dreams, I'll tell you mine." Jen caught a glimpse of herself in the rearview. She noticed the dimple in her cheek, something that appears only when she laughs. She realized how infrequently she had seen it of late.

"Well, I'm really good at finish carpentry, faux finishing, remodeling, restoration, that kind of carpentry. Not hanging your ass out in the wind, three stories high, praying you don't miss a step. Maybe if I were younger, I wouldn't mind, but I'm only getting older, you know?"

"So you'd like to have your own remodeling company?"

"Sure, I guess, someday. I don't know. I'm great with my hands, estimates, reading blueprints, that kind of thing. But the truth is, the economy is in the crapper, everybody's out of work, broke; I mean, it's a helluva downturn at a time in a field I thought I could make a good living at."

"People will always need work done on their homes. I'm counting on the fact that people are going to have to start moving because of foreclosures and jobs . . ."

"Geez, Jen, there's a little buzzard circling the dead thing in you, isn't there."

"No, no, it's just reality. I mean, people will also move *for* jobs, and some will buy houses, foreclosures, tons of them sitting empty out there. The market might turn around, at least I'm hoping."

"Hope won't pay your bills, though."

"True. But ingenuity can."

"What?"

"In times like these, people need to be ingenious! Meet new challenges, look for gaps, holes, patterns, newly formed needs . . ."

"Like what?"

"Like, okay, so folks want to cut down on their heating bills so they

95

insulate, put up plastic, maybe burn wood, go solar, whatever, every time one person decides to make that decision, it means work for all those people who make insulation, plastic, for the lumberman, and on and on . . ."

"So how do you apply that to us? Now?"

Jen considered this as she crossed the highway, and headed home along the river. She didn't want to end her day out of the house and away from her kid, just yet. She liked having a private grown-up conversation. "Okay, so in a time when no one is buying, no one is selling, banks are suddenly owning houses, essentially, other needs arise and these grow and support or employ other businesses.

"Gimme an example." Carrie always needed the concrete to go along with the idea.

"Okay, I don't know if this is true or not, but I bet with all these housing foreclosures, there's been a spike in the sale of those Info-Tubes."

"InfoTubes?" Carrie looked confused. "What the hell's an Info-Tube?

"You know, you see them everywhere. Those clear tubes with the red caps you see hanging on for sales' signs." She suddenly pointed to the side of the road. "See! There's one!"

Carrie recognized the item. "What are they for?"

"They hold copies of the specs on the house, that way interested buyers can just pull up and grab the info."

"What a brilliant idea."

"I know, so simple, but so perfect."

"I'm not too ingenious, though," Carrie said. "I'm not too good with the business end of things."

"I am," Jen said.

"What?"

"I'm good with numbers, organization, managing people, and I used to be good at budgeting money."

"That'll come back when you get some," Carrie joked.

"I'm *not* good with my hands, though. And I can barely read a map, never mind a blue print."

"Well, then I guess it's good thing you don't want to be a carpenter."

"No, but Carrie, I do know what I do want to be."

"A real estate agent, right?"

"To start, yes, but the real money is in flipping properties."

"Flipping properties?"

"You buy a cheap structure in bad shape, put the minimum into it, and turn back around and sell it."

"And you think you're going to make money in this economy doing that?"

Jen shook her head, "No, I don't. I used to, I used to watch all those house-flipping shows and think, I could do that, but I know that I got into the game too late."

"So, now what?"

"Well, that's what I mean about ingenuity. There's got to be something new arising out of the housing crisis; I just don't know what it is yet, but I aim to find out, and capitalize. Maybe it's something we can think of, together."

"Together?"

"Well, some of your interests are some of my interests and we seem to have some complementary skills—who knows? We can dream, can't we?"

Carrie shrugged, and suddenly detached from the conversation. "Sure, everybody's entitled to a dream."

"What's the matter? You don't think we could pull something off?"

Carrie looked out the window, but was furiously tapping her finger on her own knee. "I don't have a pot to piss in, Jen. You gotta have money to start a business. All this talk just throws me into an unattainable want, and I don't think that's healthy." Carrie was suddenly sullen.

"Don't you see, they are loaning money to people nowadays to start a small business, we just need to figure out what ours can be."

"Nobody's going to loan me a nickel, Jen."

Jen's mind was reeling. She'd already been thinking through some of these obstacles. She offered, "There are community services that help new business owners get started. I've been to some of their meetings. On my own, they would front me a few grand at a low interest rate. If you came on board, they'd double it."

"Came on board?"

"Carrie, did you ever think there was a reason for us to be friends? I mean other than you getting me out of jams all the time?"

"'Cause we're a couple of broke welfare mothers living in Section Eight?"

"It's not only that . . ."

"Oh no?" Carrie interrupted. "Let me ask you straight up, Jen. In our other lifetimes, would we have even given each other the time of day?"

Jen hesitated, listening for the bite in Carrie's words, and when she didn't feel it, she looked to her eyes to catch the bitter cynicism, but it wasn't there. Her friend was just saying the plain truth. "Probably not," Jen admitted. "But things are different for both of us, and we are a couple of welfare mothers living in Section Eight, and I think there's an opportunity here for us."

"Do you now?" Carrie looked out the window, following the river. "An opportunity to go down in the same sinking ship?"

"Stop it!" Jen smacked her palm on the steering wheel, again.

Carrie turned in her seat.

"Look, can either of us get much lower?"

"I don't guess so."

"Carrie, listen to me, you want to remodel and restore old homes and buildings. I want to buy old homes and buildings to remodel and restore."

"A match made in heaven," Carrie said.

"Or Section Eight. Who cares where the match was made? We are a match, don't you see? Maybe if we find the right business today, we can make our dreams happen down the road."

"Maybe so," Carrie said, more seriously than not.

"We could be a team."

"Sweet revenge."

"What do you mean?"

"My mama used to say the sweetest revenge was living a good life."

"That might be true." Jen tapped her cup. "But, every time I think about Tiffany selling off my stuff, I just want to rip her hair out! That's the kind of revenge I'm after. What about you?"

"I just pray that everything Dill puts out in the world comes back to him threefold. I pray that Dodi's twitch gets three times faster, that they have three more kids, three new cats, three in-laws coming for three weeks, and that he can handle three jobs all at once, just to pay for it all."

"That's very Zen of you."

"Thank you."

"Would you seriously consider this business venture with me?"

Carrie's brow raised, and she seemed to be considering. "I guess I would. This is the closest I've come to believing in the possibility rather than dreaming about the fantasy."

Chapter Eight

Between Pressley making her do shit-work all day and Tex's play opening this evening, Carrie was feeling frazzled. For all that sitting in those weekly Anger Management classes learning to breath, think happy thoughts, meditate, express frustration constructively and even remove one's self from ignitable situations, she wasn't sure how well she was managing her anger at all. She'd honked the horn and grumbled at Casper this morning after he took too long to run upstairs to retrieve his pink-ribbon Breast Cancer Awareness pin—a cause for which he had suddenly become an advocate. She dropped both boys off at school, sat in bus traffic, and arrived late at the jobsite only to discover it empty. It took many calls to find the new location, something Pressley had obviously told everybody else on the job but her, and as a punishment for her tardiness, he made her haul truck-loads of deconstruction materials to the dump all day.

Carrie sat down at the table and looked through the mail. She ripped open the official-looking envelope and read the court summons to decide custody. "God damn it!" She slammed her fist against the countertop.

"What's the matter, Mom?" Casper asked, sitting upright, looking away from the TV.

"Nothin', sweetie. I just forgot to get milk." Carrie smiled reassuringly. The last thing Casper needed to worry about was this.

"Want me to run and get some?" he asked.

"No. That's okay. We'll pick it up on the way back from the play. Where's your brother?"

"Over at Emily's. Did he tell you that Dad and Dodi are coming tonight?"

Carrie cringed. "No, he didn't mention it." This was not a good day to have a meeting.

"Well, he also said he'd be at my last meet and he never showed up."

Carrie knew she should say something reassuring like, *I'm sure he wants to* or *he's very busy right now*, she didn't have the stomach to work up the lie. She opened the fridge. "Want some cookies and milk?"

"I thought you said we were out of milk?"

"I was wrong," Carrie said, pulling the nearly full gallon from the fridge.

"Man, I sure hope they can keep their hands off each other this time."

"Who?"

"Dad and Dodi. Remember Tex's fifth-grade play?"

Carrie shook her head, trying to forget the visage that burned in her mind every time she thought about those two tonguing it for the whole elementary school and PTA. "I'm sure the passion has waned." Carrie set the glasses of milk and plate of Oreos in front of Casper.

Just then the door swung wide and blasted wind into the apartment. They turned to see Tex sauntering in, nearly majestic in his costume. His natural dark red hair had grown out, and a jaunty coil sprung above his eye. The lace of his shirt collar tucked below his chin followed a flowing path of ruffles, puffing up his chest. His tartan and kilt matched the swatch of plaid embroidered on his beret, set cockily on his head; a short plume of a peacock feather served like a mantle. His sporran was newly tooled with metal rivets in swirling Celtic patterns.

"Wow! You look great, Tex," Carrie said, standing up, clapping. Suddenly a bright slash of light caught her eye; her palm shielded against the glaring sparkle from his shoes, where big shiny buckles glinted.

Casper looked down. "Man, you better go put on a pair of tightie-whities under that skirt."

Tex looked down, then up, seemingly confused, and frowned at his brother.

"You don't want innocent bystanders to get a load of your loose Johnson swinging above those mirrors on your feet, do you?"

Tex ran to his room.

With a good number of others, they filed into the auditorium. Carrie, Sheckie, and Jen had split from Casper and Emily, who were finding seats with friends. Dill and Do were nowhere in sight. By the time the place filled up, Carrie had just about settled on the idea that the deadbeat wasn't going to show after all. However, as the orchestra's clumsy warm-up notes fluttered around the cavernous hall and the houselights dimmed, Carrie watched Dill and Dodi make their way to the front of the auditorium. Silhouetted against the lighted stage and sliding across the first row, Dill and his heavily pregnant wife managed to find two front row seats together.

Flanked by Sheckie and Jen, she focused on the curtains as they opened to the mystical world of *Brigadoon*. Bagpipe music blasted into the large auditorium. Walling the stage, cardboard mountains and hillsides dusted with feathery heather were layered behind large painted foam rocks. Bright lights lit scenery, and then the actors appeared, all a little clumsy in an endearing kind of way.

Tex, in all his glory, came out as part of the chorus, but also had a singing part playing Charlie Dalrymple. When his turn came, center stage, Carrie held her breath and squeezed both Sheckie and Jen's hands. His voice came at first a little shaky: *I used to be a rovin' lad.* Then he relaxed a bit, and strutted across the set, arms swinging, head bobbing. By the time the troupe belted out the first chorus, *Go Home, go home, go home with Bonnie Jean. . .,* Tex was bouncing on his toes, doing a near version of the Highland Fling.

Carrie was both smiling and crying as she watched her son in his triumphant moment. She'd almost forgotten Dill and Do until, as Tex was smiling down at the audience, his eyes locked, like a startled deer, on the first row. Carrie followed his gaze to the seats where Dill and Do sat, afraid of what she would see, but what she saw wasn't

Dill making out with Do, but Dill whispering into the ear of a woman on his other side, leaving Do to watch the show by herself. Then Tex clapped his hands, smiled, and continued without the slightest hitch. He grinned as he sauntered off stage, obviously pleased with himself.

They all stood for the ovation; Tex pranced across the stage beaming as the roar of applause rose with his appearance. Carrie wept.

After the show, they gathered at the car, waiting for Casper to join them. Tex arrived, having been delayed over and over by well-wishers. He was ecstatic, his arms loaded with roses, his face covered with lipstick kisses, and someone had sprinkled glitters in his hair. His eyes danced. As fortune would have it, Dill and Dodi appeared from around the corner.

"Oh look, the village can stop the search, we've found the missing idiots," Carrie said loud enough for Dill to turn his scowl on her.

He said to Tex, "You did a good job."

Tex nodded.

Dodi chimed in, "You were the best in the whole play!"

Tex shrugged.

"You did soar beyond the rest," Jen chimed in.

Tex smiled.

"Good thing we don't live in Scotland," Dill said. "You'd be in a skirt every day if you could get away with it."

Tex sagged, and the roses in his arms sagged with him.

"Do you have to ruin everything?" Carrie asked.

"What?" Dill asked.

"Why can't you just leave it at *Good job, son.*"

"I'm just pointing out the obvious."

"What obvious?" Carrie stepped toward Dill, arms folded.

"He's wearing a *skirt!*"

"It's a kilt," Tex said, his voice small. He grabbed hold of a pleat, scrunching it in his fist.

"You're turning gay!" Dill spat. "And you don't even know it!"

Everyone became silent. The group shuffled. The twitch in Dodi's cheek repeated a rapid convulsion. Carrie backed up to Sheckie, taking his hand, anchoring herself, knowing how easily she could land another punch.

The flowers in Tex's arms dropped to the pavement. He joined his father in the ring of light from the street lamp. Carrie could see his lower lip tremble, but then he took a deep breath, and said, "I *might* be turning into a queer, Dad, but you're a lot surer of it than I am."

"Well, Christ, just look at you." Dill swiped at the air, at his son, as if he were an example to be noted, dismissed—discarded. He did not make eye contact.

"No, *you* look at me," Tex's voice got quiet.

Disgust wrinkled Dill's face.

"This is me, Dad." Tex held out his hands. "Queer or straight. Like it or not—me—skirt and all."

Dill shook his head, and looked at Carrie, near growling, "You did this to him."

"What, Dad?" Tex asked. "What exactly did she *do* to me? What terrible horrible thing happened here?"

"Do you want to be a fag?" Dill asked.

"Do you want to be an asshole?" Tex asked. And then he stepped away; crushing the roses beneath his feet, he made his way to the van. Emily broke away from her mother, and followed him. They got in the back seat together.

Carrie extracted herself from Sheckie's hold, and turned on Dill. "Look what *you've* done to him!" She bent to pick up one of the scattered roses. "His one big night! You've ruined it."

"Yeah, right! The big highlight of his life!" Dill's sarcastic tone matched the scowl on his face. "A fag in a skirt playing a fag in a skirt. What a stretch!"

"Do you hear yourself?" Carrie gathered the broken flowers one by one. She stopped and stood. "This is your son, Dill. Your son! Do you hear the things you say to your son?"

Dodi stepped in, "She's right, Dill. Leave it alone."

"Yeah, well if he acted more like a *son*, I might not have to say these things."

"You fucking loser!" Carrie yelled. "You fucking jackass loser!" She couldn't help screaming and spitting, but she dug her nails into her palms.

"Fuck you, and the fucking system you rode in on!" Dill matched her in volume, and their matching epithets echoed off the nearby hills.

"No fuck you, and your fucking self-righteous morality!" Carrie yelled.

"At least I've got some!"

"Is that what you call it, tearing down your own son?" Carrie was just revving up when she saw Casper across the parking lot. He was in mid-approach, slowing beneath a street lamp as he took in the scene between his screaming parents; he was holding hands with a tall, dark-haired girl. Carrie watched him turn away, as if he were searching the parking lot for another family to belong to; he guided the young woman into darkness away from the feuding adults.

After Dill and Do roared away in the big truck, they'd waited for Casper until Carrie spotted him seated in the backseat of a black sedan, staring out the window. He didn't smile when she met his serious eyes. As the car passed, he rolled by without a wave. Looked like he'd found another family after all, she thought, and couldn't blame him.

"She loves me: Thirty-five. She loves me not: Thirty-Six. She loves me: Thirty-seven." Casper said between clenched teeth as he chinned himself to the bar he had bolted across the doorway to his bedroom. He'd worked himself up to fifty-five chin-ups a day; his goal was an odd one hundred and one. He ended on odd numbers so that he'd always land on *she loves me* instead of *she loves me not*. "She loves me: Thirty-nine." In the distance, beyond his imagining, the phone started ringing. He tried to ignore it by squeezing his eyes shut and quickening his pace, "She loves me: Forty-one."

"Hey! Casper *Goodson*!" Tex yelled. This was his newly dubbed moniker for Casper; only Tex thought it hilarious. "Get the phone."

"You get it: Forty-two," he said, more under his breath than not. "She loves me. Forty-three:"

The phone shrilled again.

"I'm busy," Tex yelled. "And *I* don't care who it is."

"She loves me not: Forty-four: She loves me:"

"*The Pony* is going to wonder why you're ignoring her." Tex taunted. "You better answer soon."

Casper's determination to stay focused was losing to the possibility that it might be Sara calling. ". . . Forty-six."

"*Casper, the goodly son, the goodliest son I know . . .*" Tex jingled his childish tease. The phone rang again.

Heaving himself from the bar, Casper leapt down the stairs, tripped on a pile of books, skidded into the wall, righted himself, smacked the back of Tex's head while reaching the phone, then it stilled.

"Dag, damn you, Tex!"

"Casper, is that any way to talk to your brother?" Carrie rounded the corner with a laundry basket.

"Look at him!" Casper pointed to Tex seated at the kitchen table, a foot away from the phone. "He couldn't just lean over and pick it up!" Casper was red in the cheeks.

"Look, Casper, you're experiencing frustration," Carrie began. "This is natural. But expressing this frustration by yelling at your brother is only going to create more frustration. Remember your *safe* word."

Oh, God, not the *safe* word, thought Casper. He could never remember his. And, anyhow, didn't he have a right to get mad *sometimes*?

Carrie's anger management coach had made the class come up with a word that they would repeat, like a mantra, if they started getting pissed. Carrie's was *Mary Poppins*. "A more calming presence does not exist," she had declared. "Not even Jesus. After all, remember his tantrum in the temple?"

Pam, her counselor, had said that *it is imperative for us to have the support of the most important people in our lives.* In tears, Carrie had said to the brothers, "And you two are by far the most important people in my life." That was when Casper and Tex had agreed to choose their *safe* words. Casper kept forgetting his—*nickel*—which was what he was looking at when Carrie had insisted they pick one. He could tell by the number of times Carrie uttered *Mary Poppins* that it was all she could do to stay calm whenever Tex sputtered his *safe* word—*shit.*

"Shit!" The sewing machine would jam.

"Shit, shit, shit, shit." A needle would prick his finger.

Tex was brilliant, Casper thought.

When Casper had found out that Carrie was going to take anger management classes, he thought it was probably a good idea. He had seen his mother get enraged over too many little things too often: slow drivers, dim-witted cashiers, ex-cons selling light bulbs over the phone. Once, in a movie theater, Casper had been mortified as his mother accused a rather large woman, "I don't see *your* wheelchair!" as she made to sit in the extra large seat meant for the disabled. And that was just the small stuff you are not supposed to sweat; when the big stuff landed, watch out. But there was the good side to his mother, too. The side that was fiercely protective of him and Tex—like a lioness with her cubs. Casper knew that deep down his mother was vulnerable, not weak, but inside she was a lot softer, warmer, than most anybody on the outside knew, except maybe Sheckie.

"Let's *identify the conflict*," Carrie was saying.

It was all Casper could do not to roll his eyes.

"I'm busy," Tex reached into a stack of stiff rectangular paper, inserts to be precise, primarily white, some blue, and one yellow, all with a toothy edge, having been torn from slick magazines.

"Doing what? Huh?" Casper demanded, reaching into the stack. "It's not like you're balancing an egg on the end of a spoon or hot-gluing a model airplane! You're just *sitting* there!" He picked up the pile of cards. "What the heck is going on, here?" He flipped through: *Book of the Month Club, Record of the Month Club, Fruit of the Month,* and *Meat of the Month* . . . "What exactly *are* you doing?"

"Let's *activate our listening* skills," Carrie said, softly. "Tex, why don't you tell Casper what it is that kept you from answering the phone."

"Well, Casper, my boy, I'm signing up the Dildo family for free introductory offers. Look here," Tex said, holding out a few cards he had already filled in with red ink pen. "*Polka for Perennials: The Five*

CD Collection!" He flipped to the next card. *"The Abridged and Translated Good News Bible and Study Guide.* That oughta be a reliable source. Oh, and you gotta love this one, *Pick Your Pig Parts: Knuckles, Pork Rinds, and Fat Back."*

"I don't understand, Tex," Carrie said carefully.

"I'm sending Dill and Do free introductory offers to join these clubs. They don't have to pay anything and they'll get all this stuff for nothing."

Casper smiled when he slid onto the chair beside Tex and fanned the cards in front of him. "Where'd you get all these?"

"Emily and I were looking through the magazines at the grocery store and we started pulling them out. Here, check this one: free hair removal kit if you join the *Jinxu Knife of the Month Club!* Can't beat that, now can ya?"

Casper had to admit it was brilliant. He could just imagine Dodi with her cheek a twitchin', opening the giant tweezers and hot wax kit, seeing Dill's name as the recipient and wondering what it all meant.

Casper read the conditions in fine print, "You don't have to *join,* but you do have to *cancel* if you don't want to *automatically* join by *accepting* all this free stuff."

"Exactly," Tex said. "Just think how much time they'll spend sending all that shit back."

"Yeah, and knowing Dad, he'll want to see the stuff *before* he decides. He'll either join up or start boxing up." Casper grabbed a pen and started filling in the little squares for the *Makeup of the Month Club.* "*You* are brilliant, big brother."

"Thank you," Tex said. "It was a stroke of genius, I have to admit. Postage included."

"This is going to *ignite* anger in your father," Carrie said, snapping mismatched socks apart and rolling them up with their respective mates. "It's our job to *diffuse* these situations, not create them."

"Oh, Mom, it's just a little innocent fun," Tex said. "Can't you just see Dad trying to find out if he's getting free oranges or grapefruits, only to discover that by cracking the seal on the crate he owns a fifty dollar coconut?"

Carrie tried not to smile. "By increasing our *forgiveness skills* we automatically decrease our *vengeful urges.*"

While all this *letting go* was turning Carrie Angel into some kind of calm Zen Madonna, it was causing both Casper and Tex to vent their own *vengeful urges.*

"I'm sorry, Mom. It's too late. I have forgiven all I'm going to. *Vengeance is mine, sayeth the Lord.*"

"Tex, you are not the Lord, and I think you should remember that."

The phone rang again, and this time, Casper did jump to grab it. He closeted himself in the bathroom while he made plans to have dinner at Sarah's. Then he left his vengeful brother and blissful mother to their respective tasks.

It was but a few hours later that Casper arrived home to an empty apartment. He'd had a great time with the Lashes. Mrs. Lash always made some amazing dinner that usually involved a whole carcass or large limb of meat, and mounds of potatoes prepared differently every time. Mostly, he liked how Sara's dad, Dr. Lash—or *Bob,* as he'd invited Casper to call him—would ask him questions, and listen to his answers as if they mattered. Sometimes, when Casper was having dinner with the Lashes, he would fantasize that he and Sarah were older and married, and they were having dinner with his in-laws; or sometimes he'd pretend that they were siblings, instead, and they were the beloved son and daughter. Once, though, Sarah had been kept late at her babysitting job, leaving Casper to dine alone with the Lashes, and he recalled, a little guiltily, that he'd imagined himself an only child—with no Sarah at all.

The note left by Carrie said she'd gone to the grocery store and that Tex and Emily were at the library. Casper guessed that even with all that anger management training his mother was getting, a little part of her was happy that Tex was taking out a small revenge on her behalf. Because, according to the court documents, Carrie had better calm down—or else. He was munching an apple and wondering what to do with himself when the phone rang.

"Casp, hey, yeah, it's me, Sheckie, is your mom home?"

"Nope. She's at the grocery."

"Damn."

"What's wrong?"

"I need a phone number I left at my place. I'm at the shop."

Casper eyed Sheckie's apartment key on the ring next to Tex's, which he, as usual, forgot to take with him. "I can go get it for you. Your key's hanging right here."

"Awe, Casp that would be great. It's on a yellow legal pad by my phone. Just call me back when you get it."

Casper twisted the key in the lock to Sheckie's place and pushed into the darkened room, which smelled of cinnamon and apple pie. The scent emitted from little plastic air fresheners plugged into sockets throughout the house. When Casper had asked him about the cinnamon-y aroma, Sheckie had said, "What else could you possibly want to smell all day long other than baking pie? They don't make beer scent."

Flipping the switch on the wall illuminated a couple of table lamps on either side of the plaid couch. Casper made his way through the tidy room. There was a lounger in one corner facing a television set in another. A stack of motorcycle magazines sat on a side table; hidden at the bottom, Casper knew, were the latest *Playboys*. These he would occasionally *borrow* and return, unbeknownst to Sheckie, though he thought Sheckie probably suspected.

Casper found the number right where Sheckie said it would be and quickly dialed the shop.

"No problem," he said into the phone, after relaying the information. As he was about to leave, he noticed a photo album on the kitchen table. Carefully, he lifted the thick wide cover, and opened to the first page. All alone on the big page, was a small black and white photo of a newborn baby swaddled in a blanket, its head distinguished only by two round dots for eyes. On the next page, again alone and centered, was a long shot of a small child seated in a baby swing in a playground. As Casper flipped the pages, each containing its own singular photo, he watched the child grow and morph, like one of those speedy flipbooks where you can watch a dog jump through a hoop as you fan the pages. In this case, the child turned into a little girl with long brown braids in a team uniform running across a soccer field. In another, this time on a baseball diamond, she was in motion rounding the bases. She had grown taller, shoots of hair sprung from beneath her cap, and a spark of sun glinted from the braces on her teeth.

This must be Sheckie's daughter, Casper guessed. He often forgot Sheckie had a kid; he really didn't talk about her very much, at least not to Casper.

Once, after a visit, Casper came upon Sheckie crying in his shop. They both pretended like he wasn't, pretended not to notice, but Casper knew Sheckie missed his little girl more than anything in the world; he could see that it was so bad that it hurt him. Then Casper turned the page and there squarely in the center of the next one was that same little girl, suddenly, in a wheelchair. There were no casts on her legs. She wore a long skirt, just the girl in the chair and Sheckie standing behind her, gripping the handles. Casper turned to the next page and the next, and from the middle of the book onward, she was forever in the wheelchair. On the last page, she was seated in front of a cake; it had the number 16 lighted in candles. Poor Sheckie. No wonder he was sad. Something terrible had happened, something that didn't appear to be going away. He closed the album and set it back in its place.

"Mom?" Casper said, tentatively, stepping into the kitchen, returning from Sheckie's.

Carrie was at the sink, washing up dishes. "I'm right here, honey."

"You know Sheckie's got a kid, right?"

"Yes. A daughter. Amy."

"Have you ever met her?"

"No. She lives in Raleigh with her mother. Sheckie goes to visit her there."

"Why doesn't she ever come here?"

"I don't know. Never thought about it."

"What's wrong with her?" Casper helped himself to a carrot stick.

"What do you mean *wrong* with her?"

"I mean, she's in a wheelchair."

Carrie stopped chopping and looked at her son. "What are you talking about?"

"I went over to Sheckie's to get him a phone number he needed, and there was this photo album on the table."

"Casper, you snooped?"

"No, not really. It was open. To the second page. I just flipped through it. I figured it was Sheckie's kid. From when she's a baby. But then, from one page to the next, she suddenly goes from being some kind of junior high school athlete to a wheelchair."

Carrie eased herself into her seat. "Are you sure?"

Casper nodded. "All the way to a picture of her sixteenth birthday still in the chair."

"Wow," Carrie said, stunned by the revelation.

"You didn't know?"

She shook her head. "No, I mean, I knew he had a daughter. I knew he called her a lot, e-mailed, sees her every other weekend, takes her places, but he never mentioned she was in a wheelchair."

"Sheckie keeps a lot inside, Mom."

"Yes he does, Casp."

"Are you going to ask him about it?"

"What? Tell him you went poking around his stuff and discovered his disabled daughter?"

"Guess not, huh?"

"I think we should let Sheckie tell us when or if he's ever ready."

He made for his room, but turned back. "Mom, Sheckie's been a good dad, right?"

She smiled, "He's a good man, that's for sure."

Casper hesitated, "I mean, he's been like a dad to me, you know?"

"I know, honey."

"Better than Dill," Casper said quietly. He felt a tightening in his throat.

His mother looked hard at him, as if trying to come up with something wise to say.

"You're right," was all she finally allowed.

112

"I wouldn't mind if you, you know, hooked up with Sheckie," Casper said.

"*Hooked up with?* What am I, sixteen?"

"You know what I mean."

"Get outta here," Carrie said, and waved him on.

Carrie was more than surprised not to know that Sheckie's daughter was somehow disabled. He never talked very much about her in those kinds of terms. He might tell a story she'd told him on the phone, or report on her grades, talk a little about a trip to the zoo or the beach, like any other dad might.

If what Casper was saying about was true, it would explain a helluva lot about Sheckie's financial situation. Between his gig at the complex and his motorcycle shop, Carrie always thought he should be doing better than he appeared, even with child support to pay. But, if this girl has special needs, well, it would be just like Sheckie to be covering a whole bunch of stuff he would never even mention.

The more she learned about Sheckie, the more she thought about his difficulties, the softer her heart.

Chapter Nine

"Georgia" read the nametag on the older woman standing beside Jen in the office of Edible Feast. Bonnie, the assistant manager, quickly introduced them.

"Georgia is going to do your training, Jen. She has been with us for six months and she is one of our best cashiers. You're learning from a pro!" Bonnie said, her ponytail wiggling behind her. She was about twenty-three or four years old. She'd been made assistant store manager just last week.

Jen stole a quick glance at the woman who was to train her. Beneath the green smock that all cashiers were required to wear, Georgia wore a flowing (expensive) designer tunic in soft shades of lavender, silver threaded her auburn hair pulled into a beautifully woven French braid, and her fingernails were painted a subtle soft pearl. She seemed out of place behind the register, as if she should be conducting an orchestra rather than pushing produce through a scanning machine.

After a few trial runs, in which Jen practiced her way through the keyboard, she realized it was not so different from the self-serve lanes she had used at the local chain grocery store. The computer pretty much did it for you. Things had changed since she'd last had a job in retail, back in college. Georgia was a good teacher, patient in ways that Jen appreciated; they were like two old dogs learning new tricks, and somehow they both knew it.

"So, why are you working here?" Jen asked, seated across the picnic table from Georgia while they took their thirty-minute lunch-break together. "If you don't mind my asking, I just get the sense that this is not your *field*."

The older woman shrugged. "I was a music teacher before I got married. My husband was military. We moved all over with four kids. Then, we were in Virginia and, well, he was gone a lot, and I met someone else . . ." Georgia poked at her salad.

"I see," Jen said. Both cheater and the cheated, she knew neither was an enviable position. "But, that doesn't explain why you're no longer teaching . . ."

"The person I met was involved in the school, and it got messy."

"Oh, like *that* never happens," Jen said, thinking of her own role in academia. "Were you teaching at some religious institution? Who gets fired for affairs nowadays?"

Georgia shook her head, "You'd be surprised."

"Why? Were you sleeping with the principal?"

Georgia looked directly across the table. "No, I was sleeping with his wife."

"His . . . *wife*?"

"Her name was Chris, and we met at some faculty gathering. She was a little older than me at the time; I was in my late thirties, and she in her early forties. Neither of us had ever been with a woman, and I don't believe either of us ever intended an affair."

"What happened?"

"Well, we wound up working on a charity fundraiser together, and what can I say?" Georgia smiled; a hint of nostalgia played on her lips. "One thing led to another. We fell in love. Simple as that."

Jen was surprised by these words, since the complexity of all she'd just heard had her mind reeling some. She said, "I may have just come out of the suburbs, but *this* was no *simple* matter, at all, at the time, I'm sure."

"Well, you're right about that. When the shit finally hit the fan, it was a disaster. She was the daughter of a prominent family in the town where we lived, I lost my job, she lost her home, and then my husband took custody of my kids."

"No, how? How could that be?"

"Oh, honey, this is the South, where children are taken from gay parents every day. It was a nightmare. I was only allowed supervised visitation with my kids until they neared their teens and had a voice in the matter."

"Georgia, I'm so sorry." Jen reached across the table and took the woman's hand. "I can't imagine what that must have been like."

"Do you have children?" Georgia asked her, not letting go of her hand.

"Yes. A daughter, Emily."

"Then you *can* imagine what that must have been like to have your babies taken away—I believe you can imagine that quite vividly."

Tears sprang to Jen's eyes, and welled. Georgia tilted her head some, looked intently at her. "See, you know."

"Please tell me everything worked out. Please tell me you see your children and you and your—" she stumbled for the word "—partner, are still together, and it was all worth it."

Georgia withdrew her hand, and laced her fingers together in front of her. "I can assure you, it *was* worth it; to live unloved is wrong. My children are grown with families; we see each other regularly. Only my middle boy won't speak to me."

"I'm sorry."

"Well, he and his wife are good *Christians,* you know. I'm an 'abomination'—*that* was the word he used to explain why I would never see my first grandchild."

"What's the matter with people?" Jen asked, more rhetorically than not. "And Chris?"

"Twelve amazing years together. She died of cancer last February."

"No . . . oh no, I'm so sorry."

"Wouldn't change anything—well, except the cancer part, but we had a good life together. I still have our home, our memories, and our love. Chris was wealthy when I met her. She had her trust fund, thank God, or we would have starved—no one would hire me to teach after the scandal. Finally we moved to Asheville; very gay-friendly town, good friends, I taught at a small Quaker school. We traveled, life was good, great even, until the cancer hit."

"So, how'd you get to Fayetteville?" Jen asked.

"My daughter is here. Her husband's in Iraq, they've got three kids. When Chris died, and Annie, my daughter, asked if I could come help take care of her children while she finished nursing school, I decided I could use a change of scene. Too many memories back in the mountains, so I packed up everything, and bought a darling little cottage in Haymont. The grandchildren come to visit."

"If you don't mind my asking, why are you working here, if you could be teaching?"

"Oh, I don't really need to work at all, Chris made sure of that. I just need to get out of the house. To be honest, I love the atmosphere of Edible Feast, I love to cook, I love the smells, ambience, and the people who come here—I wanted to be out in public so I won't go mad." The woman gave a weak smile. "If that makes sense."

Jen nodded. "Perfect."

"What about you?" Georgia turned the tables. "What's a smart girl like you doing in a place like this—what heartbreak led you here?"

"You sure it's heartbreak?" Jen said.

"Written all over you."

"Damn, and I thought I hid it all so well."

"Nah, your heart's pounding away, right there on your sleeve, sweetheart." And Georgia reached across the table and smoothed a palm over Jen's shoulder.

Jen was grateful for the compassionate touch. She confided. "I got married right out of college and never worked."

"Let me guess, you were a literature major," Georgia said, matter of fact.

"How'd you know?"

"My roommate was a lit major. She pretty much went to college to find a husband. Most girls back then majored in literature because the boys were so *sensitive*, passionate, if you know what I mean. You just remind me of her. Am I right?"

"Probably," Jen said, and unexpectedly thought of Barb, her lit-major roommate-slash-lover, and felt herself reddening.

"I knew it," Georgia said.

"Your roommate, did she find a husband?" Jen asked, composing herself.

"Of course. Classic case. She married her professor."

Jen nearly choked.

"Oh don't tell me, you're a cliché, too?"

"I guess I am."

"So this is where your worthless degree has landed you, huh?" Georgia asked, her Long Island accent and manner rising. Jen found her abruptness refreshing somehow. The same way she found Carrie's gruff façade more honest than any of the so-called friends she'd made during her marriage.

"So, what are you going to do? You can't stay at this job for long, can you?" Georgia asked.

"No, I'm taking a real estate course. As soon as I get on my feet, I'll be getting out of here."

"Well, that's smart." Georgia nodded. "You're young."

Jen immediately, somehow, wanted Georgia for a friend. She realized that as her life changed, so too did her social circle. Those so-called friends from her Robin's Egg Lane years no longer left even half-hearted messages on her machine. The last she saw of most of them had been at the last cocktail party to which Jen had been invited instead of Hempy. The only problem was that everyone was coupled. The married women, once her friends, seemed to be eyeing her differently; while watching closely as their men gathered around Jen, laughing at her quips, refilling her wine glass, flirting just a tad. She wasn't invited again.

Near the end of her shift, as she'd checked out her fiftieth customer, Jen turned to find herself staring directly into the eyes of Tiffany.

"Oh, Jen. I didn't know you were working here."

Georgia was quietly scanning products while Jen bagged the imported coffee.

"I had no idea you'd been reduced to this," Tiffany said.

"Reduced to what? Tiffany?" Jen felt her cheeks burning. She shoved the sun-dried tomatoes and three spice blends into a little brown paper bag. She could feel a trickle of sweat begin to slide down her cheek. Jen slammed a cantaloupe into a bag.

"Well, that you would be actually *bagging* groceries."

Jen threw the spices on top of the melon.

Before Jen could toss one more grocery, Georgia inserted her body between them.

"Ms. Manners?" Georgia took the carton of eggs out of Jen's hands. "Thanks for your help; I can take it from here."

Jen frowned, confused. "But . . . I . . ." she began.

"No, really. You can go back to your office."

"Georgia?"

"I insist, managers have better things to do than bag groceries. Go on, I'll call you if I need you, again."

"It's no problem, Georgia," Jen said.

Before either had a chance to utter another word, the credit card Tiffany swiped beeped invalid. Second and a third swipes were equally ineffectual.

"It appears that your card doesn't work, *Mrs.* Manners," Jen said, evenly.

Tiffany's cheeks flared red.

"Would you like to pay cash?" Jen asked.

The woman turned and fled the store.

After Georgia voided the bill, Jen plucked the gourmet coffee from the *returns* basket and paid two bucks with her employee discount. A good day after all, she decided as she cashed out her register.

"Georgia," she said, as they walked out to the parking lot together. "Thanks for jumping in with that woman. She's my ex-husband's new wife. Number three, if you can keep track of all of that."

Georgia held up her hand and said, "You don't have to explain her to me, cookie. I know that kind of female. Been up against many of them, myself. I won't allow anyone to go through that kind of torture. Not for seven bucks an hour. Don't worry, I got your back. And I trust you got mine."

Jen suddenly felt awash in some kind of relief, as if the woman before her had gifted her with a shield. As if they were warriors on some kind of battlefield backs up against each other, leaning into each other while they pin wheeled, crossing swords with the onslaught of oncoming enemies—Jen reached for Georgia and wrapped her arms around her, pulling her into a grateful embrace; Jen held onto the woman as she'd not held onto another in a long time. She felt the gentle power of Georgia's arms pulling her close, and the hushed whispering, *shh-shh, there-there,* of the woman's breath at her neck. She wanted to curl into this moment, stay here forever, where everything outside felt far away, and Georgia's strength seemed to envelope her, seep into her, ignite something in her—something she immediately recognized as desire, something she had not felt for a woman since college, since Barb. It surprised her, confused her, and scared her a little—she gently pulled away.

"Thank you, Georgia. I feel like I've made a friend, today," she said, and meant it.

Jen could feel the wine warming her middle; she was on her third glass, as she cleaned up the dinner dishes. She didn't care if she was drinking it like it was Kool-Aid; it was about the only thing that could put her to sleep. She had never been in such dire straits in her life, and it was keeping or waking her up every night. It was with this thought that she had drained her glass, and poured another. She suspected that she was drinking too much, but sweet Jesus, what else was there to do? She suspected it was cheaper than the shrink she'd have to go to for the Ambien she really needed. She wiped off her hands, and took the wine glass to her bed with her. After a few more sips and a couple of turned pages, she slowly drifted off.

She was in a bit of a fog when the ringing of the telephone awakened her. After shaking the cobwebs from her brain, she pressed the answer button and spoke into the wrong end of the phone; flipping it quickly, she repeated, "Hello?"

The panicked voice on the other end was female and not immediately recognizable. For an instant Jen ran through the collection of women in her life, and when no face matched the garbled words, she stopped them mid-stream. "Who is this?" she asked.

"It's me. Tiffany," the voice came, slower. "It's Hempy. He's had a heart attack! We're here at the hospital. They don't know if he'll make it. I . . . I . . . didn't know who else to call." She stumbled along. "I was hoping maybe Emily could come sit with the girls," Tiffany's words crumpled into sobs. "I know she hates them, but I don't know what else to do . . ."

"All right," Jen said, suddenly alert, looking for her shoes. "We'll be right there."

Jen went to wake up Emily, and thought of Sylvia Manners, Hempy's grown eldest daughter. She knew that Hempy's marriage to Tiffany had been something of a last straw for Sylvia. From what Emily had told her, Hempy had not seen Sylvia for years, in spite of living just miles away. *They don't know if he'll make it,* Tiffany had said on the phone. Jen hesitated for just one moment before she picked up the phone and dialed information. "Manners, Sylvia."

Hospitals, at night, glow. It's as if they are lighted from within by a giant fireplace, making you believe that whatever ails you on the outside of that building could be cured by the soft radiance on the inside. Hospitals never shut down. It's comforting to know that your healthcare was on no time limit, Jen thought, swinging the van into the parking deck. Not like a restaurant or bar that dictated when you could eat and when you could get drunk. Hospitals were comforting the way an airport is comforting: you know it'll never close. Even if you have no suitcase packed, if you need to get out of town? An airport will accommodate. If you slip and fall? The hospital is open.

She looked over at Emily as they approached the big glass doors of the tall modern building. The girl hadn't spoken a word since they'd gotten in the car. Jen wasn't sure if it was sleep or fear that had quieted her, but as they walked up to the desk, she caught a look in her daughter's wide eyes that was matching her own unease. What may have been Emily's exhaustion, Jen realized, or in her own case, wine, was being replaced by fear. The receptionist directed them to an elevator at the far end of the hallway, the one leading to the heart trauma center. As they ascended, Emily suddenly grasped Jen's hand.

121

"Mom, is he gonna be okay?" Her voice was strained, held somewhere in the back of her throat.

"We'll have to see, honey." She squeezed her daughter's hand.

"I was mean to him last time we talked," Emily said, a tear rolling down her cheek. "I've been mad at him."

Jen could feel the girl's anguish in her palm. "Kids get mad at their parents all the time. Your dad knows you love him."

As the elevator doors opened, Jen saw Tiffany seated against a wall, both little girls asleep on some part of her lap. When they reached her, Jen could see stains of tears that had been washing down Tiffany's face, which turned up to Jen, sprouting another crop of them.

"I . . . I . . . couldn't help him," the younger woman struggled. "We'd just put the girls to bed. He was going, too, said he'd been tired all day." She sniffed and managed to compose herself some.

"What happened?" Jen asked.

"I went to get him some herbal tea, decaf," she hiccupped. "You know he likes it when he's watching *Jeopardy*. Suddenly, I heard a crash upstairs, and when I reached him, he was on the floor. He'd fallen and knocked all the pill bottles off the nightstand." She sobbed.

Jen knelt and reached a hand to the shaking shoulder. "It's all right, Tiffany," she said soothingly.

"No, it's not. I couldn't find the digitalis to put under his tongue. The pills were scattered everywhere." She nearly wailed. "I couldn't tell the blue from the green from the white. They were all mixed up."

"But you called the ambulance?"

"911. I called 911." She shook her head. "It took so long for them to come, Jen. I didn't know how to help him. I just held his head and kept talking to him till they got there."

"How is he?" Jen whispered.

Tiffany petted the little blond heads on her lap. "Not good," she managed. "The doctor says it's a waiting game."

"I want to see him," Emily said, looking down the long corridor.

"He hasn't woken up since we got here. I don't know if he'll even know you're here."

122

"I want to see my dad." The young girl hugged her arms around herself.

"Third door on the right," Tiffany looked down at her daughters and burst into tears. She said to Jen, "They're so little."

Jen followed her own daughter rushing down the hallway.

They gently pushed open the door into the dimly lighted room. There was a hushed whoosh and soft beeping of machines behind Hempy, whose arms were hooked by tubes and wires to them. A young male nurse with a chart looked up, and Jen whispered that they were family. He nodded and quietly exited the room.

They stood looking down on the peaceful face of the sleeping man. There were tubes coming from his nostrils, and Jen could see little round white patches connecting threads of wire to his chest. She recalled another time when they were in a hospital together; the three of them, only their positions had been reversed. It had been Jen and a baby asleep in the bed, with a younger, more robust Hempy looking down on their peaceful faces.

Emily picked up her father's hand, stroking it lightly to avoid the needles feeding into his veins there. "Daddy, it's me, Emily," she whispered, tears falling freely. "I'm sorry, Daddy. I'm sorry I haven't called."

Jen stood behind her daughter, placing her hands on both shoulders, leaning into her.

"I'm not mad at you, Dad. I'm really not," she sniffed. Tears streamed down her cheeks. "I just get stubborn. You know?"

Her pleas were met by the rhythmic pulsing of the machine measuring heartbeats.

"Mom, he can't hear me." Emily turned up a wet face to her mother.

"I'm sure he knows you're here, honey."

"Do you, Daddy? Do you know I'm here?" she asked, her words coming more urgently now.

Slowly, Hempy's lids fluttered and he narrowed his focus on the face above him.

"Daddy, it's me. Emily. I'm here."

He gave a weak smile and whispered, "Hi, princess."

"Daddy, I'm so sorry. I'll come over. I'll babysit. If you just get better."

He attempted a slight nod; his eyes closing, he took a breath.

Emily slid onto the edge of the bed. "I swear I will, Daddy. Cross my heart."

He opened his eyes, and whispered. "How about you follow *your* heart, and I'll worry about mine?" He looked over Emily's shoulder toward Jen. "We made a beautiful baby, didn't we?"

She found herself weeping. "Yes, Hempy, we really did."

"I love you, Daddy." Emily kissed his forehead and slid back off the bed.

"I love you, too, princess."

"Come on, Em," Jen eased her daughter away from the bedside. "Let's let your dad get some rest."

Suddenly Hempy's chest heaved up, and the heart monitor jumped erratically, and a high pitched squeal sounded from it. The door burst open and in sped the same young nurse. Following him at a clip came three other nurses dressed in green hospital scrubs.

"We'll have to ask you to go!" the nurse said to Jen and Emily, tearing back the sheets from Hempy's chest. Jen pulled her daughter from the room, stepping into the hallway as Tiffany rushed toward them, dragging one little sleepy moppet and carrying the other. Jen reached down and picked up the pajama'd body and hoisted the child to her hip.

"What happened?" Tiffany asked, craning her neck, trying to get a glimpse of the activity going on behind the swinging door as medical personnel entered and exited at a heated pace. There were shouts of STAT! and ASAP! coming from within the room as the five females, mothers and daughters, huddled together in the corridor. As the commotion continued, Jen looked down the hallway and watched the young woman tentatively approaching.

Just as Jen predicted for Emily, Sylvia Manners had grown from a pretty girl into a beautiful woman. Her shoulder length hair was stylishly cut and highlighted. She had her father's big brown eyes, wide with worry. The torn jeans and sweatshirt she had obviously

124

thrown on made her look like a college kid. In spite of this appearance, it occurred to Jen that Sylvia must be about Tiffany's same age. As Sylvia recognized Jen, she quickly approached her stepmothers and half-sisters as doctors and nurses whipped in and out of Hempy's room. Jen reached for Sylvia's hand and pulled her into the circle.

It was the doctor, a young dark-haired woman, who approached them. Her expression was somber. She unclipped the stethoscope from around her neck and spoke to Tiffany. "I'm sorry, Mrs. Manners. We did all we could. He had a massive coronary."

"What does that mean?" Emily stepped forward, pressing her hand against the doctor's arm. "Where's my Dad?" She looked past the doctor to the closed door of the room. "I want to see him!"

The doctor placed her hand on Emily's shoulder and looked at her anguished face. "I'm sorry, honey. We could not save him. He's gone."

The group was cast in a dark shadow as the doctor removed herself from them. All but the sleepy babies were enveloped in the sorrow. Sylvia wrapped an arm around Emily. Jen with Vanessa on her hip and Tiffany by her side managed to guide them all away from the doorway and down the hall. They moved as one mass, as if any fracturing off from the cluster might cause the whole to fall apart. They had each suddenly become widows and orphans.

Chapter Ten

"Later!" Emily yelled as she slammed the door behind her. She was going over to Tiffany's to go through Hempy's library. Tiffany had told Emily that she could have whatever books of his that she'd like, and even invited her for dinner. She told Emily that she wanted the twins to know their big sister, because they wouldn't remember their father, and Emily could share stories when they got older. It had touched Emily in a way that she hadn't been touched before, and she'd even gathered up some old books and pictures to bring to her sisters. She'd be gone for the evening. Ever since Hempy's funeral, Emily had been spending time with Sylvia, and Jen thought this might be giving Emily a new perspective on being a big sister.

Jen wandered around the small room listening to the quiet that takes over when there is only one breath—your own—filling up the space. What to do with all this *spare* time, she wondered, pouring herself a glass of merlot: lie about the empty apartment all weekend in her pajamas, watch old movies and eat ice cream out of a carton, or quickly go find a man, any man, drag him home, and have her way with him. Except there was no man to bring home, no man she'd even considered, and lately—oh, god, lately—ever since she had met Georgia—and each encounter since had Jen reeling in confusion. They'd had lunch together every day at work, and every evening when they parted, Jen found herself mostly looking forward to the next time she'd see her for lunch.

Each time they spoke, Georgia revealed something more intriguing about herself, and the more Jen found herself drawn to her. She

126

was something of a renaissance woman; she played the piano in a band of lesbian folk musicians back in Asheville. She was also a potter and had a studio in some arts-district there. Chris had always been a philanthropist, a patron of the arts, and had opened a number of galleries for the starving craftspeople of the mountain community. Together, they had renovated an old warehouse space, where studios looked out to the river, and they lived above, watching the blue ridges change colors with the seasons. As Georgia described, Jen could picture the gallery openings, evening soirées, and salons the pair apparently hosted; gathering artists, musicians, poets and writers, along with connoisseurs and collectors. To Jen, it all sounded exotic and romantic. Unlike her own life.

With her wine glass and latest edition of *Cosmo* tucked under her arm, Jen locked the front door and made her way upstairs to the bathroom. First stopping the drain of the deep tub, she turned on the water and then sprinkled perfumed bath crystals into the pool. In preparation for this alone time, she had scattered small votive candles around the tiled room. After lighting them, she turned off the overhead light and slid a Nina Simone CD into the player. Flinging her clothes onto the floor, she sighed and eased herself into the warm, fragrant water.

There was nothing like a hot bath, she thought, sipping from her glass. A small warm trickle of water plunked soft rhythmic drips from the spout. Between the rising steam, the flowery air, the low dancing candlelight, and her vivid imagination, she could nearly believe her tropical setting backed by Nina Simone's soft, sexy melodies. Jen closed her eyes and leaned against a damp roll of towel that served as a pillow.

In her mind's eye, she anticipated the image of the young muscular stud in a loin-cloth who would be delivering her next drink from around the island palms. Conjuring in the light of flickering candles, she could see long hair flowing freely across shoulders hidden behind shadows, stepping into the soft, yellow light, lips fully pouting, seizing her with an intense gaze—with eyes that belonged to Georgia, blazing blue, capturing Jen without even touching her. Her insides warmed with wine and weakness; tentatively, she touched herself. As her imaginary Georgia drew closer, kneeling down, whispering sexy words against her ear, she intensified her search for nirvana, allowing her fingers to go where no man (or woman) had been in years. Georgia's long loose hair tickled Jen's belly, her breasts; soft lips pressed her neck; her smooth tongue slid across Jen's chin, shoulders, down the globes of her breasts; Jen imagined Georgia's mouth on her slick nipples. Jen hurried her search, quickening her own rhythm, discovering the button of heat scorching her fingertips. Georgia sucking as Jen pressed onward, and as her hardened nipple clenched and pinched between soft lips, she arched from the water, toward heaven—

"I fucking *hate* her!" The bathroom door flung wide, banging the wall, as Emily burst into the jungle oasis. Jen crashed back into the water, jolting upright, before Emily flicked on the fluorescent above.

"Turn it off!" Jen yelled, shielding her eyes and her exposure from her daughter's view. Emily quickly flicked the bright light off and turned her back to her naked mother. "My God, Emily, you about gave me a heart attack!" Jen said, and then felt bad about it since Hempy had just died of one; she clutched the towel to her chest and downed the rest of the wine.

"Sorry." Emily frowned and then mumbled, "I didn't know you were in the tub."

"What are you doing here?"

"I hate them," Emily said, her back still toward her mother. "*All* of them."

"What happened?" Jen's voice sounded weary, even to herself.

"First, Tiffany invites me over to go through some of Dad's books. Says she wants me to have whatever I want, but by the time I get there, half the books have been packed up and given to the library. Then, she asks me all nice to have dinner with her and the twins, tells me how she wants me in the girls' lives since they won't remember Dad and I do, and on and on . . ."

"Yes?"

"So, right in the middle of dinner, her phone rings, supposedly it's a *friend* 'in need' of a ride." Emily gestured the quotation marks. "She asks me can I just stay with the girls for a minute while she gives this friend a lift home?"

"Did you?"

Emily stamped her foot. "Yes! Damn it! And once again, Tiffany manages to screw me over. I waited two hours for her to come back! Two! By the time she walked in the door, I'd bathed both girls and put them to bed."

"Did she apologize?"

"No, that's just it, she didn't think it was a problem at all, and on top of all that, she brings some guy home!"

"What?"

"You heard me. Some young guy name Tad or Brad or Chad, I don't know, but not a whole lot older than me, I can tell you that."

"Whoa," Jen managed to punctuate the diatribe, giving Emily a chance to catch her breath.

"Then that bitch told me, basically, that Daddy would want me to know my sisters, and that instead of whining about babysitting, I should be grateful for the opportunity to spend time with those little devils."

"Emily, they're only little girls. They *are* your sisters."

"Do you know what that little Vanessa did, Mom? She peed . . ." Emily looked carefully at her mother. "Yes, I said *peed* in my book bag! I caught her!"

"Oh Em, I'm sure it was . . ."

"It was the act of a spawn of Satan. She had a *gleam* in her eye. Just squatting over it like a cat, I swear to God." Emily folded two fingers across her heart. "Scout's honor."

"What did Tiffany do about it?"

"*Tiffany? Do* something about those monsters? Oh no, no, get this, she says they do it to get my attention. That if I spent *more* time with them, they wouldn't act out! That it's *my* fault!"

"What did you say?"

"I told her they were devils, and that I didn't want to be in the same room with them, never mind spend time with them."

"And?" Jen could feel the turmoil in Emily. It was all so complicated.

"It's *my* fault the little goat pissed in my book-bag! She said that my father was disappointed that I didn't try to foster a relationship with my sisters. She said that, Mom!"

Jen saw Emily's bottom lip begin to quiver, and she softened. "No it's not, honey. I'm sorry."

"I can't believe Daddy died and left me with that witch and her changelings."

"So what happened?"

"Well, I'm standing there with the piss-dripping book bag, with Brad/Chad staring at the scene like he wants to change his mind and leave, that maybe screwing a cougar isn't all it's cracked up to be."

"A cougar? I don't think Tiffany's old enough to be a cougar."

"Or something. Sow, more like it. So I ask her to bring me home, and she tells me that Brad/Chad will give me a ride home when he leaves, and then he popped a beer!"

"So how is it you're here?"

"I called Elise, you know, from school; she came and picked me up."

"I'm so sorry, honey." Jen emerged from the water, wishing she'd never insisted Emily try to get along with Tiffany for the sake of her father and the twins. She wrapped the towel around herself. Emily quickly turned away. When did they become so modest with each other? Jen wondered, as she often wondered how, after nine months of carrying a child inside you, there could be anything but a comfortable exposure.

"One more thing, though. I, uh . . ." Emily looked away, guilt written all over her.

"What?" Jen stared at her child.

"I didn't tell Tiffany I was leaving."

"You mean she thinks you're still there?"

"Right."

"You mean sulking in your room?"

"I guess."

"Emily, you get on the phone this minute and tell her where you are. She'll be worried sick when she finds you gone."

"*If* she finds me gone. If she can tear herself away from Brad/Chad. If she even cares to check on me."

"Well, if she does, she'll, *rightfully*, young lady, have a beef with you."

"Good."

"Emily, she *is* . . . *was* . . . your father's wife and your sisters' mother . . ."

"You know, Mom, I don't know why you defend her. She certainly doesn't defend you."

"What's that supposed to mean?

"What's a gold-digger?"

"Is that what she said about me? That I'm a gold-digger? Right, like Hempy Manners had such a treasure to mine. What about her? She pulled her U-haul right up to 21 Robin's Egg Lane before I had the last dishtowel packed. What does that make her? The nerve." Jen wrapped herself in her robe and twisted her hair up into a towel.

"Tiffany also said that you were doing a bad job of raising me, considering how I was turning out."

Jen's heart thudded. "Exactly *how* are you turning out?"

"She said that the way I was wearing *makeshift clothes* was the first sign. That's what she called my designs—*makeshift*! And then she said that my dyed hair, pierced eyebrow, and associations with other *disenfranchised youth*, that's what she called Tex, were all obvious *cries for help!*"

"Oh, for God's sakes."

"Then she said that you didn't have a clue."

Jen stopped and looked at her daughter. Emily's newly black hair, cut in a hip shag, along with big silver hoop earrings, accessorized her latest design: black and white checked bell bottoms topped by a silver satin and black velvet Nehru jacket. She'd salvaged an old pair of platforms and covered them in silver glitter. She looked terrific, Jen thought, even if she wasn't wild about the eyebrow stud.

Emily continued to recount the rest of Tiffany's diatribe against her, "She said she'd lay bets that I was doing drugs and having sex."

Jen's eyes narrowed. "Are you?"

131

"Mom, I'm not an idiot."

Somehow Jen believed her.

"Can I go to the movies with Elise? She's waiting in her car."

"Are you going to call Tiffany?"

Emily folded her arms across her chest. "No. I want to see how long it takes the perfect stepmother to even notice I'm missing."

"I'll call," Jen conceded. She couldn't blame Emily for her anger. "All right, you can go, but I want you home by midnight. Curfew, right?"

Emily scampered over and kissed her mother's cheek. "Thanks, Mom. Thanks for understanding. I love you." And she was gone.

"I love you, too," Jen muttered at the already closing front door. She hesitated before picking up the phone, and then held the receiver to her ear as she dialed the number. How dare Tiffany criticize her parenting? Jen thought, and slowed her motion. Tiffany's own parenting was more than questionable. From what she had witnessed and what Emily had said, those two little girls were a couple of hellions. But worse, it was Tiffany who turned Jen into a *single mother*, forcing her to deal with *everything* all the time, *alone*. Emily was a good kid. The phone was answered by a male voice; Brad/Chad, Jen surmised.

"Is Tiffany there?" Jen asked.

"Sure, hang on, just-one-sec," he said, sounding as if he were waking, or stretching, or . . . there was a muffled shuffle of the phone, Jen was sure, across bed sheets. "Babe, it's for you," she heard his voice echo through the lines as he juggled the phone to Tiffany. Jen hung up the phone. This time she'd let Tiffany do a better job at parenting, she thought.

It was two in the morning when the shrill ringing of the telephone sent Jen scrambling from her bed. It was Tiffany. She was hysterical. She couldn't find Emily, she cried. Oh God, she said three times in a row, and was praying with all her heart that Emily was there, safe at home where she belonged.

"You've *lost my daughter?*" Jen asked, trying to shake the wine-induced fuzziness that filled her head. "My God, Tiffany, I trust her

132

in your care for one evening and you're telling me you can't find her?" Have you called the police?" But then the evening's events came back to her. She remembered Emily coming home from Tiffany's and going back out with Elise, but she didn't recall Emily's return from the movies, and immediately headed for the teenager's bedroom. One glance across the closet-like space revealed its emptiness. She hung up the phone on Tiffany without another word. Jen tore down the stairs to see if Emily was asleep on the couch. She punched in the numbers of Emily's cell, the one Hempy had given her just before he died. It rang and rang and finally her voice mail, *Welcome to Ghost World–Leave a word for Emmy at the beep.*

"Emily Jane Austen Manners! Where are you? This is your mother. You better call home immediately!" She near screamed into the phone. Then hung up. Then redialed. This time more calm, she said, "Honey, I'm just worried. Sorry for the outburst. I love you. Please call home."

The phone rang, and it was Tiffany in a total tailspin, crying and begging forgiveness, and because Jen couldn't deal with her, she told her to relax and that she'd call as soon as she'd heard from Emily.

Jen paced around the apartment. Was it too soon to call the police? *Every minute counts,* they say on *America's Most Wanted*; it had been two *hours*. Did she know this Elise's phone number? Elise—who? What was that girl's last name? Oh, God, she couldn't remember. Watson! Yes, that was it. Running to the phone book, Jen found nearly three full columns of Watsons. There was no time for this, she ran back upstairs to Emily's room. On her desk, thankfully, was an address book and sure enough, in Emily's scrolling hand, a cell phone number for an Elise Watson. Jen quickly dialed. There was no answer on this one either. Jen attempted to leave a seemingly calm message, asking Elise to call as soon as possible.

Her daughter was missing, and she had no one to turn to, no one to share her mind-numbing fear. After some thought, she dialed Carrie's number. Her daughter was missing. This was her punishment. God was punishing her. The phone was on its fifth ring. No answer, no answering machine. She hung up. She looked to the clock. Four minutes had passed. *Every minute counts,* she replaced the phone and flew down the stairs and out the door to Carrie's apartment.

Pounding loudly on the door, Casper, with Carrie fast on his heels, let her in. Jen blurted out her fear and panic about the night's escapades and her missing child. It was then that the threesome noticed another missing child. With all the commotion, it was strange that Tex had not emerged from his mice-infested room. Casper checked on his brother.

"Gone," he announced.

"Okay, well, we can probably assume that they are together," Carrie stretched sleepily. "I'll make some coffee. Casp, go get Sheckie."

"Shouldn't we call the police?" Jen asked, anxiously wringing her hands.

"Let's think this through for a minute, before we do anything rash."

"But every minute counts," Jen nearly cried.

"Look honey, I've been raising boys for years. You gotta think like a boy before you panic like a girl."

"But Emily's a girl, and Tex is, well, Tex is . . ."

"Tex is Tex, for sure, but that doesn't mean he still doesn't think like a boy."

"Mom!" Casper lunged through the door. "Your car's gone. The Toyota."

"What'd I tell ya?" Carrie put a hand on Jen's arm. "He doesn't even know how to drive. See, that's how boys think." Carrie confirmed. "Casper, we need Sheckie, *now*."

"I'll go cruising around," Sheckie said, strapping on his helmet. "They can't have got far, that old heap is falling apart."

"That's what worries me, they might be stuck somewhere."

"Emily's got her cell phone," he said. "Just keep calling it. And call me on mine if they come back." He rolled out of the parking lot.

"I'm gonna go run around the neighborhood," Casper said, tightening his sweatshirt hood.

"No you are not," Carrie said. "For crying out loud, I don't need another kid to worry about. Sit down right there," she pointed to the chair at the table.

134

"Where could they have gone?" Jen paced the kitchen. "I mean, I can't believe they would do this. We don't really know that they're together. Do we?"

The phone rang and Jen rushed it.

"Hey? Mrs. Manners? This is Elise? Elise Watson?"

Jen could barely hear, it seemed there was a party going on in the background. "Elise? Where are you? Is Emily with you? Are you at a party? If Emily is there, you put her on the line right now, and tell her she's in *big* trouble . . ."

"Mrs. Manners, that's why I'm calling back? Emily's not here? I am at a party and please don't call my parents, but I just I wanted to tell you that I dropped Emily off around 11:30 last night?"

Why did every sentence sound like a question? Jen wondered. "Did you see her come into the house?"

"Sort of?"

"Was she alone?"

"At first? And then that guy, Tex? He walked over and they were, like, talking? So I thought it was cool and I left?"

Jen hung up and reported the latest sighting. "So, I guess we can be sure they're together."

"Casp, was Tex acting strange tonight at all?" Carrie asked.

"Mom, you're asking about Tex," he arched his brow. "I mean, what's *not* strange about Tex?"

"Okay, let's say *out of the ordinary* for Tex. Let's put it that way."

"Well, come to think of it, he was waiting for a phone call all night. I don't know if he ever got it. I went to bed."

"Who was calling?"

"I don't know, but I do know he had some money on him."

"Money?"

"A wad of it."

"Drugs?" Both women burst out.

Casper looked at them. "We're not idiots."

Suddenly they heard the rumble of Sheckie's motorcycle followed by the familiar sputtering engine of Carrie's Toyota. All three leapt and raced through the door.

"Where'd you find them?"

"Where have you two been?"

"You are in so much trouble Emily Jane Austen!"

"*Emily Jane Austen?*" Carrie leaned into Jen.

"You should talk—*Casper Wyoming? Amarillo Texas?* Kind of like calling the kettle black, dontcha think?"

"*Anyway,*" Sheckie's big voice interrupted the side conversations. "These two were out buying *hot* property."

"What?"

"I caught 'em making a deal out of the back of a big rig, stolen material from India is my guess. Come here, I'll show ya." He led the group around to the back of Carrie's car and pulled out a bolt of turquoise-colored silk, like nothing Jen had ever seen before. It was exquisite. She could just feel it against her skin. She could just see it fashioned into a long, luxurious, tight-fitting cocktail dress.

"It's not *stolen,*" Tex defended. "It was *acquired.* The guy said so, fell off the back of a truck on the Jersey Turnpike."

"Anyway, we didn't break any laws or anything," Emily defended. "We just bought it cheap. No crime in that."

"Oh, no?" Carrie stepped in. "You make a deal that has to be conducted out of the back of an eighteen-wheeler in the middle of the night, and you don't think you might be breaking some laws?"

"How much did you pay for it?" Jen asked.

Tex gleefully wrapped himself in the bolt of shimmering silk; another in burgundy still occupied the backseat. "Five dollars a yard," he whispered.

"My God," Jen nearly fainted. "Five dollars a yard? This must be worth . . ." She held it against her cheek, ". . . ten times that. Fifty . . ."

"Seventy-five," Emily interrupted. "It goes for seventy-five."

"We've got fifty yards," Tex bragged.

"Amarillo Texas, you just be quiet, right now. I haven't decided what I'm going to do with you, yet. It's not bad enough that you snuck out, bought hot property, but you drove my car without a license! Do you understand how big a deal that is?"

"I do, Mom, I do, and that's why I was especially careful. I mean, it's not like I've never driven. I am taking driver's education at school, after all. I mean, I did just fine, didn't I Emily?"

"Oh, yes, yes, Mrs. Angel, he was very careful. Stopped at all the signs and lights, and used his turn signal. I watched."

Carrie took a deep breath and pressed the heel of her palm against her forehead where a vein was threatening to burst. Quietly she said, "You kids all get to bed. This is something we'll all have to talk about in the morning."

"And don't think you're not grounded, young lady," Jen yelled after Emily. "I just haven't decided for how long."

After the three skulked off to their respective homes, the adults stood huddled together on the sidewalk. The sun was coming up, turning the sky pink.

"I could kill them," Carrie said.

"They sure are enterprising," Sheckie said. "You gotta give 'em that."

"If you had any idea of the quality of that silk, you'd see their genius." Jen said.

"What are we going to do?" Carrie asked.

"They could make a lot of money with that fabric and their designs," Jen considered. "Emily said they were thinking of handbags and scarves."

"Pretty smart, if you ask me," Sheckie said.

"But what kind of message are we sending them," Carrie asked, "if we let them think that buying stolen goods is okay?"

"What else are we going to do? Make them hunt down the truck and give it back?" Jen asked.

"They could donate to charity," Sheckie suggested, solving the moral dilemma.

Chapter Eleven

Casper had just about finished cleaning out the last mouse tank when Tex and Emily walked into Tex's room.

"Do you know how many freaking mice you have?" Casper dumped the clean cedar shavings into the terrarium, set the water bottle at the edge, and placed a small bowl with nuggets at center. Then he picked up a bucket from the floor and poured the mice back into their home. "You have eighty-nine! Eighty-nine, Tex. That's a shit load of mice."

Tex looked around the room. There were shelves of cages and glass boxes lining his walls, each teaming with wiggly white mice. Then Tex looked at his brother. "I thought there were more."

"Eighty-nine *is* more. You have to make a decision," Casper mopped his forearm across his brow. "We can't keep living like this. Everyday there's a new litter. It's starting to smell like a zoo in here. I can't keep up."

"No worries, little brother, something will happen."

"Why do you say stuff like that?" Casper was disgusted. "Like *what* will happen, Tex? Like the place will catch on fire? Mom walks in, lights a cigarette and we all blow up 'cause of the ammonia fumes coming from the mouse piss?" He tied up the trash bag full of old bedding.

"You don't have to be so dramatic," Tex said.

Casper dragged the garbage bag out of the room. "No? Well how 'bout if I just quit cleaning this stuff up? How 'bout if I quit feeding them? Watering them? How about that? Then you'll not only have mouse mess, you'll have *dead* mouse mess. You'll have corpses and carcasses rotting away. Freak mice will be copulating and then eating each other. It'll be *Lord of the Mice*. How 'bout that? Wanna live in that?" He slammed the door behind him.

"Mom, you gotta make Tex get rid of the mice," Casper said, passing Carrie with an armload of grocery bags. "It's outta control in there."

"I know. But Tex has to make that decision. After all they are *his* mice."

"No. They are not *his* mice. The first two were his mice. Lord knows whatever happened to *them*. But these last eighty-seven? No one owns these mice. I'm just keeping them clean and fed, but they are multiplying and taking over that room. It's a mouse coup, I'm telling you."

"Eighty-seven mice?"

"Eighty-*nine*, altogether."

"Dear God." Carrie shook her head.

"See? And who's cleaning them?"

"Well, Casper, no one said you had to do that."

"Oh right. Are you going to do it? 'Cause Tex surely isn't. We'd all asphyxiate if we left it up to him." Casper checked his watch. "Now look at me, I'm late." He slung the garbage bag over his shoulder and headed for the front door.

"Where are you going? I'm just about to make supper."

"Running. With somebody from the team," he, said, feeling his face getting hot. He turned away from his mother.

"Who is she?"

"I didn't say she was a she . . ." he stumbled, glancing over his shoulder.

"No, you didn't have to," Carrie said. "The tips of your ears are pink."

"God, Mom." He pawed at his gossipy ears. "I hate it when you say stuff like that."

"I know but it's my job. What's her name?"

Casper paused, "Mustang Sally. There, you happy?" Then he bolted from the house.

139

□□□

He threw the trash bag into the dumpster and then sped down the hill, leaping a fence and a flowerbed, turning into an alley, scaling a wall and finally landing upright at the forest edge of the Knob Knoll gated community. It was the shortest cut he'd determined after many trials along other routes. He'd got online and did a Google search of the area. This particular pathway was thirty-two seconds faster than either of the others.

Leaving the tree-lined limits of the neighborhood, Casper picked up an easy pace. He waved to the neighbors who were just arriving home from work. He'd come to know some of them. On these nightly passes, Casper made polite conversations with homeowners returning from work around this same time each day.

Chugging along the tree-lined streets, Casper noticed that birds seemed just a bit more colorful here. Their songs just a bit more chipper. In this neighborhood, people had time to paint hearts and pineapples on their mailboxes. They had time to blow leaves off their driveways. They washed their cars, trimmed their lawns, and rearranged tools and boxes in their near-empty garages.

There were a few more neighbors who knew his name, others who would wave or nod as he ran along, grinning. When asked where he lived, as he sometimes was, he'd point to the direction he'd just come from and say, "Over a couple streets." Then he'd change the subject. And so these last few weeks, as he and Sarah jogged through this neighborhood, it appeared that it was Casper who knew more of the residents than Sarah even had, in spite of living here since she was a baby.

She was waiting for him at the end of her driveway, he saw. Bending from her hips, her palms flattened on the pavement, Sarah formed a perfect triangle. She was exquisitely geometrically designed, Casper thought, a gem of nature. As soon as he reached her, the front door opened and Sarah's mother poked her head out.

"Hi, Casper. I made brownies, did you want one?"

He did, but he was about to run.

140

She interrupted his hesitation. "I'll pack up some when you're through. Stop by before you go home, okay?"

"Sure, Mrs. Lash. Thanks. Mom said she appreciated the chocolate chips you sent last week." This was something of a lie because Casper hadn't actually brought the cookies home with him. He hadn't wanted to explain to either Carrie or Tex where they'd come from. So he ate the whole lot on his way home, and had regretted it the rest of the night. The cookies and his deception had roiled in his stomach. This time he would take the brownies home and give Carrie the chance to really say thanks; then it would all stop being a lie. Well, not all of it would stop being a lie. Because there were some other half-truths and omissions that were starting to function like lies. And this made Casper squirm a little bit.

He hadn't *said* he lived in Knob Hill. Sarah and her parents and a lot of the residents just seemed to assume he did. It wasn't as if he had claimed it. It wasn't like anyone was asking which house or who his parents were. Not exactly lying, he'd decided.

Sarah said, "We're going to have to keep running just to fend off the cookies and brownies my mother is determined to stuff into us."

"She is a great cook."

"Oh, no, this is more than that. She thinks you're my *boyfriend.*"

Casper went white.

"I told her that you were better than a boyfriend, you were more like a *brother.*"

No! Casper cringed inside. Not *that* word. *That* word stopped all hope. *That* word left no question as to the nature of the relationship. *That* word—*brother*—meant that if you had any notions of kissing the girl standing in front of you, you've not only lusted in your heart, you've committed an act of incest. *No, no, no,* thumped the beat of his heart. If only Sarah had said *friend* instead of *brother.* At least a friend has a chance. There's always the possibility of friends morphing to . . . well, *more* than friends. But when someone reminds you of a *brother?* There's nowhere to go from there. They might as well have been in the womb together, he considered.

The pair took off jogging down the sidewalk. "I mean," Sarah continued. "We have so much in common. We both like peanut butter and chocolate syrup sandwiches. Together we have the entire collection of the Beach Boys. We want to go into medicine. I mean, Casper, I've never had a brother." Sarah wrapped her arm around his waist for a moment and squeezed, sending his pulse into triple time.

"You are the only girl I know who can eat a whole pepperoni pizza and burp louder than me."

"See what I mean? And you don't have a sister, either."

Casper considered this. "My brother's more of a girl than you are," he said. "He can out-dress, out-sew, out-primp, out-accessorize, and out-perform any girl I know."

"Yeah, but he's still your *brother*, not your sister."

"True." He hesitated, wanting to share but not wanting to burden. "I *do* sort of have a sister, though." He looked to gauge Sarah's response. "Her name's Destiny. She's my father's kid with his new wife."

"How old is she?"

They turned the corner and began an uphill trek to the cemetery, where they would run past the granite *dead*-stones, as Tex called them.

"She's around three," he said. "I barely see her."

"Why not?"

"Well, for one thing, my father is Dilberto The Magnificent! Ever hear of him?" Casper looked at Sarah, who shook her head. "Ah, well, then you are unfamiliar with the greatest magician of all time. He travels the world with half his wife, Dodi, performing tricks for dukes and queens."

"Half his wife?"

"Yes, the Do-half. The Di-half stays home with the children."

"The Do-half?" Sarah was eyeing him suspiciously.

"That way, the headliners read, The Marvelous Dildos! Tonight at the Palladium! See Dil saw Do!" Casper bowed in front of Sarah.

"So, really, why don't you go there?" Sarah asked, only mildly amused.

"No room."

"Oh come on." She pushed against his shoulder, prompting him.

"Bunch of stuff."

"Like what?"

"Just a bunch of stuff."

As they ran quiet through the cemetery, Casper ticked off the familiar names on the passing headstones. The long dead families: fathers and mothers buried side by side with infant babies at their feet. Siblings and their mates and children and grandchildren were all close by. Nowadays there wouldn't be enough room for a whole blended family in a plot.

They finally rounded the corner and made the last stretch to Sarah's house. When they landed on the front porch steps, Mrs. Lash appeared, on cue, with milk and a plateful of brownies. After each plucked a chocolate square, she covered them with Saran Wrap. "Don't forget to take these to your family, Casper. There's just the three of us here, they'll go to waste or they'll go to *my* waist," Mrs. Lash cackled at her own joke, and made her way back into the house.

"Parents can be so embarrassing," Sarah said.

He got up and grabbed the plate of brownies. "I better get going before it gets dark."

"Can I walk you home?"

He shook his head. "Then, I'd have to turn around and walk you home. And then you'd walk me back home, and then—"

"Yeah, yeah, I get it," Sara said, only mildly amused, Casper could tell.

"Casper, why haven't you ever invited me to your house?"

He could feel the sweat rise on his upper lip, and he knew that the patches of heat flaming his cheeks would be pink going to red; he could feel them. He shrugged. Kicked his toe against the step. He couldn't lie. Up till now, he'd merely not been *forthcoming*, and that wasn't lying, not technically; although, he'd felt a similar kind of guilt, he found he could assuage it with *trade-offs*. The trade-offs in this situation were things like: even though he sort of pretended to live in Knob Hill, he never really *said* he did, and even though he didn't live here, he'd made a point of getting to know his neighbors as if he *had* lived here. And being a good neighbor is what's important, no matter where you live. So, his less than honest living was voided by his stellar citizenship. Something like that. But, here was Sarah asking him outright. He wondered if he closed his eyes, and waited long enough, if either he or she might just disappear.

"Casper, I know where you live."

"You do?"

"Of course, everybody knows where everybody's from around here."

"So you know I don't live in Knob Hill," he clarified carefully.

"Right. I know you don't live in Knob Hill."

"So, you know I'm Sex8," he said the word, but tasted its bitterness on his tongue.

Sarah stood on the rising step. "If that's what you want to call yourself, sure; I know you live over in the housing complex right around the corner, and you've never invited me over."

He glanced into her face to see that she was actually a little hurt by his neglect. This surprised him. He was sure that his residing in Section Eight would totally turn Sarah away. He'd been trying to save her from the embarrassment of associating with his living conditions.

"I just never thought . . ." he fumbled. "It's just not the greatest place in the world.

"And you think I'm someone who cares about stuff like that?"

"Well, no, of course not, but . . ."

"But you kept it from me because you thought I'd judge you?"

Oh, crap, he thought, he was just digging himself deeper. Sarah was looking less hurt and more angry every time a word fell out of his mouth. "No, Sarah, no . . . it's just that . . . well, it's just that . . ."

"It's just what, Casper?"

He stood with his hands dangling at his sides. He didn't know what to say, he felt lost. "It's just that *I* care about stuff like that. *I* judge people who live in Section Eight," he finally confessed. "It's *me* who is ashamed, Sarah. It's more about me, than you. Do you understand?"

Then she leaned over and kissed Casper right on the mouth.

Wait! This was no *brotherly* kiss. It did not even contain the same characteristics of a friendly kiss. If he wasn't mistaken, was that a small tongue touch? Then he peeked and noticed that Sarah's eyes were closed. They pulled apart and Casper could feel the fire in his cheeks.

"I do understand," Sarah said, quietly, smiled shyly, and then turned and headed up the steps. She stopped before entering the house and looked back at Casper. "Maybe I didn't exactly mean that I liked you like a *brother*. Maybe I meant like a *friend*," she said. "Maybe more than a friend." And then she was gone inside her house.

More than a friend! Casper kept repeating over and over, as he ran home. She likes me *more than a friend!* He felt like Rudolph the Red Nosed Reindeer leaping his way home. There was a kiss, and Sarah had done the kissing, even.

He finally knew what it would be to die happy.

Jen and Carrie were going out for lunch. They'd planned it. They'd saved for it, and Jen was hoping she could further convince Carrie about the great business opportunities she foresaw for them. The yellow ski jacket she'd chosen had gotten too big. Nothing like poverty to make you skinny. It was cold outside. Winter was definitely upon them. She pulled the coat tight, frowned at her waiflike appearance, and was about to hunt for something else when the doorbell rang. Jen heard Emily cheerfully invite Carrie in out of the cold. She grabbed her gloves, smoothed her hair one more time in the mirror, and hurried down the stairs. Emily was flipping through a magazine and chattering away.

"Oh, Mom," she said, and smiled. "There's this great little coffee shop just down the block from where you're going. It's called *Coffee It Up*. It's very hip. All the college kids go. You should go."

Jen let out a snort, and laughed, saying mostly to Carrie, "Oh, I'm sure to fit right in with a bunch of college kids."

Emily slapped the magazine flat with a bang, startling the two women. The teenager stood and shouted "Fine! *Don't* go! Don't *ever* listen to anything I say!" She pushed back the chair, nearly toppling it, and rounded the table at a clip. Red faced and grimacing like she had a pain somewhere, Emily stomped her foot. "You know, I *try* to be nice. I *try* to be polite. *Engage* in conversation with your *stupid* friends—"

"*Emily Manners!*" Jen barked the warning.

"*This* is the *thanks* I get for even *believing* you *could* fit in?"

"Emily, for God's sakes, I didn't mean it was a bad idea, I was just thinking how long it's been since I was in college . . ."

"Yes, Mother! That's the point. I was trying to give you a little advice about maybe meeting some new *friends*, students, professors, people with educations who aren't so—" she looked at Carrie and scowled, "—*pedestrian*," she said.

"Emily! How dare you!" Jen stood. "You apologize to Carrie right now!"

The girl spun in a circle, and yelled, "For what? Telling the truth?" I mean, talk about lowering your standards! I can't believe you even *ever* went to college, never mind *graduated;* although, that's questionable too, isn't it? I mean, did you graduate because you slept with your professor or did you sleep with your professor so you would graduate?"

"*Emily!*"

"Oh, *what*, mother? Truth too hard to hear?" With that she stormed up the stairs. "I *hate* my fucking life!" And slammed her bedroom door.

Jen was shaking when she sunk to the kitchen chair. "I'm so sorry," she said.

Carrie asked, "What does she mean, *pedestrian?*" She patted down her jacket. "Something about my shoes?"

"Oh, Carrie, never mind. She's just a brat. I don't know what just happened. Do you see what I'm putting up with? I am walking around on eggshells every day. Never sure whether she's going to kiss me or kill me. Her moods, lately, are as unpredictable as a . . . as a . . ." She looked at Carrie, helpless.

". . . As a teenaged girl who just lost her father?" Carrie finished for her.

Jen shook her head and sighed. "I don't know. That's certainly a compassionate way to view someone who just insulted you. Maybe.

146

Maybe it's just Hempy's passing that has made her worse. I'd like to put all the blame on him—alive *or* dead, but . . . I don't know."

Carrie looked toward the stairwell, where noises from Emily's room were echoing. "You mind if I go up there?" She asked Jen.

"At your own risk," Jen said.

She listened and heard Emily crying on the other side of the door. Carrie wasn't sure exactly what she was doing, she had no patience for all this girl-drama, and thanked God for giving her boys—even Tex didn't emote this much. She took a deep breath and knocked.

"*Go away!*"

Turning the knob, Carrie gently cracked the door.

"*Argh!* Didn't you hear me? I said, *Go away!*" She flung a pillow across the room.

"Whoa!" Carrie said, ducking.

Emily sat up, wiping her face. "I didn't know it was you. I thought you were Mom."

"So, hurling pillows at your mom is okay?" Carrie leaned against the door frame.

Emily scrunched her knees to her chin, and wrapped her arms around them, like a tightly bound knot. She looked away, but Carrie noticed that her eyes could not rest anywhere, and when they returned to meet hers, they were scowling. If Emily were a gypsy, Carrie would be hexed, for sure.

"Mind if I come in?"

Emily shrugged.

Carrie pulled out the chair by the desk, tossed the damp towel clumped on its seat to the floor, and perched on the edge.

"Look, Emily, these temper-tantrums of yours have got everybody around here thinking you're just some rotten spoiled brat—me included."

The girl rolled her eyes and looked away.

"And maybe that's what you are, but I'm not so sure."

Emily frowned at Carrie, as if curious to know why she wasn't so sure.

"I was like you, ya know—an only child worshipped by my parents—only mine didn't have a lot of money. My dad was a mechanic and mom worked checkout at the grocery store. My parents got killed in a car wreck when I was sixteen, and at that time I could barely think for myself, never-mind do for myself. I got shipped off to an aunt I hardly knew and her creepy husband who liked to watch me undress through the bathroom keyhole—"

Emily's scowl turned surprised, and she tilted her head, like an alert puppy, listening.

"—till I shoved a pencil in his eye." Carrie shrugged as Emily's mouth opened.

"What happened?"

"He went off in an ambulance. My aunt gave me a fifty-dollar bill, drove me to the bus station, bought me a one-way ticket back here to Fayetteville, and wished me good luck."

Emily narrowed her gaze. "What'd you do when you got here?"

"Well, it was about two in the morning—"

"You were alone at the bus station? Was anybody waiting for you?"

Carrie shook her head, and smiled. "Nope, back then there were no cell phones. It was pretty much me and a really old man with no teeth—"

"So, what'd you do?"

"I had a thumb—"

"You hitchhiked?" Emily's eyes widened.

"It wasn't the smartest thing in the world, but I wasn't thinking very smart back then."

"Were you scared?" Emily hunched forward.

"Scared, hurt, confused, frustrated, nobody knew what I was going through, but mostly, when I think back, more than anything else, I was angry.

Emily glanced quickly away.

"I was mostly angry with my parents."

"Why?" Emily asked, now interested.

"For abandoning me. For leaving me unprepared for, well, just about everything. For loving me so much that when they were gone, my whole world disappeared. I was a daddy's girl. Spent most of my time in his workshop. I liked being with him better than just about anybody, and he didn't discourage it, so when he died, I was pretty much alone."

"Where'd you hitchhike to?"

"Well, luckily, I did have a good friend growing up. Lucy. I went to her house. Her parents let me live with them till we graduated high school. Then Lucy went to college and her folks retired to Florida. I got a room in a boarding house, worked waiting tables, tending bar, that kind of thing."

"That sucks."

Carrie shrugged. "The point here is that I understand what it feels like to have a parent die. I know what it's like to lose the people who love you, who take care of you—"

"Yeah, well, that happened long before my father died."

"No, that's not so, and you know it."

Emily frowned.

"Look, I'm willing to give you some room for your feelings, but I can't abide made-up stories. When your folks divorced, things changed for sure, but you still had two parents, you still had their love, their attention. You didn't lose your father, not really, not even like Tex is losing his." Carrie paused to let that one sink in, and saw that Emily was considering. "You had to share your father with his new cunt of a wife and your succubus half-siblings—"

Emily snorted a giggle. "Good one," she said, a tad begrudgingly. And then, as if trying it out, she said, "Suc*K*ubus" with the emphasis on the hard C. She raised an eyebrow at Carrie, seemingly suspicious of the source.

"Got it from Tex," she said. "He Googled it. He's been study Succubus mythology. I like the word." Carrie grinned.

"Me too," Emily said.

"Listen, Emily, I hate that your dad died," Carrie said, noticing tears spring to the girl's eyes. "I hear being a teenager sucks even with both around, but I don't know how my teen years could have been worse had that tractor trailer not run mine over. I was safe with them—and then I wasn't."

149

Emily nodded. "That's it. I don't feel very safe." She gave a small choked sob.

"I know you don't. But here's the deal, you do still have your mom, and even though she's having a hard time right now, she's trying to make things safe for both of you. And she will because she's smart and determined, and because there's nothing else to do but make it better. You see?"

Emily slid to the edge of the bed, across from her. She was crying and droplets splattered on her hands resting in her lap.

Carrie said softly, "You aren't exactly helping things, Emily. These crazy outbursts just add to the stress. You're stressing everybody out— me included. Mostly yourself, though. You gotta get a handle on all that dark energy, and get it behind something positive instead of throwing up all over your mother and splattering any nearby innocent bystander. Your mother loves you. She even needs you, if you can believe that." Carrie reached a hand across the chasm between them and ruffled Emily's already ruffled hair. "Look, you know I have to go to anger-management classes, right?"

Emily looked up and nodded. She swiped a sleeve against her wet nose.

"Well, that didn't happen because I suddenly woke up one day and threw a shoe across a room. That happened because I punched Tex's father in the nose during a session of *mediation.*"

Emily's eyes widened and she tried to stop the tug of the smile playing on her lips.

"It'd be funnier if it didn't land me in this position where I might lose my kids in court on account of it, ya know?" Carrie said soberly. "I mean, you're a lot smarter than I ever will be, you've still got a mom who is breaking her back to take care of you, and you've got college all paid for because your dad died and left you that college money he'd been putting away, so even he's still doing his part from the grave. If you keep acting out like a crazy woman every time something happens that you don't like, well, you too could be going to anger management when you're my age—get it?"

Emily sniffled and nodded, finally she managed, "I'll try harder."

"Good. That's all any of us can do."

"Thanks, Carrie."

"No problem. If you ever want to talk, you know where I live." She stood to leave.

"Carrie, I'm sorry about what I said about you being *pedestrian* and all; I didn't mean it. And it's so not true. I was just being a bitch."

"Yeah you were," Carrie said. "Hey, what do you mean I'm *pedestrian*, anyway?"

Emily visibly pinked.

"Look, I may not be educated, but I'm smart enough to know two things: One, I will never know everything, and Two, there's always a way to find out what I don't know. So, since you somehow insulted me, tell me how."

"Can I just say one thing before I tell you?"

"Sure."

"The thing is—I mean the truth is—you are *so* not *pedestrian*. Seriously, you're one of the coolest women I know. You do stuff most girls can't do, you can build things and use power tools and know fractions, I don't mean to be sexist, but I don't know a lot of women who can do all the cool things you know how to do." Emily explained.

"So, being pedestrian is not being cool?"

"Well, more like someone who's ordinary, not very clever, someone lacking in vitality, kind of dull, unimaginative—"

Carrie held up her hand. "Okay, I get it. You can stop."

"I'm sorry, really, I didn't mean it, and you are *so* the opposite."

"No, I get it. Apology accepted."

"Just like that?"

"Just like that."

Lunch had been a wonderful little getaway, and Jen was so grateful to have gotten out on a Saturday afternoon. Carrie was the one who reminded Jen of Emily's suggested coffee shop. And so they decided to make a trip to Coffee It Up! Carrie returned with two lattes as Jen claimed their table.

"This is nice," Jen said.

"All the kids rave, so I guess this must be the new hip. Feels crowded and a little grungy if you ask me."

"Well, I guess grunge is still in," Jen said. "Good latte, though. Did you see they have live music on Friday nights? We should come down sometime."

Suddenly a woman brushed past their table, the soft black fur of her coat lightly caressing Jen's cheek. Its familiar feel was nearly electrifying to Jen. Following the figure wearing the short black jacket, Jen nearly lost her breath. As if punched in the stomach, she leaned heavily across the table.

Carrie caught hold of her arm. "What's the matter? You look like you've seen a ghost!" She tossed a glance over her shoulder and then offered Jen a sip from her water glass.

"I . . . my . . . I . . . my . . . !" Jen stared at the blond head of Tiffany, whom she recognized, wearing Jen's own sealskin jacket. Directly behind Carrie, Tiffany removed the coat and draped it over the back of the chair. She sat down across a table from a woman, about her own age.

"That's *my* sealskin jacket," Jen hissed.

Carrie turned around. "Are you sure?"

"My God, look at it. Have you ever seen anything like it? It is one of a kind—look at the ermine trim! I kept it in a cedar chest in the storage unit. That's Tiffany. Coincidence?"

"Hey, you don't have to get snotty with me. I'm just checkin'."

"I want it back." Jen made to get up.

Carrie stopped her. "What are you gonna do?"

"I'm going to grab it, then I'm going to tear out her hair."

"No, wait a minute." Carrie rose. "She's got a friend there."

"I don't care. I want it back right this minute! It's mine!"

"Jen." Carrie pulled her back to the seat. "Sit. Look, I promise, we will not leave this coffee shop without that jacket, but you gotta be smart."

Jen breathed out and sat back. She looked into the eyes of her new friend and saw a kind of tenacity she felt herself lacking. How do you

152

get what you want when everything seems to go against you? It was there, in the steadiness of Carrie's gaze, that Jen found some strength. She decided to trust the promise.

The coffee shop was bustling with students hefting book bags, customers chattering, Celtic music drifting above, and wait-staff weaving in and out of it all. With all the commotion, it was easy for the Dynamic Duo to move into action when Tiffany got up and headed toward the bathroom. Carrie rose, turned, and stopped just in front of Tiffany's coffee companion.

Jen watched as Carrie approached the younger woman.

"Don't I know you?" Carrie asked her.

"I'm not sure," the woman smiled, looking puzzled.

"I think our kids go to the same pre-school," Carrie kept up the charade, stepping in between the woman's view of the sealskin coat.

"*WunderKindlings* on Bragg Boulevard?" the woman offered.

"No, the one over on Raeford!"

"Oh, well, then, we must have met at the Christmas pageant at the Civic Center last year."

"That's probably it," Carrie agreed.

"Do you have a girl or a boy?"

Carrie blocked the view as Jen made the switch.

"Two boys."

"Oh, nice. I have *three* girls, if you can believe it."

"That's a lot of emoting going on," Carrie sympathized.

"For sure. That's why it's nice to get away every now and again."

Jen slipped the sealskin jacket from the chair and replaced it with the old ski jacket she wore that morning. She listened while Carrie continued to distract the young mother.

"I hear ya," Carrie agreed. "It's key to keeping our sanity, isn't it?"

The woman laughed. "That and Xanax," she said.

Jen swung around with the coat and her bags gathered, then stealthily slipped from the shop.

As Tiffany emerged from the rest room, Carrie said, "Well, it was nice meeting you."

"You too! Enjoy your time off," the woman encouraged.

"And, you," Carrie said and made her way out of the coffee shop. When she arrived at the car, she was out of breath.

"What happened?" Jen asked. "Did she notice the coat switch?" They made their way to the car at the end of the block.

"No. Not even, it was all clear when I left," Carrie said, sliding into the driver's seat. "Roll down your window, it'll make the heat come on faster."

Jen protested against the cold.

"Trust me. I know my car," Carrie said, and rolled down her own. They pulled onto the street. "So, you and your jacket are in the clear," Carrie said, coming to a stop at the light. "Tiffany never saw me. I got out of there before she even came out of the bathroom."

Jen pulled the fur jacket around her. It was warm and silky soft. "Touch it," she said to Carrie, holding out the sleeve.

"No."

"It's so soft."

"Well, yeah, it's soft. It's from a fucking baby seal. What'd you expect?"

"No, it's not. I would not wear one from a baby. It was adult. I'm sure. Male."

"I've never seen a grown seal with fur."

"I don't care. I love it."

"Well, good, I'm glad you're happy."

Suddenly a blood-curdling scream shrieked from the sidewalk. Jen watched as Tiffany flew out of Coffee It Up. She was carrying the yellow and orange ski jacket Jen had left on the back of the chair. First Tiffany ran in one direction, stopping strangers, flailing her arms as she spoke.

"You would have thought she'd lost a kid," Carrie said.

The screaming commenced as Tiffany spun around, this time heading up hill. Jen scrunched down in the seat with her nose just above the car's window ledge. The car behind them beeped for the green light. "Go," Jen said, and buried her face in the fur.

Later, Jen crawled naked onto the bed with the jacket. Turning it inside out, she slid her arms into the silky fur-lined sleeves. Then wrapping the luxurious softness against her bare back and breasts, she slipped her skin into the sleek baby seal fur. She didn't care where it came from; nothing had ever felt so good.

Chapter Twelve

Carrie and Jen had both arrived home from their respective days at the same time. Carrie was covered in sawdust, and Jen was loaded down with thick heavy manuals. Carrie swung her arms, loosening the joints. "Feels good just to walk, you know?"

"True. Been on a twenty-four seven mission, lately. You?"

"Finishing a job over in Spring Lake." She patted her jeans, watching the white tufts of dust billow in puffy clouds around her. "That bastard, Pressley, I work for, takes great pleasure in giving me all the punch list at the end of the day."

"Punch list?"

"All the little nickel and dime stuff that gets left dangling at the end, like making sure doors have locks, switches have plates, molding cracks that need filling and on and on, that kind of junk."

"Sounds tedious."

"It is tedious. I swear, it's putting all my anger management techniques to test, that's for sure."

"Are you done with that class?"

"Next week, then I get some kind of badge." Carrie laughed at her own joke.

Sheckie was coming around the tool shed as the women passed by. "Hey, you two." He waved. "Where ya going?"

"Bus stop."

"The kids'll hate you," he said, squinting down the road.

"We know. We don't care. That's why we're going. To remind them to hate us."

"Mind if I join you?"

"If we did, would it stop you?" Carrie said, laughing.

Jen noticed Sheckie's quickly masked hurt and said, "We'd love for you to join us."

"How's the real estate class going?" Carrie asked, knowing that the reason she hadn't seen Jen around for the last few weeks was because of her job and this class.

There was a guaranteed placement with a high score, and so Jen had been focusing all her attention on her studies. She had no doubt she would make that score. "I just need to get through it. I've always been a whizz at test taking," she said, confidently. "It's never been a problem for me. I've got a bit of a photographic memory."

"Well, lucky for you," Carrie said, but commenting more to herself.

"Too bad she couldn't take your carpentry test for you," Sheckie said.

"No kidding."

The bus pulled up and all three adults waved as it emptied its load. The three teenagers jumped to the road, looking at each other and then the mothers.

Tex was the first to drop from the bus, sauntering toward the adults. "Did Dill finally ditch Do? Have you come to break the news? Go ahead, I can take it." Tex didn't wait for an answer, though, instead he skipped around in a circle singing, "Ding Dong, the Dildo's dead . . ."

"Is there something wrong?" Casper wondered, immediately alarmed and worried.

"What are you doing here?" Emily demanded when she landed.

"We just wanted to greet you when you got off the bus," Jen said.

"God, Mom," the girl said under her breath. "That is so embarrassing."

"That's why we did it," Carrie interjected. "Get over it, kid. We love our babies," and with that she ruffled Casper's hair.

"Mom, stop it," Casper said.

"How was your day?"

Tex hitched up the Afrikan skirt he'd been wearing. "Golf has never been my thing, but coach said he'd pass me if I quit twirling my club before every swing."

"Slam-dunked a history quiz," Casper said.

"Same on a math test for me," Emily mentioned.

"Wish you *all* could take my carpentry test for me," Carrie said.

"What's up with this carpentry test?" Jen asked.

"Oh, I've been taking and failing this last stupid test for my certification over and over again. I just cannot pass multiple-choice. I don't know why. I've got some kind of block that won't unclog. I've tried everything. Been studying my ass off. Right, Casper?"

"It's true. We even made flashcards."

"I decorated them," Tex piped up.

"Nothing seems to work," Carrie continued. "In just weeks, I'll be failing it again, and then I'm sunk."

"Multiple choice?" Jen asked. "Oh, that's simple."

"Easy for you to say, Miss *Photographic Memory.*"

"No, I mean it's simple to understand, once you get a system down. I mean, there are tricks to helping you memorize. I could show them to you. Really, it'd be my way of paying you forward again; after all you did for us."

"Would you knock it off with that *paying it forward* business? I'm sorry I even mentioned it. You don't owe me anything. I gotta figure this one out myself. Maybe I'm not meant to be a carpenter."

"Mom!" Casper said. "Stop talking like that. You know you love it. You're already a carpenter. You should let Ms. Manners help you."

"Yeah, Mom," Tex concurred. "That's what you're always telling us: if you don't know how to do something, go find the way."

"She helped me learn the multiple choice thing way back in fourth grade," Emily spoke up in defense of her mother. "It really works."

"Whatdya got to lose?" Sheckie finally weighed in. "Do you want to get out of this shithole or not?"

Carrie shrugged. "I don't know, Sheck. What would I do without you living next door?" She punched him affectionately. "I'd miss your big mug in my face everyday."

"Guess you could take me with you," he flirted, just a little. "I could live in your garage, next to my motorcycles. You could invite me up for pancakes in the morning."

At this, both Casper and Tex sputtered, "Pancakes? Mom?"

"All right now," she cautioned the men. "Never see you three turning down a burger or spaghetti, do I?"

Jen put her hand on Carrie's shoulder and said seriously, "I really can show you the way to ace that test."

"A passing grade would do."

"Okay then?"

Carrie shrugged, "Like Sheckie said, I guess there's nothing to lose. At the rate I'm going, if I don't pass it soon, I'll be too old to do the work at all."

Sheckie and Casper were off to the batting cages, and would be dropping Tex and Emily off at the mall on the way. The space had been cleared for a night of preparing for Carrie's exam. After the gang piled out of the house, Carrie and Jen turned to each other, and Carrie laughed. "Why do I feel like I'm back in elementary, stuck after school with the teacher."

"Did you drink wine with your teachers?" Jen offered and Carrie sank into the kitchen chair.

"If only. English would've been so much easier," she said, reaching into her backpack. She heaved the giant *Finish Carpentry* textbook onto the table between them.

"Are you sure you want to help me with this stupid multiple choice test?" Carrie asked.

"Look, practically speaking, you know all this stuff, right?" Jen asked. "I mean, from what I've seen of your work, and heard from the word on the street, you're a great finish carpenter already."

"The *word on the street?*" Carrie repeated. "What, are we living in the *hood*, now?"

"You know what I mean. You *know* this stuff. Can you at least admit *that?*"

"Sure. I admit it." Carrie straightened her shoulders some. "I'm good."

"So the only thing between you and your certification is this ridiculous test. It's a mindset. Once you get some of these tricks, you'll blast right through."

"I hope you're right. If I don't pass it this time, I'm done for."

"Not going to happen." Jen set their wine glasses down on the table and got out some paper and pens.

Carrie sipped, her hand shaking a little. Jen felt for the woman. It was horrible to be an adult and feel like a child in front of anybody. She opened the sample test in the workbook.

"First of all," Jen said gently. "Always cover up the answer-part with your hand while you read the *stem.*"

"*Stem?*" Carrie threw her hands up. "What the hell's a *stem?* See already it's too late. I've been studying this for three years and I don't know what the fuck a stem is. I can't do it. Thanks a bunch, Jen. You've been great, but this is a big fat waste of time." She leaned back against her seat.

"Are you through?"

Carrie shrugged.

"The *stem* is nothing more than this part." She pointed to the question. "So as you read it, cover up the possible answers."

"Why?"

"Because your first instinct is often the correct answer. If you choose it in your mind first without mucking it up with the other possibilities, you're probably going to get it right." Jen demonstrated the technique. "See? Take your hand away and the right answer is usually glaringly obvious, especially if you know it in the first place. Which, I bet you do."

Carrie took a deep breath. "Hmm," she muttered. "Wouldn't have thought of that." She leaned forward, checking out the example.

Jen continued. "If you see the one you think is right, mark it. Then check to see if there's a closer one. Try it."

Carrie carefully covered the choices to three stem questions and each time she revealed her correct answer. She seemed pleased, but then quickly asked, "What happens if I don't see what I think is right?"

Jen nodded. "Good question. And this is a bit of a gamble, but more often than not it can be reliable. If a choice contains absolute words like *never* or *always* they're probably wrong."

"Why?" Carrie asked, scrunching forward. Setting aside her glass, she peered into the book.

"Maybe because there are no absolutes in the world," Jen said, and then reflectively, "There was a time I didn't believe that. There was a time when I believed in absolutes."

"Like what?"

"Like love."

"You thought love was an absolute?"

"Sure, I mean, I was born into it. I'd had it unconditionally from my parents my whole life. I know I am lucky in that way. You?"

"Yeah, till they got killed in a car wreck and left me, alone, when I was sixteen. Oh, they absolutely loved me, but what good's all that fondness after people die? I learned real quick what a hot pile of moving shit *absolute love* was: Dill Angel."

"But that wasn't your parents' fault; it wasn't betrayal. It was an accident. Like when my mother died. I know she still loves me from heaven."

Carrie said, "Oh, don't get me started on heaven, church, or God, for Christ's sakes. If I had to rely on all that hoodoo for comfort, I'da blown my brains out. I got more faith in me than I do in the man behind the curtain, sitting on his gilt throne with winged angels flapping around, doing his bidding, fucking up the world in general and my life in particular . . . ugh, Geezus, Merry, and Sane Josef."

Jen laughed. "Tell me how you *really* feel about it, Carrie."

The sarcasm was not lost on her. "Sorry. It's a sore spot, for sure. After Dill married Dodi, he wound up going to church, getting *saved*, whatever that means, now he's this so-called *Christian*, whatever that means; just an excuse when you fuck up, and judgment when everybody else does."

"Well, that's true, but I was talking about the way, like you, really believed in absolute love, thinking it could be with another person, figuring out it's mostly between children and parents, ya know?"

"Yeah, I do know. Love is a many splendid thing until it isn't, then it's fucked up."

"Do you really feel like that? I mean, don't you ever dream of having that perfect absolute love with someone else?"

Carrie took a deep breath. "Jen, if I don't pass this test, the judge could rule in Dill's favor and make the boys go live with him, so, no I don't really wonder about much beyond this—if you need an answer, then, sure, as a mother, there's absolute love, but, I don't expect or want it from anyone else. All I care about right now is Tex staying put with me."

"I'm sorry, Carrie. Of course you're upset. Of course that's what's on your mind. I was being stupid."

"No, it's not you. It's just—well, how do you think living with Dill is going to affect Tex? You've met Dill, seen him in action, you know how he feels about . . . homosexuality. He'll probably send him to one of those places to get *cured.*"

"At best," Jen concurred, her stomach doing a little flip, thinking of her own current situation with Georgia, the woman she'd been sleeping with for two weeks, the woman she couldn't get off her mind, the woman who walked into a room and made Jen feel all of sixteen and giddy all over again.

She wasn't really surprised when it happened the first time. Jen had gone to Georgia's for dinner that night with lust in her heart, if she were going to be honest. She'd had dreams about Georgia, fantasies she'd played out in her own private moments; she loved talking on the phone, sent e-mails and texts all day long, and in a school-girl kind of way, found herself doodling their names together on a sticky note while talking on the phone. When Georgia invited her to come for supper to her quaint little cottage in Haymont, the historic district of Fayetteville, Jen couldn't sleep for three nights, imagining every scenario that could ultimately land her in Georgia's bed. The fantasy wasn't half as awesome as the real deal, when it happened.

They'd begun with fruit and cheese appetizers on the wide open porch with its blue ceiling; made their way to the kitchen, where the flirtation involved the tasting of so many parts of the dinner. Georgia was a gourmet cook, and spoon-fed Jen nips of sauces, a tender piece of steak, a savory hot pepper, in-between sips of wine. When the dessert of raspberry sorbet was followed by a fine scotch, the likes of which Jen had not tasted in years, the intimate stories led to more intimate whispers, confidences, confessions, and before she could stop herself, Jen slid close on the loveseat, reaching and twisting a finger around a lock of Georgia's hair, drawing her near. Their mouths hovered, brushed, until Jen felt Georgia's tongue touch her lips, and her wet mouth pressed softly, gently pulling, sucking; Jen thought she would liquefy, and began her own probe. When Georgia's fingers grazed her already hard nipple, she felt an urgency, and had to pull herself away. Jen gulped air as she paused the intimacy, while Georgia's lips kissed her knuckles, but the break did not last long, and when Jen could finally breathe again, Georgia took her hand and led her into the bedroom. One by one she unbuttoned Jen's blouse, all the while holding her gaze with shadowy eyes. She slid her hand between Jen's legs, cupping and massaging. Jen moaned, pressing against Georgia, who guided her backward and pushed her down on the big bed. Beginning at her toes, Georgia licked, caressed, and teased between Jen's legs, driving her into a near frenzy. She grabbed at Georgia's long hair, pulled and pushed, begged her to go on, pleaded with her to slow down, and nearly screamed when she felt Georgia's tongue between her legs, parting her lips, plunging her fingers into Jen's hot wetness, sucking and drawing the very life out of her. Jen had never felt herself so swollen, so throbbing, and she came in cataclysmic spasms, over and over with Georgia' fingers plunging deeper, fucking her to an ecstasy that Jen could not believe; she thought she could finally die happy.

Even after she thought she was spent, she was not, and Georgia brought her around once more, before Jen even touched the soft wetness of Georgia, even before Jen kissed and licked her way down Georgia's belly, gently searching with her own tongue for Georgia's velvety clit, and when she found the sweet juices dripping into her mouth, she couldn't believed she was aroused all over again; fucking

Georgia meant coming again and again, until they both lay limp in each other's arms.

"Are you listening to me?" Carrie snapped her fingers in front of Jen, bringing Jen from her reverie.

"I'm sorry, I was thinking. You said something about, about Tex being cured?"

"I said if he went to live with Dill, that he would probably send Tex to one of those places to get *cured.*"

"That's horrible," Jen agreed. "So what if he's gay?"

"I don't care if he's gay! I mean, I'm really okay with it, I thought he was gay when he was three, and wanted to be the princess of his toy box all the time. But, it's not an easy life, and it's one more reason for Dill to ride the kid instead of just loving him. I mean, he's his son."

Jen thought of how terrified she was to tell the people she loved about Georgia. While she knew Emily was very open-minded and adored Tex, and had recently confided that she herself might be bisexual (which had elicited a startled gasp from Jen and a warning eyebrow raised by Emily), Jen wasn't all that confident that Emily would be quite so supportive if her mother beat her to the proverbial punch. Teenaged girls were so unpredictable. Then there was Carrie; while she supported her own son, she might feel betrayed, somehow, to know that Jen was with a woman. So, yes, she completely understood how scary the notion of Tex living with Dill was for Carrie.

She said, "Well, let's make sure that the jackass homophobe doesn't get to torture his gay son 24/7, okay?"

Carrie nodded, calming down. She took a sip of wine. "Let's do this thing."

Jen pointed to the sentence on the page. "So if there's a word like *probably* or *usually*, see here?" she tapped, "you can nearly count on including them in the possibility of right answers."

"Okay, that makes sense, I can buy that—but!—" Carrie smacked her hand on the book. "What about that God-awful mind-crippler *All of the Above*? I fucking *hate* that one."

Jen laughed. "Actually, *all of the above* is often a correct answer."

"No shit."

"If you can prove that more than one of the answers is true, then more than likely the rest are, too."

They tested the theories between sips of wine and the bread and cheese Jen had brought home.

"Here's my favorite *clue* to a correct answer," Jen laughed.

"Man, you *like* this shit, don't you?" Carrie looked at her suspiciously.

"I admit it. I *love* it." She emptied her glass and pointed to a *stem* in the book. "See here? This stem ends with *an*."

"So what?"

"So, that means the true answer begins with a vowel!" Jen hailed her glass high in triumph. She grabbed the bottle and refilled their glasses to the brim with the last of the wine. "Go ahead, read the answers and tell me if I'm right."

Carrie did as she was told and her mouth dropped open in disbelief. "You are a fucking genius," she uttered.

"I know."

"Anything else?" Carrie asked.

"If all else fails, pick *B* or *C.*"

"That doesn't sound very scientific."

"It's not, but many testers like to hide the answers inside the grouping. So, you'll find more true answers there than anywhere else."

It was quite late and almost two bottles of wine later when the clatter from the returning troupes interrupted Jen and Carrie's study time. They'd pretty much finished, anyway.

Emily and Tex were first through the front door, and they were practically glowing. Their matching smiles spread across their faces, rosy cheeks glistening, eyes sparkling. The chattering between them filled the apartment and blasted both women, who'd been feeling cozy and warm with their wine. Sheckie and Casper sauntered in and made their way to the couch and flipped the TV to ESPN.

"We've already heard *all* about it," Casper explained their distance.

"Oh my God, Mom, you should have seen it! Tex and I were

walking past the *Bridal Fare*, and there was this obviously unhappy, crying bride-to-be with an even unhappier, yelling mother, and a salesgirl who looked like she wanted to run away. Then, Tex, here, runs into the store, and says, 'Sweetheart, never fear, Tex is here!' And he proceeds to go through the gowns and dresses, mixing and matching veils, capes, trains, and on and on until he came up with just the right combination!"

Tex nodded, laughing. "The bride was happy, the sales girl was relieved, and the mother was *so* pleased that she invited me to the wedding and offered to pay me one hundred dollars to help Joselyn, that's the bride, get ready!"

"That's great, Tex. You really know how to step up. I'm proud of you," Carrie said.

Jen looked over at Sheckie and Casper, the latter glued to the television set. Sheckie caught Jen's eye and nodded at the boy on the couch beside him. Jen nudged Carrie, who glanced beyond the (finally) calming Tex and Emily.

"How was your night, fellas?" Carrie called over, asking the men on the sofa.

"Got a lot of good hits," Sheckie said, uncomfortably.

Casper remained silent.

"Are you hungry?" Jen offered. "I've got some cold cuts."

"I'm good," Sheckie said. "We packed away six or seven hot dogs. Didn't we, buddy?" He turned toward Casper, who didn't move.

"How 'bout you, Casper Wyoming," Carrie said to her son. "How was your night?"

Casper stood and headed for the door; before he exited, he turned. "Saw Dad, tonight."

"Where?" Carrie asked.

"At the batting cage."

No one spoke.

"He was there with Dusty." Then Casper left the apartment.

No one moved. Finally Carrie turned to Sheckie. "What happened?"

He rose and shrugged his shoulders. "That was pretty much it. We

166

look over and there's Dill showing that little fat kid how to hold a bat. He looks over and sees Casper and me. He just stares at us."

"Did he say anything?"

Sheckie made his way to the door. "Nope. He takes the fat kid by the shoulders and leaves. After a few more swings, we left to pick up these guys." He thumbed over toward Tex and Emily, immersed in a music video.

Jen asked, "Did Casper say anything?"

"Not really. Something about it being the first time he'd ever seen the kid without food in his hand."

Carrie sighed.

"Poor guy," Tex said. "Imagine envying a benign blob because you want the attention of a dim-witted moron."

"Tex, that's enough," Carrie scowled at her elder son. "Your brother is hurting; have a little compassion."

"I don't know why he's hurting. Good riddance to bad rubbish, is my motto," Tex said, flatly. Jen suspected his bravado might just be masking his own hurt.

Carrie rose. "I better go talk to him," she said, worry apparent in her brow.

"Want me to walk you home?" Sheckie asked her.

She nodded. "Thanks for tonight, Jen. It really helped a lot."

"I think you're going to ace that test this time."

"For the first time, I might agree with you."

"We'll do a couple of rounds before you have to go do the real thing."

"That'd be great," Carrie said, and stepped next to Sheckie. "You coming, Tex?"

"Can he stay till after this movie?" Emily asked.

"Okay with you, Jen?"

"Of course. He's like the son I never had."

Jen wandered up to her bedroom. From her view at the window, in bright moonlight, she watched as Carrie and Sheckie walked together toward Number Two. Carrie was leaning into the big man, and he'd wrapped his arm around her shoulder. When they reached the apartment, they didn't part immediately, but stood together like that for a long while. Jen imagined they were probably talking about Casper. They were obviously staring at the moon and stars. Jen watched as Carrie slowly turned to Sheckie, placing her head on his big chest, wrapping her arms around his waist. He held her and cradled her head in the glove of his hand.

She imagined that Carrie might be crying, but she had difficulty imagining the hard little woman breaking down. Sheckie leaned over, leaving little kisses on the top of Carrie's head. After some more time, she wiped the edge of her shirtsleeve against her cheeks. Sheckie took her face gently in his big hands, tilting her eyes to him. He bent and kissed her mouth. They lingered together like that and then Carrie hurried inside. Sheckie stood there for a long time. In the darkness of her room, as Jen watched him staring at the stars, she wrapped her arms around herself, longing for the touch of Georgia's arms around her, protecting her, calming fears—real and imagined—giving into the cradle of assurances, as she had just the night before. It was the same feeling, she knew, Carrie had as she caved into Sheckie's strong arms. There was no difference when it came to absolute love.

Casper tried to ignore Tex's whining from the front passenger seat as their mother drove them to Christmas dinner at the Dildos. This wasn't exactly what either of them wanted to be doing, but why Tex had to make it worse by listing (again) all the reasons why it was going to be the most god-awful, torturous, mind-numbing evening of their lives, Casper hadn't a clue.

"I cannot believe you're making us go through with this, Mom," Tex said for the millionth time. "He didn't even call till yesterday. *So* last-minute, if you ask me." Tex heaved his arms across his chest.

"Look, your father has the right to see you. He wants his family around his dinner table for the holiday. It's perfectly reasonable," Carrie's voice held an even tone.

"Oh yeah, and what a *family* it is, yes indeed. We got the Kosher Dill, himself," Tex said, turning in his seat to face his brother.

"Understood," Casper said.

"Then there's his twitchin' wife," Tex continued. "I mean, can we just say that it's really hard not to stare at that eye and mouth when it gets going. Like she's a hooked fish." And with that, Tex snagged his cheek with his curled index finger and tugged.

"Oh, don't forget this," Casper said. Leaning forward between his mother and brother, he began an incessant winking timed with his own jerking smile, watching himself in the rearview. "Like a clown with Tourette's syndrome."

"Now, boys," Carrie cautioned.

"You're right, Mom," Tex said, "It's not nice to make fun of the handicapped."

"Tex."

"So let's make fun of the fat kid instead," Tex said, "I mean, why did Dodi name him *Dusty*? Can we just consider this for a minute? What does one expect from a *Dusty*, exactly?"

"Kind of cowboy-ish, don't ya think?" Casper asked. "Home on the range, tumbleweeds, men in chaps."

"Hey, that's *my* line," Tex pouted.

"*Dusty Trails to you* . . ." Casper warbled.

"Or, maybe Dodi thought he could become a folksinger. Weren't there a lot of folk singers named Dusty, Mom?"

"Dusty Springfield."

"Yeah. And who else?

"That's the only one I can think of . . . Dusty Springfield, she sang, *I only want to be with you.*"

"No, there were more," Tex complained. "Anyway, that fat kid is no cowboy. He's no folk singer, either. Dodi missed the mark by not just flat out calling him Tubby, or Lard-ass! I mean that's what everybody's gonna wind up calling him, anyway."

"Tex, that is just plain mean," Carrie said. "He's a little boy. He has a problem."

"Yeah, it's called Moon Pies." Tex squirmed around in his seat to face Casper again. "You think anybody calls that kid *Dusty*?"

"Not all by itself. Dusty-butt, Dusty ass, maybe."

"Moon Pie Boy." Tex shook his head. "Kid looks like a moon pie."

"All right, Tex, that's enough!" Carrie said. "Not like you two got off Scott-free in the names department."

He swiveled his head around and whispered, "You think that little Destiny still wears underpants on her head?"

"Not another word, Amarillo Texas!"

Casper watched as Carrie drove off to have dinner with Sheckie and Jen. He longed for a seat at that table, where he could be watching football with Sheckie. Instead, he dragged his feet after his brother and approached the Dildos' front door.

"You knock," Tex said.

"No, you."

"What if we just stand here and see if anyone comes?"

Casper knocked.

"Oh, boys," Dodi said, swinging back the door. "You don't have to *knock*. This is your home!"

"Not if I can help it," Tex whispered in Casper's ear.

She hugged a stiff-limbed Tex and then stood back, waiting for Casper to enter her outstretched arms. He leaned forward enough to receive a pat.

Dodi looked out toward the street. "Your mother dropped you off early."

"Want us to wait on the porch?" Tex asked.

The threesome stuffed in the vestibule, squished together by surrounding stacks of suitcases: large hand-truck type, carry-ons, and a colorful diaper bag. Cramped up in another corner of the tiny entryway were a stroller and a folding playpen.

This was only the second time Casper had seen his latest half-sibling. The new baby had come fast, popping out in the ambulance on the way to the hospital. The first time was not long after the birth; they'd been summoned *for the viewing*, as Tex called it.

"Dill, the boys are here!" Dodi called out as Dill rounded the corner with a box of canned baby formula. He set it down on the floor next to the stroller.

"Well, nice of you two to finally grace me with your presence." He was dressed in a bright red turtleneck sweater sporting a large Christmas tree at its center; it matched Dodi's. "Thought I'd have to get cancer before you'd grant me an audience," Dill continued his lament. "And even then, who knows?"

"Hi, Dad," Casper lifted his hand in a limp wave.

"Stunning sweaters," Tex reached for a feel of his father's sleeve, he said, "Forty percent nylon, fifty percent acrylic, thread-count . . . four," and smoothed the material between his thumb and forefinger before letting it drop.

Just then, four-year-old Destiny danced into the full-to-capacity foyer, bouncing and weaving like a little top. She, too, wore a red sweater with a giant Christmas tree.

"Well, let's get out of this hallway and move into the living room," Dodi said. "With all these suitcases, there's no room."

"Going someplace?" Casper asked about the packed foyer.

"Disney World!" Destiny chimed in, jumping up and down on Tex's feet. Casper watched Tex wave her off, as he would an annoying gnat.

In the living room, side by side on the couch, were Dusty and the new baby, who was strapped into a plastic chair. They were each wearing appropriately sized versions of the red sweaters.

"Epcot!" Dusty piped up from the sofa. The potato chips crumbled from his mouth to his belly, sprinkling his Christmas tree.

"They're so excited," Dodi said, and then, as if suddenly aware of their presence, she explained, "My parents are taking us." She held out her hands for Tex and Casper's coats. "Here, let me hang these up in the guest closet."

Casper was not wearing a red Christmas tree sweater (he didn't have one) but his usual yellow and black school sweat suit with his white running shoes. Tex unbuttoned the long red cape with the high collar (à la Dracula) that he'd designed, and handed it to Dodi. The *reveal*, Casper considered, was stunning. There stood Tex in a pair of tight shiny red satin pants, knee-high black patent-leather platform boots, and a gold lamé shirt laced in white rabbit's fur. He had two faux diamonds in each ear, and when he bent over the bobbing Destiny, Casper saw him stick out his tongue and click his stud.

"Oh, for Christ's sake!" Dill moaned and walked into the kitchen. "I need a beer."

"My, my, my . . ." Dodi muttered, staring at the spectacle in her living room.

"Brilliant, brother," Casper whispered.

Dodi's father, Grampa Dick, appeared, wearing, again, another matching sweater. He pointed his soggy cigar at Tex. "What the hell are ya? Some kinda drag queen?" he asked, chomping on the cigar. "Back in my day it was burlesque," he said, except it sounded more like *boy-lesque*. "And you," he poked a knobby finger into Casper's abdomen. "Ya look like a bumble bee. That any way to dress for a holiday? Dot!" he called behind him, "Get out here, ya gotta getta loada Dill's kids."

Tex leaned into Casper's shoulder and whispered, "Do you realize we're not wearing matching sweaters?"

Casper pulled back, feigning shock, "My God, you're right! I was too busy noticing how our names don't start with the letter D!"

Whipping into the room came Dot, Dodi's mother, a small, wizened woman sporting a bright orange beehive and rhinestone eyeglasses. She was also bedecked in a red sweater, but her Christmas tree had been bedazzled with extra tiny sparkling gems. "Oooh, there they are!" She was sipping from a martini glass. "Let me remember, you're Tex," she said, reaching up and grabbing his cheeks. Dot smoothed a hand over his shirt. "Good fabric. How much you pay?"

"I made it," Tex said.

"You made it? Didja hear that Dick? A regular Coco Chanel we got on our hands, here."

Casper went to make his way to the kitchen when Dot grabbed him.

"Oh no you don't, you big handsome boy." Dot pulled him down and planted a bristly kiss right on his lips. She sloshed the martini on Casper's uniform and he pulled away.

As he wandered into the empty kitchen, he noticed that the turkey was sitting on top of the stove, covered in foil. He lifted the tent and saw that the bird was all plump and brown. Sliding his finger up under the skin, he ripped a piece of breast meat free and stuffed it in his mouth. While he was alone, he carved another hunk out and devoured that one. He was starving.

Dodi came up behind him and he swallowed quickly.

"Casper, honey, I'm glad we have this chance to be alone."

He looked around, panicked, praying Tex would pop in, but then he heard Dick ask Tex if he knew the words to *These Boots Are Made for Walkin'* and started singing. Tex was just as trapped.

"I hear you're running track." Dodi plugged in the hand-held mixer.

"Yup."

"I used to run track in high school, too."

"Huh!"

"I have to admit, I was pretty fast back in those days. Oh, sure, you wouldn't think so to look at me today, three babies and fifty pounds later, but I could sprint the quarter mile in no time at all. My coach even thought I might make it to the regionals, maybe even the nationals."

"Cool."

"But, then I fell and broke my ankle."

"Tough."

"Yeah, it laid me up for the whole season, and then of course, I wound up getting pregnant with Dusty, and that ended that career . . ."

"Sorry."

"Pretty much ended all careers," she said—more to herself, Casper thought, than to him, so he kept mum—and she went on.

"If I'd only just kept running, after my ankle got better. It'd be a lot easier to lose this extra baby weight if I was still running. You know what I mean?" And then she started up the mixer, mashing up the potatoes.

Casper gently lifted the tin tent off the turkey and carefully sliced a knife under the brown skin. He slid a chunk of breast meat from beneath it and stuffed the turkey in his mouth. Under the loud buzz of whipping potatoes, Casper wandered out of the kitchen.

173

The group assembled around the dinner table, and Dodi brought the platter carrying the beautifully round brown turkey. With a bit of fanfare from Dill clashing the knife and fork together, he poked into the already gouged bag of skin.

Casper, sleepily feeling the effects of the tryptophan in the turkey, watched as both Dill and Dodi peeled back the skin, revealing the pocket where breast meat had been.

"What the hell's going on?" Dill noticed the picked-over legs, and he dropped the fork and knife, leveling a look at Dusty. "For crying out loud! Didja have to eat the whole freakin' bird?"

"Dill, we don't know that Dusty did this. Did you do this, Dusty?" Dodi asked.

The boy shook his chubby cheeks.

"See, he didn't do it, Dill."

"Well, hell, he's not going to admit it!"

"He knows he can tell the truth."

"Let me smell your breath," Dill made to round the table, but Dodi grabbed his arm.

"Dill, stop. It's Christmas."

"Aw, give the kid a break," Dot said. "He's a growing boy."

Dick said. "Jeez-us boy, could ya have left even a leg?"

With that, Dusty stumbled crying from the table.

"Now, look what ya went and did," Dot reprimanded her husband. She said pointing at the turkey. "Look, I see some meat. Dill, get back in there and slice it thin."

Casper felt a little bad about Dusty but not enough to 'fess up; the little porker was going to Disney World, after all. Casper was grateful for the elastic waist of his sweat suit. His stomach, he could feel as he ran his palm over it, was distended like balloon.

"Let's all join hands and go around the table and say what we're thankful for," Dodi said, reaching to Dill and Destiny on either side of her. "I'll start. I'm thankful that our whole family is here—well, except for Dusty, but he'll be back—to share this joyful and precious day. I'm thankful that Casper and Tex are with us."

"For *dinner*," Tex whispered to Casper.

"I'm thankful for you, Mom, and you, Grampa Dick."

Casper leaned into Tex. "Why does she call him Grampa Dick?"

Tex shrugged, "Maybe he's her father *and* her grandfather."

Dill mumbled something about being thankful the Panthers were winning this season.

Dusty rejoined the table, sniffing and still wiping tears away, and he went next, saying he was grateful for his dog, Dippy.

"I'm grateful for going to Disney World!" Destiny piped up. "I'm grateful for Mickey and Minnie, Donald Duck, Dumbo, Goofy, Winnie's Pooh, the Seven Dorfs, Lady is a Tramp . . . and . . ."

"Okay! Okay, Destiny," Dill snapped. "We get it. Good job. Next!"

"I'm grateful I'm still regular every morning," Dick said, reaching for peeled leg.

"Oh, Grampa Dick," Dodi said disapprovingly.

"What? I am. Can't I say that? I'm a seventy-eight-year-old man who can still take a crap every morning, seven-oh-five, like clockwork, just as I'm getting to the sports page. It's a miracle, I'm telling!" He slapped the table.

"He's right, you know," Dot said. "A miracle." "My turn!" she called out. "I'm thankful that I outlived my sister, Myrna—she would've hated what was happening in this world, today—what with a colored president and all."

"Never mind that he's a socialist-fag-lovin' Muslim, who was born in Kenya, and wants healthcare, green energy, education, and jobs for everybody," Tex added. The sarcasm seemed lost on everyone but Casper.

"Exactly," Dot, said, but confusion crease her brow.

When it came to his turn, Casper said he was grateful for the school break.

"And?" Dodi urged.

"And that I get to sleep in late," he said, noncommittal.

Finally it came around to Tex, who stood above the group, raised his glass and said, "I hope you all have a great time in Disney World."

"What's that supposed to mean?" Dill demanded, suspiciously.

"Just what I said. I'm glad you get to take your family on this vacation." He lifted his glass.

Everyone hesitated. Dodi's cheek jerked. There was an uncomfortable group shuffle as all eyes turned to the table, landing on the turkey as if it were the toast, instead. Finally, Casper tapped his brother's glass. "I'll drink to that, big bro! Bon voyage! Here's to the Angel-family vacation!" He nodded to his father. The brothers drained their glasses, while all but Dill toasted to the trip.

Shortly after dinner, Dill suggested that he drive the boys back home. Casper suspected his father just wanted to get away from the madness. He knew he sure did. The two of them were silent—unlike Tex, singing Christmas carols and pointing out the more *fabulous* of the holiday house decorations.

"Have a great vacation!" Tex waved as he leapt from the truck after it had pulled into Number Two.

Casper stayed in his seat. "Yeah, Dad, have a blast in Disney World."

"Thanks, Casp," he said, a tad sheepishly. "You know Dodi's parents are paying for most of this."

"Sure." Casper picked at a ragged fingernail.

"I can barely afford staying home, never mind going on a trip."

"Then why go?"

"It's Dodi. And the kids. Dick and Dot. I mean, I can't deny them."

"No. I guess you can't."

Dill shifted uncomfortably. "There's just a lot going on right now. Work sucks. Same shit, different day. I never should've left the Air Force."

"Why did you?" Casper asked.

"They kept moving us around. Your mother hated it. I kept getting stuck with these asshole commanders who were nuthin' but a bunch of pencil-pushin' pussies. If they'd left me alone and had just let me fly—you know, do my job—everything would've worked out."

"But they didn't?"

Dill shook his head. Casper noticed a faraway look in his father's eyes, as if he were trying to catch a glimmer, a glimpse, of a life that would have been if he'd made one different choice.

"Between all that bullshit military bureaucracy and your mother nagging the fire outta me, well, the pressure was too much, so I got out."

"And that's when you met Dodi?" Casper dared.

Dill looked over. The lines around his eyes creased in permanent bitterness, his mouth set tight. He nodded his head slightly. "Yeah. I was feeling lonely. Frustrated. Dodi, we had some good times for a few years, and that's where they should've ended. But, I can tell you now that you're getting older, marrying her, well, it was a big mistake, I admit." He was confessing as never before, and Casper squirmed. *Don't do this*, he thought. *I do not want to hear how the twitching woman you ditched us for isn't worth it, after all.*

But Dill kept on, as if to a priest. "If Dodi hadn't gotten pregnant with Destiny, we wouldn't be together. You know?"

Casper shrugged.

"It's complicated."

Casper looked hard at his fingernails.

"Like what happened with your mother."

Casper clenched his fists tight, and released, and did it again.

"Getting pregnant with Tex. Supposedly faulty birth control pills. Yeah, right."

"You didn't have to marry her," Casper said. "You could've just supported her."

"No kidding," Dill agreed. "She wound up sucking me dry, anyway. I could've just cut to the chase without ruining my whole life."

Casper stared.

"I would've paid for the abortion. I told her that. But no, she wouldn't even consider it." He was looking out the window, talking as if to himself or a close buddy, but not to the son whose mother he was crucifying. "She told me she'd raise it with or without me. What was I supposed to do?"

Casper thought to say something. He thought to say: *Are you hearing yourself? Are you hearing how you're talking about Tex? Your*

177

own kid? Better off aborted? What about me? Am I part of the ruination of your whole life? He wanted to scream all these questions, but instead said, "Tough breaks, all around, Dad."

"Yeah, well. That's only part of what's going on. Never mind we got *another* kid. Dodi's got that spasm in her face, and has to have some brain scans. Dusty eats enough to feed a small village. Destiny's allergic to every goddamn weed, animal, dairy and wheat by-product on the planet. The medical bills this year alone have cost a mint, never mind what your mother's bleeding me."

"Yeah, well, Dad," Casper mustered a defense. "It's not like Mom's not working. I mean, you are our father."

"Yeah, well, it wasn't exactly on purpose."

Casper sucked at his lip.

"I mean, I'm glad you're here, and all—of course, but if you can just see it from my point," Dill pleaded. "I mean, I was a kid myself. Not much older than you. Can you imagine? I got tricked out of a whole big life."

"Yeah, too bad you fell for those manipulative women." Casper's sarcasm missed his father.

Dill nodded. "That's the truth. You know, Casp, you're old enough to understand relationships. Do you have a girlfriend?"

Casper felt mortified. He hadn't had an intimate conversation with his father since, well, since forever. He nodded slightly.

"'Course you do," Dill grinned. "You're a handsome devil. Take after the old man, an' all. I'm sure you've got 'em lining up."

Casper shook his head. "No, just one."

"Yeah, well, see how long that lasts. You know, there are some things a man needs more than a woman does . . ."

Casper thought to leap from the vehicle, roll across the lawn, slither under the door, crawl on his hands and knees to the bathroom where he might just hurl his entire Christmas dinner . . . *Stop! Do not do this,* he wanted to yell, but it was too late.

"Sex is one of them. You know, Casp, sometimes we men have to take care of our needs in other ways, and I don't mean with Mr. Handy," he chuckled and waved his fingers. "I mean, sometimes it

178

helps to release the valve outside the marriage, you know, in order to keep the inside of it together. If you catch my drift." He winked.

Casper frowned, and Dill must have registered the look to be confusion rather than revulsion.

He went onto to clarify, "It's best to find someone you can have an *arrangement* with in a similar situation. No messy divorces, just a little relief on the side, you know? I can't expect a woman who just had a baby to be interested in sex, now can I? But why should I have to go without? You know what I'm saying?"

Casper was afraid he knew exactly what his father was saying. The revelation brought up burning bitter bile in the back of his throat. He suddenly felt a kind of loathing for his father creep over him. Similar to the loathing he had for liver or spinach, but in a way he could not distance himself. *Why tell me this?* He wished he could shout. *Why would you tell your son that you cheat on your wives?* But, instead, with his hand on the door handle, he managed, "We all do what we gotta do." He slid out. "Hope you have a good trip, Dad."

"You know I'd take you if I could, Casp," Dill said, lamely.

"Sure, Dad." Then asked, "Tex, too?"

There was silence.

"Someday, Dad," Casper said, feeling emboldened somehow by his new-found loathing; "you'll have to take responsibility for something."

"What's that supposed to mean?"

"I guess when you finally do, you'll finally know."

When Casper got to the apartment, Tex called him into his bedroom. "Look what I got," he said, opening his backpack and pulling out Dill's Air Force pilot's uniform; the one that had last been seen tacked to the wall in Dill's den.

"Holy crap, what are you doing with that?" Casper's eyes widened.

"We're going to burn it."

"What?"

"We're going to build a fire and we're going to burn it up."

Casper swallowed. "Why are we going to do that?"

"Because he didn't take us to Disney World."

Chapter Thirteen

It was days later when Jen bumped into both Carrie and Sheckie at the mailboxes. Each was reluctantly unloading their slots of bills that neither wanted to collect. As if on cue, they tucked the piles underneath their respective armpits. But Jen sifted through her stack, finally finding what she'd been awaiting. It was the envelope containing the insurance settlement for the "loss" of her sealskin jacket. She tore across the back and yanked the check out.

"Crap!" She exclaimed and then frowned, re-reading the front of the check.

"What's the matter?" Carrie asked.

Jen rummaged in the envelope and unfolded the sheet of paper accompanying the check. "Unbelievable," she muttered as she read. "Five hundred bucks. That's all the insurance company reimbursed for my coat."

"That's good, isn't it?" Sheckie asked, confused.

Jen turned an angry stare on him. "Good? That was a five thousand dollar coat when I bought it!"

Carrie snatched the sheet out of Jen's hand and read. "*Depreciation*, they're calling it."

"Depreciation! You saw that coat; did it look depreciated to you?" Jen was huffing. "What a bunch of idiots. I'm going to appeal! I have pictures!"

Sheckie said quietly, "Actually Jen, you have the coat."

Jen and Carrie both looked at him. No one spoke for a moment, and then Carrie said, "He's right. I mean, what are you going to do? Drag it out and *prove* how much it's *really* worth?"

"No," Jen said, begrudgingly. "But you don't understand; it's insulting to the coat."

"Jen, the coat is insulting," Carrie said.

"What do you mean?"

"Baby seals? Do you realize that they club them to death? That's how they're killed. Clubbed to death on a beach. It's like a freaking Roman blood sacrifice."

"All the more reason to get the full price," Jen said, matter of fact.

"What?"

"Well, let's say you're right and it truly is a horrible sacrifice. Can you really *depreciate* the value of a life?"

Carrie stared at her.

"What?" Jen held her hands up. "Hey, *I* didn't club them."

Neither Sheckie nor Carrie said anything.

"I'm *honoring* the lives lost!"

Still the pair stared.

Finally, she conceded, "Okay, okay, I'll shut up and be grateful."

"Blood money," Carrie said.

"Tell you what, I'll buy the pizza and beer," Sheckie said, trying to soothe the moment.

"Your place, Carrie?" Jen asked. Tex and Emily were at Jen's, watching a movie. When they entered, the first thing Jen noticed was the strong cedar-y smell, and an odd humming noise, like a motor on the fritz.

They gathered around the table, popped some beers and were happily devouring the pizza in the box between them. Jen again noticed an irritating hum in the air, at first sounding like a high-pitched whine of a fast spinning wheel, like the way a belt sounds on a vacuum cleaner or the fridge right before it snaps. Then she noticed that the whine was just the first layer of sound. Underlying this was a scratching, a rustling, like someone walking through leaves in the fall. She could see by the way Sheckie was tilting his head, like a dog perking to a noise, that he heard it, too.

"What the hell is that?" He turned to Carrie.

She looked up from her slice. "What the hell is what?"

"That noise. You hear it, don't you, Jen?" he asked.

"I hear something."

Sheckie got up. He paused mid-stride. "There it is, listen." The sound pervaded the apartment.

"I don't hear a thing," Carrie said and shrugged.

"Oh, there's definitely a noise," Jen said. "High pitched."

Sheckie stalked toward Tex's room. He leaned across the darkened threshold and then flicked the switch. "Mary, Mother of God!" he yelled.

"What?" Both women leapt to the room.

Not only were mice wiggling in wall-to-wall glass tanks stacked on top of dozens of cages but on the floor at the foot of the bed were a milk bottle, a mop bucket, a covered casserole dish (lid tilted), and a large empty plastic water jug, each also containing squirming mice.

"Oh my," Jen muttered and backed away. Mice in general gave her the willies, but seeing hundreds squirming around like that just made her skin crawl.

Carrie sighed. "It's getting worse now that Casper has refused to stop cleaning them, it's bad." She shook her head. "I've been ignoring it. I admit."

Sheckie closed the door and turned on some music to drown out the chattering and scurrying of the little critters. They made their way back to the table.

"You really should make him get rid of them, Carrie," Sheckie said. "Casper's right. Aside from the noise, they stink. It could be a health hazard."

Above them, asleep in his bed until he heard his name float up through the vent from the kitchen table below, Casper rolled to his side, rubbed sleep from his eyes, and put his ear to the echoing box. They were discussing Tex's mice, he could tell right away. Crossing his fingers, he was praying that these two grown-ups, Jen and Sheckie, might possibly convince his mother to make Tex get rid of the freakin' mice. Casper was sick of taking care of them, sick of the smell, sick of the noise they made, sick of the fact that, while he loved them both, he thought his mother let Tex get away with too much laziness, all because she felt sorry for him because he was gay and kids had picked on him for it since he was in pre-school. Everybody had known Tex was gay ever since he insisted on being *Teela* to Casper's *He-Man* always rescuing *Strawberry ShortCake* from *G.I. Joe* and making her go live with *Barbie* sans *Ken*. Just because he got picked on, Casper considered, was no reason for special treatment. Casper knew for a fact that Tex really didn't care very much what other people said because, half the time, Tex was oblivious to it. And in the meanwhile, Tex had been milking his mother's guilt for years, and Carrie was so full of guilt, Casper didn't ever think the well would dry. He listened and crossed his toes.

"I suppose he should get rid of them," Carrie said, half-heartedly. "I just hate to make him give them up. He got them from Dill after we'd split. They took his mind off things. I don't want to revive any of those old feelings of loss and abandonment in him."

"I think he's over it," Sheckie said. "I'm pretty sure those first two mice are long dead and he doesn't even know it."

"They don't really last very long," Jen agreed.

"We've had mice for over seven years," Carrie said.

"'Cause they keep reproducing," Sheckie tipped his beer to empty. The women followed suit. "Their whole existence is to eat, sleep, copulate, and do it all over again."

"Just like men," Jen said. "Eat, sleep, copulate; that's all they think about," she said, as if Sheckie were not one of the *they*. "First they get a wife, use her up, and then go get themselves another one and another. All near replicas of the first."

"But dumber," Carrie mentioned her own nemesis in Dodi.

"Hey, now!" Jen said, considering her second-wife status.

"Sorry. Present next-wives excluded," Carrie apologized.

Jen continued, "Then the already old geezer goes and gets himself a younger one still, and in this case you're right, Carrie, much, much dumber."

"It happens somewhere along the line."

"You two are making big assumptions," Sheckie tried to interject for his gender, but was immediately overrun by Jen.

"By the time they're onto their third or fourth wife, they're so old that they gotta take pills to get it up and drugs to make the little buggers swim faster."

"Not me!" Sheckie raised his hands.

"And having already produced two female offspring, this possibly being the last chance before he dries up or drops dead—we already know how that turned out—he shoots for one more, praying for that male heir to carry on his name—*Doctor* Manners . . . *PhD.*, translation: Pathetic human Dolt." She finished. Liberated by her diatribe, she smiled and guzzled her beer.

Sheckie sat quietly between them.

Casper was losing interest in the conversation, and he could tell Sheckie was too since he hadn't said a single word since he offered mice-advice. He was probably sitting there wishing for a way out of the house now that the women had left mice and moved onto men. Casper himself could feel his eyelids begin to grow heavy again.

"Let me tell you," Jen blurted. "Now that he's dead—rest his soul—he's like God to Emily! Never did or could do any wrong. Jesus would have a hard time competing with the recently deceased Hempy Manners, at least according to his daughter. Can we just say that?"

"Jen, don't you think that's a little harsh?" Sheckie asked.

"Harsh? Harsh? No, not harsh when I'm selling off jewelry to keep a roof over our heads, and that Tiffany is living in that big damn house on Robin's Egg Lane!" It was obvious the beer had made its way quickly to Jen's head.

"Well, that is true, it's hard being the custodial parent—" Carrie started, but then remembered Sheckie's situation and let it go. He'd give anything to be the custodial parent, she knew for sure.

"It's not just men," Jen conceded, and finished her second beer. "Tiffany's already taken up with some man-boy." Jen snorted, "Some crackling pubescent male voice answered the phone the other night.

She's on the prowl for young cock if you ask me!" Jen smiled, obviously delighted by her use of the word *cock*.

Casper sat suddenly bolt upright, just as his eyes were finally closed and his breathing becoming steady. To hear Mrs. Manners use *that* word *that* way, oh my God! He shook his head and climbed off the bed and hunkered next to the vent, beside the wall.

Sheckie stood and stretched. "You know what, ladies? I'm about to call it a night."

"*No!*" They shouted in unison.

"I thought we'd play cards," Carrie suggested.

He ambled to the door. "Nah, I'm kind of out of the mood. I gotta get up early tomorrow anyhow. Thanks for the beer." And he left.

"Something we said?" Jen asked.

Carrie nodded. "Probably *everything* we said. It hurts his feelings. Sheckie doesn't like to be thrown into the stereotype of *all* men."

"Well, I will say there aren't a lot of Sheckies in the world." Jen looked over at Carrie. "He's a good one, don't you think?"

"Probably as good a one as you'd find anywhere. Deep down, at least."

"So what about you and Sheckie?" Jen asked tentatively.

Casper usually hated when the kitchen-table conversations went this way. Whenever Carrie had a friend over and the conversation moved onto men and feelings and relationships, it was often just too hard to listen, to think of his mother actually having any of these thoughts going through her head made him uncomfortable, but he had to admit to a mild curiosity about her answer.

"What about us?" Carrie asked. "We've known each other since I moved in here. We've helped each other out of a couple of binds. He's good to Casper." Carrie said, "And we slept together once, a long time ago. That what you're asking?"

185

Damn, Casper wished he didn't have to hear that one. He popped some knuckles, and stared at the map of the world he had tacked to the wall, making the image his mother just conjured go away.

"He just seems to really care about you." Jen got herself another beer. "I think you two are cute together."

Carrie dismissed her with a wave. "My days of being cute with another human being have passed. I'm more interested in being financially secure with another human being. And that is something that Sheckie is not."

"I know your reasoning, but that can backfire, too. I thought Hempy was financially secured, which he had been when he only had *one* wife, child, and mortgage, but that changed with me and Emily. Money got tighter still with Tiffany and the twins. What really pisses me off is that she is going to keep getting his royalties; the royalties on college text books *I* helped edit. I was such an idiot."

"You don't see a dime of that money?" Carrie asked.

"Not a penny. Emily does. It goes into a trust for her and the sisters."

"It's the principle, though." Carrie guessed.

"Yes, *and* we about paid off two mortgages with the Houghton deal. Emily and I should be in that house on Robin's Egg, not Tiffany. She contributed nothing to that place. And now she's got a boy-toy in there with her. Barely skipped a beat, the bitch."

Carrie nudged Jen. "How about we go depreciate her property just a little?"

"What do you mean?"

Casper had been taking apart a pen he'd found on the floor, when he heard his mother's tone, and sprung the spring from between his fingers. What were these two mothers up to? He leaned closer.

"Rodents," Carrie whispered. "A terrible scourge of mice to hit Robin's Egg Lane. White mice. Hundreds of them."

Jen smiled nervously. "We couldn't."

"No? We've got the mice."

"Carrie, how would we?" Her heart started beating. She felt a rush of energy pulsing to her face, like when she said *cock,* causing her grin to widen uncontrollably.

Casper couldn't believe it either. He knew it was wrong, and he couldn't believe his mother was suggesting it. On the other hand, he could understand Mrs. Manners' desire for revenge. He stood, not knowing what to do. He couldn't risk revealing his listening spot. He could wait; catch them in the act, before they could leave; confront them, remind them they'd been drinking; or if he wondered if he should join them, help them get rid of the stinking mice—or just sit tight. He decided to sit tight.

"Come on," Carrie said, beckoning Jen to follow her to Tex's room.
"I can't. I hate mice. I'm . . . I'm afraid of them."
"Oh for god's sakes. What can they possibly do that scares you?"
"They wiggle."
Carrie opened the door, looked inside and then looked back at Jen, who had plastered herself against the farthest wall. "They *do* wiggle," Carrie admitted, "But that's all they do. Once we get them all into this jug," she lifted the big plastic container once used in a water cooler and held it up so Jen could see it, "you won't even have to get near one."
"I can't touch them."
"All right, fine. You hold the jug and I'll dump in the mice. Deal?"
"Deal."
Together the women had filled the ten-gallon plastic water bottle with every single one of Tex's mice, leaving just enough wiggle room, and the pair carried it to Carrie's Toyota. It was after midnight when they circled the cul de sac that harbored 21 Robin's Egg Lane. Jen pointed to a small opening in the trees beside the driveway, and Carrie slid the little compact into the shadows. They lifted the giant water bottle out of the trunk and rolled the big cylinder like a bingo drum with mice tumbling round and round. Jen confirmed that there was, indeed, a cat-door at the rear entrance, and so they decided that this would be the way in for the mice.

Through the hinged panel at the base of the back door, the dizzied little white blobs of fur spilled from the wide mouth of the jug, and plopped down onto the linoleum on the other side. Some made valiant escapes across the porch; others tried to crawl back up into the bottle, not sure what was happening.

"Grab 'em!" Carrie whispered, as another escapee made a dive for the yard.

But Jen only made a lame attempt at recapturing. "I can't. I just can't. Yuk." She shivered uncontrollably. "We have enough, don't we?"

Carrie had scooped up a few loose stragglers and deposited them through the slot; they could hear a scrambling on the other side. A loud cat roar came from somewhere within. Jen could hear the big tabby racing around the kitchen, claws tapping tiles. Suddenly there was a crash of glass, and light came splashing from an upstairs window.

"Let's get out of here," Carrie hissed. She tilted the bottle and spilled the remainder of the mice onto the lawn. They fled down the hill. With headlights extinguished, they rolled past 21 Robin's Egg Lane. Jen could distinctly hear shrieking coming from inside the house, where every light was ablaze. Through the windows, she watched as dark shadows raced from room to room. She couldn't help but smile.

Chapter Fourteen

Jen was lolling back against the pillows in a state of sweaty euphoria. "I want a cigarette," she said, and rolled over and ran her hand along Georgia's smooth stomach, tracing circles with her fingers.

"Do you even smoke?" Georgia asked.

"No. At least, not anymore. I did in college. Something about sex always makes me want to, though."

"All those movies we were raised on," Georgia offered. "Oh, I'm not sure I remember any movies like this growing up."

"Not even the *Prime of Miss Jean Brodie?*"

"Oh, do you remember that saucy movie?" Georgia laughed.

"I remember that girl's naked breasts in it. It probably turned me gay before I knew it."

"Well, you're very good at it."

"Thank you very much, I try."

Jen nuzzled against Georgia's warm naked body. "Did I mention that making love with you is the most amazing sex I've ever had in my whole life?" she asked.

"Hhhmm, nope, I don't think you've said a word about that," Georgia said. "Unless that's what all that screaming and panting and begging was all about."

Jen suddenly sat up. "Did you hear something?"

"No. Like what?"

"Like the front door opening."

"I don't think so," Georgia said. Then there was definitely a sound of a door closing.

"Mom?"

"Oh shit! Emily's home!"

Jen and Georgia jumped from the bed. Staring at each other's bare bodies, they jumped apart as if they'd suddenly realized they were naked. Jen flew to her closet, slipping on jeans and a t-shirt, backward.

"Shit!" Jen whispered. "Shit, shit, shit!"

Georgia was on her feet, throwing on her shirt, jumping into slacks, hanging her Edible Feast apron around her neck, and clumsily hopping around on one foot, looking for her other shoe. "I thought you said she was at school?"

"I thought she was too! She's supposed to be. It's only two; she's not supposed to be here for another hour!"

"Mom?" Emily's voice was echoing in the tunnel of the stairwell. "Are you up here?" And then the door swung open before either Jen or Georgia could hide or duck or block her entry; they stood caught, like deer in headlights. Emily stood at the threshold, frowning first at her mother, then at Georgia. Then her eyes scanned the rumpled bed, and again the rumpled Georgia, and another once over at her rumpled mother holding a shoe in her left hand and one sock on her right foot.

Finally Jen spoke. "Honey—what are you doing home?"

"Mother, are you really going to start there?"

"Um—I, this is, well, this is my friend, Georgia. The one I've been telling you about."

"You mean, talking incessantly about!"

Jen felt her face get hot.

"Hi," Georgia said.

I knew it!" Emily clapped her hands together. "I knew it! I swear to God, I told Tex just yesterday, *I think my mom's a lesbian*—I swear. Those were my words! I am so good about these things." She folded her arms, triumphant. "Tex said, *Now don't go jumping to conclusions;* he said just because your mom's been talking about Georgia non-stop since she met her, just because they're on the phone together, constantly, that just because lately she's been spending all her spare time with her new lesbian best friend doesn't mean she's a lesbian; I told

190

him he was wrong, and I was right!" She looked over at Georgia and said, "Mom didn't say how beautiful you are, though."

"Well, thank you," Georgia managed.

"Emily, I'm sorry—"

"Sorry? What are you sorry for? Don't be sorry. God, Mom, this is the twenty-first century! I'm just glad you've found someone. You haven't had a date in years. You've been miserable. You've been depressed. Ever since Georgia came along, well, you've been nearly pleasant to live with!"

"Oh, well thank you, I guess."

"Georgia," Emily stepped forward and put her hand out. "I feel as if I already know you. I feel like you are already part of the family." And then Emily not only shook Georgia's hand, but pulled her in and hugged her tightly. "Can I just say? Having a lesbian mother may be the coolest thing that has ever happened to me?"

"Well, I assure you, I didn't do it for you," Jen managed, not exactly sure how she felt about this all this enthusiasm for what to her had been a big decision.

"So, Mom says you've been gay for quite some time now?"

"Well, yes, it's been a while—"

Jen interrupted, "Do you think we could maybe all go downstairs?" She was beginning to feel real discomfort since they were gathered around the rumpled bed where she and Georgia had experienced glorious ecstasy rolling around those sheets not thirty minutes before.

When they entered the living room, there was Tex sitting in front of the TV watching a cartoon. Jen was mortified. She had no idea that he was here. And when the three women piled at the foot of the stairs, Emily shouted, "*See, Tex!!*" Gesturing to her mother and Georgia on either side of her, "I *told* you my mom had gone gay!"

Tex stood, his curls bouncing all around his head. "Mrs. Manners! Congratulations! I'm so happy for you! I wouldn't have guessed. But hells bells! The more, the merrier!" Then he walked over to Georgia, took her in a squeezing embrace and said, "Thank you. Thank you for helping Emily's mom find herself. We've all been worried about her, and well now—"

Jen thought he might cry.

"Now, we're all just *family*—aren't we?"

Georgia was nearly in tears with laughter. She winked at Jen, and said, "Tex, I've heard an awful lot about you, and I am so glad to finally meet both Emily and you," Georgia managed after prying herself from Tex's embrace.

"I can't *wait* to tell Mom!!" Tex said.

"No, whoa, hold on there, Tex," Jen said. "Please, Carrie's my friend; I'd like to introduce her to Georgia, myself, if that's all right—"

"Of course!" Tex and Emily both shouted. "We'll go get her!" and they ran out of the apartment.

When the door slammed and they were left alone, Jen looked at Georgia. "I am so sorry."

"For what?" Georgia put her arms around Jen. "You should be happy. That was the easiest family outing I've ever been through!" She laughed, and shook her head. "Did you see Emily's face when it finally dawned on her what she had walked into? Priceless."

"It *was* kind of funny," Jen admitted.

"It was perfect." Georgia wrapped her arms around Jen. "Emily's perfect."

"She is, isn't she?"

"Like her mother."

"Hardly."

"For me."

"Okay, I'll give you that one."

Tex and Emily invited Carrie, Casper, and Sheckie to Jen's "coming out dinner" where Georgia entertained everyone with stories from her trips abroad, and wooed them with her Fettuccine Alfredo. After the meal, the men and Emily agreed to clean up the kitchen, while Carrie smoked outside and Jen walked Georgia to her car.

"That was a great night," Jen said. "Thank you."

"Thank me? For what?"

"Dinner for one, but making it all so easy."

"I didn't do that," Georgia said. "You've got a great kid, great friends, that's what made this easy. Do you feel better?"

"Oh my God, like a weight lifted. You know?" Jen said.

"I do." Georgia pulled her into her embrace, and the pair stood like that for a long time.

"I have never felt so—I don't know the word for it," Jen said, "And me, an English major."

"Isn't that why they invented poetry?" Georgia considered.

"I've never felt so *whole*, is the only word I keep coming back to, every time I think about my life, I keep coming back to the idea that now that I've found you, I somehow feel whole."

Georgia smiled and touched Jen's cheek. "I know what you mean. I felt it with Chris, and I believed it had everything to do with her and very little to do with me—or us, but when she passed, I never felt so loose and so *un-whole*, as I have for the past year, until . . ."

Jen looked at her, into her beautiful face that at times she could not take her eyes from—as if Georgia were some kind of miracle that might disappear.

"Until tonight, Jen. Tonight made me realize that I've somehow been blessed all over again. Given another chance. Somehow, I must've done something good to deserve you and your beautiful daughter and friends in my life."

As Georgia drove away, Jen joined Carrie, smoking on her stoop and waiting for her. They looked up at the night sky. It was brisk and cold, and neither wore a jacket. Jen smiled at her.

"She's nice, that Georgia," Carrie ventured.

"She is, yeah, she's great."

"How come you didn't tell me?" Carrie asked.

Jen could tell her friend sounded a little hurt. "It's not exactly an easy thing to tell, you know?"

"But, I've got Tex."

"He's your son, you're going to love him no matter what; I was afraid to risk it."

"Risk what?" Carrie asked, crushing her smoke under her boot.

"Losing you."

"What are you talking about?"

"Carrie Angel, you're the best friend I've found in the last ten years, there is nothing that would pain me more than to lose your friendship."

"Well, not telling me when you're falling in love and finding happiness is no way to keep me around—"

"I'm sorry. You're right. I—well, to be honest, I wasn't really sure about it until recently—it's a big leap, in case you hadn't noticed."

"Oh, I noticed all right."

"Before I went announcing my dramatic life change—I wanted to make sure."

"Are you?" Carrie put her hand on Jen's shoulder, an act of affection that Jen was unaccustomed to with her friend. She pressed her palm against Carrie's cold fingers.

"I am sure, Carrie. I can't exactly explain my feelings, except to say they're no different from the ones you have for Sheckie . . ."

"Let's not go getting me or Sheckie involved in this—*I'm* not even sure of those feelings."

"Yes, you are; you're just afraid of them."

Carrie shrugged. "Maybe so. But you're happy, right?"

"Very."

"Then you won't lose me. Not as long as you're happy and straight-up with me, from now on—deal?"

"Deal," Jen said, and then hugged her friend.

"And if that Georgia does one thing to hurt your feelings—I'll just have to kick her ass."

"You're so butch, Carrie Angel."

"That I am."

Chapter Fifteen

Carrie pulled into the parking lot of the community college and slid into a slot near the building she would soon be entering. The lot was still empty, and considering it was just seven in the morning and classes would not begin for another hour, it made sense that she would get prime parking. She had planned it this way. Grabbed a full mug of coffee before leaving the house; dropped both grumbling sons at school, even before the doors opened. And against Jen's advice, was determined to glance, one more time, through the textbook before attempting to pass her carpentry certification. Her heart was steadily and loudly thumping against her chest, and the mid-section of her body was one tightly wound gastrointestinal knot.

Flipping through the pages, Carrie skimmed with her finger, squeezed her eyes shut and held her breath, as if capturing the answers inside her brain. The nutty parts of her wanted to stick both fingers in her ears and somehow plug up her nostrils to prevent the information from escaping, but the sane parts (small as they were) stopped her just short of it. Jen's test-taking tricks helped a lot, she comforted herself. Casper had devoted every evening of the last month to quizzing her. Tex and Emily had designed new flash cards in psychedelic colors that matched word associations, and when she closed her eyes she could see the answers in hot-pink, fuchsia, electric blue, and lime green. I must be ready, she thought.

There was a sudden rap on her window, and she nearly spilled her coffee into her lap.

"Hey Angel, trying again, are ya?" The male voice came from the other side of the glass. "You sure do have perseverance, I will give you that."

Carrie opened the car door and stepped out onto the pavement. "Hey, Tony. How's it going?" Tony, a young handsome Italian, was one of the latest students in the carpentry apprenticeship program. She had seen many others like him come and go. He was taking the test for the first time. He had told her just last week that he already knew he could ace it. *No sweat,* he had said. *If worse comes to worse, I got an uncle in the system.* Carrie wished she had an uncle in the system. Hell, even a second cousin would do.

"Are ya ready?" he asked, his chipper-ness a tad bit too enthusiastic for her.

"As I'll ever be," she said, heading into the building. She stopped off at the ladies room before making her way to the classroom. After relieving herself for the tenth time this morning, she washed her hands and then splashed cold water on her face. As she peered in the mirror, she thought that her eyes looked big and her face looked small. A deer caught in the headlights, she admonished, and breathed in and out into her cupped hands.

"Hey, Carrie," Pat, the young baby dyke, banged into the rest room. "How's it hangin', Mama?" Her name, short cropped hair, and flat chest, not to mention all the leather and chains jangling about her belt and boots, blurred the gender-lines around this androgynous creature. Not until Carrie had met her in the ladies room did she realize there was another woman in the class.

"It's hanging," Carrie replied. "How about you? Ready?"

"My girlfriend tried to help me study last night, but then we got into this really big fight. She walked out, and after a few hours of hanging up on each other, she finally came home. By then, we were both a little drunk, so the after-fight-before-sex-processing was taking even longer than normal, so by the time I finally got to sleep . . ." she glanced at her watch, ". . . two hours ago," she said, and shrugged. "Who the hell knows? Maybe it'll be a miracle."

"I'm sure you'll be fine," Carrie said as Pat closed herself into a stall.

"Well," the woman said from behind the door, "I do take comfort in knowing that you have done this part over and over. I mean, if *you* can't pass it right away, and you're really smart, why should I beat myself up? I mean, you're a good ten years older than me and you haven't quit. Right?"

Carrie knew that Pat had meant this as a compliment, but there was an uncomfortable truth she did not like hearing. "Right," she encouraged the young girl-boy and then left the bathroom.

In the classroom, the overhead fluorescent lights cast an institutional pallor on everything, including her own skin. If she passed this test, she'd never have to sit under those buzzing bulbs again. Pure ultra-violet sunlight would radiate her skin golden instead of green, and she was looking forward to it, in spite of the cancer warnings. Seating herself in the back row, up against the wall, nearest the door (in case she needed a fast exit), Carrie pulled out her sharpened pencils and aligned them neatly on the desk. She stuffed her book bag beneath her, sipped the tepid coffee from her mug, and began her mantra, *Mary Poppins*, evenly. The meditation was working when suddenly, at her right shoulder, a thick and looming presence huffed stale coffee and cigarette breath into her face.

"Angel! Didn't think you'd have the guts to show your face in here, again!" The little wiry man with the yellowed mutton chops and slicked back duck-tail jostled her. "You got bigger golf balls than me, sweetheart."

Carrie slid down in her seat. *Not Pressley.* She wanted to cry. Why did he have to be the exam proctor this time? This was his chance to have *real* power over her. On the job, even though he was her boss, she was the superior carpenter; there was no denying it. She was faster with a miter saw and more precise with a saber; she could drive a nine-penny nail in four swings compared to his five. Slicing a coping saw through a piece of crown or shoe molding, exacting a tight fit around a room, was her specialty. In addition, she was a woman. She was exactly the kind of woman-carpenter that Pressley wanted to keep out of the brotherhood.

"I thought I told you to go take that hairdresser's class across the hall," Pressley bellowed. Making his way to the front, grinning at the other fifteen or sixteen test-takers, all men with the exception of Carrie and Pat, he continued yelling. "Or maybe manicuring fingers and toes would suit you more."

She could feel her temperature rise and her cheeks flame. There were some snickers from across the aisle. A couple of miniature versions of Pressley, whom he'd cultivated into sycophants, bullied in his stead. "You gotta give the little lady credit, coming back here year after year, failing over and over." He passed out the tests, one at a time, leaving her for last.

She clenched her fist into her lap and her teeth behind a set jaw. Pat and Tony and a few of the other classmates she'd befriended were all looking at their desks or shoes, her own discomfort replicating in their hunched shoulders and downward gazes.

"That right, Angel?" he asked, waving the test back and forth like a bone. "Remember, this is your *last* chance."

She glared at him.

He let the paper flutter to her desktop. She reached to steady it.

It didn't matter, she tried to reassure herself. She was going to pass this test, and not just because of some fucked-up new law, either. She would pass this test to keep the boys with her. She was going to get the certification, get a job, and get the hell out of Section Eight.

The clock above the door clicked loudly as Pressley told them, "Begin . . ." He held a stopwatch, ". . . now!" and punched the button on top. "That includes you, Angel. You *can* read, can't you?" he cackled as he sat at the teacher's desk in the front of the room and slung his legs up onto its top.

Carrie mistakenly looked up to see Pressley's hands folded behind his head and his gaze fixed upon her. Knowing the kind of prick he was, she knew he could hold that pose for the duration of the two hours. She decided she wouldn't look up again.

At first, everything—letters, numbers, punctuation marks, words, sentences, phrases, even the little circles to match the right answers— seemed to roar across the page right before her very eyes, as if the questions and answers were smearing. She sipped from her mug of what tasted more like warm ice coffee than cold hot coffee and managed to calm her eyes down enough to bring sense to what lay in front of her. As letters aligned and sentences straightened, Carrie tried to block out the ticking of the clock as it seemed to echo more loudly with each second-hand spin around its face. With each sweep, she could feel the panic rise. Four minutes passed, then seven, and somehow she could not touch her pencil to the paper, as if it were being restrained by some invisible force. Tick, tick, tick; the clock picked up the pace of a speeding metronome. She could hear the scratching of lead on paper as her classmates frantically filled in circles. Some tapped a finger or foot. A few gazed upward. She noticed Pat's pencil dancing down the paper. Two hours of sleep and she was fine. Nine minutes; Carrie eyed the clock and then the open doorway to her right. She could bolt, before she blew her chances, wait an extra six months and *then* be sure she wouldn't blow it.

Get yourself together! She yelled in her own mind and then imagined reaching around her shoulders and shaking herself back to sensibility. She would not let Pressley or Dill or any fucking state legislator decide she was too lazy to get herself onto her own two feet. She began to read the *stem*.

Hearing Jen's comforting words in her mind eased her shaking hand. *First instincts are usually right.* Carrie breathed and filled in some answers that she just plain knew. *Answers with* **never** *and* **always** *are usually wrong.* Carrie found them and eliminated them. **Probably** *and* **usually** *in the answer could be counted as good bets.* She included these in her choices. *And remember,* **all of the above** *is your friend.* Jen's voice and words filled Carrie's calm as her pencil filled in circles. The only problem she faced was that time was closing in on her.

As the clock continued its perpetual motion, her palms were sweating, making her grip the pencil tighter. Her own bladder, in some malicious conspiracy, began to fill and increase the pressure. Droplets of perspiration hit the paper, just missing and almost blurring answers. Without stopping, she tapped her foot to distract her bladder and chewed her pencil to stop the ticking from entering her ears. Her breath came as if she were jogging. What had once passed for coffee in her cup was beyond recognition. It did not quench her thirst. Without having once given Pressley the satisfaction of a glance, Carrie's pencil marked the last quick answer as his stopwatch brought the scribbling students to a halt.

"All pencils down!" Pressley called out. "All faces forward."

There would be no time to go back and check her answers, she thought, disappointedly, as she passed her test forward. Leaning over, she grabbed her book bag and, like an arthritic old man, rose from the hard plastic seat. She ignored Pressley as she made her way from the class.

"Guess we won't be seeing each other again, no matter whether you passed or failed," he called out after her. "But my bets are on the latter," he laughed, "Anybody want in on the pool?"

Someday, she thought, I'm gonna fire *your* ass off *my* jobsite; but she said nothing. She climbed back into her car. Now, with a newly refreshed sense of dread, she set her sights on her next most difficult challenge. It was the upcoming court battle to keep her kids. The showdown. Not even having one moment to digest how she had done on *this* test, she steeled herself for the next one. The one with the greater stakes.

It was late, just the right time of night to get centered, Carrie thought, as she sank further under her covers. A cup of *Sleepy Time* herbal tea sat cooling on the bedside table. She had come to relish this time alone. Boys in bed, everything closed up for the night. It was here, at the end of a long day when, as her counselor, Pam, from her anger-management class suggested, *managees* should give attention to themselves. Long luxurious baths, cups of hot tea, soft music or total silence were just some of the ways to quiet their minds so they could dedicate themselves to writing down *cynical thoughts* in their daily *hostility logs*.

Carrie opened the journal that served this purpose and slid the brown envelope from the first page. She pulled the thick paper from the sleeve. Smoothing her fingers over the raised letters of the diploma-like certificate verifying that she had successfully completed the Anger Management class, she smiled. Now, when she went to court with Dill, she would have this *and* her carpentry certification (if she passed) as evidence of her newly acquired temperament and professional skills.

She leafed through the last entry, the one she'd written the night Casper and Tex had arrived home from Christmas dinner—"with the Dildos" is what she'd originally written and then scratched out, replacing it with "Dill & Dodi's" instead.

Reading over her entry, she realized just how aggressive her thoughts turned against Dill upon hearing of the trip to Disney World.

A tragic mishap on Space Mountain (she'd detailed) *where Dill's harness breaks and he is flung to the far reaches of the domed Milky Way. Front page featuring a press conference photo framing a distraught Mickey Mouse dabbing an oversized handkerchief to his eyes in response to the tragedy.*

She smiled. While she still hadn't mastered putting herself into *the other person's shoes*, as she was encouraged, she had, through her journal, found a way to find humor in it, as was also encouraged.

Carrie glanced up from the page, and a sound outside her window caught her attention. When she pressed her nose against the glass, she saw an odd glowing light outside. She slid from her sheets and tiptoed toward it. Leaning closer cupping palms around her eyes, she squinted. There seemed to be a fire flickering down below in the playground of the housing complex; it appeared to be the size of a campfire. As the shapes of the jungle gym and swing set came into her view, she could also see silhouettes of bodies mingling in and around the shadowing casts of light. What the heck was going on? she wondered. Then, suddenly, something familiar struck her as two figures poised facing one another in profile. Those shapes were unmistakable! One long, lanky, skinny frame was flapping his arms as the shorter one pranced on his tiptoes, flitting like a ballerina moth against the flames.

She flew out the door, streaking across the parking lot and through the chain link fencing that surrounded the playground. As she climbed over the seesaw and swished around the merry-go-round,

Carrie saw that there were three, not two forms around the fire, the third a female body draped in flowing fabric. Carrie's run brought her to the edge of the yard, to the large sand box where the campfire was burning. Plastic trucks and pails and shovels had been tossed clear of the fire. Tex and Emily and Casper were gathered round, each dressed ceremonially in long, flowing scarves. As Tex turned toward her, she could see his face painted like a warrior chief in stripes of blue and green and yellow. The headdress of colorful feathers waved back and forth as he danced around the fire. Emily and Casper were also garbed in war paint and feathers, and all three were ringing tiny bells as they tripped around the sand. Only Casper, Carrie noticed, seemed less enthused by the macabre rite than the other two, who were singing *Ding, Dong, the Witch is Dead.* My God, what were they into now? Carrie thought.

She stepped into the glow of the flames. "What the hell is going on?" she shouted, startling the revelers.

"Mom!" Casper froze and dropped his bell. "See, I told you, Tex!"

Both Tex and Emily had also stopped their gyrations and were facing Carrie. The threesome were swapping glances and shuffling.

Near Tex's feet, a bundle was folded. A sudden spark of light bounced from it, catching Carrie's attention. She leaned down, lifting and unfolding the long blue and white jumpsuit. In her outstretched arms, she recognized the familiar *Captain D. O. Angel* on the nametag over the right breast pocket and the shiny silver flight wings across the left. On each epaulet were pinned captain's bars. She frowned. Looking up from one son to the next, she finally managed, "This is your father's. What are you doing with it?"

Not one of the teenagers would look at her. As she took a step backward, her foot hit a small red, plastic gasoline can. Horror filled her as she made the connection. "Casper, do you want to tell me what this is all about?"

He remained silent.

"Emily," Carrie's eyes did not leave her son. "I think you better go home."

The girl fled.

Finally she turned to Tex, "Was this your idea?"

"Maybe."

"But why?" She held up the uniform.

"Because it's the only thing he cares about," Tex said.

"This is no answer to that," she tried. "There are other ways to deal with all this. Retaliation is wrong."

"Mom, do you remember that Christmas he didn't come and get us?" Tex asked quietly.

Carrie's heart sank and throat tightened. She felt the same sickening rise as she had every time she recalled that morning. It had been soon after the divorce. Dill and Dodi had been away on some vacation, and the boys hadn't seen him in weeks. Casper was about six years old. They woke that Christmas morning not with toys on their minds but with excitement about seeing their daddy.

"He won't be here for another thirty minutes, Casp," Carrie said to the little boy seated on the couch. Even though he was scooted to the sofa's edge, his toes did not quite reach the floor without a stretch. He was dressed in a red and green plaid vest, crisp white shirt, and bow tie. His hair was slicked back, and he was wearing his winter jacket. "You're going to get hot sitting there in that coat." She reminded.

On his lap, Casper was balancing the Christmas gift he'd made for Dill. It was a snow globe fashioned from a cleaned-up mayonnaise jar. A molded clay Santa waving from an airplane could be seen within the water and sparkle-filled dome. Casper's heels rhythmically tapped the front of the couch.

Tex, on the other hand, was still in his pajamas, hair out of kilter, and playing video games.

"You better get moving, mister," Carrie said to her older son. "You know how your father hates to wait."

"He's not coming," Tex said, not moving.

"He is too!" Casper yelled from the couch.

"Is not."

"All right, Tex, enough." Carrie pulled the plug on the set and scooted him up the stairs. By the time he descended, it was ten minutes past the pick-up time. He'd changed into a pair of sweat pants and shirt and had slippers on his feet.

"Where are your shoes?" Carrie asked.

"He's not coming," Tex said.

"Shut up!" Casper elbowed his brother.

An hour later, Tex went back to the video screen. Casper had remained planted on the couch in his jacket, checking both the time and the window every few seconds. Finally, the phone rang, and he leapt from the sofa.

"Daddy! Where are you?"

Carrie watched Casper's optimistic expression waver some.

"Are you coming later?" he asked, hopefully.

She could see the tremble begin in his bottom lip.

"Tomorrow, then?" he asked, more tentatively. Trickles of sweat popped from his hairline.

"When, then?" his voice getting smaller.

Carrie could not move fast enough; she could not reach her child in time to save him. Casper's face crumpled. The receiver dropped from his grip. He grabbed the mayonnaise jar snow globe, and thrust his way out into the yard. His little legs pumping down the drive, jacket flying behind, he was yelling, yelling, yelling. Before she could catch up to him, he hurled the snow globe at a boulder jutting from the ground, smashing glass and scattering glitter, Santa and the airplane mashed into one glob of clay. She grabbed him from behind as he sank to his knees, sobbing. They rocked together like that until they were cold and exhausted. When they re-entered the house, Tex, without glancing from his game, said, "Told ya so."

Now, Tex kicked at the sand, scattering it over the fire. "You remember that, Mom? It's been since then. Let him take the whole damn dysfunctional Dildo division to Disney in their matching red, Christmas sweaters."

"But I don't get why you want to burn the uniform," Carrie said, still confused.

He held it outstretched. "This thing hangs right in the center of a wall in his den. All around are pictures of him in that uniform, next to a plane, with the Dildo family. There are even a couple of Casper, really young, but still. Do you know how many pictures of me are in that room?"

Carrie stared at her son.

"None, Mom. Not one." Then he turned and left the playground, leaving Casper to deal with their mother.

She could see Casper's shame, which she could not see in his brother. "Why did you go along with this?" she asked.

He shrugged. "I don't know."

"Casp, this is so unlike you."

Swiping at his face with his sleeve, he smeared the green and yellow stripes, turning his cheek blue.

"Do you want to go live with your father?"

He shook his head.

"'Cause this'll sure give him one more thing to complain about." She held up the uniform. "Why didn't you stop Tex?"

He looked at his mother. "When Dad dropped us off, he told me that he would've taken me to Disney if he could've."

"Okay, so that's even more reason for you not to be a party to something so diabolic. I still don't get it."

"He also told me that marrying Dodi was a mistake."

"He said that?"

"Yup."

"So?"

"So he screwed up our lives for her," Casper said.

"What do you mean?"

"He left us for Dodi and it turns out not being worth it, after all."

"I'm still not following this line of logic, Casper." Carrie was becoming impatient.

"He said lots of things," Casper shouted. "He said he wished he'd never gotten you pregnant with Tex! He said he begged you to get rid of him! He said *we* ruined *his* life!"

"Oh, Casper, you must have misunderstood."

Casper wiped tears. "He told me he's cheating on Dodi."

205

At this, Carrie just stared. She believed her son, knew he was not exaggerating. What she couldn't believe was that Dill had told Casper. "He said that?" She asked quietly.

Casper nodded. "Said it was a way to keep his family together while Dodi's all twitchy and not interested in sex since she had that kid. Said men have *needs.*"

"Used those words?"

"Said I was *old* enough to understand." He swiped both hands across his face, and composed himself with a deep breath. "Like I ever want to know this stuff at *any* age; seventy-five wouldn't be old enough."

"I'm sorry."

"I don't want to be around him. It makes me sick."

"I don't blame you," Carrie said.

"Good, because Dad's got enough blame for everyone, even that poor little new baby."

"I'm sorry you have to go through this, Casp," Carrie said.

"He said we ruined his life!"

"Prick," she tried to sound sympathetic, but she was just pissed.

"When he said he'd take me on his stupid trip," Casper took a deep breath, tears had begun, again. "I asked if he'd take Tex, too."

"And?"

"He just drove off."

Together they kicked sand over the fire. Carrie handed him Dill's uniform. "You give this back to him. Tell him why you took it." She put her arm around his waist as they walked home.

"Can Dad really make us go live with him, Mom?"

"Let's hope not," she squeezed. "Then *I'd* have to go set his house on fire."

Chapter Sixteen

Snow was beginning to fall and Carrie stomped the frozen ground, trying to keep her toes warm. This was the last time she would be on this jobsite. Scanning the landscape sprinkled with newly occupied mini-mansions, she realized she had had a hand in building some part of nearly every one of them. For the last three years, this had been her classroom. She had learned a lot more than just carpentry. There was much more to it than cutting boards and banging nails. Through freezing cold and scorching heat, stinging bees and wasps, hammers nailing thumbs, saws slicing skin, Carrie had pretty much mastered all that kind of figuring out.

She noticed that the weasel was absent from the job again today.

Standing amongst a cluster of other apprentices awaiting the arrival of Ketchum, the director of the program, Carrie looked over to the circle of regular carpenters to see if Pressley was hiding in the crowd. There was Mick, Don, a few of the sycophants Pressley had groomed, but not the jerk himself. For the first time, she was disappointed by his absence. She had been fantasizing about this certification ceremony for the last week. As was tradition, Ketchum would present the awards here on the jobsite, and all the newbie-master carpenters would get to pick an old-timer to be her helper for the last day. Carrie had her heart set on picking Pressley and tormenting the fire out of him.

"Where's your pal?" A familiar voice came from behind.

Carrie turned to see Pat's boyish buzz cut.

"What pal would that be?" she asked.

"Pressley."

"No pal of mine. One good thing will come out of today: whether I passed this test or not, I'll never have to see that prick again."

"What do you mean, *whether you passed this test?* Of course you passed it." Pat said.

Carrie lit a cigarette. "If I did, I swear, I will quit smoking. No. Swearing, I swear I will quit swearing. You're my witness."

"Me and Jesus," Pat said.

Carrie looked up to see a long, black sedan making its way down the road leading to the subdivision. She bumped Pat on the shoulder and pointed. "Here comes Ketchum. This is it." She felt her heart double-time.

Ketchum emerged from the sedan along with two other government officials. The tall gray man with the big, round glasses leaned back and squinted skyward as if he were gauging the velocity of the falling flakes.

"Let's do this inside," he called over his shoulder, leading his entourage, which included all apprentices and carpenters, into the open bay of a nearly completed garage. A makeshift podium quickly assembled from sawhorses and boards centered the space. The suited men stood on one side opening briefcases, and those in denim stood on the other side sipping from coffee mugs.

After a brief speech about hard work and determination, Ketchum began calling the names of the newly certified master carpenters. As soon as it became apparent that the list was in alphabetical order, Carrie felt a sweat break on her upper lip. Ketchum had skipped from Alvarez to Axelrod (no Angel in between), and was onto Finn . . . Jackson. Why had they not called her? She was sure she had passed the test. Seeing the disappointed faces of those other by-passed names, Carrie could feel her insides tightening.

"Nelson . . . Peters . . ." The director called out.

Carrie turned to push her way out of the crowd. Gulping swabs of air as she moved toward the open doorway, she felt like she was choking. Whatever was about to burst from her was primal, and she would soon lose control of it. She needed to get to her car where she could safely be sick or scream or howl, whatever it was her body needed to do to rid her of the mind-numbing fear that gripped her. She would lose her boys. Without the certification, she would lose them for sure. Dear God. What would she do? She staggered through to the edge of the circle, past the apprentices, past the row of rowdy man-boys, beyond the old-timers who begrudgingly parted for her.

"... Quinn, Rodriguez ..." Ketchum called out.

The path to her car was slippery, and she slowed her pace as the wind whipped the snow around her. The court date was in weeks. She had blown it. Tears would no longer obey and spilled down her cheeks. She was going to lose her boys. Carrie swiped her face with the back of her sleeve. Taking a deep breath, she straightened her shoulders, keeping the onslaught of wracking sobs at bay.

"... Wasylak ..."

She reached the Toyota and yanked on the door. It stuck, frozen from the falling ice and snow. She kicked the side panel. Fuck. The ache in her center gripped tighter. Wrapping her arms around her middle, she leaned back against the car. Snowflakes landed, melted, and mingled with the hot tears on her cheeks. She had failed the test. Failed her family. Her sons. Most especially, she had failed Tex. Eyes, jaw, and throat clenched against the mounting explosion rising within her. Holding her breath and squeezing her arms tightly around her torso, she attempted a restraint that threatened an imminent implosion. Just as she was about to bust wide, her own name reached her ears. Like the snowflakes, *Carrie Angel* whirled by on a draft of wind, and she opened her eyes, and squinted through the snow at the crowded garage.

"Angel?"

She saw a dark figure coming toward her.

"Hey, Angel? They want you back there," said the approaching carpenter.

Through her nostrils, she let out the deeply held breath, as if she were a slowly deflating balloon.

"You *are* Carrie Angel, right?" he asked.

She nodded and straightened.

He thumbed over his shoulder, back to the ceremony in the garage. "Ketchum's waitin' on ya."

Pat rushed her. "Ketchum wants you," she whispered into Carrie's ear as she made her way to the front.

"There you are, Ms. Angel," Ketchum greeted her. "I thought we'd lost you."

"I'm not following you, sir," Carrie said, as the room quieted.

"By our records, eighteen students had taken the exam, but we only received seventeen tests back from the proctor." Mr. Ketchum looked up into the crowd and addressed the group as a whole. "It seems that Mr. Pressley had a grudge against Ms. Angel," he said, looking from face to face. "And neglected to turn her exam in with the others."

A murmur went through the crowd.

"This was brought to our attention by Mr. O'Reilly, who reported Mr. Pressley and his scheme," Ketchum said. "Mr. O'Reilly, would you step forward?" He pointed to the back row.

Carrie watched as Mick, red-faced, made his way to the front of the crowd. He shuffled from foot to foot and mostly looked down at the floor. The tips of his ears glowed bright purple. His Irish was rising all over him.

A few sporadic claps came from the crowd, and one or two boos.

"It took integrity and courage for Mr. O'Reilly to do the right thing. Some might have ignored the situation." Ketchum scanned the crowd. "Some might even have played along with it."

Many searched randomly between their feet.

Ketchum continued, "In recognition of his integrity, we have promoted Mr. O'Reilly to the foreman's position vacated by Mr. Pressley."

A hearty round of applause went up from the crowd.

"All good deeds should be rewarded."

"Thank you, sir," Mick said.

Ketchum turned back to Carrie. "As for you, Ms. Angel, I wanted to save the best for last. This too might have eluded us were it not for Mr. O'Reilly's vigilance in bringing justice to the job. "It is my honor to announce that you have scored a perfect 100 on this test!"

A perfect score. She had not failed the test. She would not lose her boys. She was flooded with relief that gave way to tears, and while she was mortified to be spilling in front of the guys, she saw that even some of them were welling up. Mick for one could not stop a loose drop from rolling over his lashes and onto his smooth cheek. Ketchum was handing her the diploma and another envelope. "And on behalf of the commission, here is a gift certificate to the Lime-Light Restaurant," he said. "Congratulations!"

As Carrie made her way back into the crowd, which had begun to shuffle toward the doors, Ketchum raised both his arms and his voice, stopping everyone in their tracks.

"Hold up! Everybody, listen up! I've got another announcement."

They all turned back toward Ketchum, and Carrie saw that the contractor for the sub-division, Rob Keller, had joined him.

"Folks," Ketchum said almost quietly to the attentive group of trades-people. "I, I mean we, Rob, here, and I have some bad news."

The crowd murmured.

Rob stepped up, cleared his throat. "It's no news that the housing market's tanked. Foreclosures. Bankruptcies. Folks losing everything. It was just a matter of time before it hit us, I guess." His voice tapered off as if he were still trying to figure it out. "It was just a matter of time before it hit me," he clarified, then held up a notepad.

Heads turned, and worry appeared in furrowed brows.

Rob continued. "I'm afraid, I'm goin' to have to shut down most of this development operation. We're gonna finish the houses we got deals on, and we're gonna board up the rest till somethin' changes."

A murmur rose from the crowd. Whispered and not so whispered expletives could be heard pinging off the walls.

Rob put his hands up. "I'm sorry, fellas, but the best I can do is keep a skeleton crew—"

"Bone this!" Someone yelled from the back.

"We're gonna do it the fair way—"

"Fairway, my ass! We're goin' down the dole hole while you're playin' through the 9th hole."

"First to hire, last to fire—"

A groan went up.

"Fuck this shit." Many had already started packing up, knowing they would not be on the list.

Carrie didn't wait to hear anymore. She slung her tool belt over her shoulder and made her way to the car. Ketchum seemed to have fallen in step with her. He nodded, and she gave a weak smile back.

"Looks like I picked the wrong career, after all," she said.

"Well, at least you got through in time. They're shutting down the program. No government money left. I'm out of work starting next month."

"I'm sorry," she said. "I guess this economy is hitting everybody."

"At least you've got some good skills to rely on."

"Skills with no work do me no good."

"Maybe not, but your skills are handy, you'll always be able to rely on them, you just have to be creative."

"I suppose you're right. Even if there's no new construction, eventually, somebody's going to need a door hung, eh?"

"Exactly."

"What will you do, Mr. Ketchum?"

"Me?" he seemed surprised that she had asked. He stopped beside his big black car, huffing small puffs of air as he slowed his breathing. "Honestly, Ms. Angel, I don't know. I'm fifty-five years old. I've got a kid in college. My wife's had breast cancer. She's fine now, but with a pre-existing condition, I'll never be able to get her health insurance. I lost most of my retirement in the market crash." He smiled and then shrugged. "I've already applied for unemployment, but with this useless government, I don't know what I'm going to do. I just hope I can keep my house."

Carrie thought he nearly sounded in a daze and she guessed he was, because what was a way of life for her was something this kind of old man was just about to begin, and she felt sorry for him. "Well, good luck, Mr. Ketchum. You've helped me a lot, and so if you need anything, give me a holler."

He waved as he drove off.

Carrie caught up with Mick before he got in his truck.

"Hey," she said.

"Hey."

"Congratulations on the promotion."

"My wife is happy."

"You?"

"It's a lot of extra responsibility, you know?" the Irishman said.

"You'll be good at it."

"Thanks."

"Listen, I want to thank you for what you did," Carrie said.

He shrugged.

"Why'd you do it, though?" she asked.

"I thought about what you said, that time, about Pressley being a bully and me always standing by watching people like you get beat up."

"Hey, I'm sorry about that . . ." Carrie said.

"No. You were right. It was time for somebody to step up."

"Well, I appreciate it."

"Congratulations on the top score," Mick said.

"Shocking, huh?" she grinned.

"Not really. You're one of the best carpenters to come through." The Irishman blushed and dusted snow from his truck's windshield. He pulled up on the windshield wiper and knocked ice from its blade, and then jumped down.

"How'd you get my test, anyway?" Carrie asked, more curious than anything else.

Mick turned and shook his head. A dark shadow crossed his brow. "Pressley was showing it off."

She could see his temper flare in his green eyes.

"He bragged on how he swiped it from the stack and replaced it with a blank one. He was passing yours around the site."

"I don't understand," Carrie said. "Why didn't he just burn it? Why keep it?"

"He said he wanted to make you sweat. Make it disappear until the last minute. Then give it back before you had to take it over again."

"Where was I when all this showboating was going on around here?"

Mick's voice calmed when he said, "You were home with a sick kid." He glanced over her head and stared off into the snow. She could see that he had weighed the stakes. Somehow, the sick kid had brought it home to him.

"I saw the test lying out in plain sight on the front seat of Pressley's truck. So I took it."

"Didn't he notice?"

Mick stepped up into his big truck. "As soon as I swiped it, I drove to Ketchum's and explained the whole thing. Never saw Pressley again."

Carrie held onto his door. "I don't know how to thank you."

"We all gotta do what we all gotta do, right?"

"We do, Mick, we do."

"Sorry about the job. Wish I could hire you. I'd trade my top three veterans for you."

"Thanks. Keep me in mind if anything comes open, wouldja?"

"You bet."

"See ya, Mick."

"Carrie?"

She turned, she couldn't remember if she'd ever heard Mick use her first name. "Yeah?"

"Don't give up," he said.

"I won't, Mick. I can't, I have kids."

When she pulled into slot Number Two, Carrie noticed that the windows of the apartment were still dark. Stepping across the threshold, she took off her wet jacket and damp boots. She clipped her hat and mittens to the drying rack by the door and then stripped down to her long johns. She lit a candle and placed it in the center of the dining room table. Finally, she reached back into the spice cabinet and pulled out a small airline-style bottle of Grand Marnier.

Sitting at the kitchen table, she carefully slid the embossed certificate from its brown sheath. There was a raised gold medallion in the lower corner. Its date and notarized lettering made her official. She was a tried and true finish carpenter. Alongside Mr. Ketchum's signature was that of the governor, which Carrie guessed had been stamped from some machine. Her name centered the document and she traced the swirling calligraphy with her fingertip. She had kept *Angel* even after the divorce, in spite of the fact that she considered herself a feminist. It was easier for the boys to have everyone with the same name. The second reason was vanity. For the first eighteen years of her life, she had been Carrie O'Harrie, and not that she wasn't proud of her heritage but she had just suffered enough.

Uncapping the tiny bottle, Carrie closed her eyes and wished on the candle. She wished until she visualized it. She wished until she could trace the lines of its structure: the windows and doorways and stairwells and the pitch of its peaked roof. She wished until she could hear the sounds of her family coming from within it: Casper's chin-ups, Tex's sewing machine, and Aretha Franklin cranked to the roof. Carrie imagined waltzing around her own new home with a broom. She wished until the smell of her sons' sweaty socks and spaghetti night reached her nose. She wished until it was no longer a wish but a truth. She could see the house with its white picket fence, a chord of wood stacked ready for the fireplace, and small patches of bright flowers lining its pathway. It would be hers, soon.

This certification was supposed to be her way out of Section Eight, out of poverty, out of a story that went something like *Carrie Angel is a loser.* Instead, it felt more like a punch in the gut. Ha ha, all that hard work down the drain, here's a license to do nothing. Cheers to me. No, she wouldn't go there, not completely. She had done some-thing good. It would help them out. She just didn't know how or when, but she had to keep thinking it would, or she'd go insane. *Cheers to me!*

Not long afterward, the school bus pulled up and both Casper and Tex, quietly, entered the apartment. She heard them tiptoeing into the candlelit room. Their whispers hissed through the air. She smiled, watching their curious but hesitant expressions as they tentatively made their way nearer. Some part of her felt a flush of guilt knowing that their worry came from the last two times she had failed the cer-tification test. Then, she had thrown a couple of whopper tantrums,

215

leaving punched walls, busted phones, and a few shattered dishes in her wake. This morning before leaving for school, the boys had hugged her tightly, kissed her cheeks, head, and nose, and left her with supportive hopeful salutes: Good luck! Break a leg! We know you did it!

They approached the table and each sank into a chair. Tex was wearing a charcoal gray pinstripe suit with a black shirt and a shiny maroon silk tie. A matching handkerchief peeked above the breast pocket, and Carrie noticed silver cufflinks at his wrists. He was chewing a toothpick.

By contrast, Casper was, as always, dressed in those damn yellow and black sweats. Carrie thought she should talk to him about it.

From her lap, Carrie pulled the certificate and slid it across the table to them. Tilting their heads, each read from side to side. Tex smoothed a finger across the raised gold medallion and lettering. "Embossed," he said, reverently.

Casper read aloud, "The State of North Carolina and Fayette-Roberson Community College, in recognition of the successful completion of a program of studies in Journeyman Carpentry, it is hereby certified that *Carrie Angel* has completed all the requirements for the degree of Master Carpenter. And is accordingly granted that degree with all the honors, rights, and privileges which it carries." He looked up, solemnly. "Cool, Mom."

"Brava!" Tex stood. "Brava!"

Casper jumped from his chair and ran to the front door. With a long sweep of his arm, he pulled it open and revealed the waiting group in the foyer. "She did it!" Casper announced, ushering in Jen and Emily loaded down with food and wine. Bringing up the rear with a bundle of red roses in his arms was Sheckie, his big body filling the doorway.

"Congratulations!" the group shouted. They surrounded Carrie and the table, setting out the prized specialties Jen brought from Edible Feast. Emily and Tex arranged the roses in a tall Tupperware pitcher. Sheckie uncorked the bottle and poured into the glasses that Casper held for him. A swallow of wine for the teenagers, and Sheckie made a toast.

"Here's to Master Carpenter, Carrie Angel—the fastest nail banger in the county!"

They all tapped and sipped.

"Here's to Mom," Tex lifted his empty cup. "My hero!"

Carrie refilled the teenagers' glasses with soda, and raising her own glass, she said, "Here's to Jen Manners, without whom I never would have scored a perfect hundred!"

All glasses paused mid-air. They looked first to each other and then all eyes landed on Carrie.

"You got a perfect score?" Casper asked.

Carrie nodded.

Sheckie wrapped an arm around her shoulder and kissed the top of her head.

"Oh, my God, Mom! You're a genius!" Tex gasped.

Carrie made her way around the table to Jen. "I don't know how you did it," she said. "If it wasn't for you . . . I don't know what would have happened."

"You already knew it all," Jen said, modestly.

"I couldn't get it down, though."

"You had a block. We just unplugged it. It wasn't that big a deal, Carrie."

"Not a big deal? I owe ya." Then surprising herself and everyone around the room, she wrapped her arms around Jen and hugged her tightly and for a long time. Carrie disengaged and laughed, embarrassed by her tears. "Look at me, I'm a mess," Carrie said and sniffed. "I just don't know how to thank you."

"You'll just pay it forward, then," Jen said, and hugged her.

Later, after all the celebrating, Carrie, Jen, and Sheckie sat at the kitchen table while Tex and Emily left to go watch a movie at her place, and Casper went to his room to do homework.

"Carrie, I am so happy for you. So impressed," Jen said, again for the hundredth time.

Carrie shrugged and sipped her drink.

"What's the matter?" Sheckie asked. "You don't seem all that happy about it."

217

She started to laugh. First, it was a giggle, a small hiccupping sound, and then it took over her body the way a laugh can and will if you give it enough room, and when Sheckie and Jen looked confused and worried, well, this just made it worse, and those giggles turned to guffaws, turned to choking, crying, red-faced, nose running, until Carrie could take it no more, and she was clutching her stomach and gasping for breath. "Oh God," she finally managed and rubbed her eyes with the heels of her palms.

"What is so funny?" Jen asked.

Carrie shook her head. "It's not. No, really it's not funny, but it sure is friggin' ironic. The way my life goes." She laughed again.

"What do you mean?"

"Today, not only did I get my certification, I also lost my job."

"What?" Sheckie asked. "How can that be? You scored highest."

"I did, and right after the ceremony, the contractor got up and told everybody we were fired, all except a small crew of first hires. The economy. Foreclosures. No bank loans. Days of housing market millions are over. Did I pick the right trade or what? Carpenter. Shit. I could've at least been an electrician, or even better a plumber, everybody is always going to need a plumber."

"Can you go back to the program and become a plumber?" Sheckie asked, earning a raised eyebrow from Carrie.

"*Even* if I wanted to, which I don't, that's all over, too. Apparently, the state's going broke and there's no money for job training. Program's dead."

"That's terrible," Jen said, "Think of all those women, single mothers, who just lost their opportunity," Jen said.

"Mick said if anything came open, he'll call me, but I can't rely on that. Not one of those old-timers are going to give up their places. I know I wouldn't. No, this time around, I can't count on somebody else. It's going to take some ingenuity on my own, I'll figure something out. No matter what, I've got some jobs lined up. It'll get us through."

"Ingenuity," Jen said. "That *is* exactly right; you just have widened your horizons."

"True. And you, Jen. I mean, it's bound to affect you too."

Jen frowned. "What do you mean?"

"Crapped out housing market; I mean, it's a disaster out there. Nobody's flipping houses nowadays. Banks aren't lending, people losing jobs, there's a gazillion houses standing empty, or partly empty, basically rotting away. People are so pissed they just leave them, a lot of times trashed, too, it's a mess out there."

For some ridiculous reason, some ignorant, blinded, arrogant reason, none of this had occurred to Jen. She'd thought, like she'd seemingly naively always thought, that these kinds of things happened to other people, but why she thought this, after these things had happened to her, she did not know.

"I'm screwed," she said.

"We're both screwed," Carrie said.

"Now, wait a minute," Sheckie said. "Didn't you just both agree this was going to take some ingenuity? I think you're selling yourselves short. You're both smart, put your heads together and figure out what you *can* do, instead of focusing on all the things that are getting in your way."

"He's got a point," Carrie said. She looked across the table at Jen and saw a look of pure dejection. As if she'd just been told that after eight years of mastering medical school, she would not become a doctor, not because she wasn't good enough, but because people weren't getting sick anymore.

"Carrie, what are we going to do?" The woman's face was lined with hopelessness. Carrie had never seen Jen so deflated. She was the one who'd buoyed everyone else when things seemed dismal. Now there was that deadened look in Jen's eyes. Carrie had seen the look in others around the complex, she'd watched her own hair begin to gray and her little boys turn into young men here in Section Eight, and she imagined, she too, got that look. But seeing that sad dawning flicker behind the woman's eyes, pulled Carrie from her spot. She rubbed her friend's shoulders and said, "No worries, Jen. This is just a bump in the road. We're just going to have to get super ingenious!" Even though, in her mind, she hadn't a clue about what.

□□□

Upstairs, with his ear to the heating vent, Casper heard this part of his mother's news, the one she didn't share with *the children*, sparing them once again from another harsh reality. He swallowed hard as he listened to her bravely talk about her future. His mother, it seemed, just couldn't get a break. No matter how hard she tried, there always seemed something in the way. It wasn't fair. Fairness mattered a lot to Casper. It was in the Constitution.

He stayed propped on his elbow and listened to the details of fore-closures, and the way people were walking away from homes, leaving belongings and trash scattered through rooms, sometimes leaving rage in holes punched and kicked in walls. He heard his mother use the word *ingenuity,* which made him sit up. He grabbed his laptop, a hand-me-down from Dill after Dill bought a new one and Casper helped paint his house the previous summer. He'd heard the word before, but wasn't sure of its exact meaning and so he looked up *inge-nuity: noun: the quality of being cleverly inventive or resourceful . . .*

Casper thought himself to be cleverly inventive. He was known by family and friends alike to be extremely resourceful. Why, this quality in him alone had earned him many a compliment, award, and even some money here and there. Like the time he helped Sheckie rig a lift in his broken down shop using air hoses and a compressor. Somehow Casper knew it was up to him to discover what ingenious business *could* Carrie the carpenter and Jen the realtor do now that the economy's tanked, empty broken houses, people losing jobs.

He typed a Google search, and opened a *USA Today* article entitled "Trashed Out Firms Clean Up in the Foreclosure Biz." The article described the growing need for *foreclosure fixers;* there were hundreds of thousands of empty homes in need of cleaning out, repairs, and in many cases, where the homeowners were so pissed about what happened, they kicked in doors, broke windows, stole cabinets—the list went on.

Next, Casper, typed in *foreclosure fixers* in their surrounding area. There appeared only three: one was a *Merry Maids* gone rogue; the other two seemed more versatile, one advertised as three guys, two chicks and a dumpster, the other a former construction company turned *Trashed-Transformers*, located in the most southern part of town. Not much competition, he thought. He then searched farther to discover the number of foreclosures within a hundred-mile radius, and when he did, he was stunned to see over six hundred homes listed. This is what Mom should do, Casper thought. She and Jen, together. There was plenty of work to go around, and given the economy he was sure there were more on the way.

He started to take his news downstairs, but then realized if he did his mother would know that he'd been eavesdropping, she'd find out about his secret listening spot, and that would be the end to all his privileged information. He had to think. Finally, he realized that Carrie had to come upon this information herself. Casper disguised the document as a bogus outline for a Social Studies research paper entitled "One Man's Bust is Another Man's Boon!" He sent the document along with the articles to the ancient printer located in the corner of the living room down below and hit *Print*.

The next morning, rather than retrieving the papers from the printer dock, he left them, knowing his mother would see them. Casper felt quite confident that Carrie was the kind of mother who would look through the pages to see that they were Casper's. She'd worry that he needed them for class, and would drive them to school even without his phone call asking for them. During homeroom, he couldn't help the grin widening on his face when his name was called over the intercom to report to the office to pick up schoolwork his mother had dropped off.

Chapter Seventeen

As they drove through the near empty streets of Spring Lake, Jen glanced over at her companion and could see the sleepiness still in Carrie's face. She sipped her coffee and stared out the window. Both Jen and Carrie had been working double and triple time, lately, trying to save enough money to move out of Section Eight, and to try to get some kind of foot-hold in their new business. Carrie seemed more determined than ever to push ahead, even now in the most dismal economic downturn since the Great Depression. Somehow this spurred a kind of tenacity in Carrie that Jen had not seen in all the months she had known her. Ever since Carrie'd learned about a new emerging business—cleaning out and fixing up foreclosed homes—she'd been hot to pursue the endeavor. In fact, when Carrie showed Jen the news' articles and the national data and local statistics, Jen had to admit, it was a real possibility for them; maybe even better than the business Jen had first envisioned.

For weeks, Carrie had been scrambling to line up as many handyman and foreclosure cleaning jobs as she could manage alone. Carpentry, at least the kind she'd learned, was the least of what she was doing. Painting, wallpapering, laying floors, grouting tile, refinishing cabinets, hanging sheetrock, hauling crap to the dump, she even put in a ceiling fan. This was the work that was coming in; she'd build dog houses if it paid enough, she told Jen.

Watching her friend's vigilance, and understanding her exhaustion,

Jen knew better than to try to cajole a conversation out of Carrie Angel at this time of morning.

Jen's own newly evolving scheme to get them out of Section Eight was relying heavily on Carrie's participation and cooperation. Over the past weeks, Jen had been concocting a plan. The whole deal relied on convincing Carrie that the benefits were greater than the risks.

While Jen had aced the real estate license exam in one long multiple-choice test, it did not land her the job she'd anticipated, just as Carrie had forewarned. Jen stayed on as a cashier at Edible Feast while working part-time as an "administrative assistant" (or slave) to the wife of one of Hempy's former colleagues. Rona was a top realtor in town who made it known that Jen was a pity-hire, out of respect for Hempy, *God rest his soul*. Rona did encourage the possibility of an agent position when the market shifts—*as it always does*, she said lightly—but a shadow crossed her brow and Jen wondered what Rona knew that was making her less confident than she sounded. And this prompted Jen to take matters into her own hands.

Beside her in her briefcase were listings of foreclosed properties, fire and flood-damaged houses, and condemned residential and commercial real estate. She'd managed to gather the material on the side, making copies when Rona was out of the building, book-marking websites, taking phone messages regarding potential foreclosure sales and keeping a copy for herself.

Well into the night she studied statistics, compared ratios, drew charts, and followed markets. On Sunday afternoons, she and Carrie drove around looking at all the foreclosed houses, and taking down the mortgage company contact information. There were so many abandoned, and they were quickly deteriorating, inside and out. Whether left clean or trashed, these homes soon bore the weight of their neglect on their facades: lawns brown and bushy, paint cracked, mailboxes stuffed and tilted, shingles curled, doors sagged, and windows shut tight.

For weeks, they had focused on the business, but Jen had also kept her eye out for something else, something that could get them out of Section Eight and into their own place without having to rent. But her plan relied not only on Carrie, but Sheckie as well, and without Carrie she'd never get Sheckie, and they'd all be exactly where they are—nowhere. Carrie Angel, Jen thought, was going to be the hardest sell of her whole budding real estate career, she knew it.

"So, what's this big secret you made me get out of bed for on a Saturday morning?" Carrie finally piped up from the passenger seat.

Jen glanced over. "Oh, you're here? I thought that was just a bag of bones riding along."

"Funny." Carrie smiled. "Sorry, I am just wiped out. I didn't get home until four this morning. I couldn't start installing those doors over at the mall until after it closed. Took me all friggin' night."

"I'm sorry. How'd it go?"

"Casper and Sheckie helped, so it wasn't so bad."

"No Tex?"

Carrie shook her head. "He doesn't know a door jam from a door knob and informed me that he has no wish to be informed. Said that he can't imagine a time when he would ever need to know the difference."

"Those kids of ours are like two peas in a pod," Jen said. "Emily told me that she didn't need to learn how to do laundry because she would be hiring someone to do it for her."

"What is it about *our* lives that give them these ideas?"

"Maybe that's exactly it. Maybe they look at our lives and think, not me."

Carrie sipped from mug. "Where exactly *are* we going?"

They had wound their way along the river, near Sheckie's shop. Old brick warehouses and storefronts stood boarded up and destitute. As they slowed around a curve, Jen flicked her blinker and made a right hand turn up a bumpy driveway whose pavement was crumbling away in chunks.

She stopped in front of a large, three-story brick building set atop a double bay garage. The rickety front porch sagged in the middle, and someone had propped a long two by four under it. Off to the side and behind was a detached garage. Both buildings were falling in on

224

themselves. Out front, a wrinkled For Sale sign was barely visible through the tall grass.

After moments of silence, Carrie finally asked, "What's this?"

"It's a four-plex apartment house with a detached garage. Residential *and* commercial in one. It was condemned and has been on the market for three years."

"What a dump."

Carefully, Jen lifted her briefcase and pulled out the specs on the property. She shuffled through the papers and handed Carrie the appraisal. "It's not as bad as it looks really. All the plumbing and electric is new. They went into foreclosure before they could finish the renovation work."

"What a bear of a job that would be," Carrie said, glancing from specs to structure. "No wonder they went broke, they should have just turned it into a parking lot."

Jen took a breath and handed Carrie another sheet of paper. "Look here," she slid a finger across the bottom line, "They're asking fifteen thousand."

"So?"

"So, it could be a great investment."

"Ever see that movie *The Money Pit?*"

"I'm serious," Jen started.

"I am, too," Carrie shook her head. "Somehow, you're imagining some clever little *paint and go* job, but I'm telling you, as a *professional*, you're looking at serious structural damage, never mind all it would take to make it even *look* decent." She nearly glared at the building. "I mean, geez, you'd have to shore up that whole porch. That is, if you didn't just yank it down." Carrie's frown had narrowed, and she leaned forward. "Half the windows are broken and those upper four have mullions missing. You'd need to replace all of them, if you wanted them to match."

"That would probably be better, anyway," Jen, ventured. "Don't you think?"

"Well, if you got double-paned, it would definitely help with the insulation. That chimney's crumbling." Carrie pointed to the peak.

"Look, there's friggin' *holes* in the roof, and I'll bet you ten to one that the trusses underneath are rotting."

"But that could be replaced, right?"

"Nah, we don't want to clean up this piece of shit."

"I wasn't exactly thinking of cleaning it up."

"No? What were you thinking of doing, *buying* it?" She snorted.

Jen cleared her throat. "Well, I was kind of thinking that *we* could buy it."

"*We* who?"

"You, me, and Sheckie."

"You're out of your mind!"

"No, I'm not. Listen to me. Back there," Jen said hurriedly, and pointed beyond the building. "That garage used to be a mechanic's shop. It has hydraulic lifts in the floor. It is totally equipped, and even has a small office space and bathroom. Sheckie could own his own shop."

Carrie shook her head, but before she could protest, Jen turned their attention to the brick building in front of them.

"There are four apartments. We could all have one. We could rent the fourth!"

Carrie frowned. "You mean we all move in here? Together?"

"Why not? Together we will be stronger than apart. Together we can fix this place up. Between my design ideas, your carpentry skills, and Sheckie's big strong back, we'd make a pretty good team."

"You're forgetting something."

"What's that?"

"Together, the three of us can't afford a pot to piss in."

"But we could." Jen said, bringing out yet another set of papers. She'd figured out how much they'd each need to contribute to buy the property outright. "I know you've been saving to get out of housing, so have I. Look here," she said pointing to the numbers. "I have my third. I bet you're close to that with the money you've been saving. Am I right?"

Carrie considered and said, "Pretty damn close. But, Sheckie can barely buy a beer on a Friday night. Where do you think he's going to get that kind of money?"

"He could sell his motorcycle," Jen said, already having thought this through.

"Ha! Now I know you're out of your mind, Sheckie'd *never* part with that bike. No way."

"But, it could be temporary. He wouldn't need it if he were working right where he lives. Both you and I have cars if he needed one," Jen said.

"How long have you been spinning this little fantasy of yours?"

"A long time," Jen said, quietly. She stared up at the building; it would be the beginning of the empire she was planning. "Carrie, this could be our chance. A new beginning. If we pay cash, we'd qualify for a home loan, and then it'd be a matter of doing the renovation. But this could also give us collateral for the business."

"And where are we all going to live for ten years while it gets done?"

"It won't take ten years."

"It'll take that long and a miracle to make that thing livable."

"Would you at least look inside before you pronounce it dead?"

Later, as the women huddled around the heater at the back of Sheckie's shop, they blurted out their scheme while he straddled an old chopper with its parts scattered at his feet. His mustache twitched as he listened, but he did not interrupt.

"So, after she stomped on every floor, rattled every stud, and poked behind every piece of sheetrock, she was convinced!" Jen blurted out.

Carrie said, "The biggest problem is the roof, well, and the porch and chimney. All three need shoring up. But all the studwork is up, new sub-flooring down, and the first two apartments have working plumbing and drywall in place. Honestly, Sheck, it'll take some work, but it'd be worth it."

He looked back and forth from each woman as she rattled off the next and the next piece of information. Finally he said, "Sounds like you girls have got it all figured out." He did not seem very enthusiastic.

Jen nudged Carrie, who stuttered, "See, that's just it . . . we weren't thinking it'd just be us . . ."

"We thought that maybe the three of us could go in on it together," Jen said.

"The three of who?" Sheckie wiped his hands with a rag.

"You, me, and Jen."

"Right," he climbed off the machine and moved away from them. He was circling the skeleton of another motorcycle like a painter approaching a canvas.

"There's a fully equipped mechanic's garage in the back." Jen followed him around the bike. "You could give up this place and work from home. There's an office and a bathroom set up, too."

He stopped and she bumped into him. When he turned on her, he was not smiling. "Just exactly where do you think I'm going to get the money to do this? You think I'm a janitor in Section Eight housing out of the goodness of my heart?"

"Sheck, it's only five thousand dollars. Maybe even three, if we can talk them down."

"Might as well be five million, Carrie. You know I don't have that kind of money *or* credit."

They women exchanged glances, and Carrie stepped over to him. She reached up and tugged on the straps of his overalls. "You've got the bike," she said softly.

He flinched and then looked across the shop to the black and white Harley propped near the front door. Slowly lowering his gaze back to Carrie, he whispered, barely audible. "Sell my bike?"

"I know it sounds drastic, but just think, you'd have your own home. Your own shop."

"And what? Walk everywhere? How will I get up to see Amy?"

"We'll share our cars until we can get you a new bike."

"It's asking a lot."

"It's a temporary car situation but long-term living situation, don't you see?"

"Sheck, it's security," Carrie nudged. "You might even be able to bring Amy here to visit."

He looked at Jen. "You would want me to be part of this?"

"We wouldn't want to do it without you," Jen said.

"My own shop, huh?"

"Sounds pretty good, doesn't it?" Carrie asked, and hugged him to her.

By the time Carrie had tiptoed downstairs and got the coffee going, the sun was on the rise. There was a quiet knock on the door, and Jen stepped across the threshold and handed Carrie the rolled newspaper she'd picked off the porch.

"What are you doing here so early?" Carrie poured a second cup.

"Came to see if you're okay," Jen said, easing into a kitchen chair, and Carrie sat across the table.

"I guess." She took a deep breath and exhaled slowly. "I'm as ready as I'll ever be," she said, and patted a thick accordion file-folder set on the table. I've got all the records the lawyer told me to bring to court: carpentry certification, my Anger Management diploma, and my W-2." She glanced at Jen. Carrie had been hoping they'd know by now about the purchase of the Phoenix Street building. They were both praying they wouldn't have to rent something—throwing their combined savings down the toilet.

"You can show the judge the paperwork for the building. You can say that it's just a matter of time." Jen patted Carrie's hand. "You know that, right?"

Carrie shrugged, "Let's say I hope that. Look, I know that all the odds are in my favor. All this *proof:* letters from guidance counselors, teachers, coach, and on and on. I mean, even the lawyer said they were just backup. That we wouldn't need them."

"Then, why so worried?"

"I'm just afraid Dill will say something to make me blow my top. Then the boys'll be living in his basement *because* of me."

"You know that's not going to happen. You know how to stay calm. Better than he does, nowadays. I'll remind you about the nasty phone tirade after he discovered his uniform missing."

"To be honest, if it hadn't been so ridiculous, it might have been scary," Carrie said, blowing across the top of her cup. "I mean, he was talking crazy. Threatening to call the cops on Tex, threatening to come search my *premises*," she laughed, repeating his words. But then she didn't laugh, because recalling his tone and intensity made gooseflesh rise on her arms and scalp, and she thought about how often he'd been calling lately, sometimes she thought he might be drunk, or e-mailing his threats, or . . . she hadn't mentioned it to anyone, but she was sure he'd been driving around the complex. She'd seen an APS truck parked twice across the street from number two. The closer they were getting to court, the meaner Dill seemed to be getting.

She brought herself back to her conversation when she realized Jen was waiting for her to finish. "Steal something *precious* of mine . . . he said." Carrie shivered. "That's when it got a little creepy."

"Too bad you don't have that vile-ness on tape."

"No, I don't. I don't want the boys to hear it."

"You sure you don't want me to come with you to the courthouse, today?"

Carrie shook her head, and then looking at the clock she stood. "No, thanks. I appreciate it, but I need to do this myself." She gathered keys and her shoulder bag, into which she stuffed the fat file-folder. "The boys might try to come, so could you please stay and just make sure they get to school?"

"I'll drive them, myself." Jen walked to the door. She placed her hands on Carrie's shoulders and said, "Just remember, this is the very last hurdle. When you get home, we'll be popping corks!"

"Let's save that for the building contract."

"Let's decide it's already happened."

Dill was seated at one end of the long front . . . *pew* was the word that came to Carrie's mind, although there was nothing churchlike about this court-room; fluorescent lights glaring, green walls, steel chairs, nothing like what you see on television. There was brown carpeting, and Carrie found this disconcerting. She eased into the next row, crossing the laps of two women whose appearance led Carrie to imagine their after-hours occupation, and sat only feet from a shackled man dressed in an orange jump-suit with blue tattoos on his knuckles; he winked at Carrie, and when he grinned his gold front tooth gleamed. She closed her eyes. Never had she imagined her life would lead her seated in a courthouse between pimps and hoes, and then she stopped herself from these thoughts.

Dill had turned and was staring at her when she glanced in his direction. She noticed he was solo, sans Dodi and company. She thought he might bring them to prove his family values. When he wouldn't look away, she began rummaging in her bag and pulled out the folder. It wouldn't hurt to have everything ready. With the help of Mr. Solomon's lawyer friend, Mr. Biggs, who gave her some free and encouraging advice over the phone, she had felt like she could do this, but as she faced the task, her hands shook as she sifted through the papers.

Dill was turned sideways into the arm of his seat, fixing his eyes on her, unsettling her. How had he gotten so mean? she wondered. So angry, Casper had noticed, and she'd tried to reassure her son that she hadn't *married* a jackass, that Dill hadn't always been so vengeful. But those days of gentle thoughts for Dill were dim in her memories, and overshadowed by the more recent, immediate version—a man bitterly disappointed by his life, and blaming everybody but himself for how it turned out.

She'd read the contents of her folder from top to bottom, twice, as the courtroom filled and emptied of citizens; as cases for fraud, prostitution, child custody, bad-checks, domestic disturbances, and minor drug possession charges were tried and settled—one way or another.

She'd imagined the way she might answer the questions asked of those people up on the stand. She noticed how many couldn't just give a straight yes or no answer, and she could tell it was irritating the judge, and she made note not to do that. She imagined swearing on the Bible, and when she did, she'd look the judge right in the eye, because she noticed when people didn't, he was paying attention. She thought about all the things Dill's lawyer could ask: about Tex being gay, about Carrie's bad temper, about Casper and the stolen uniform;

although, Casper had yet to return it, so Dill didn't have proof of that, yet.

Punching Dill in mediation was going to be the hardest and most embarrassing to explain away, but the anger-management would help with that. When she imagined herself acting as her own lawyer questioning Dill up on the stand, after *he'd* sworn on the Bible, she let her fantasies take over. While she had a list of three specific questions her lawyer told her to ask, there were tons of things she wanted from him while she had him under oath: how can you live without seeing those boys? How can you not call them every day? How could you so easily trade this family for that one? These were the things that she wished she could ask while he was up there, but her pro-bono lawyer warned her to keep on task. Having spent all morning and afternoon witnessing all those people wasting so much time giving so much useless information, she could see exactly how that line of questioning was not a matter for the courts. She instead envisioned asking Dill questions about his income, Dodi's home-based job, and how to describe the basement room where the boys would sleep. With her thumb, she smoothed the slick ocean stone in her pocket; the one Casper had given her, trying not to care as Dill's heavy-lidded eyes bored through her.

Finally, just thirty minutes before the end of the day, their case was called by the little robed man up in the big chair. They were the only ones left to be heard, and Carrie was grateful that she wouldn't have to miss another day of work to come back. She leapt to her feet, fumbling the folder a little, but recovering before she spilled everything. She was grateful that the pimp and prostitutes (she was right) were gone. So she slid easily out of her pew, and approached one empty lawyer's table, alone, while Dill and his attorney, both dressed in gray suits, settled at the other.

"Mr. Fox, representing Mr. Angel," the judge read the file from behind low half glasses. I see you're asking for full-custody and child-support of the minor children Texas and Casper Angel?"

"Yes, Your Honor," Dill's lawyer answered, and shuffled some papers before him.

"Mrs. Angel, who is your attorney?"

Carrie stood, "I don't have one, sir. I, uh, I did talk to a lawyer, and he told me all the things I should bring today." She held up her folder. "I've got proof of my job, my education, I've got letters." Carrie nervously rifled through the envelopes, scattering pieces of paper across the table, a pen skittered to the floor. "Here." She slid them into her thick manila folder containing the rest of her defense, and handed it to the bailiff, who handed it to the judge.

"Yes, well, then you'll be representing yourself, Mrs. Angel? Is that correct?"

"Yes. That's correct."

"Fine, then, Mr. Fox and I will meet in my chambers." He rose.

"But, wait—" Carrie called out, even though she knew she wasn't supposed to. "I'm sorry, I mean, who, I, who will . . ."

"Yes, Mrs. Angel?" The judge asked.

"Who will speak for me in there?" she finally managed.

He stared at her, as if he hadn't thought of this, as if he was reconsidering, and then he held up her file. "You will, Mrs. Angel. It's all here, correct?"

"Yes, sir."

"If we have any questions, we'll ask."

Everything she expected to happen did not happen. She sat on one side of the courtroom, and Dill sat on the other. Neither spoke. He appeared to be texting everyone in the whole world. She flipped through a *People* she'd found on a bench outside the courtroom. Strange how the same magazine could make time fly on the can, but had a way of slowing it here; for each celebrity scandal, a minute passed. She saw that Dill was furiously jabbing at this phone.

Suddenly the chamber's doors opened and the judge and Mr. Fox came briskly back into the courtroom, Mr. Fox joining Dill at the table, and the judge stepping up to his chair. His Honor leaned back against his massive seat and looked tired. "I read your complaint Mr. Angel, and I read your paperwork Mrs. Angel."

"There are no custody issues. I have dismissed this part of your claim, Mr. Angel. Your sons are doing just fine with their mother."

Dill stood. "What about her temper? She hit me in mediation!"

He turned to his lawyer. "Didn't you show him the letter from the mediator? Solomon?"

"Mr. Angel, you will sit down. Mr. Fox, please remind your client of the observances of this court."

Carrie raised her hand, she didn't know what the observances of the court were, either, but she was pretty sure she wouldn't get yelled at for raising her hand.

"Yes, Mrs. Angel?"

"So the boys are going to live with me?"

"Yes, ma'am."

"And you don't want to ask me anything about my job, or my temper, or anything?"

"Do you want me to, Mrs. Angel?"

"No! I just expected that you would."

"It's not necessary, here. In the letters from your almost grown sons, I have learned that they are happy, healthy, and well cared for; they speak highly of their mother, and they made it very clear where they want to live. Mrs. Angel, you appear to be a good mother, a good person, who hit some hard times."

"Yes, sir," she almost whispered, and felt herself wanting to cry.

"You also appear to have turned your life around, and are on the upswing."

"I hope so, your honor."

"Mr. Angel, according to the state guidelines, you are underpaying your child support, and so we'll be raising that to meet the minimum standards."

"What do you mean I have to pay *more?*" Dill turned on his lawyer. "This was supposed to be about getting custody, not about raising child-support, again!"

"Mr. Angel, you'll refrain from any more outbursts." The judge banged his gavel. "Court adjourned."

Carrie left the room as soon as the gavel landed, but the elevator was taking forever. Dill slammed out the big double doors. He got as close as he could without actually touching her. "You want those little bastards you tricked me into giving you? You got 'em. You bitch!"

The security officer, whom neither had noticed, stepped into their view and Dill turned and scurried down the back stairs. "Are you all right, Ma'am?" the officer asked, as they listened to Dill's fleeing footsteps.

Carrie laughed nervously, "Well, I am now that you're here," she said half seriously.

"Can I walk you to your car, then?"

Carrie looked to the windows, which were darkening with the quickly setting sun, and decided it wouldn't hurt to have an escort; if nothing else, it would stop a confrontation if Dill was waiting for her. But it appeared he wasn't. The parking lot was pretty empty except for the Toyota and a couple other vehicles.

"You need to get that fixed," the officer said, as they approached her car.

"Get *what* fixed?"

He pointed to the left, broken taillight. The one that wasn't smashed just hours ago.

"Shit."

"Wasn't broken when you got here, was it?" he asked.

"What do you think?' She shoved her hands into her pockets, and kicked at the tire.

"Want to file a complaint?"

"No, I think I want to get home and just be glad it's over, you know?"

"Well, I'm going to write down some notes, keep the information, file an incident report with my boss. If you don't mind."

"I really don't have time," she said. "I also don't want the hassle."

"I understand," he said, and smiled. "I can't say as I blame you. But, if you change your mind, you can just call." He handed her his card. "My name's Mike. Mike Ross."

Carrie noticed that he had a nice smile, his front teeth were a little crooked. He was about her age. Tall and gangly, but wiry—fit, she could see by the sinewy muscles of his arms. His green eyes were kind, and went with the Irish of his reddish, thinning hair. There was something familiar about him, and then she remembered.

235

"Don't I know you?" she asked.

"I don't know," he seemed surprised, "do you?"

"Did you go to Fayetteville High?"

He grinned and a dimple creased, "I did, but only for my last two years. You must have a good memory?"

"I do," she said. "I'm Carrie."

"Carrie? Something funny," he said, trying to remember her last name.

"Hey now."

"Carrie *Barry* or something like that?"

"*O'Harrie*," she admitted. "It's Angel."

"You're married?"

"Was. To that prick who smashed out my tail lights."

"Yikes."

"Kept the name for my sons. Carrie Angel. You always wore a plaid cap." Carrie remembered.

He straightened some, and pointed his pen, "That was my grand-dad's cap; I still have it."

"Didn't you go into the Army or something, after high school?" she tried to remember.

"No, I went to the police academy; I was a state trooper until last year, and then I got shot—"

"Oh, no! Are you okay?"

"I am. They've got me on courthouse duty for a few more months, till I can get back to my car."

"I'm so sorry," she looked him over to see if she could see where he'd been wounded, but there was nothing visible.

"Thanks."

"I'm glad you're all right," she said.

"Yeah, me, too," he said.

"I'm sure your family, your wife, must have been a wreck."

"Oh, there is no wife. Like you, there's an ex, but no kids. Less complicated, I suppose."

"You'd think," she said, because she didn't know what else to say. She wanted him to keep talking, she liked the softness of his voice.

236

The freckles on his nose seemed brighter when the streetlight came on, and he looked young, reminding her of a time before—before everything complicated happened.

"Yeah, you would," he said.

"Well, I gotta go," she said, gesturing to her car, for some reason wishing she didn't have to, wishing she could stay and chat about old times.

"Sure, sorry to keep you."

"No, it was great running into you, after all this time."

"Yeah, you, too." He patted the hood of her car. "Don't forget to call if you change your mind. Or, let me know if that jerk tries anything, just call."

She waved his card, and slid it into the visor, and pulled out of the parking lot.

Once on the highway, she could breathe easier. What they said about that fine line between love and hate was pretty true, she thought, pressing into the back of her seat. She might stop down at Paddy's Tavern and have a beer before heading home. She needed a moment to herself. One that was suddenly unburdened of the dread of this day and its *other* possible outcome. She wanted a moment where she could toast herself for all her good hard work, and reflect a bit about *her day in court;* which, considering all she'd prepared for, wound up being a tad anti-climactic. Not that she was complaining. Turning off the main road, she headed down the winding lane that would bring her to the little Irish bar by the river she loved to get away to.

Suddenly a pair of headlights was fast on her tail, filling the Toyota with stark bright light, sending blinding shards to her eyes. She smacked the rearview to tilt it out of her view. "Jesus Christ!" Pressing hard on the gas, but to no avail, the vehicle behind her was big and bearing down. As she fixed the mirror, trying to get a view, the truck was flashing its lights. Slowing only made it worse, as she felt it ride closer. This stretch of road was dark and winding, with nowhere to pull off, and no way to turn around, there was nowhere to go but forward. Speeding up seemed only to encourage the pursuit, and so with her palms sweating, Carrie slowed to the speed limit hoping the jackass would go around. He didn't, and just as they swerved the first steep curve, the front bumper of the monster truck smacked her back end, and she could feel the little car fishtail beneath her. Gripping the wheel, she pulled away from the embankment. "You fucker!" She yelled as he tapped again, this time pushing her into the opposite lane, where luckily, there were no oncoming cars. Sliding back, she caught a glimpse of the painted orange flames decorating the front of the truck. Just as they came to the straightaway, Carrie heard the big engine behind her roar. Holding tight as the truck slammed again, pushing her across the road, she spun off the pavement down into a small ravine, landing slightly tipped and at the edge of a ditch, nearly teetering into it. As Carrie looked up from her vantage point, she saw Dill's truck speed by.

That night, after Carrie got home, and after she'd celebrated her court victory with the boys and Jen, she and Sheckie settled at the kitchen table, and she told him about Dill and his courthouse threats, the broken tail light, and finally how he ran Carrie off the road. She watched as Sheckie flexed his muscles, cracked his knuckles, and paced the length of the kitchen, all the while swearing to *go cut the fucker's throat.* She'd managed to talk him down off his caveman's ledge, and promised to let him know if any other incidents occurred. Later still, Carrie walked Sheckie back to his apartment, but rather than turn around and walk the fifty yards back to her own, she went inside at his invitation.

They made love for the first time since the first time. They loved each other with a new kind of passion that culminated in quiet slow ecstasies, tears, and finally exhausting laughter. Together and separately, they ran the gamut of emotions, all within each other's clutches. When spent, Carrie curled into the hollow of his arms, resting her head on his chest, listening as his heart slowed to a steady rhythm. He held her close.

The moon was shining through the window onto Sheckie's big bed, slanting a bar of light across their entangled naked bodies. Carrie liked the feel of them together.

"I love you, Carrie," Sheckie quietly admitted.

She swallowed. How she wanted to return his words. She certainly felt them, but they remained deep within her. Her brain was holding them at bay. *Measure twice; cut once,* the old carpentry adage ran through her mind. She had measured Sheckie once a long time ago when they were far out of alignment with each other. Now, though, she measured again. This time around, they were down to fractions. "I know you do," was the best she could do.

Chapter Eighteen

Casper gave free rein to his thoughts as he ran in the predawn light with Dill's Air force uniform tucked tightly under his arm. There was the conversation he'd overheard between Carrie and Sheckie after his mother had come back from court the other night. They'd won; she told them when she entered the apartment. She was smiling a bit too broadly, he reckoned. Not only would he and Tex remain with her, but the judge even increased Dill's child-support; for this, Carrie had said, she was ecstatic. Except, she didn't seem ecstatic; she didn't seem happy at all. She seemed on edge, skittish and distracted, and while she smiled and laughed, Casper watched as her eyes darted around the room, and the way she kept smoothing back her hair, a habit that always increased with her nervousness.

Casper knew the look of fear in his mother's eyes. He could feel the danger she was fending off; it was old in him. They'd been through everything together, and he knew when something was not right, and there was definitely something not right. The first thing he noticed when she came through the door was how pale she seemed, and this alarmed him, thinking things had gone horribly wrong at court, and that he and Tex would be moving in with the Dildos, but that was not the case. No, the case was even better than any of them had hoped for; they'd all live happily ever after together, and Dill would have to pay even more for abandoning them.

Whatever it was that had Carrie all worried on the inside, was knotting the fist in Casper's middle during the celebration. It wasn't until Jen and Georgia and Emily had gone home, and he and Tex had gone to their respective rooms that he finally heard the *whole* story of what had happened at court, including what had happened afterward. He lay in bed listening while Carrie's whispered account of Dill's road rage came floating up through the heating vent, as she relayed it to Sheckie.

As Casper had listened the night before to the terror in his mother's trembling voice, he had an urgent, primal desire to hurt his father for hurting his mother. In the same manner, he imagined, as he must have had in his past-lives. Cro-Magnon Casper would club Caveman Dill to death for dragging his mother around by the hair. He imagined his every incarnation through the ages, because this was something he was coming to believe in—karma, reincarnation, and all that repetition-until-you-get-it-right-stuff—and he imagined the different fathers that the different Caspers would have confronted throughout history.

There would be Prince Casper beheading King Dilbert to save his mother from the chopping block, and the Texas Ranger Casper hunting down the Desperado Dill, who'd robbed the fair Carrie of her last penny; Casper's favorite fantasy, though, was where Indiana Jones. Casper swoops in, rescues his mother from the showers of Bergen-Belsen where the diabolic Nazi Hitler Dill has had her imprisoned—proud and vindicated; this is Casper's noblest of scenarios. This morning, though, the real Casper would be defending not only his current mother's honor but also her life against the very real and very dangerous Dill.

It was still dark when Casper got to Dill's driveway. The big truck was parked in the driveway, and its giant tires lifted so high that Casper could nearly crab-crawl under it. On his back, the underbelly of the truck was a grid of lapping dirty metal and greasy steel, and Casper knew enough from working with Sheckie, which were the moving parts and which were structural, and once he'd identified an inert rod close to the rear, he threaded the leather shoelaces from his pocket, through the grid, and tied the uniform securely. He slid out, leaving the tidy bundle hidden behind the back tire.

From here, Casper jogged back toward home, but before he

reached the street that would take him to the housing complex, he veered across the highway, and made his way, instead, down to the river, and followed the road to the APS, American Package Services; the warehouse distribution center where Dill worked. The sky was turning gray when Casper got to the grounds, and he picked out a cluster of picnic tables at the far end of the parking lot where the APS trucks were idling, and where Casper knew his father would be entering soon. Men in their mustard-colored uniforms, caps, and jackets began arriving, getting out of their small pick-up trucks and American-made cars, carrying lunch bags and thermoses. One had already switched to the shorts versions of his outfit; Casper thought he was nuts, there was snow on the ground in places.

He watched as the men circled around each other, standing at the entrance to the building. They had just enough time for one last smoke before they had to punch-in; Casper had heard many stories from Dill about these morning *huddles*, recapping games, laying bets, and listening to the young fellas brag about their scores with the ladies the night before. Casper heard them joking and laughing with each other, sipping coffee and telling lies, as Dill would say. They seemed like a bunch of jerks, Casper always thought. All the stories these guys and his father thought funny, just reminded Casper of the jackasses exactly like them that he'd encountered at school. They were the guys who picked on Tex, got fighting drunk on Friday nights, and tried to get into the pants of any girl that would let them. That was the guy his father must have been in high school, because that was the guy his father was now. And so were all his jackass friends, all perked like hound-dogs. He heard the roar of Dill's engine arrive before the monster truck came bouncing into the lot.

The big machine seemed to leap forward, racing across the black-top, aiming for the fellas by the door, bearing down until the group sprung apart, men ducking for cover. At which point the giant truck came skidding, fishtailing, swinging around, and sliding to a grumbling halt facing the opposite direction. The workers re-grouped: laughing too loud, brushing off their sleeves and backs and pride, poking at each others' leaps to safety; Casper imagined they were all ignoring the tightness of their collectively and respectively puckered sphincter muscles.

One of the men elbowed another and pointed to the back of Dill's truck, and the others followed suit. A few were venturing forward, staring at something on the ground. One guy bent over and toed the mass. Casper stood, and came a bit closer, but still no one had noticed him. He watched Dill get out of the cab and join the men at his tailgate. He was laughing really loud, busting their chops about scaring their pansy-asses when his eyes were also drawn to the clump on the ground. He slowly set his lunch cooler down, and bent over and picked it up the ragged heap. Snagged on the bumper, Dill jerked until the laces snapped and freed the bundle from the truck's frame. He shook it out in front of him. The group of men widened, instinctively, giving him space.

"Ain't that your fancy Air Force Uniform you had tacked on your wall?" Casper heard someone ask, as he made his way closer, standing on the outskirts of the circle, nearly blending in. They ignored him as they watched his father gently drape the uniform over the tailgate. One of the legs was torn off, and what remained was tattered and frayed. The once blue suit was black with grease and road dirt, tire marks striped one sleeve. Whatever *fruit-salad* collection of medals and ribbons that had once decorated the chest, held only his flight wings, bent like a butterfly. Dill fingered the collar, and stared at the uniform. Some of the men slowly left the circle and went inside. A couple backed up, but you could tell they wanted to stay and watch what happened next. When Dill finally looked over his shoulder, it was just a couple of guys and Casper standing there. He watched his father squint and seem to try to place his son's face in some sort of context. When it became clear, when Dill's gaze unclouded, he looked from Casper to the rag of a uniform and back again, suddenly making, if not understanding, the connection.

"You?" he whispered, looking wounded. "You did this?" He lifted an upturned palm. "Why?"

"You really *do* need to ask, don't you?" Casper said, his own realization settling on him. The one he could never-quite believe, the one that Carrie had come to know, and the one that Tex had seemed to know all along—Dill truly believed that *he* was the victim in all of this; not the abandoned Carrie, the poverty-stricken single-mother of his first-born children, not poor father-less Tex, the boy rejected by the man because he had too much girl in him. And, not Casper, who would have killed for a dad to toss a ball around with. No, by the hurt in Dill's eyes, Casper could tell that his father had no clue what he'd done to any of them—only what had been *done* to him.

"Yeah, I have to ask," Dill said, "I can't believe you'd do this to me. Sure, I can see why your brother would want to hurt me; we've never been close, but you and me, Casp—"

"You and me what, Dad?" He approached. "There hasn't been a *you and me* without Dodi and company since I was four years old."

"It was all I had left . . ." Dill trailed off, lifting the sleeve of the suit, and then grasped the uniform to his chest. "Why this?"

"Why do you think?"

Dill shook his head. "Figures."

"What *figures?*"

Dill had to look up to narrow his gaze on his son. "You're just like your bitch of a mother."

Casper lunged at his father, shoving him with his full body up against the tailgate of his truck, his forearms pressing across Dill's throat.

"Hey!" Dill tried to twist away, but Casper grabbed the beaten uniform from Dill's clutches and pushed the suit into his father's chin. Casper could smell the oil and dirt and burnt rubber singed into the Nomax material.

"Why *this?* You want to know?" Casper hissed in his father's ear. He could feel Dill's breath quicken, his chest pumping beneath Casper's own weight, the rapid heart-beating against Casper's, slower paced, stronger one. He hadn't been so close to his father since he was a little boy captured in an embrace. This was no embrace. He was no little boy. They were two men, now.

"*This* is a warning." Casper leveled the bunched material with his father's widening eyes. "Try to hurt my mother again, and next time, *this* will be you. I will drag you behind your own truck the next time you get it into your head to run my mother off the road, or any other schemes you might have to harm her." He let go of his father with a shove, and dropped the tattered uniform on the ground.

"Your mother—"

"Stop." Casper shoved his fists into his father's chest, pinning him. He stared at the man pressed against the truck. Dill had once been a proud, handsome man: tall and lanky and angular. Casper remembered him that way, and he saw it every day in the mirror as his own physical features were becoming more like his father's. But Casper vowed never to become this man. This victim of his own non-choices.

"You have never taken responsibility for one fucking thing in your life, Dill." Casper used his father's name. "You are just full of fucking excuses!"

"Casp, let me explain," Dill straightened. "That judge screwed me. Your mother—"

"My *mother* what, Dill? What? *Made* you start a new family? *Made* you sue her for custody? *Made* you bust out her taillight? *Made* you run her off the road? Are you hearing yourself?"

"Casper, please—" Dill nearly whispered. "You and me, we got something special. You were the best thing to come out of that marriage. Let's you and me talk this out?"

"No, there is no talking this out. If you want a relationship with me, you've got to start manning up. You've got to take responsibility for your own shit. And leave my mother alone." He shoved his elbow against Dill's throat, making him hunch down.

"Sure, Casp, whatever you say."

"One more thing." He loosened his grip on his father.

"What's that?"

"You better start treating my brother better. He's a good person. So what if he's gay? Better than being a prick like you. If you can't accept Tex, you don't get me." He let his father go, and the older man slumped on his truck, gasping for air. The other few men in the lot were all looking at their feet.

"If things don't change, we are done," Casper said. "Done, for good." He turned and started the long jog home.

It was as he was rounding the corner, the sun on the rise, turning everything from purple to blue, that he saw a silver car pulled up to Sheckie's apartment. There were two people inside, Casper could tell. They appeared to be talking seriously, and as he passed on the opposite side of the road, he saw that it was Sheckie and a woman with blond hair sitting behind the wheel. Casper slowed, and then slipped behind a bush, and watched from behind the car whose tail-lights were glowing red. The couple talked for a few more minutes, then hugged and kissed on the lips, Casper noticed, and then Sheckie climbed out. Before he closed the car door, he reached be-hind the seat and hoisted a small overnight bag to his shoulder. He stood and watched as the car drove off, and then made his way into the apartment. Casper suddenly felt sad for his mother, sad that she would be disappointed, sad that she'd be alone, sad that Sheckie had lied. Then Casper realized that he was already experiencing all those feelings, himself, right then and there, and it was horrible, heart-breaking, really. Why do people do these things to each other? Part of him didn't want to grow up, just so he wouldn't inflict his bad de-cisions on good people in ways that mattered. So, he decided to keep the information to himself; maybe it wasn't what it appeared, maybe it was something more innocent than he could even imagine; some-times things are not always as they appear. But, he decided, most of the time they are.

Later that afternoon, when Casper emerged from the track-house, he saw an old blue Dodge Caravan at the curb, and Dodi at its wheel. She leaned out her window, gesturing to him.

"Can I talk to you?" She asked.

"I guess."

"Come, get in the car, I'll drive you home," Dodi said.

Casper loaded his duffle bag onto the floor and climbed in after it.

"Dill told me what happened this morning."

Casper looked out the window. "Did he tell you why it happened? Did he tell you what he did to my mom?" Casper could feel his cheeks burning as his eyes filled with tears. He swallowed back his fury, something he thought he'd run out of his body at practice when he ran eight miles instead of just the four he'd been required. He wanted to kick the windshield out, but clenched his fists, holding back his rage as best he could. Seeing Dodi just reignited it all inside of him. "He ran her off the road, Dodi! He could have killed her!" He began to cry. He pulled his knees to his chest and crossed his arms, covering his face. Dodi pulled the car over and parked. She reached and pressed a hand to his head, smoothing his hair. "I know, honey, I'm sorry. I couldn't believe it when he told me what he'd done. I'm scared, too."

And Casper could see that she was, and then felt bad to know that there was another person in the world who'd been terrorized by his father. He took a couple of deep breaths and composed himself. Pressing the heels of his palms to his eyes, he wiped them dry, and then wiped his running nose on his sleeve. "What's the matter with him?" he was finally able to ask.

"I don't know. I know he's angry. I know he's frustrated. I know he blames a lot of people for stuff he brings on himself. But, I don't know how to answer that question, sweetie. I really wish I could pinpoint his behavior to one thing, one terrible incident that changed him, or drove him to do what he did to your mother. I really wish I could, because then I would know, too."

"Mom does her best, Dodi. It's not easy on her. She's alone. He's made it harder. You've made it harder," Casper said, quietly, but not caring anymore about anybody else's feelings.

Dodi shifted in her seat, but didn't stop him.

"You and Dad never give her a break. She doesn't bother either one of you unless her child support doesn't come and then whose fault is that? She's doing it all alone, Dodi; you were alone once, too, don't you remember?"

She nodded, but was looking out the window. Casper thought she looked sad and far away. For the first time since he'd met her, he felt sorry for her. Sorry for the mean things he'd said and thought about her, the mean things his father was doing to her, sorry they were all in this mess.

"I'd rather not have a father than the one I've got," he finally said.

She took a deep breath, "I can't blame you. I feel the same way about the husband I've got. You, unfortunately, are stuck with him, he's your father. In my case, there's always divorce. She wiped a renegade tear from her cheek. "That's what I wanted to tell you." She turned toward him. "I also gave him an ultimatum, today. I told him that if he didn't get some help, find a therapist, that I am taking the kids and moving out. He has till next week."

"Is he going to?" Casper managed, hopeful.

"We'll see."

"He's got a lot of ultimatums hanging in front of him," Casper said, and smiled.

"He's got to start owning up to the things he's done, or we're done."

"I'm sorry, Dodi. I hope he does, but I'm not holding my breath," Casper said.

"Well, I am."

"If only therapy could work miracles."

"Casper, I know you won't believe me, but I'm glad you did what you did."

"You are?" he turned to look at her.

"I am. I think what happened this morning really shook your father up. I think this might have scared him enough to make him get help."

Casper reached for his bag. "I hope you're right. I hope he sees that he's about to lose everybody," he said, and meant it. "I'm sorry he's been treating you crappy, too," he said, and then regretted it when tears welled in her eyes, again. But, she stifled them.

"I'll let you know what I do."

He opened his door. "Yeah, do that."

"Don't you want me to drive you the rest of the way home?" she asked.

"Nah, thanks. I could use the walk."

He watched the van pull away and amble down the road. He

thought about what Dodi had said, and how the two of them talking like adults with a common problem made him, somehow, feel better about his father, instead of worse. Then, he was a little surprised to realize that the whole time they were talking, Dodi's tick was gone. Not one little twitch. Not a spasmodic jerk, no winking and grinning at the same time, just normal. Casper considered, for the first time since he could recall, Dodi's face was as calm as an ocean after a storm.

Chapter Nineteen

"What is she doing?" Jen paced back and forth in the parking lot, watching Carrie come out of the building only to turn around and go back in. Jen looked at Georgia, who was walking toward her from the car. Jen continued, "You know, up until two days ago, Carrie Angel couldn't wait to start this project. She's been chomping at the bit to get moving. She's been up nights, working weekends, planning every last detail, and all she's done all morning is walk in and out of the damn building."

"Did you ask her what the problem is?" Georgia handed Jen the cup of coffee they'd picked up on the way to the Phoenix Street four-plex.

"She wouldn't say. She said she'd tell me when she'd figured it out."

"Have some faith in your partner, there. She's got her reasons."

Today was the big day, the first day of the project. Neither Jen nor Carrie had slept in days. While Jen took care of the business end of things, Carrie had rented tools, gotten permits, and hand-picked a crew of skilled women she knew from the apprenticeship program, who were now standing around smoking cigarettes and chattering, Jen noticed.

Carrie worked hard readying for today. For days prior to this one, she'd marched intently around the site, examining every possible pitfall, testing machinery, rechecking measurements, and recounting materials. The entire roof was to be skinned, moldy plywood and rotting trusses removed and replaced.

It was all Jen could do to remain calm as she watched Carrie come out of the building again. Georgia brought dozens of boxes of donuts and a cooler full of steaming coffee, enough for the whole crew.

"There she goes again," Jen said, and sipped from her cup.

The sun was rising and steaming up the dewy grass. It was a perfect spring morning to begin the job.

"I'm going down there." Jen said, and headed into the yard.

"Oh, for Pete's sake," Georgia hurried on her heels. "Now you calm down." She caught up and then placed a hand on Jen's arm. "This is going to be a long process," Georgia whispered, "Let's be gentle."

"I will," Jen said, but didn't feel it.

"What's the matter?" Jen asked, entering the building as Carrie was climbing down off a ladder leading to the ceiling.

"I'm worried."

"About what? Everybody's ready to start."

"This load-bearing truss." Carrie said, pointing upwards.

"Meaning?"

"I hadn't noticed it till yesterday after we got the flooring up, my boot hit a spongy section."

"What does that mean?"

"It means that there's bad termite damage. I just checked the length of the beam. It's sawdust that's holding up the second story."

"What are we going to do?" Jen asked.

"We have to replace it."

"Okay, so do it. We've got all these women on the clock."

"It's not that simple. We need a crane, and I don't see us getting one here today, on a Saturday."

"Is there any other way to do it?" Georgia asked.

Carrie took a deep breath, "Let me think."

"The carpenters and this equipment are all on the clock."

"I understand," Carrie said. "But, people can get hurt if we don't do this right, never mind the long-term consequences."

Jen was getting impatient. "No, *you* don't understand, every minute we're standing here discussing this is costing us a dollar!"

"Better than a life," Carrie noted.

"Why didn't you know this before?" Jen asked, accusingly.

Carrie looked pained, but remained composed. "I didn't know because until yesterday, the floor and ceiling were covering it up. Now they're not, I can see it."

"Okay then," Georgia stepped in, and took Jen's arm. "Let's not go there, let's think this through. Carrie is not making the board rotten, so let's don't go killing the messenger."

"Yes, you're right. I'm sorry, Carrie."

"What's going on down there?" Sheckie yelled from the top of the scaffolding. "We gonna rock on this thing or not?"

Carrie raised her palm to him, but leaned into Jen when she got close, "A dollar a minute is nothing compared to the damage that can occur if a load bearing beam cracks and comes down our heads—okay?"

"Okay." Jen took a deep breath. "But damn it! I want to get this started!"

"Let me think," Carrie said, pulling away from Jen and Georgia, beginning a small circle walk around the yard. She tugged on her bottom lip and searched the ground.

While Carrie and Sheckie went to get the materials, Jen dropped Georgia off at home, and then drove back to the apartment. Today's glitch put them over budget, and not in a little way. It was going to hurt them. Jen had sold every last piece of jewelry she owned, so her options were limited, but was one last resource, and she knew it was time to use it. Climbing the steps two at a time, Jen went straight to her bedroom closet and reached to the dark back corner where her sealskin coat was hanging in a garment bag. She yanked it from the rod, and slung it over her shoulder.

"Evan!" She called out as she entered the jewelry store.

"Ah, Mrs. Manners," the wispy man said, slipping from around the counter and taking her hand. "How might I help you today?"

"I know you don't deal in furs, Evan, but today, I am desperate. Today, so many people are depending on me. I need your help in getting as much as fast as possible." She unzipped the bag, and pulled out the luxurious fur. Evan reached a hand and smoothed his palm over the jacket. He then took it from her, slipping it off its hanger and right onto his own shoulders. Somehow, the jacket fit Evan better than it had ever fit Jen; she couldn't believe it, but the man transformed the coat. He catwalked toward the mirror, twirled twice, pressed his face into the sleek collar, and when he returned, he offered her better than half of what she'd originally paid. On the way out, she kissed the bills and slid them into her bra.

It was noon before Carrie and Sheckie returned from Davies' Steel Company. While the fabrication shop was closed for the weekend, Sheckie happened to know Lou Davies, a fellow biker, and convinced the guy to roll out of bed and open his shop doors for them. Carrie found what she was looking for almost immediately in a pile of irregulars: a twelve foot long by twelve inches wide by one inch thick length of a steel beam that had irregular holes the size of quarters and dimes bored along its length. Lou gave it to her for nickels; he said, "You're doin' me a favor gettin' that piece a shit outta my shop." But Carrie knew that in reality, Lou was doing Sheckie a favor—for what? She didn't know, she didn't ask, but she was grateful the debt was there to get called in. With the robotic hoist they loaded the heavy unwieldy beam onto Lou's big flatbed truck, and he followed them to the apartment site.

"I wish I could stay to help," Lou said, "but I gotta take my kid to baseball."

Carrie shook his hand, thanked him again, and then hugged him.

Carrie had all eight of her crew lift the beam and set it across four saw horses, and then they followed her into the building, along with Sheckie, and trailed by Jen and Georgia who were mostly onlookers.

"Okay," Carrie said to the group, and pointed up. "You see that blackish beam running from there—" her arm swung from the north wall "—to there?" and landed on the opposite southerly wall. "We are going to take that out." She looked at the serious expressions of the faces in front of her.

Pat asked, "Load bearing?"

Carrie nodded.

The group inhaled and murmured.

"Then, we're going to replace it."

"With the steel beam?"

"Yes."

"How're we going to get it up there without a lift?" one of the women asked.

Carrie grinned, "With leverage, of course."

She put four of the carpenters to the task of sandwiching and bolting the steel beam between two equally sized lengths of pine board—"making it even heavier," one woman noted as she tightened the last lug with her wrench.

The others set to the job of knocking out the rotted board without the entire building coming down on their heads. They braced two-by-fours lining the length of the beam under the adjoining joists, and with a Sawz-All and hammer claws, the infested old board was so soft, holey, and dry that it came down quickly and dustily. Carrie said to Jen, "It's a miracle this place is still standing."

The whole operation of getting the huge beam up twelve feet and onto the side ledges that held the original beam relied on the following: four wheeled scaffolds (each one-buck high), eight concrete blocks, two sheet rock lifts, two ropes, nine women, and one Sheckie.

It happened in slow, meticulous stages, and Carrie's orchestration of what appeared to be a monumental task mesmerized Jen, who stood on the sidelines with Georgia and watched her friend and partner take control to accomplish the seemingly impossible feat.

First, the women lifted and then slid the long wood and steel beam onto two of the wheeled scaffolds and easily pushed it into the building. Once in place, the women lifted one end to shoulder height and placed the board on the left scaffold, then repeated this on the right scaffold. At turns, on either side, the women stepped the beam six inches at a time up the staggered concrete blocks until the length of it hovered above them at around eight feet. It was here, while the beam steadied on the top block, that two carpenters below simultaneously hand-cranked the sheetrock lifts to meet the beam. Above them still, swinging from the ceiling rafters of the second story, long lengths of rope were looped. On the ground to the left stood Sheckie with the first length of rope, and Pat to the right with the second. The women on each scaffolding slung the ropes under the ends of beam, and on one-two-*three*, Sheckie and Pat pulled them, lifting and guiding the beam while women on either side slid the big board onto the sheetrock lifts. All together, they worked like a finely tuned mechanism: pulling, lifting, guiding, and slipping the beam onto its ledges: "Like butta!" Carrie called from the top of her ladder where, twelve feet up, she smacked the board into place with a mallet while another carpenter on the ladder across the room did the same—making it perfectly straight.

After securing the board, and shuffling down the ladder, Carrie ordered the bracing to be removed. They stood, eyes skyward, breaths held, as the two-by-fours were knocked away, and the ceiling stayed in place.

"Yeah!" The cheer went up as the last two-by-four came down. The women circled Carrie, patting her back, congratulating her and themselves all the way around.

Later, after the crew had gone home for the day, Jen, Sheckie, and Carrie sat at the picnic table under the big tree at the apartment complex.

"Carrie, you were amazing, today," Jen said.

"Seriously," Sheckie concurred. "I can't believe we got that all done."

"I can't believe you knew how to get that all done," Jen marveled. "Without a crane, even!"

"And with a bunch of girls, even!" Sheckie said, teasingly.

Carrie shook her head, "You joke, but the fact of the matter is, I've watched men on crews do the stupidest most dangerous things with sheer brute force, when in my mind, the whole time I'd be watching them, I'd be thinking—but if you just used a board to pry that up, or a rope to lower that down, or even a little WD-40 to loosen the muther . . . but more often than not those jugheads would be huffin' and puffin' and blowin' a hernia or disk or wreckin' a neck because they wouldn't take the time to figure it out how to do it without all that hurt. Women? We, on the other hand, know we can't rely on our strength, and so from our beginnings we've been using leverage for everything."

"Too, true," Jen thought, considering how far this extended to everything from carpentry to sex. Women understood very well how leverage worked in every situation, but leverage, she considered, did not always translate to power. It was merely a means to an end, and if you didn't think out the long-term, as she had not with Hempy, then leverage is no more useful than a nail without a hammer—or a marriage without a partnership.

Carrie unpacked the last box of the move. She looked around. The place was still unfinished but livable. It was the first of the renovations to be done. While the walls were not yet painted and the ceiling mud was still drying, the kitchen and bathroom were in good working order, and the place had gotten the city's certificate of occupation.

She and the boys moved in first, since she wanted to be first on the work site in the morning. She'd wrangled every unemployed female electrician, plumber, and carpenter who had gone through the state-sponsored program onto the jobs. *I can't pay you what I'd like, but I'll pay at the end of every day,* she promised, and she knew the trade-off was worth it for them. Having spent so many hours of a life waiting for money to come in, she knew the daily wage was much needed.

So many had heard about Carrie Angel's renovation project and offered her services that Carrie had to limit the daily workforce, but they were all on the list Jen had compiled for the *Angels & Manners Complete Home Services* file, and she could pretty much count on a full crew most days. Sheckie'd moved his shop operations over since the garage was in pretty good shape; built tough like a garage should be, so it was mostly a matter of cleaning out the wreckage and replacing the roof. Sheckie and a couple of his motorcycle buddies had the hydraulics working soon after the electric was hooked up. There was a lot to take care of, a lot more to do, and not only for this building. They had their first customer for a foreclosure clean-out lined up.

Now that she and the boys were settled right here, and summer was upon them, she thought she'd have more time to get the other units ready. Jen and Emily, and Sheckie were hoping to move in soon, but Carrie was concentrating on the next rental; without its income, things were going to be tight.

Feeling the ache in her back, she looked at her watch, confirming the late hour. The boys were both tucked into their rooms; she could hear Casper doing his evening exercises (hundreds of repetitions of sit-ups and push-ups) and Tex chattering away on the phone to Emily when there was a light tapping on the front door. Carrie didn't like the way the hairs on the back of her neck raised. Only Sheckie, Jen, and a handful of others even knew she'd moved out here, away from civilization, with the exception of a few dark businesses across the road and one or two houses behind them. She could hear the river rushing by, down below. The tapping came again, only this time a bit louder. She glanced around the kitchen and grabbed a rolling pin from the countertop. On tiptoes she was able to squint through the peephole and called out "Who is it?" but she saw who it was before he had a chance to identify himself. Dill was standing right there on her doorstep, unannounced, after he'd driven her off the road. She hadn't seen him since that day, and she was doing her best to keep it that way. She slid the barrel of the deadbolt into place, and kept a tight grip on the rolling pin in her hand, her wooden club.

"What do you want?" she asked through the door.

"I want to see Tex," he said, his voice low, and something else, something she couldn't quite identify, but somehow familiar.

"Does he know you're here?"

"No."

"How'd you find out we moved?" She was not sure what to do. She was stalling. He was Tex's father, but he'd never dropped by to see the kid.

He shook his head and seemed to grin. "Did you forget? You changed your address for the support payments."

"Why didn't you call first?"

"I didn't think anybody here would see me," he said, and then she recalled that old familiar softness in his tone, the one belonging to the kinder, gentler Dill. The one she'd married, not the prick she'd wound up divorcing.

"Hang on," she said, and went down the hallway, knocking on both boys' bedroom doors.

"Your father is here," she said when they'd joined her in the hallway.

Tex craned his neck. "Where?"

"He's outside. I didn't let him in."

"Are you going to?"

"It's up to you." She looked from son to son, so different from each other: Tex, built solid with dark red curls and pale green eyes, and Casper tall and lanky, blond and blue-eyed, yet, both at this moment were each hovering between his four-year-old self and the man he was meant to become.

"What does he want with us?" Casper asked.

"Not you, Casp," Carrie said. "He asked for your brother."

Tex looked startled.

"Alone? Not by himself, he can't," Casper said, his fists balling up.

"What do you want to do, Tex?" Carrie asked him.

For a moment, he looked like a lost little boy. Then he pushed back his shoulders and lifted his chin. "If nothing else I'm curious about what the sperm-donor has to say." He walked tall down the hallway till he got to the door, then turned and waved Carrie and Casper nearer. "Don't leave me," he mouthed, and then opened the door.

"Dad." Tex pushed his curls back from his forehead, and then shoved his hands into his pockets.

Carrie noticed that Dill had to look upward to meet his son's gaze. But there were those same piercing green eyes, that same strong chin, the tilt of the head, nearly mimicking each other. While Dill's sandy hair was cropped close, showing gray at the temples, Tex's curls cascaded to his shoulders, and he was attempting a faint reddish goatee.

Dill cleared his throat. "Tex things have been tough lately. I, uh, I've been doing a lot of thinking, worrying, to be honest, and well," he laughed nervously, "and going to therapy, even. I realize that I've not been around . . ." He seemed to search the porch light for words, as if they were riding the backs of the kamikaze moths smashing themselves against the hot lamp. "I don't feel like we've spent much time together and that's wrong." He stopped, seeming to need a breath. "I just wanted to say I'm sorry about that . . ." He paused as if waiting for some sign from Tex that his words hadn't, like those kamikaze moths, exploded on impact.

"Go on," Tex said, with little emotion in his voice. Carrie could only see his profile. She could tell he was holding himself very still, but beyond that, she had no idea what was going on in her son's head or heart.

"I want to make things better," he said, and then looked over Tex's shoulder, toward Carrie. "I'm sorry for making things hard for every-body," as close to an apology for running her off the road as she was going to get, Carrie figured.

"That it?" Tex asked, officiously.

"Almost," Dill said, and then dug into his coat pocket and pulled out what appeared to be a piece of shiny silver metal, but Carrie couldn't quite make out what it was. Dill was looking down at it, and then he held it out to Tex. "I, uh . . . I want you to have this."

Tex looked at the object in his father's hand but didn't immediately take it. He'd ducked to see it better, and then leaned against the door jam with his fists still shoved in his pockets.

"What is it?" he asked.

Dill smiled a little, and looking over Tex's shoulder toward Casper perched on the arm of the nearby couch. "In better times, these were my flight wings." He held them out. "They're a little bent. They had a run in with an idiot, I'm afraid." He smiled.

Slowly Tex pulled his hand from his pocket and took the wings from his father. He turned them over.

"I want you to have them," Dill said, again, only more tentatively.

Tex looked at him. "Why?"

"What?"

"Why do you want me to have them?"

For a moment, this seemed to stop Dill. And then Carrie saw him swallow hard, watched as his eyes glistened, and heard the tremor in his voice when he said, "Because you're my son. My first born and I love you."

Carrie couldn't help the stinging at her eyes as tears filled and spilled.

Tex nodded, staring down at the bent wings. He shoved them in his pocket. "Okay, then," he said, and watched his father swipe a coat sleeve against damp eyes. Tex held out his hand to shake, and Dill pulled him close for an awkward shoulder-patting hug, and then the two stepped back to their respective sides of the threshold. There they shuffled, and then gripping the doorknob, Tex said, "Well, see ya."

Instead of turning, Dill stopped the closing door with his foot, startling all of them. Tex jumped a little, and Carrie noticed Casper on the rise, but Dill said, "I was thinking that maybe we could go do something together, sometime."

This seemed to startle Tex even more. "You and me?" His voice rose just enough to hint at the fear of the unknown. "Alone?"

"Sure."

"What would we do?" Tex seemed to be posing this not just to Dill but to himself; prior to the moment, the possibility of spending time alone with his father was so remote that he hadn't even toyed with the idea in ages.

Dill shrugged, "Whatever you want. We'll do something that *you* want to do."

"Really?"

Carrie could almost hear the wheels spinning inside her son's brain, concocting a most awkward venue for his father to sweat through: a fashion show, ballet performance, or maybe he'd really make him squirm and make him sit through a literary reading, or even a drag show.

But instead, what she heard her son say seemed the kindest thing of all. "I'm interested in the military uniforms from the past; I think there are some interesting elements that I'd like to incorporate into my new designs. Would you be interested in going to the Military Museum on Post sometime? Can you get me in with your ID?"

Dill seemed to brighten, relief smoothed his face, and he said, "Sure! We could do that. There's a whole section on all the different time periods."

"That'd be cool."

Then Dill ventured, "Have you ever been to the Army Navy store over in Raeford?"

"Nope."

"They've got some cool stuff there. Maybe we could go do that, too?"

"When?" Tex asked, as if he didn't pin Dill down, it might never happen.

But the man kept surprising them all when he said, "Saturday? Morning?"

"I could do that," Tex said.

"All right then. I'll pick you up at nine."

They all three watched Dill walk down the steps and toward his big truck, the load on his shoulders a little lighter than when he'd arrived.

"Well, that was something new," Casper said, pleased.

"Wonder what got into him?" Tex thought out loud.

"What matters is that he made the effort," Carrie was able to say, and actually mean it.

"We'll see if he shows up on Saturday," Tex said, closing the door on the retreating tail lights of the big truck. Carrie noticed the bent silver wings gripped tightly in Tex's palm as he went to his room.

"Do I look okay?" Casper asked, standing in front of the mirror, slicking down a suddenly spiking cowlick for the hundredth time only to see it spring again, as if it had a mind of its own. He'd swapped his yellow tracksuit for a light blue V-neck sweater and a pair of pressed khakis. Carrie hadn't seen him dressed like a human in months. He'd begun to remind her of a giant bee perpetually garbed in his school colors: yellow and black. Forever wearing his sweats, uniform, or his pricy, Letterman jacket (the one Dill had bought him for his birthday.) She was relieved to see him in other colors.

261

"You look great, honey. Your sweater brings out your eyes." She smiled as his ears pinked at the tips.

He went to the window and searched the road.

"Casper, come away from there and set the table," Carrie said, trying to distract her nervous son. He straightened an un-crooked picture frame on the way to the cupboard, swiped a clean counter with his palm, and rubbed shiny utensils with a towel before setting them on the table. In between, he checked the windows.

"Honey, it's not even four, Sarah's not due until five; you need to calm down," Carrie finally said after all his fidgeting started making her jumpy.

"I know, I know. I just want to be ready."

Carrie stopped herself from laughing. They had been *ready* four days ago. When Carrie suggested Casper invite Sarah over for dinner, so they could all meet and get to know his new *friend* (he insisted on calling her), you would have thought they were preparing for the Queen of England. Casper went into hyper-cleaning-mode. Up at all hours, dusting, wiping, sweeping, vacuuming, a week before the girl was due to arrive.

When Carrie pointed out that the apartment was only just a month old, brand new everything, and asked how dirty it could possibly have gotten, Casper merely gave her an exasperated look. While she and Tex tolerated his rules about taking off their shoes, not eating in the living room, or even sitting on the couch (they'd watched television from the kitchen table for three nights), Carrie put her foot down when he demanded they have Filet Mignon for the dinner, and instead decided on lasagna and salad.

"Mom, remember, try not to ask her too many embarrassing questions, okay?"

"I'll do my best."

"And, try not to swear. Especially don't drop the F-bomb, okay? I mean, Sarah's not a prude or anything, it's just, well, you know . . ."

"I get it, Bud. No fucking F-word."

"Mom!"

"Sorry. I'll shut the fuck up."

He stamped his foot.

"I'm kidding, Casp. Lighten up. It's going to be fine. I'll be on my best behavior, I promise."

"Are you wearing that?" he asked about her jeans and black turtleneck.

"What's the matter with this?"

"Don't you have a dress?"

Carrie put down her knife, and bunched a fist, propping it on her hip. "Listen, mister, I—we—are not going to be anybody but ourselves tonight—do you understand? I am not wearing a dress, your brother will probably paint his fingernails, we're not serving fancy steak that we, ourselves, have never tasted before, and I'm not going to scrub at dirt that doesn't exist. If this girl doesn't like us for us, then, well, I don't know why you'd like her to begin with . . ."

Carrie went back to chopping the vegetables for the salad, and Casper could tell by the shift of her shoulders that he'd hurt her feelings.

"Mom, I'm sorry. It's not Sarah. It's me. Sarah wouldn't care if you showed up in your work boots and served hot dogs. She's not like that. It's me who's being a jerk. I'm sorry, you look great, and the lasagna smells great, and the house looks great." He hugged his mother's shoulders. "I really appreciate it. It's just . . ."

"I know, honey, it's just the first time you've ever had a girl over."

"Right."

"I'll do my best to make you proud."

"Mom, you do make me proud. It's Tex I'm worried about."

"Well, you might as well give that up. You're not responsible for him, and lord knows, you can't control him."

"Too true, little bro!" Tex said, appearing from his bedroom. His now long reddish curls were tied back in a ponytail with a modest blue ribbon. He wore a white cotton oxford with a loosely knotted navy tie, khakis, and loafers, and he was clean-shaven. He was also sporting gold-rimmed glasses that he didn't need, completing his prep-school boy appearance.

"Holy crap!" Casper exclaimed.

"Oh, my, god . . ." Carrie was stunned speechless. She'd seen her eldest son in every wild costume she could imagine and then some. Lately, the more outrageous they'd become, the less startled she was, but this? This was the most shocking outfit she'd ever seen him wear. "Tex, you look, well, you look amazing. So very handsome."

He grinned, and pressed his palms against his slacks. "I feel like a lawyer," he said.

"How do you feel like a *lawyer?*" Casper asked.

"I don't know. Something litigious about a rope around one's throat, I suppose."

"Help your brother set the table, would you?"

"Of course," Tex said, more than cooperatively, as if it were second nature to him. "Casp, I'm assuming bed-wetting, thumb sucking, and breast-feeding until you were seven are off-limit subjects, tonight, yes?"

"*Mom!*" Casper whirled around.

"Tex, don't upset your brother."

At exactly five o'clock, a black Mercedes pulled up into the driveway. They all huddled at the door, watching it circle and stop.

"A Mercedes, huh?" Tex noticed.

"Her dad's a doctor, is all. It doesn't mean anything," Casper defended the car.

"Well, let's don't all stand here gawking." Carrie stepped back. "Casper, you go out, say hello to her father. Tex, you wait at the door."

"Shall I greet her with a martini?"

"Tex, I swear if you say or do anything to embarrass your brother tonight, I will personally tell the story about how, when you were three, you painted your penis green, stuck a flower shaped butter-cookie onto the end of it, and ran naked from room to room yelling, "I'm a daisy! I'm a daisy!"

"Mother!"

"I swear I will."

"Fine. I'll behave."

The evening had gone just as awkwardly and politely as it should have considering it was a *meet the family* moment, Carrie told Sheckie the next morning when she wandered to his shop with her coffee.

"She's a cute girl. Smart. Self-confident. Not like I ever was at that age. Or this age for that matter," Carrie said.

"So you liked her?"

"Sure. She's sweet. She complimented the apartment, asked about my carpentry work, flattered Tex by telling him she thought he'd been the best in *Brigadoon*. Tex asked her things like *Did she believe in fairies*, but rather than getting flustered, she told a story about how she'd once seen a fairy in Ireland when she was a little girl on a visit. Shut Tex right up. Other than that, it was pleasantly uneventful."

Sheckie laughed. "Well good."

She looked at her watch. "So, you called me here for this *meeting*, what's up?"

"Want me to top off your mug there? I've got a pot on," He thumbed over his shoulder.

She sat down at the table, and he poured the coffee.

"How's the job going?"

She shrugged. "Good. I mean, it's good to be working. Not what I expected to be doing, but it's paying the bills. If you could see what people leave behind in these foreclosed houses, it would shock you. Sometimes it's disgusting to see the waste and loss, or chilling to witness the anger in a smashed-up toilet, or the desperation in an appliance-gutted kitchen, but worse is how heartbreaking the small things can be, like a little girl's doll left in a closet, ya know?

He nodded, "Sad," he said, but Carrie didn't think he was really listening. He sat across from her, and sipped his coffee.

Carrie thought something was going on. Actually, she'd thought there was something going on for a couple of weeks; Sheckie'd been preoccupied at best, distant at worst. She'd let him get to it. Her days of figuring out what bothered men were long gone.

"There's something I need to talk with you about. About Amy," he said, quickly, as if rushing each word to pass the other.

"Your daughter?"

He nodded. He painfully described the car accident, the one that had paralyzed her from the waist down and had killed her grandfather, the driver, in vague details. He talked about her condition and progress, since, and how—he had to stop to take a breath.

Carrie reached a hand across the table. "Sheck, when did this happen?"

"Right after we met."

"Why didn't you tell me?"

He shrugged. "I don't know. I think it was because I couldn't deal with it myself. After that, I just didn't want to burden you; you had enough of your own shit going on. After a while, it just never came up."

"Is that why she's never visited?"

"That and a bunch of stuff." A shadow crossed his brow, and he frowned. She could tell he was trying to find words, and so she sat still, and waited.

"There's this special clinic in LA that might help Amy walk again. We're not getting our hopes up, but we want to give it a try."

"That's great! So when does she go?"

"Actually, we're all going to go."

"What?"

"I'm going to go, too. I need to be there."

"But you bought into the duplex?" Carrie was confused.

"It's new information. We just learned about this place. We were surprised they could take her so quickly."

"Sure. I understand." She smiled. "Guess we'll just have to collect your mail for a while." She watched him turn his back to her, and then as if deciding, he turned and looked at her. There was sadness in his eyes.

"We're going to do it as a family," he said. "These are ongoing treatments, probably for the rest of her life."

Carrie sat upright. "Forever? You're going forever?"

He nodded.

"You're getting back together with your ex?"

"I'm sorry," he said.

266

"The apartment? The shop?"

"I'll talk to Jen about buying me out."

"Us?" She let slip.

"She's my daughter, Carrie. I can't fly back and forth while she goes through this. I need to be there."

Carrie thought about how hard it had been to get Dill to even make a phone call to his sons, never mind visit them, and here was Sheckie willing to move all the way across the country for his kid.

"Of course you do," she said, knowing she would do the same for her own. She stood and rounded the table, wrapping her arms around him, kissing the top of his head; she couldn't help the tears that came, nor could he.

"Always seems like bad-timing for us, Carrie."

"Maybe not so much bad, but never right, that's for sure." She squeezed his neck, gave him one last pat, and then headed for the door.

"I love you, Carrie," he said, before she left.

"I know you do. I'll see ya around."

She fled the shop as if fleeing the scene of a crime. Once she closed the door behind her, Carrie tore down the hill, raced past the apartments, out the driveway, across the road, and to the river. She found the head of a path that Casper had shown her, and once she'd been enveloped by its brushy edges and shading trees, she slowed her trot, and began a foot-dragging walk as if she'd just been kicked in the stomach; Sheckie's news had been a sucker-punch.

Finding a clump of sun-warmed boulders on the edge of the lapping water, she climbed up and sat down. She pulled a crumpled pack of cigarettes from her pocket, lit one and inhaled, holding the smoke in her lungs like she used to do as a teenager smoking pot and getting the *most from the toke*, as she and her friends used to joke. But this was no flowery bud, this was tobacco and it burned, and she let it, because that's exactly how she was feeling in every other organ, so she might as well tear up her lungs, too. Finally, she exhaled.

Sheckie was leaving. She finally let her mind settle on it. Just like that. She thought he said that he was back with his ex, but admittedly, she'd barely heard much after he'd said he was leaving. Blind-sided and stupid, that's how she felt, both at the same time. She threw a pebble into the water and watched it sink into the muddy bottom.

He'd said there was a faraway hope in a faraway place that might help his crippled daughter walk, and even if that possibility were as remote as the moon, there was still the possibility that his little family could make a new beginning in LA. Carrie took a long drag and slowly released a plume of smoke, letting her lungs, shoulders, brow, and finally brain rest with that notion—if Sheckie had made any other choice, she would, she had to admit, have been disappointed in him.

She thought of Casper, and her heart ached. He would be devastated. Another man disappointing the boy. Another father-figure ducking out. How he would resolve this in his own manhood, she didn't know, and worried for him. Would he decide against kids altogether? Or have a baseball team's worth, become *Super-Dad* just to prove the contrast to these other so-called *dads*? It was only when imagining her son's pain that tears welled, and she choked back a sob, surprising herself. She swiped a sleeve against her cheek. She'd miss Sheckie, for sure. He was a great guy. They would all miss him. Then, a feeling arose that confused her; took her completely off-guard. She did a *feelings check,* as Pam her one-time counselor called it. *Which emotions are arising?*

Reconsidering her feelings since receiving Sheckie's news, she could intimately trace her morphing emotions: shock, panic, fear, confusion, disappointment, anger, sadness, up to this very moment. Now *gauging her middle (*where the *truth* lies) she discovered she was feeling relief.

Relief.

This was surprising. Confusing and surprising. She understood the succession: *fear* to *anger* to *sadness*—predictable, really. Grief? Sure. But, relief? Odd, she considered. Wiping her face dry, taking a deep breath and stubbing out her cigarette on her boot heel, she pocketed the remains. That was the feeling—the confusion—that was what was odd—she was *relieved.* Sheckie was leaving. How could that be?

Lately, they'd become closer than ever. Obviously, the business partnership, the living arrangements, occasionally sex in each others' bed. Everyone, she guessed, including herself, was figuring that eventually she and Sheckie would move in together, and one day probably get married.

As this exited her mind, she felt the only word she could come up with was—*expansive*. This made her smile. She said it out loud—*Expansive*—and laughed because it sounded like a drawled version of *expensive*, and when she said it again, her giggles led to hiccups.

My what an expansive *mind you have, Carrie Angel.*

Yes, it'll cost you to pick it.

And your heart—equally as expansive?

No. Not open for business.

Well, not exactly, she thought. More like not willing to go back in time. Not willing to settle for the obvious. Not after so long, not after so much work. It wasn't like she wouldn't have made a good life with Sheckie, she could have, but if she had, she would never have known if there was another life she could have made for herself—one completely of her own doing instead of from happen-stance that came rolling in. It's why she married Dill after her parents died and left her alone and unprepared; it's probably why she took up with Sheckie in the first place, needing someone big and strong to lean on, but she was no longer alone nor was she unprepared. A huge part of her wanted to see what she could do with her own life, rather than sitting back and watching what other people might do to it, and for this she was relieved that Sheckie was going, because now she wouldn't have to wonder about whether she could've done it on her own without some man to cling to, and she wouldn't have to ruin it, later, in order to find out.

Chapter Twenty

Jen stood at the window of her makeshift kitchen-slash-office, looking across the landscape that included a glimpse of the nearby river. Still hoping that purchasing the Phoenix Road property was a smart move, in spite of the fact that nothing was going as she'd anticipated. This last bit, with Sheckie suddenly announcing his leaving, well, she'd spent many a sleepless night going over the books, looking for ways to cut corners, but they'd cut so many there was little left to shave. She tried not to burden Carrie too much with the money side of things. It wasn't that Carrie couldn't handle the bad news. In fact, for Carrie the next "hard-knock" always seemed inevitable; she took them in her stride, as if expecting them, always more surprised when things went right. Perhaps this attitude eliminated a lot of disappointment. It certainly wasn't one Jen had mastered.

Jen was still triple-timing it between Edible Feast, Rona's Real Estate, and *Angels and Manners Complete Home Specialists*. Carrie was managing the field-side of the business, but she too was still working a bunch of little jobs here and there, trying to make it all break even. The only bright spot of the day was that someone was interested in renting Sheckie's shop, so she had her fingers crossed.

They hadn't been able to lease the fourth apartment. Well, that wasn't exactly true, they'd rented it to a bachelor who threw a giant party that included liquor, naked girls, and marijuana. Jen had called the cops; they evicted him on the spot. With Carrie and herself occupying only two of the four apartments, and Sheckie moving out of the third, it was all they could do to stay above water. She was so lost in her own thoughts that she was startled to feel the arms slip around her waist from behind, and welcomed the soft lips on her neck, happy for this one peaceful spot in her otherwise harried world. "I forgot you were here," she said to Georgia. "You're so quiet."

"You weren't here," Georgia said, massaging Jen's shoulders, "You were over the river and through the woods," she soothed.

"Only to discover that grandma's house included a big bad bill collector who's about to huff and puff my little house down, if I don't rent one of these apartments ASAP."

Georgia stepped away and reached for the two cups of coffee she'd set on the desk when she walked in, and handed one to Jen. "Is that all?"

"It's the beginning, I'm afraid. What with Sheckie leaving. Well, it complicates the already complicated. You sure you don't want to leave that darling little cottage in Haymont and come live in a dinky apartment next door?"

"Very tempting," Georgia said. "But I'll have to pass. No luck at all with renting?"

"No. It seems we're just a tad too far from Post, and a tad too close to the railroad tracks and a tad too isolated or a tad too populated, people are so picky. And if they're not picky, well, after we had to kick out the Blues Brother, I'm picky. Do you know that six female GIs wanted to rent it?"

"Six? That'd be awfully tight."

"Oh, they had a grand scheme for saving money: since they were all on different schedules and would be in the field, deployed, or working nights, they figured they'd save on quarters by all piling in here. What they didn't figure, as they were reeling off all the reasons it made sense for them, was that it conjured all the reasons why it didn't make sense for us."

"Can you imagine all that racket?"

"In and out, day and night."

"And women? All cramped together?"

"All cramping together, how 'bout that?" Jen laughed at her own joke.

"No kidding, though, right?"

"It's been hard enough renting out one apartment, but having to rent out two; it's just one more headache."

"When does Sheckie leave?"

"End of the month. So we've got a little time."

"How's Carrie doing about Sheckie leaving?" Georgia ventured.

"Honestly, I think she's relieved."

"Relieved? I thought they were together? You know—lovers and all."

"I think they have been, casual, or maybe cautious is a better word. But she seems at peace with it."

"Has she mentioned her feelings?"

"Mostly she said she didn't think she was ready to settle down since she'd just got *upright*," Jen said, and smiled. "Her word, not mine. She said it made everything clear for her. She admires Sheckie for sticking by his kid, and then confided that she was worried about her own. Right now, I think she's more concerned for Casper's feelings about Sheckie leaving than her own; he's taking it pretty hard."

"Poor little guy. He loves that big man, doesn't he?"

Jen sipped her drink. "He does, and considering the dickweed he got stuck with for a father, I can't say as I blame him for wanting a replacement dad."

A powder blue Volkswagen pulled into the driveway, and Jen watched Sylvia Manners climb out. Her long legs carried her gracefully like a dancer and Jen could see the resemblance between the half-sisters more clearly as each matured. Since Hempy's death, Sylvia and Emily had been spending time together. Today, they were going to dinner and a movie. Before the young woman made it to the office, Emily came flying out of her room, waving as she passed. "Bye, Mom! Bye, Georgia! We're going to the movies later! Don't wait up! Love you!" And she was through the door. Jen watched as she met Sylvia with a hug. They watched the younger girl chattering away, and Sylvia smiling and nodding.

"It's nice that Sylvia spends time with Emily," Georgia remarked.

"Yeah, she's a great role model. Smart, independent. I like that

Emily has that connection. It hasn't always been this way. They were quite estranged for a long time. My fault, really. I really was a wicked step-mother."

"Oh, come on, I can't imagine you being wicked."

Jen raised an eyebrow.

Georgia grinned, "Okay, I can imagine you being *that* kind of wicked."

"I was young and jealous of Sylvia and Ruth and any involvement Hempy had with them. I didn't make it easy for Sylvia to have a relationship with her father, any more than Tiffany made it easy for Emily, and for all the same reasons."

"I can see that. What that man put all of you women through is despicable. Look at all the female lives he fucked up while attending to his needs."

"This is going to sound bad, but," Jen bit her lip, "I honestly think all of our lives have improved since he died."

"That's not bad, that's just the truth."

"I feel liberated by his absence, in a very different way than when we divorced. With divorce, somehow the continuation of the financial and parental relationships without the love and partnership is more entrapping, more shackling, than when you're married to him. If that makes sense."

"Sure it does. Bonded by the courts rather than the hearts. How can it ever turn out good? Whatever happened to the first Mrs. Manners?"

"I did ask Sylvia about Ruth, and she told me that her mother had remarried a nice dentist, they have a son together; they live in Arizona where they play a lot of golf."

"Good for Ruth."

"Yeah, good for Ruth. Good for me. And good for Emily and Sylvia, only they don't know that his passing has liberated them, too."

"Oh, they might know it. Look at them, yammering away to each other, they didn't have that before he died."

"The only one who's not been liberated is Tiffany,' Jen said. "I heard he left them in financial shambles. The house on Robin's Egg is on the market; I saw the listing in Rona's office. She's going to take a beating in this market, not to mention the second and third mortgages it's carrying. She'll never get enough to pay them all off."

As if mentioning her name could conjure her, a silver Volvo station wagon, like Tiffany's, pulled in. Jen couldn't imagine what she would be doing here. Jen and Georgia watched to see Tiffany emerging from the vehicle, then rounding to the back door where she retrieved twin toddlers.

"Holy shit," Jen said.

"Who's that?"

"That's Tiffany!" Jen turned to Georgia, surprise taking over her face. "Can you believe it? It's like I summoned her!"

"That's creepy. Why'd you do that?"

"I didn't."

"She looks familiar."

"You remember her. She's the one who tried to embarrass me at Edible Feast, my first day. You came to my rescue." She leaned over and kissed Georgia's cheek. "My hero from the get-go."

"Oh, yeah, I remember. She looks a lot rougher today than she did then, I have to say."

The doorbell rang, and when Jen opened it, there she stood; holding two somewhat disheveled little girls by each hand. Jen hadn't seen them for months.

"Tiffany?"

"Can I talk to you?"

"Sure, come in." Jen stepped aside and allowed the little pod of Manners into the room.

Tiffany glanced around the room, quickly, before landing her eyes on Jen, who noticed a familiar recklessness in them. She appeared thrown-together, Jen thought, with some satisfaction. Tiffany's dark roots were well past their six-week touch-up. Were it not for the similarly rumpled appearances of the twins, whose growth spurts were marked by the high-rise of their matching pants' legs, Jen might have savored the moment. Instead, she noticed that Tiffany was shivering, as if she were cold.

"Would you like to sit down?" Jen offered a seat at the kitchen table.

Georgia was returning from the kitchen with a third cup of coffee, and as she handed it to the shaking woman, Jen said, "This is my friend, Georgia."

"Nice to meet you, thank you," Tiffany said, taking the cup, and managed a weak smile. The little blond-headed girls stared at Jen with the same big-eyed worry that she'd seen in Emily in those early days of the divorce, and if she were to admit it, she'd seen it in Sylvia's eyes when Hempy was leaving her. Fear emanated from the three standing before her; it was an all too familiar scent. They were another calamity left in the wake of the parting of Hemphill Manners; this time, though, no follow-up wives, no fourth Mrs. Manners to crown, no new little princesses to de-throne. These two father-less girls, much like their older sisters, were each left with an abandoned, desperate mother: *Fuck you, Hempy,* she thought, as she saw the quiet terror Tiffany's fear was inspiring in them.

Georgia directed the twins to the fish tank on the far wall, the only pet Jen had allowed Emily in lieu of the cat she'd asked for; the girls busily poked their little fingers against the glass.

"What's the trouble?" Jen asked, sitting down across from Tiffany.

"We're broke," Tiffany managed. "Between Hempy's medical bills, all the credit card debt, they're threatening to foreclose on the house." The young woman sobbed, reaching into her purse and pulling out the paperwork. The little girls rushed to her side and danced nervously around their mother, her outburst of emotion spurring their own worries. "I'm barely hanging onto my adjunct position at the university," Tiffany continued, seemingly unaware of her children who disengaged and started chasing each other around Jen's desk. "But that barely covers food." Tiffany blew her nose with the tissue Jen handed her.

"Adjunct pay is pretty meager, that's for sure," Jen said. Through Hempy, she'd met many adjunct professors who had taught at a number of different colleges, just to make ends meet.

"Here," Georgia said, attending to the little girls. "Let's get you two some cookies and milk." She took them by their hands. "Would you like that?" she asked, herding them into the next room.

When they exited, Jen watched Tiffany unfold, completely breaking down. She sobbed into the wet tissue, unable to catch her breath. Jen let her get it out; she'd been there, she got it.

Finally she took some deep breaths and composed herself. "If I'd only finished my dissertation," Tiffany said, softly.

"Well, there aren't a lot of jobs in teaching these days, as you know. Maybe you're lucky you don't have those loans on top of the rest of it," Jen pointed out.

"You're right about that. I can't find a job teaching anywhere, not college or high school. I'm going to have to go bankrupt on top of losing everything." Tears welled and spilled all over again. It was obvious that she was at the end of her rope. Being a single mother could age you faster than anything, Jen thought. No matter how you got to be single.

"I just don't know how to handle any of this . . ." she dabbed at her eyes, and Jen watched as she twisted the tissue between her nervous fingers. "You must think I've got some nerve coming to you?" Tiffany looked across the desk. "But, you did it, Jen. You survived divorce. I mean, look at everything you've done on your own, as a single mother. Who else knows better what I'm going through?"

"How can I help you?" Jen finally asked, not knowing what else to say.

Tiffany blew her nose and leaned forward. "I listed the house a few months ago, but nothing is selling. Rona doesn't want to try for a short sale, I know you work for her, I was hoping you could convince her to try to find a buyer."

"Well, a short sale might not be in your best interest. You might have to owe money."

"I know, but I don't know what else to do."

"It's tough times. You might not have a choice. Foreclosure might even be preferable. I'll talk to Rona, see what she thinks."

"We have to move out. My lawyer says to distance ourselves from the whole situation. I don't know where to go, nor do I have much money."

"There's always housing," Jen ventured.

Tiffany's face crumpled. "I know you were forced to into Section Eight because of us. I'm so sorry, but Jen, I can't do it. Not with the girls. They're so little. It's so dangerous . . . so many unemployed . . ." she stared out the window, and the tears flowed.

She seemed to drift away, Jen noticed, and remembered how easy it was, in desperate times to disconnect.

Then she came back, and said, "I've got to find a place to live and a better job. I'm applying all over the country, but in the meanwhile . . . Section Eight . . . shit, it terrifies me, Jen."

"Have you applied yet?"

"Yes, and that's the other thing: Even if I qualify, there's no housing available. It'll be weeks, maybe even months." She broke down again, as if by revealing each piece of horrible news it made them all the more real. "I'm going to have to go live in a hotel, or God forbid, take the girls to live with my brother and his bitch of a wife in Vegas."

"That sounds horrible."

"Oh, believe me, he's a rich bastard. Big giant house with a big mouth wife with big giant tits, two lazy over-grown sons with gambling and drug habits, and chihuahuas, they have dozens of chihuahuas."

"That doesn't sound good, either."

"No, there's not one thing good about it," Tiffany said. "Except maybe with my new tits I could strip my way out of poverty."

"Well, let's not stoop to such drastic measures," Jen said, horrified, thinking of the little girls.

Tiffany shrugged. "I just really need Robin's Egg to sell quickly." she blew her nose, and appeared to be coming back to reality. "I understand if you want me to leave. I can't believe my own audacity being here." She looked at Jen, tears flowing. "I just feel like I'm chasing myself in circles. I don't know what to do. Where to turn. I'm sorry."

Jen reached a hand across the table, and placed it Tiffany's arm. "Look, I will try to help you sell Robin's Egg." Admittedly, she felt a tad guilty, now, about the mice incident, and even though she'd never 'fess up, she felt like she could do a little paying it backward *and* forward.

"Really?" The young woman looked surprised, and seemed to calm a bit. "It would be such a big help. You just don't know."

"Yes, I do, Tiffany."

"What a relief." She started to pack up her purse, and shuffled her chair back, making to leave.

"Wait," Jen said, stopping her retreat. "Look, I know this may sound crazy, and I can't believe I'm saying it myself, but I have an apartment, here, in this building that I can rent you. It's small, and upstairs, but could be a temporary solution to going into housing."

"Jen, I don't know what to say."

"Would you like to see it?" She stood, grabbing the key from her drawer.

"After everything . . ." Tiffany sat motionless.

"Look, we might as well help each other out. Our daughters are sisters. We should try to start acting like a family, because we are."

Tiffany's stared at Jen. "You would do that for us?"

"Didn't you come here for help?"

She nodded.

"Well, that's the kind of help I can give you."

"Why don't you hate me?"

"For what? Doing exactly what I did to Ruth and Sylvia Manners? I'd have to hate myself then, wouldn't I?"

"I'm grateful, Jen. Truly, I am. I've been horrid. I'm so sorry," and she began to weep. "Do you understand?"

Jen reached a hand and patted Tiffany's shaking shoulder. "I wish I were saying something similar to Ruth Manners, right now."

Tiffany nodded knowingly.

"Come on, I'll show you the apartment," she said.

"I'm not sure how much I can afford, Jen."

"We'll figure it out."

Later that evening, Jen, Georgia, and Carrie sat out on the front porch. The weather was warm, and there were fireflies flickering. They could hear the rush of the river across the road, but all else was quiet.

Carrie tipped her beer, and for the second time asked, "You really rented the apartment to *Tittany Manners?*"

"Carrie, you have to stop calling her that. When she moves in, you're liable to slip and call her that to her face."

"I wasn't planning on calling her anything, to be honest. I still don't get it. And do *not* tell me that you are *paying it forward.* I should never have told you that; you way overused it."

"I don't think you can overuse it."

"You wouldn't think so, but you've managed it." Carrie squinted across the road, intent on nothing. "Really? She's going to live here? What does Emily think about that?"

"Well, I haven't exactly told her yet. She's at the movies with Sylvia."

"Oh, boy, that's gonna go over like a lead balloon. Do me a favor; don't tell her till the morning—I'd like to get some sleep, tonight. I have a better idea, don't tell her at all, and just let them bump into each other."

Jen sipped her wine. "Yeah, well, Emily doesn't pay the bills around here, so she has no say-so."

"Well, that doesn't mean she won't scream one." Carrie said. "Just give me some notice before you tell her, I want to clear the premises."

Jen laughed, and leaned toward Georgia. "Carrie is afraid of teenage girls. She can't deal with the high art of the drama, the emotional intensity . . ."

"The roller coaster ride you mean," Carrie clarified. "All that energy swirling, emotions emoting, all that naval-gazing/boy-crazing/hyper-ventilazing . . ."

"You're a poet!" Jen laughed.

"A rapper, no less," Georgia concurred.

Carrie grinned. "Anyway, let's just say it's a good thing I am the mother of sons."

"Speak of the devils," Jen said, seeing Tex and Casper walking up from the river. Casper was carrying an obviously heavy pail, and Tex was swinging the flashlight to and fro.

"Hello, fair maidens," Tex waved the light in their faces, making them blink and raise their hands in self-defense.

"Tex! Knock it off!" Carrie shouted.

Instead, he held the beacon under his chin and affected some pretty scary monster faces. Casper set the bucket down with a thud.

"What'cha got there?" Georgia asked.

"I am going to make a sacred mandala out of river stones," Tex said.

"Mandala?" Carrie asked.

"It's a symbol representing the cosmos through shapes containing images or attributes of deities; I am going to represent myself as the cosmos, and pick my own personal deities."

"Casper?" Carrie asked. "Are you making a mandala, too, son?"

"No. I'm just carrying the rocks."

"Why is that?" Jen wanted to know. "I mean, why are you carrying the rocks?"

"I lost a bet. I have to carry three-and-a-half buckets of rocks up from the river."

"What was the bet?" Carrie wondered.

Casper sighed. "Tex said Mormons believe in aliens."

"So you bet him?"

"Wouldn't you?" Casper asked. "I mean, what were the chances of him being right?"

"Mormons believe in aliens?" Jen asked.

"And then some," Tex said.

"Why do you even know this?" Carrie asked.

"I'm fascinated by polygamy."

"Now, Tex," Carrie said.

"They don't do that anymore," Jen said. "Do they? Have a bunch of wives? I thought it was illegal?"

"Actually, there are fringes that still practice polygamy, today, but not mainstream Mormons," Georgia said.

Casper interrupted the women. "So yeah, that's why I'm hauling rocks, on account of Mormons worshipping aliens."

"What would you have won had the Mormons not believed in aliens?" Carrie asked.

"Three-and-a-half days of Tex not talking."

"Tex?" All three women laughed. Carrie said, "Oh, Casp, why didn't you Google the Mormons before you bet?"

"I know, Mom, imagine the peace and quiet."

"Fine!" Tex stamped his foot. "Come along little brother, that's only bucket number two . . ." He glanced toward the darkening sky. "Do you think we'll have time to get the third load tonight?"

Casper hoisted the pail and climbed the stairs in two long strides. "No, Tex, I am not going back down there in the dark, tonight. You go if you want a snake up your ass."

"No need to get personal," Tex said, and followed him inside.

"Those two," Jen said.

"Couldn't be more different," Georgia concurred.

"Yeah, well, they're both Dill's, unfortunately; don't go thinking I had any time for an affair back in those days," Carrie said, as if reading the women's minds. "If *only*."

Headlights blinded them as Sylvia's VW pulled up and into the drive, but she quickly circled around, swinging the spotlight away from the group on the porch.

"Uh, oh," Carrie said. "I'm getting out of here."

"Don't you dare," Jen said.

"Come on, Georgia, make the break with me," Carrie goaded.

"I'm pretty sure if I did that, I might be all alone in my big cold bed, tonight."

"Oh, you can bet on that," Jen said. "Nothing alien about *that* outcome."

Emily emerged from the car, pretty much still chattering, only carrying a couple of bags; the girls had obviously done some shopping. Sylvia beeped the horn as she exited.

"Hi honey, did you go to the mall? What did you buy?"

"No, we went to Sylvia's and she and her roommate, Gail, gave me all these old clothes—" she pulled a shirt from one of the bags, "—shoes, jackets, sweaters." She lifted out a bit of each as proof. "And, best of all?" From her pocket she slid out a thin black rectangular device with a white cord attached.

"What's that?" Jen asked.

"Sylvia's old i-Pod! Still loaded with all her music, too. She upgraded, and gave me this!"

"Very nice," Jen said. "Glad you had a good time."

"Yeah, we really did." Emily placed one of the round pods into her ear, and appeared to be making her way into the apartment, when Jen put out a hand and stopped her.

"Honey, I have some news."

Emily backed up, and pulled the second cord from her other ear. She immediately squinted, suspicious. "What news?"

"Well, you see, something happened today . . . you know I've been having a devil of a time renting the apartment, and so Tiffany came over, upset, and those poor little girls . . ."

"*Tiffany* was here?" Emily asked.

"Yes, she drove in as you were driving out, this morning."

"I *told* Sylvia I thought that was Tiffany's Volvo, but then I decided it wasn't because I couldn't figure out why she'd be coming here."

"She's in big trouble, as it turns out," Jen said.

"Well, yeah, I'd guess so," Emily said, "Dead husband, twin girls, no job, and from what I've gathered, Dad didn't exactly leave his finances in order."

Jen was cautious listening to Emily's seemingly adult understanding of the situation, but she couldn't quite read her tone. This was the kind of moment that could go either way with the girl; she could be on the verge of exploding or not, although it was quite difficult to tell.

"That's pretty much it in a nutshell," Jen said, "You nailed it."

"So, what does that have to do with you?"

"She wants me to help her sell Robin's Egg."

Emily's eyes widened. "Are you going to?"

"I told her I'd try."

"Wow, Mom, that's big of you. Is that the news?"

"Yes, but there's something—"

"Oh, well, I don't have a problem with that; maybe if you're in charge, I won't lose all my trust fund."

"You can't lose a trust fund," Jen said. "That's the point of a trust fund, and by the way, yours doesn't exactly have much to lose."

"Whatever. I'm going to make my own money, anyways."

"That's the spirit," Georgia said.

"It's nice of you to help her, Mom," Emily said, distractedly, and then stuck in the ear-pod, and made her way toward the door.

"Wait," Jen said, again.

"There's more?" Emily, a tad impatiently, pulled the plug from her head.

"Yes, you see, Tiffany might have to move into Section Eight. It's terrible for the girls."

"Don't *we* know it," Emily said.

"So, after we talked, and she said she was looking for jobs, and since it's all just temporary, there didn't seem any harm in it . . . and we need the money . . ."

Emily was staring hard at her mother. "What are you saying?"

Carrie finally piped up; "What she's saying is that she rented the upstairs apartment to *Tittany* and her twins, I mean daughters." She grinned at her own joke, and giggled when Georgia covered a laugh.

"What?" Emily backed away. "You mean they're going to *live* here?"

"I know it sounds crazy," Jen started weakly.

"After everything that's happened?" Emily nearly whispered.

"They are in some pretty dire straits," Georgia ventured.

"It's only until they can get on their feet," Jen assured.

The women at the table seemed braced for the eruption as Emily stood, seemingly fuming. Jen had never seen her daughter so quiet and in a state of such deep consideration. Finally, Emily picked up her bags and said, "Well, Sylvia says that the only way you know how somebody else feels is to stand in their shoes, I guess we've been in theirs." She started to head toward the door.

"You're okay with it?" Jen asked.

Emily shrugged. "What-ev. I mean, live and let live, right? They are my little sisters; just like I'm Sylvia's little sister. I guess it would be good to get to know them, maybe be a big sister to them. You know."

Jen could barely speak, and so it was Georgia who filled the lapsed response. "That's awfully adult of you, Emily. And, those little girls will really benefit from having a sister like you in their lives."

"Yeah, well, somebody's got to have their backs. Their mother's a kook."

"I'm sure Tiffany will really appreciate your attention."

"I'm not babysitting, though, just to warn you." Emily stuck the other ear-pod in. "I'll hang out with them when I feel like it—not when *Tittany* asks."

"Emily!" Jen scolded.

But she'd already turned up the music as she went into the apartment.

"See what you've done?" Jen smacked Carrie.

Chapter Twenty-One

Sheckie was making trips back and forth to the U-Haul. Casper watched from his bedroom window. He'd hoped to avoid this day; he hoped Sheckie would've moved on a school day. Ever since Sheckie told him he was moving, leaving, splitting town for good, Casper had been avoiding him; he hoped to come home and find Sheckie just gone, poof, disappeared into thin air, and that would've been the end of it. But his mother had knocked on his door for the second time, telling him that Sheckie wanted to see him, and "*Would you please go down and talk to the man?*" Casper tied the laces of his running shoes, zipped up his sweat suit, and grabbed his water bottle. He really didn't want to talk to him. What more was there to say?

The day Sheckie took him out to the track to watch the Formula One cars practice, was the day he told him he was going. It had been a great day, and then on the way home Sheckie told him all about his kid and how she might walk again by going for this treatment in California, and how he needed to go with her. Casper couldn't blame the guy, and he kind of would've been surprised if Sheckie didn't go, but it didn't mean Casper wasn't going to miss him. It didn't mean he had to like it. It didn't mean he wasn't disappointed, and, if he was going to be honest, it didn't mean he didn't want to cry—but it was this very thing that made him not want to talk to Sheckie again. *There's nothing left by the cryin'.*

He was on his way to the track to get in some laps, and he'd been hoping Sheckie would've left before he did, but he didn't and if Casper didn't say goodbye, it'd look bad; he didn't want Sheckie leaving thinking he was mad.

He took a deep breath and headed upstairs to Sheckie's. The door was open, and so he stepped inside the cavernous room, his footfalls echoing on the hardwood floor. He found Sheckie in the kitchen of the emptied apartment. He was taping up what seemed like the last box in the place.

"Hey," Casper said, clearing his throat.

Sheckie turned and grinned. "I thought I might've missed you."

"Nah, I was just leaving for the track." He thumbed over his shoulder.

"You got a meet today?"

He shook his head. "I'm just going over to run some laps. You know."

"Meeting Sarah?" He winked.

"Probably." He toed the corner of the threshold.

Sheckie shoved his hands into his pockets. "Want a drink? Pepsi?"

"Nah. It'll make me belch when I run."

"Can't have that, not with a pretty girl running next you."

Casper looked around the room—at the nothing-ness of it. "So, you're going," he finally managed.

Sheckie nodded. "Yep. Looks that way."

"Long trip."

"Three thousand miles as the crow flies."

"Wear out a pair of wings, I'd bet."

"You think you'd ever come visit?" Sheckie asked.

Casper shrugged. "I guess I could."

"If I sent you a plane ticket, would you come?"

"You'd do that?" Casper looked up, genuinely surprised.

"I'm gonna need some help getting my new shop together out there. Maybe you could come out before school starts back up in the fall. Whatdya say to that?"

"That'd be cool."

Sheckie took a breath. "Listen, Casp, before I leave, I've been meaning to . . . I wanted to say something about your dad . . ."

"What about him?"

286

"Look, I know he hasn't been a model father—"

"—or even a mediocre one, or a model husband, friend, brother, son, officer, pilot, truck driver, human being . . ."

"I know. I get it. I've heard it all and seen it all, but can I just say that, as a father, especially one who doesn't live with his kid, it's not always easy to know the right thing to do."

"You'd think it'd be the easiest thing to know—pay attention, spend time, support, encourage. Really, Sheck, are you saying those things are too hard to know?"

"Look, I'm not defending your old man, how he treats you guys, what he did to your mother, all the lowest of the low, but what I do know—as men—it's up to us to figure out how to make those things right."

"You'd think an almost forty-year-old guy would know by now."

"Yeah, you would, but, we've all got our own timing."

"Maybe it'll never be right with Dill," Casper considered.

"Maybe, but maybe not," Sheckie considered, and finished taping the box. "We men," he grinned, ". . . at least some of us more base ones, have this tendency that when we get frustrated, we get angry and stupid, which can make things a lot worse, it seems."

"That what happened to you and your wife?"

"Something like that; let's just say I messed things up pretty bad—I was a dumb kid, back from a war, my head up my ass. But, you know, Casper, my ex and Amy both gave me a second chance, and here I am, getting another shot at doing the right thing."

Casper looked to the floor. Inside he was battling his good self, the one that was happy for Sheckie and his kid, and even for his ex whose second chance gave them all something to hang onto, but Casper's bad self, the selfish self, wished that the woman had taken her kid and fled to California, leaving all of Sheckie to Carrie and him, giving *them* something to hang onto—and so he said nothing.

"I think it'd be okay to give your dad a second chance. Look at Tex, he's even got the old man shelling out for ballet tickets." He nudged Casper with a playful punch.

Casper grinned.

"You know, I'm not supposed to approve of your methods, but what you did by confronting Dill, making him own up, take responsibility, making him work for your respect and Tex's, well, that was you being a man, Casper. That was you owning up, taking responsibility, working for your own self-respect. That was you being a good man, the kind of man who'd make any father proud."

Casper absorbed every word, memorizing the emphasis of each syllable, recording the soft timbre of Sheckie's voice as he said them, repeating them over in his own mind: *a good man. . .who'd make any father proud.* Casper had captured them, exactly, so he could replay them over and over—when he needed them. "You didn't tell Mom about that, did you?" he asked.

"'Course not. That's between you and me. If you hadn't done something, I might have, and so for that I'm grateful. I could've landed myself in hot water."

"Or the big house," Casper grinned.

"True," Sheckie said.

"Thanks for keeping it to between us—man to man."

"Thanks for trusting me in the first place. Casp, you told your father that if he changed his ways with Tex, he might get another chance with you—right?"

"Something like that."

"Well, he's trying to live up to his part of the bargain, wouldn't you say?"

"I suppose," Casper said, non-committed.

"Just think about it, at least," Sheckie said, and left it there.

Casper shuffled, and thumbed over his shoulder. "Listen, I probably should get going."

"Sure, sure," Sheckie said. "Hang on a minute, I got something for you." He headed for the hall closet and returned with his scuffed, black leather motorcycle jacket. It had seen better days. Covered in patches, worn elbows, a ripped cuff, and his silver jump-wings tacked to the lapel. He handed it to Casper.

"Sheck! No, man. That's your jacket! Your Harley jacket. You earned this jacket. I can't take it." But as he was protesting, Sheckie helped him into it. He slipped his long arms into the sleeves, and the big jacket swallowed the tall skinny boy, even over his sweat shirt.

"Casp, I want you to have it."

"But, I can't . . ."

"If you've got it, I'll know that we'll always be friends. No matter where we are, you understand? I'm always at the end of a phone, okay?"

Casper nodded, biting back tears. He stretched his long arms out, the cuffs covered his knuckles. He reached behind his head and lifted the chain from around his neck, and dropped it into Sheckie's palm. "You know how we Angels can't be beholding. So, here . . ."

"Just like your mother," Sheckie said, his eyes glistened. He fingered the gold disk at the end of the chain.

"It's my first gold. For cross-country," Casper said. "Seems appropriate."

Sheckie draped the chain around his neck, and held the medal in his fist. "Thanks."

"Sure."

Casper looked over his shoulder. "I gotta go."

Sheckie pulled him into a bear hug. "I love you, Casp."

I love you too, Sheck." Then he pulled away, and darted out the door.

Casper didn't stop at the apartment to take off the leather jacket, he didn't stop running to cross a busy intersection that was, thankfully, empty of cars; he also didn't stop running when he got to the track house. In fact, he didn't stop running until he'd finished the cross-country route, and had done two more laps around the track. When he finally looked up, connecting beyond his tears-blurred vision, beyond the pounding of his aching heart, focusing on the familiar form of Sarah, who appeared to be putting her jacket back on, he trotted over.

"Hey," he managed as he approached.

"Good grief, Casper," she said, seeing his drenched appearance, his red face, sweat-soaked hair plastered to his scalp. "Where have you been? Are you okay?"

He nodded, gulping swallows of air.

"I've already done my laps."

"I'm sorry." He bent over, pressing his palms against his knees, attempting to catch his breath.

"What are you wearing?" she noticed Sheckie's jacket.

He stood, looking at her, his eyes brimming once more. "Sheckie left," he said.

"Awe, Casper," she put her arms around him. "I'm sorry. I forgot. I didn't realize it was today."

"He gave me his jacket."

"I see."

Casper shrugged, and then made his way to the nearby bench, his legs feeling rubbery. "We're gonna keep in touch," he said. "I might go out there this summer. He said he'd send me a plane ticket."

"See, that's great."

"Yeah, he's gonna need some help getting the new shop ready."

"Well, I know he's really going to miss your help, for sure."

He nodded, careful not to speak for fear of letting loose another bout of stupid tears.

"Listen, I hate to do this," Sarah said, as the black Mercedes approached. "But, I promised Dad I'd go hit some golf-balls with him."

"That's cool."

"No, no it's not. I wish I could stay here with you." She hugged his neck. "Would you like to come with us?"

The car came to a stop in front of them, and the passenger window rolled down. "Hello, Casper!" Dr. Lash called.

"Hi, Dr. Lash," Casper stood.

"Bob, call me Bob," he said, as he always said; it was something Casper had not yet been able to bring himself to do. Instead, he just grinned and nodded.

"Sarah and I are going to putt around some golf balls, would you like to join us?"

Casper smiled but shook his head. "Thanks, but no thanks. I told Mom I'd be home early for dinner."

"All right then, another time."

"Sure. That'd be great," he waved.

Sarah hugged him twice as hard and long as usual. He appreciated the gesture, but his neck smarted a bit; the girl didn't know her own strength. After they'd driven off, Casper sat back down on the bench. He took the leather jacket off, and folded it across his lap. He traced the lines of the little silver parachute on the front, and let himself feel sad for a few more minutes before he went home. He wanted to make sure Sheckie was gone. He couldn't go through all that again. Like going to the same funeral twice.

Slowly he lifted himself off the bench, and started to walk. He was feeling better. Imagining getting on an airplane, something he'd never done before, and *jetting* off to *LA* as he considered it. Hell, he might even get *discovered*, with his charming good looks. Some agent would sign him to some top-notch studio, but they'd discover that not only could he act but that he could do all his own stunts. He'd have Tex come out to be his wardrobe guy; he'd buy Carrie a giant house in Malibu, and fly Sarah out for weekends till she finished college, then he'd marry her.

Just as he exited the school's gate and had begun a slow trot homeward, the rumbling of a big engine roared behind him. When it didn't go around, but instead slowed down and followed him, he turned and slowed. Shading his eyes from the sun, he saw that it was Dill's truck. When the passenger window rolled down, it wasn't Dodi sitting in there, but Tex.

"Hey, little brother."

"Hey, big brother."

"Where ya headed?"

"Home."

"Hi, Casp," Dill said.

"Hi, Dad."

"We're going to see some ancient Indian Burial Mounds over by Raven Rock."

"That's cool," Casper said.

"I want to get some ideas for my mandala."

"Cool."

291

"Would you like to come?" Tex asked.

Casper looked over at his father.

"Plenty of room," Dill said, unlocking the doors. "We could stop for pizza on the way. You look hungry."

Casper's stomach growled at the sound of the word, and he realized just how hungry he was. He looked at Tex. "You don't mind?"

"Not at all. Plenty of room, right, Dad?" Tex assured.

"Absolutely," Dill said.

He climbed in behind his brother. Tex started reading from the brochure about the ancient ruins. Casper leaned his head back, saw Dill looking at him in the rearview, nodded and closed his eyes.

Carrie bustled out into the chilly early morning air. Summer was gone and school had once again started up. All three kids were on their way. Emily waved as she got into Sylvia's VW. They were heading up back up to Chapel Hill where Emily had started college, and Sylvia was finishing graduate school. Emily had been home for the long holiday weekend; mostly to have her laundry done, Jen had grumbled when Emily had opted for two nights out with Tex and friends, rather than an evening home with her mother.

Tex and Casper shuffled sleepily toward Carrie's old Toyota. The rattle-trap was still clunking along at thirty-five miles per hour, like a school-bus, Tex complained, which had made Carrie feel safe when she gave it to him. She bought a new used van and had stenciled in swirling red and black letters *Angels & Manners Complete Home Services*.

"I hate to tell ya, you look so gay in that outfit," Tex said to Casper, who was dressed in tight blue-jeans, a plaid shirt, and cowboy boots.

Casper looked down at himself. "What? Sarah and I are going contra-dancing after school."

"Which is also so very *gay*."

"Oh yeah, well, what about you, Jesus of Nazareth? That *dress* you're wearing?" Casper was referring to Tex's shoulder-length hair, scraggly beard, and newly embraced appreciation for all things Eastern.

Tex appeared appalled. "This is not a dress!" He pressed his hand against the hem of the cream color cotton tunic, ending just above the knee over what appeared to be a pair of striped pajama bottoms. "This is a Kurta Suit!" And he slid behind the wheel as if that was all the explanation required.

"Have a good day, kids," Carrie called after them, bickering animatedly as they pulled out of the parking lot.

"TGIF, Mom!" Casper hollered from the window, waving as they drove off in separate directions.

The sun was slow to rise this morning, leaving a dewy chill in the air. The job-site was already bustling with the crew from the early-shift. Because so many of the women were mothers, Carrie and Jen agreed on flexible hours, which included these women arriving at near-dawn, then leaving before the last bells rang at the elementary schools, giving them time to reach home before their children. Those women without kids or with older ones often opted to arrive later and stay to button up the job in the evening.

She watched Pat, up on the porch, whose long braid swung at her waist as she pointed and directed women hauling out bags of garbage from the garage. Pat had come to be a reliable second-in-command, and good friend, Carrie thought. She was the first full-time field employee they'd hired, and she was the only one Carrie wanted for the job. Carrie told Jen that she'd take a pay-cut if it meant luring Pat off her more lucrative contracting job. But, it hadn't taken that. After Pat had (finally) ditched her tumultuous relationship with her feisty young girlfriend, she'd sworn off women for a year, and eagerly joined *Angels & Manners.*

As the truck carrying the dumpster pulled into the yard, Carrie slid from the cab and into the familiar squeaking leather of her well-worn tool-belt. It began to drizzle, and so she grabbed her coffee and made for the porch, where Pat was sipping from a silver thermos.

"Mornin'," Pat said, but not exactly like she meant it.

Carrie clapped her hands together. "Dontcha just love the smell of rain?"

Pat shook her head. "That's what I like about you, Carrie Angel; you find joy in the little junk."

"I haven't always," Carrie squinted into a memory and back again. "One year ago it was hard getting up in the morning."

"You've come a long way. Now you're a garbage lady."

"I *am!*" Carrie smiled. "And, I'm doin' a jig every day!" She shuffled her feet.

"Might want to stick with renovations," Pat said, watching the display.

"Cranky, are we?"

"Sorry. Tired."

"Hard weekend?"

"Yeah, well, I met this woman in Raleigh . . ."

"I thought you'd sworn off women and sex?"

A blue Honda pulled up, and Carrie watched as Jen got out. She ducked as rain came down harder, and she high-footed it across the muddy lot, joining Carrie and Pat under the porch.

"Look at me, I'm soaked." Jen said.

"Good thing you've got that *durable* rain gear on, then?" Carrie said, teasingly, knowing that Jen's LL Bean rain coat had cost a mint back in her married days, but she'd always brag about its utilitarian qualities: *look how long it's lasted. . .*

"Here, have some coffee." Pat poured into her thermos cup and handed it to Jen.

"Thanks," she said, wrapping her palms around the steel mug. "We got another contract this morning," she said. "A job that runs the whole gamut, from clean up to renovation!"

"Wow."

"That's why I came by. To pick you up. The guy who's buying it wants to meet us over there to do a walk-through, in about twenty minutes. You game?"

"Sure."

There was a state highway patrol car in the driveway when they pulled into Jen's old house on Robin's Egg. Carrie got nervous. "Something going on we don't know about?"

Jen shook her head. "No, the guy's a cop. He's on his break."

294

Carrie could see a tall, lanky man standing in front of the house, craning his neck, squinting, looking at the roof. He turned when he heard their doors slam, and came toward them in just a few long strides. Carrie recognized him immediately, just as she had six months before.

Jen turned to Carrie, as he stepped before them, and introduced, "Officer Ross, this is my partner, Carrie An—"

"*O'Harrie,*" the freckle-faced patrolman said, grinning, as he extended his hand.

"No, *Angel,* Carrie *Angel,*" Jen said, confused.

"Hello, Mike," Carrie said, taking his hand, feeling its warmth, catching the same in his eyes. She found herself blushing.

"You two know each other?" Jen looked from one to the other.

"A long time ago," Mike said.

"Another lifetime, really," Carrie said.

"High school," he said.

Carrie turned to Jen and said, "Mike was the guard on duty at the courthouse, the night Dill smashed out my taillight."

"Oh, right. A bit of a knight in shining armor, you were," Jen said, embarrassing Carrie. She could tell Jen was also embarrassing Mike by the way his ears went red, just like Casper when he too was mortified. They grinned at each other.

"So, you're the *field manager* Ms. Manners has been mentioning throughout all these negotiations," he said. "I had no idea."

"Yep, that's me, the Angel not the Manners."

"Guess this means we'll be working together," he said.

"Guess so," Carrie said, and felt a little tug of excitement in her middle. She liked the way Mike's grin cracked his whole face into a smile.

Jen checked her watch. "Oh, I hate to do this, but would you mind if I leave you two alone for the walk-through? I've got to meet with the accountant, show a house at noon, run to the post office, and call that plumber about the leaky faucet in number four before that couple move in next weekend, and I haven't even gone to the bank yet. Mike, do you think you could give Carrie a ride back to the jobsite when you're through?"

"In his patrol car?"

He grinned, "I'll get the sirens and lights going for you."

"You will, huh?" Carrie asked, and his color deepened again, and then she realized the double entendre of his words, and blushed, too.

"How 'bout it? You up for a ride in a cop car?" he asked.

"Long as I don't have to be in handcuffs," she said, and immediately bit down on her tongue.

He laughed.

"I didn't mean it like that," she said, mortified.

"Like what?" he asked, mischievously.

"Like nothin'." Carrie pulled out her notebook. "Follow me."

"I'm right on your heels," he said.

"Okay," she slowed, "but not too close."

Cat Rising
Cynn Chadwick

Cat Hood's life looks good: she's in business with her best friend; she rides a '59 Harley Duo Glide; her brother has finally come back home.

Cat Hood life looks great: she's published a book; she has an agent making big plans; folks in her hometown—Galway, North Carolina—think she's a star.

It's hard to see how Cat Hood's life could look any better: she's just found the woman of her dreams, the one she's been waiting for all this time.

But Cat knows something's missing. Something she can only have if she's prepared to go back to her past. Looks like she's in for a bumpy ride …

Lesbian Fiction |Trade Paper | 296 pp | 978-1-932859-66-9 | $14.95

Girls With Hammers
Cynn Chadwick

"It's never too late to be what you might have been"
—George Eliot

Carpenter Lily Cameron first read that quote after a fight with her lover Hannah. Her best friend, Cat, had already moved to Scotland, leaving her no one to talk to. Then the person she looked up to the most, her father, died—leaving her in charge of the family construction business and forcing her to put aside her own business, Girls With Hammers. Soon after, Hannah decided to take a position in Amsterdam. Lily was alone with the George Eliot quote ringing in her ears and not knowing what to do.

Lesbian Fiction |Trade Paper | 328 pp | 978-1-932859-28-7 | $13.95

Babies, Bikes, and Broads
Cynn Chadwick

Cat Hood doesn't want to go home. She has a new life and a new love in Scotland. But her brother, Will, has been widowed and left with two small children. So there's no choice for Cat now. She must return to Galway, North Carolina, the place she left when love got lost.

But it looks like love wants to be found again. When Cat gets back, she comes face-to-face with Janey, the lover who betrayed her all those years ago. As Cat helps her brother to rebuild his life, she starts to see that her own needs attention. And maybe it's time to get over Janey. If she can …

Lesbian Fiction |Trade Paper | 240 pp | 978-1-932859-62-1 | $14.95

Greetings from Jamaica, Wish You Were Queer
Mari SanGiovanni

Lambda Literary Award Finalist

Marie Santora has always known her Italian family is a little crazy, but when she inherits her grandmother's estate, they now have a million more reasons to act nuts.

Climb aboard this hilarious roller coaster ride where Marie is left wishing "out" was the new "in" and where every lounge chair is a hot seat when the Santora family ventures this close to the equator. The island of Jamaica just may not be big enough ...

Lesbian Fiction |Trade Paper | 264 pp | 978-1-932859-30-0 | $13.95

I Came Out for This?
Lisa Gitlin

There's only one place Joanna can tell it like it is. Her journal: *My name is Joanna Kane. Jewish, 47, living in Cleveland, Ohio, which will prejudice you against me immediately because what's Cleveland, Ohio? A loser city. Anyway, I'm gay and was too stupid to come out until I was forty-five years old. Do you know what it's like to come out when you're in your forties, having menopausal symptoms, for God's sake, and then fall madly in love with someone? All of a sudden you're in adolescence for the first time. You don't even recognize yourself . . .*

Lesbian Fiction |Trade Paper | 304 pp |978 1-932859-73-7 | $14.95

Last Chance at the Lost and Found
Marcia Finical

In 1972 Bunny LaRue was young and beautiful. Days in the sun on the beach at Malibu and nights in the bars with the girls. Soon Bunny finds herself making big money modeling for a lingerie catalog. Then she falls in love and life seems to be giving her everything she has ever wanted— until the day she loses it all.

Last Chance at the Lost and Found is the compelling story of one woman's journey through twenty-five years of living as a lesbian and her determination to change with the times to find love and happiness.

Lesbian Fiction |Trade Paper | 328 pp | 978-1-932859-28-7 | $13.95

Mirrors
Marianne K. Martin

Lambda Literary Award Finalist

There are plenty of reasons why Jean Carson isn't a lesbian: she's a wife; she's a Catholic; and she's a teacher. Besides, Shayna Bradley is just a good friend. But Jean's a wife who doesn't want children with her husband. A Catholic who rejects the teachings of the Church. And a teacher desperate to help one of her students—and failing, because there's nothing she's allowed to say to "Lezzie Lin." There are plenty of reasons why Jean Carson isn't a lesbian. And plenty of reasons to announce that she is.

Lesbian Fiction |Trade Paper | 200 pp | 978-1-932859-72-0 | $14.95

For Now, For Always
Marianne K. Martin

Lambda Literary Award Finalist

Renee Parker knows what love is and what love does. She doesn't think twice about sacrificing her own future to give her brothers and sisters their best shot at life.

   But then a different kind of love threatens everything Renee has built. Meeting pediatric nurse Olivia Dumont convinces Renee there is room in her heart for someone outside the family. But the watchful eye of social worker Millie Gordon is always on the Parker family. And Millie knows what's right and what's wrong . . .

Lesbian Fiction |Trade Paper | 216 pp |978 1-932859-43-0 | $13.95

Under the Witness Tree
Marianne K. Martin

Lambda Literary Award Finalist

An aunt she didn't know existed leaves Dhari Weston a plantation she knows she doesn't want. Her life is complicated enough without an ante-bellum albatross around her neck. Complicated enough without the beautiful Erin Hughes and her passion for historical houses, without Nessie Tinker, whose family breathed the smoke of General Sherman's march and who knows the secrets hidden in the old walls—secrets that could pull Dhari into their sway and into Erin's arms . . .

Lesbian Fiction |Trade Paper | 224 pp | 1-932859-00-4 | $12.95

Bywater Books represents the coming of age of lesbian fiction. We're committed to bringing the best of contemporary lesbian writing to a discerning readership. Our editorial team is dedicated to finding and developing outstanding voices who deliver stories you won't want to put down. That's why we sponsor the annual Bywater Prize. We love good books, just like you do.

For more information about Bywater Books and the annual Bywater Prize for Fiction, please visit our website.

www.bywaterbooks.com